Attachments

A Novel

Attachments

Jeff Arch

Published by SparkPress, a BookSparks imprint,
A division of SparkPoint Studio, LLC
Phoenix, Arizona, USA, 85007
www.gosparkpress.com

Published 2021
Printed in the United States of America
Print ISBN: 978-1-68463-081-3
E-ISBN: 978-1-68463-082-0

Library of Congress Control Number: 2020917552
Interior design by Tabitha Lahr

for
Gene and Louise
and
Jenny and Greg

what a gift
to be the bridge between you

"We were talking about the space between us all."
—GEORGE HARRISON

"Mind the Gap"
—LONDON TRANSPORT

Mt. Raymond, Oregon

1972

///////////////////////////////

dear mr and mrs griffin

*i'm sorry it took so long to write to you and tell you i'm ok.
i'm at a place called the mt. raymond buddhist center, near
the oregon and washington border. i didn't know they had
places like this in this country, or people like the monks who
brought me out here. the abbot is named hataka sudo roshi
(roshi is about the highest thing they have), and you can
see in a minute why everyone here treats him with such
respect. he said i could stay here, as long as i worked every
day and also continued my education—i can get my GED
through cascade community college, and then continue on
as a regular student. i wrote to mrs la fave separately to ask
her to send transcripts. in the meantime i've been helping
roshi in the office, and since i started i've sort of become his
assistant as well. mostly his phone calls and correspondence,
his english isn't great so he has me take care of a lot of that.
and when the monks go into town for food and supplies,
he sends me with them so that the local people take less
advantage. it feels good to be able to be useful to them.*

    *i don't know what to tell you about why i left school,
and the way i did. everything about it just still hurts too
much. i know i left a mess behind, and i'm sorry about
that, very much. i just want to understand it better, and*

maybe it'll start to hurt less. i wonder if that will ever happen. anyway i wanted you to know where i am, and that i'm okay, and if you were worried at all i'm sorry about that too. also i've told my mom where i am, and why i've decided to stay. for now we're pretending it's like another boarding school, just farther away.

okay now i have to go—they have bells here too!—for the monks it means morning meditation, for me it means scrubbing the kitchen after their breakfast.

all the best and thank you, for everything—
stewart

Kirby, Pennsylvania

18 Years Later

1

Griffin

He was halfway to the floor when Mrs. Levering came in. She had the afternoon mail with her and she looked up from it and saw him reach out for the back of his chair to try and grab on, but the chair wheeled out from under him and he banged his head on the edge of the desk and dropped the rest of the way and was down.

Oh my God, he heard her say, and he had a hazy awareness of trying to answer her, but was curious to discover he couldn't. He watched her eyes turn fierce with alarm; her arms with the clackety wrist bracelets lunging out while the letters fell out of her hands and dropped in angular stabs against the other side of the desk and the chair and the floor. They seemed like bombs to him.

"Henry!"

He was squeezed in between his chair and the credenza. He saw his reflection in the walnut side panel; his face, pressed up against itself, looking contorted and vaguely surprised. Something smelled like lemons, factory-sweet, and he was thinking they overdid the wood polish again when he felt his weight shift underneath him and he smelled lavender now and saw Mrs.

Levering's reflection coming in and out as it appeared behind his own. She was trying to wiggle her way in there and get his head and shoulders up into her lap. He had never known her to wiggle before, or to sit on anyone's floor.

"Henry! Can you hear me?"

He wanted to tell her that he could—that he could see her mouth moving, but her motions seemed gummy and disjointed and wrong somehow. And he wanted to tell her how strange it was that the sound of his own name could take so long to get to him from such a short distance away. But he couldn't; he couldn't make the words come, and a cold wave of fear began to build instead—a slow thick liquid, starting at his heels and climbing his spine like mercury.

He watched her stretch for the phone and punch numbers; he knew it had to do with helping him and he wanted to thank her for that. But there was something else—something to ask her, to get her to do, desperate and essential, but still he couldn't get the words to come out. And the feeling began to dawn on him that he might die, really die, right here on this floor, with the thing he needed to say trapped tight and thick in his throat.

"Henry. Try and listen. I think you're having a heart attack, or a stroke. Can you hear me? Do you know where you are?"

Yes! he shouted. Or thought he was shouting. *At the school, on the carpet, in my office!* But she must not have heard him; Mrs. Levering only looked more worried. "Your wife's on the way," she told him, "and I called the field house for Chip."

Griffin's head went limp and heavy. He had to tell her about Piccolo and Goodman. He had to tell her, and she had to get them here, so they could be there for Chip. He felt his eyes rolling, fluttering upwards while some deeply planted instinct told him not to let them do that. He felt helpless, and inevitable, and doomed.

Mrs. Levering was talking again. Her voice like it was leaving on a train. He had to try, one last time, before he wouldn't be able to do anything at all.

2

Pick

"My client is on his way out of town," Pick announced. He watched everyone look at each other, wondering how he'd managed to sneak someone out of the courthouse already; simultaneously he had both tricked and intrigued the New York press. "He's going to take an extended sabbatical and figure out how to go on with the rest of his life. However, he has authorized me to speak on his behalf, and to tell you that he's very relieved, and grateful to the jury. Beyond that he has no statement. Thank you."

"That's it?"

"What can I say, Rowan. Not everyone wants their fifteen minutes."

"Mr. Piccolo!"

"Sandy!"

"Over here!"

It took forever to get past all the cameras and back to the office. Usually this kind of attention only went to the high-profile divorce cases and celebrity drug busts, and the occasional crackpot lawsuit, like the guy who went after his dry cleaner for eight figures for losing a pair of his pants. But somehow Pick's case caught people's pulses, and the media were happy to deliver. A well-known and highly regarded surgeon loses half the nerves in one of his hands when he tries to grind up some peanut butter at a self-service machine in his local supermarket, and gets electrocuted instead. The company that made the machines was responsible for installing them, and they screwed it up—and now a guy's life was changed forever, because he liked the idea of peanut butter that you could grind up right in front of you, and had nothing else in it but peanuts.

Thirty million sounded right.

At the office, it seemed like every second person had a bottle of champagne in hand, ready to pop and get going. And while they'd all earned and deserved their victory lap, Pick didn't really have it in him to take part. Most of them knew he wouldn't; others knew not to ask. Yet, something had to be done to mark the occasion—the case took months, with everybody working monster hours—and all of them would be better off now for their efforts. Especially with the holidays up soon; Pick was always generous come bonus time.

Bottom line though, by nature he just wasn't big on cele-brations—even less on drinking as a means. It didn't loosen him up, and it didn't make things more fun the way it seemed to do for everyone else—and nothing was worth the price of feeling like hell the next day. He'd had one hangover in his life, and it probably wasn't even a bad one; still, he ended up slamming the front door on some poor innocent Cub Scout selling raffle tickets. That was enough.

And yet, when he'd needed it—when it was time to bury his daughter, and he'd relied on alcohol's promise to numb him, the stuff failed completely. He and Laura had put away a bottle and a half of grappa that morning—strong enough to knock over cattle, they were told—and it didn't do anything at all. The funeral still happened. Liana was still dead, and they still came home to a house with one less kid in it, with her brother and twin sister shaken and having nightmares, unable to understand and afraid to ask the questions you could never explain anyway. So, fuck drinking if it's not going to be there when you need it.

They were singing now. They were calling for a speech. Pick declined, but he did step up the effort to come through for these people. He shook hands, patted backs, threw the occasional high five. Always though, with his eye on the time; he knew Laura would be cooking, and putting a lot into it, and she'd want him to be home. That he didn't feel like eating, ever again maybe, wasn't a factor—Laura probably didn't feel like it either. But they had to, so they did. You went through the motions until the motions took care of themselves. That's what they were told, anyway. And they knew it was a lie; nobody gets over the death of a child. Easier to split an atom with a butter knife.

So, really. Fuck celebrations too, sometimes. What's the point if it only makes you feel worse?

3

Chip

By the time he made it across the campus there was already a crowd—whispering, spreading the word about Mr. Griffin and what had happened to him. Chip stood on a bench, to see over heads and umbrellas and shuffling. The EMTs were loading his dad into an ambulance. In another two minutes the whole school would know.

"Chip."

He'd been back at the field with Randy, working on a pass play that Coach Milpitas wanted them to learn for the Nihaminy game. They had an extra week to prepare for this one, and they needed it; the two schools hated each other to begin with, and last time they played it ended ugly—Nihaminy won, on a disputed call that would remain disputed for the next hundred years. The only thing both sides could agree on was that the next time they met would be cold and bloody. A brick fight.

"Chip."

They'd stayed after practice to work on the play, and were lining up to do it again when they heard the sirens and then saw Bostick running triple time from the field house. Standing there, dripping wet, they wondered which one of them he was coming out in such a hurry to get.

"*Chip.*"

It was Mrs. Levering. She was tugging at his sleeve—ready to climb up on the bench with him if he didn't answer this time. People were turning around now, looking at them. Chip was in his sweats, blotted through from both directions, and he did not want this kind of attention; he didn't like being exposed this way, having his guts strung out on a line. Bad enough that they all knew about Ellie, dropping him like a bowling ball and avoiding him like a disease. Now they're taking his dad away, in front of everyone, and here he was on display again which made the whole thing even worse. Sometimes he felt like he could go through anything, as long as nobody knew.

The doors closed with a sick *thunk* of finality. There were leaves stuck flat to the back windows—big wide dead brown maple leaves, plastered heavy by the rain, blocking any kind of view there might have been inside.

"Is my mom in there?" Chip asked. People were stepping out of the way now, as the ambulance pulsed forward and started off.

"She's with him. If you want to go to the hospital, I'll take you."

"I want to. I want to go."

She had to get her keys and her purse from her desk. Chip followed her into the Foyle Building, waiting in his dad's office while Mrs. Levering used the ladies' room across the hall. He listened while she ran the sink in there—then the toilet flush, then the sink again, with the water on full force. There was no way to hide it, she'd been crying.

"Are you sure all he did was faint?"

"He hit his head on the desk."

"Hard?"

"He hit it pretty hard, Chip."

Chip looked; his father's desk was unusually shiny. But also he noticed a streak along the side panel—a comet tail smear that went down its whole length. It looked like a fat smudgy fingerprint left by someone's whole face.

"What's that smell?" Chip asked.

"Furniture spray," said Mrs. Levering. "Let's go."

She drove down Memorial, wipers on high. He had never been in her car before; it was a Camry—sensible and no nonsense, just like she was. A Lexus without the flash, for fifteen thousand less. Mrs. Levering all the way.

"It felt like Robert Kennedy."

Chip looked at her. After three traffic lights and a railroad crossing where no one said anything, something now felt like Robert Kennedy.

"The night he was shot," she went on. "In that hotel ballroom, in Los Angeles." She shook her head, like this was a bad thing that had just happened to someone in the neighborhood. "He won the California primary that night."

Chip told her he knew. "Mr. Loftus is a Kennedy freak. He makes you read everything. He showed films."

"Then you know what happened. He had just made his victory speech. I can't remember the name of the hotel. Excelsior, or Embassy . . ."

"The Ambassador," Chip said. He shrugged when Mrs. Levering looked surprised: did he not just tell her Loftus was a maniac? It was like he knew the family personally—like they were lifelong neighbors in Hyannis or something, and they had him over all the time for lemonade and quoits. He took their deaths that hard.

"There was that busboy," Mrs. Levering was saying. "The one on the floor with him, with all that blood. And he looked so frightened—an immigrant, and maybe not even legal—yet there in his lap is the head of a crown prince." She shook her head. "You can't get any farther apart than that in this country."

No, Chip guessed. You couldn't.

"Anyway, that's the way we were sitting for a while. Until

the ambulance came. And I saw our reflections in your father's credenza and that's what I thought of. Bobby Kennedy, on the floor of that hotel. With all there was to look forward to . . ."

She was rambling now. Chip decided to let her; she could sing Irish drinking songs if she wanted, as long as she didn't swerve off and hit anything. They crossed the bridge into Wilkes-Barre and went through Market Square; then things turned industrial pretty quick—a furniture mart, a brewery that had just changed hands, a couple blocks where there were warehouses, then the new shopping center that already looked old somehow, and then the hospital.

That's right, he remembered. The hospital. They were going to the hospital.

"Chip. Your father said somebody's name."

"What do you mean?"

"I mean, before he—while we were on the floor there. He tried very hard, to say somebody's name."

"Whose."

"Well that's it. I don't know whose. Actually, it was two names, and I'm not even sure I got them right. They were the last things he said . . ."

"What were they?"

"One was Piccolo—I think. And one was Goodman. Or maybe not."

Chip didn't know. Piccolo was familiar, in a local kind of way. Everyone knew about Carmine Piccolo—the man was as notorious as Capone in these parts—although it was hard for Chip to imagine how he could be associated with his father. And Goodman? Never heard of Goodman. Anybody's bet.

"I guess your mom could know," Mrs. Levering said.

"I guess."

He was out of the car almost before she stopped it. He leapt over a bench and ran through the doors and kept running—blurring past the people turning to ask if they could help him. He noticed different colored lines on the floor, like racing stripes on a car. The lines intersected sometimes, ran parallel sometimes—all according to some kind of code, he was sure, but he really didn't want to have to figure it out right now. He should still be out on the football field, running that play with Randy. Bostick should have stayed in the locker room and not come looking for them. His father should be in his office and the day should have kept on going normally, like normal days are supposed to go.

He thought about Mrs. Levering, running the faucet so she could cry. Bobby Kennedy and the Ambassador Hotel. The aerosol smell of lemons, and the smear on the side of that desk; Chip knew somehow that he'd remember these things forever—that he would always connect them with the day his father cracked his head and had to go to the hospital. The way those maple leaves clung to the ambulance. How that whole crowd of people turned around, and saw him all soaked and caught short—and how Ellie, out of everyone, was nowhere to be found.

He hit it pretty hard, Chip . . .

What anyone else remembers, he thought, is totally up to them. He picked the blue lines underneath him, and ran on.

_4_

Laura

S he sat at the table, hearing the TV from the den. The four
o'clock news led with the big victory—so did the five, and
the six, and the six-thirty—all lead stories, and she had set the
VCR to record them all, so Pick could watch when he got home.

"Your reaction to the verdict?"

"He's a surgeon. He can't use his hands anymore."

"You don't think the size of the award is excessive?"

"Compared to what?"

She heard Pick mute the sound in there. He was on the
phone. "All right," he was saying. "Look. I'm gonna get a doctor,
someone from the city. Someone who knows about strokes. I'll
fly him up there. My expense. Don't worry about it . . ."

Laura wondered who didn't have to worry this time, and
knew right away she had been fooling herself to think they
might have this hour alone together. She'd had a great afternoon, a rare one, planning this meal—shopped for it, cooked
it, set out a beautiful table. She fed the kids early and shipped
them off to their rooms so Mom and Dad could have dinner
by themselves; Andy not only cooperated but said he'd read to

his sister tonight, and help her get settled for bed—and then he followed through and did it. That meant Laura was going to owe him, big.

"Wait," Pick said in there. "He hit his head and then he passed out, or he passed out and hit his head?"

In the end it all amounted to nothing. The shopping, the cooking, the arranging. The bribing of the first son. Because nothing special was going on in here tonight—nothing was happening that doesn't happen routinely, when Pick is home at dinnertime: he's in the other room, on the phone, drawing a bead on the enemy and telling his clients that he'll do the worrying, that's what they pay him for.

And they paid him a lot.

"All right . . . I'll be there. I'll—if he asked—I'll work on it. I'll move some stuff around."

Laura nodded. Of course he will. He'll be on that phone all night if he has to, and he'll take care of business like no one else—while one room away the wine was breathing, and the clock was ticking, and his wife was coming to the quiet conclusion that things might not ever be any other way.

"You can't change the spots on a leopard," her father would say, in that Good-Old-George-Appleby tone of his, and they loved him up at the Rotary for that, but it never worked on his daughter. Because what Good Old George Appleby never got, never would get, was that Laura didn't want to change the spots. She knew who she was marrying; she just thought that even leopards might stop once in a while and have dinner with their wives.

"I don't understand," she heard from the den. "Is he in a coma or not?"

She was finished with her plate and had started picking at his: crab cakes, because that's what she did best, and this was a beautiful batch. Big white tufted Chesapeake plumes, fat as a thumb, and the trick was to use just enough binder to hold them together without getting in the way. No mayonnaise, no breadcrumbs, and especially not mustard—five years waiting tables down at Chincoteague, one thing you're going to know is how to treat a hard-shell crab.

"So how can I call the ICU directly—I don't want these guys having to go through switchboards . . ."

She remembered watching a cooking show once. The chef was doing regional foods, and filmed a segment on Maryland's Eastern Shore. But when the guy got around to crab cakes—*authentic* crab cakes—Laura was horrified. He was gumming them up with more filler and junk than a cruise ship buffet. Later, she learned that he was arrested for a sex crime, and lost his show.

Figures, Laura thought. It figures.

"Goodman, too? Stewart Goodman?"

Laura stopped cold. For about two seconds she played with the fiction that maybe there just might be some other Stewart Goodman involved here—after all, there had to be loads of them. But from the way Pick's voice sounded, there was only one possibility. Only one Goodman.

"Both of us? Specifically?"

She played back in her head what she'd heard so far—wondering what to do, how to act when Pick got off the call and came back in the room, or whether she should even be there in the first place and not somewhere else by then: Singapore, maybe. Or the Middle Ages.

"Wait a minute, I don't know about that. I am really not the guy to go looking for him—believe me."

Yes, Laura thought. *Believe him. Ask someone else. Go back in time if you have to, and dial a different number.*

"Well for starters," she heard Pick say, "I'm the reason he went away."

And then he closed the door.

5

Pick

He was working when he heard her come up the stairs. He had his legal pads spread out over the bed, even though there was a full separate office off the garage, put in by the two psychiatrists who lived here before Pick and Laura did, and who worked their practice at home. No one was sorry when the place went up for sale; neighbors said there were people coming and going all day—people with *problems*—and you had to think twice about letting your kids run about, if you got their drift. By the time the Piccolos closed escrow, no one cared how they got their money, as long as they left the house every day to do it. Like normal people.

Pick liked to work in bed because of a movie he saw when he was little, where the main character was also in bed, surrounded by papers, with those half-glasses on for reading while important phone calls came in. Pick asked his Aunt Luisa what kind of job the guy did; when she said he was a lawyer, Pick decided he'd be one too. What was cooler than a job you can do while you're still in your pajamas?

Even when he learned there was a little more to it than that, Pick stayed with the vision. And right from the beginning, when a mattress was all he had, that's where he did his best work—long after he didn't have to anymore. He knew he was living out something he had promised himself as a kid. He was important; he mattered. He had people in need who depended on him, and he knew how to come through. He had a wife and a home and a family—the refrigerator was filled and there were vacation pictures on the wall. He got along just as well with the cleaning crew as he did with the Mayor; there were more plaques and awards with his name etched in than he had room for.

Amazing, he thought—one scene in a movie had sold him all that.

"The guy has a stroke," he said. Laura had come in to open the window; she liked the fresh air for sleeping, no matter what the temperature was outside. It was an argument Pick was never going to win. "Right before he passes out, he asks for me. And Goody."

Laura crossed the room in her robe; flannel nightgown underneath, with the collar turned up. Pick remembered when she didn't wear anything at all to bed—when neither of them did, even on the coldest nights, because neither of them wanted to. Skin to skin; he wondered if she remembered that too. He wondered if she missed it as much as he did—and why, if they both did, could neither of them just come out and say it.

"You two been in touch?" he asked. Hoping, if they had been, that it was Goody who'd called Laura, and not the other way around.

"No," Laura said. She was beginning the detailed bedtime routine that she carried out every night: several trips back and forth across the room, reminding herself about something, always in motion, in a pattern evident only to her. There'd be a progression of drawers opening and closing, the medicine chest with the mirror that squeaked, the water coming on and off in the sink, an item of clothing or a towel, or pillowcase to fold and put away, a trip to the toilet, something to go down the hall and write on the white board fixed to the outside of each kid's door, something else to fold and put away and then the bathroom and the medicine chest with the squeak again—before brushing her teeth and finally coming out of there, to a bed that Pick would have cleared away by the time she was ready to get in it.

Then, if she hadn't already, she'd open the window.

"You sure you haven't seen him," Pick said. "You can say so."

"I haven't seen him," Laura said.

"What about Griffin. You ever call the school?"

"No, Sandy—I don't call the school. Do you?"

"I called when Liana happened."

"Interesting way to put it," Laura said.

Pick heard someone over at Maltby's, calling for their cat. The daughter, probably. Girls and cats. Molly'd been begging for one forever. Then what—a horse? Like Lubling, the estate planner, who got his daughter a prize Arabian, and said it was the biggest mistake he ever made in his life. He wished he'd put in an infinity pool instead.

"You saw Goody in Malibu," he reminded Laura. "When that pain in the ass book of his was all hot. When it was still supposed to be a movie."

"I thought you meant recently."

He noticed she didn't swing at the comment over Goody's book. It was a damn good book, he had to admit, no matter how much discomfort it had brought. And the movie would have made things worse; thank God that the thing never got made. As far as an elephant in the room went though, you couldn't do better than that.

"What about his mother?" Laura asked. "Is she . . ."

"Can't find her. And I had Iris check the place out in Oregon. That Buddha place."

"What'd they say?"

"'Number disconnected. Everybody's gone. Iris called the Chamber of Commerce, they said the place went under. People use it for corporate retreats now. Motivational shit. They climb ropes."

"Ropes," Laura said. She curved around him, bent down and picked up a balled-up sock of his, pulling it straight on the way to the hamper.

"It's hard to believe," Pick added. "That's all. That in all this time, he still hasn't called you."

"Why would he call me, Sandy? Why on earth would he want to talk to me?"

"Because he loves you."

"You got your tenses wrong," Laura said.

Pick wondered if she meant that. Some people never give up, and he knew it—he *traded* on it. He finished stacking his papers, still hearing Maltby over there, and the drama over a cat. "Listen," he said. "Let this be about just one thing. Just for now. Griffin's sick—you care about him too, right? And he said our names, and I don't have a prayer where Goody might be, and there's not a lot of time. I got paralegals checking phone books in all fifty states. I got a detective looking, and the only thing I don't want to do is go begging to Carmine to get his people looking too. So if you could spare me that, it would be great."

"I don't know where he is."

"I'm just saying. Now would be the time."

"Just stop. All right?"

"No repercussions—"

"I said stop!"

She went into the bathroom and closed the door. Blew her nose in there—twice, always twice—and then she came out and shot right past him, past the bed and straight for the door.

"Laura—"

She kept going. He heard her say "repercussions" on her way down the steps. He could picture her shaking her head.

6

Chip

He was on a wall phone, where he could still see his way down to the ICU. They would only let him go in for five minutes every hour. He'd been in four times. It was late; almost lights out now, at the school.

"So what do they say'll happen?" Randy asked.

"They don't know. They have to watch him for a while. He's hooked up to a bunch of machines." He looked around to see if anyone was listening; you'd think from the kind of calls people had to make from here, the pay phones might be a little more private.

"How's your mom doing?"

"She's okay. Listen, what happened in Western Civ?"

Not that he cared. What Chip cared about was that he and Randy and Ellie were in the same Western Civilization class— so if there were any late developments, any signs of forward motion along the lines of maybe she was changing her mind about him, then Randy might know.

"You didn't miss much. More of the same. Plutarch speaks, nobody listens."

"Anything else?"

"Mrs. Dibley made Sussman leave the room when we got to the Vestal Virgins. He couldn't stop laughing."

But Chip didn't want to hear about Dibley, or Plutarch, or Sussman and his damn Vestal Virgins. Randy had to know that; he just wasn't taking the bait.

"You should see this," Chip said. He nodded at the window; there were some doctors down there, just outside the canopy, having a smoke. Hunching their shoulders, stomping their feet to stay warm, their breath coming out in grey frosted clouds. "They look like buffalo."

"Who does?"

"These doctors. They're smoking."

"What, like cigarettes?"

"No, Randy. They're out there in front of a hospital firing up these big giant reefers with each other. Then they're gonna steal some motorcycles and go sacrifice the mayor's cocker spaniel. What the fuck."

"If I knew what you were talking about, amigo. Buffalo, that doesn't help."

"Why would a doctor smoke, is what I'm talking about."

"Well—clearly that's for bigger minds than mine. I'm more interested in nurses anyway."

"Nurses smoke too."

"They can't all."

Chip had to concede; all nurses can't smoke. He got off the phone, but stayed at the window, watching the doctors out there—orange firefly trails stabbing at the night while they checked their watches and told jokes to each other, staving off the moment when they'd have to go back in and crank it up again. Maybe it was a stress thing, Chip thought, with the cigarettes—the way people are always saying is the reason they do it. Doctors, though? Chip thought they'd know better. Or maybe they just didn't give a fuck about staying alive.

"You're Chip, right?"

It was one of the nurses. She had a sweater on over her uniform, a button-down, and part of it went over her ID tag. Chip remembered that she was one of the first people he saw when he finally got up here and found this place.

"Heck of a night, huh?" she asked. She was friendly; she seemed pretty genuine about things.

"Yeah. I mean—I haven't been outside since I got here."

"I meant, in there." She nodded down the hall towards ICU.

"Oh." Chip's cheeks burned, from being an idiot. "How is he?"

"He's holding. It's a touchy time. But he's strong, Chip. You can really see that in him. So, be hopeful. It helps—you'd be amazed."

"Yeah, I know. Thanks. I am."

She smiled. He was full of shit and it might as well have been stamped on his forehead; at least she was cool enough to let him off the hook. Still, somehow, here in this place, he didn't mind so much how he came off to someone. He was in a hospital, for Christ's sake—with his dad all laid out, and his mother trying to hold it together, and a girlfriend who dumped him after three years and won't even say why, who won't talk to him at all. Knowing at the same time that the thing that should really be upsetting him was his father; there was nothing more important than what was going on just a few feet down the hall. And yet as close as it was, it was the thing that seemed the most abstract, and ephemeral and remote. It didn't add up, and he couldn't get his head around why. Maybe it was too unreal to be real—where something like Ellie leaving him, that was too real to be anything else.

"Sure you're all right?"

The nurse. Maybe she was some kind of counselor, Chip thought, with some special kind of training, who gets sent around to deal with it when they find people staring out of windows. "I don't know," he said. "It's not like anything's changing or anything."

"I wouldn't say nothing's changing, Chip. Not at all."

"But he's still unconscious. And they're still saying critical. So what's different?"

He watched her pause. She looked like she was practiced at this; no doubt he wasn't the first worried kid she'd had to talk to in her career. "Think of it as a holding pattern. Your father's had a stroke. And strokes are unpredictable."

"It means you don't know. No one knows—that's what it means."

The nurse turned a little. *Mogavero*, her name tag said. And he knew she was trying to be nice—she probably *was* nice, in real life—but it didn't matter to him right now. He didn't want it to matter. "Chip, I know that's your father in there—"

"It is?" He turned to her. "Then why'd he ask for someone else, people I never even heard of?"

He knew she didn't know what he was talking about—how could she? But still it was kind of cool, she sort of recognized something going on anyway. And if you went by the way she was reading him, what was going on seemed like it might be pretty fucked up, but also kind of valid. It felt strange that she might know that.

"In a stroke, Chip, nobody knows where the victim is inside. It affects the brain—it beats it up—like when you're real dizzy, and you're going around in circles and you look around for any-thing that's still, anything you can hold on to. That's what your dad's brain is doing. Searching for a time and a place that he can hold on to, so he can get his bearings and start coming back."

Again, she seemed to be giving him time to digest that; Chip couldn't tell if this was sincere or if she was working him. "And maybe where he has to come back from," she said, "is a place where he doesn't know you. Because he hasn't met you yet."

"Well that's just great, isn't it?"

"No, it isn't. Because it hurts—I can see that. And nothing that hurts is great—not while it's hurting, that's for sure." She gave him a smile—understanding, worldly wise—and was about to say something else when another nurse caught her eye. "I'm on call all night," she said. "Here if you need me."

He watched her shoot down the hall, where there was a light blinking above someone's door. He looked back out the window—the doctors were gone, but Chip found himself wishing they were still there so he wouldn't have to feel so lonely all of a sudden. He found some more change and used it to call Randy at the dorm again.

"Did you see Ellie?"

"No. Not yet."

"But she knows, right?"

Randy didn't answer. Which left one option: Ellie knew, but didn't care. Or at least care enough to say anything. Great.

"Look, I'm sure she knows," Randy said. "She probably just hasn't had a chance to call."

"Maybe someone talked her out of it."

"Why?"

"I don't know. Ramifications."

"Since when does she care about ramifications?"

"Since always. Ellie lives and dies by ramifications."

"Then why do you want her to call?"

"Because I do."

There was a pause, where Chip gave Randy plenty of time to offer up anything else he might know. Randy had only seen Ellie once that day, he said—she was with two other girls and they were all excited about something, but Randy didn't catch it.

"You should've moved in closer."

"I couldn't. One of them was Janet."

"Oh."

"Anyway, I found out later. Katie got into Georgetown. On some like super early admission deal. Full free ride, too. They were doing the jump up and down thing. Lotta noise."

"Georgetown. No shit." Chip hadn't applied anywhere yet, though he knew he was behind; most other people were already up to their essays and getting feedback from Mr. Loughnane. But they weren't already *in* somewhere. Jesus. "Since when did she even want to go there?"

"She met a guy over the summer who's a junior."

"Oh." That's all it took sometimes. "Is the guy into theater?"

"Foreign Service. That's the specialty there."

Chip gave that arrangement one semester, at best; Katie Brocksmith was nobody's long-term girl. She was born to be in the spotlight—rave reviews and curtain calls and cast parties, and men of all ages throwing themselves off bridges for her. She was about as suited to Georgetown as a duck would be in the Gobi Desert.

"But you didn't actually talk to her."

"Who, Katie?"

"Ellie."

"No."

Chip knew this wasn't true. But he forgave Randy; he'd've done the same thing.

"You want me to?"

"No."

Ramifications. Fuck.

7

Laura

She made their lunches for school while the kids finished breakfast. She cleaned up around the sink, listening to them, but still she'd turn around and see for herself—just to make sure they were there: at the table, in her kitchen, in her dominion, where Laura could see and hear them, where she could be reassured that they were still eating, and breathing and functioning—even though she knew that nothing, ever, would reassure her the way she needed it. Not when you've lost one. Not when you've shoveled dirt on a four-year-old's grave. And when the two you have left still can't figure out what hit them.

Nobody did. How could they? How could anyone.

Birthdays and holidays were a given: there would be tears. But also the tiniest, random things would set Laura off, with a jolt, like a thief jumping out of an alley—just because someone crinkled a wrapper a certain way, or someone's kid would laugh, three lines over at the store. The way the trees looked in February—bare branches, flat black and waterlogged against a grey lifeless sky, and suddenly they'd form Liana's face and it would be unbearable. That last hopeful smile, her last little whimper of a cry. The lies they told her, about how she'd be coming home soon, and how Molly and Andy were waiting at the house and would be so excited. Her special pillow with the Little Mermaid on it, that they brought to the hospital, so she could sleep on something familiar; she took her last breath facing Triton, King of the Deep.

Laura wished, all too often, that she could have died instead. Sometimes she wasn't so sure she hadn't. For now—for herself, for everyone—the best she could do, was pretend to be alive. And maybe, one day, she would be again. They'd all be.

At the table, everything was right on track. Andy had some neon cereal Laura couldn't remember buying, and Molly had an English muffin that she was taking forever to eat—which meant that all was just about normal, and soon it would be time for the *Hurry ups* and the *Come on get goings* that would complete their routine and hustle them out of the house in time for school—so that Laura could spend the day by herself, fighting off the fear that something would happen and they'd never come back.

Reassurance. Off the menu, forever.

Then Pick came in, and all the energy in the room swooped over to him—like a vortex you could actually see, and measure on some kind of scope. He put his briefcase down by the phone desk, and folded an overnight bag over the back of a kitchen chair.

"Where you going?"

It was Andy. Pick looked at Laura; obviously she hadn't briefed the kids. Molly, suddenly, had gotten busy on the English muffin and was working on a mouthful. But Andy looked right at him. Andy would stare down a Chinese tank.

"Remember I told you about Mr. Griffin?"

"Yeah, some guy from that place you went to school. So what?"

"So what. He's sick, that's so what. And I gotta go see him."

"B-b-b-but—"

Pick turned to Molly. "But what, Honey?"

"Sandy."

Pick looked over, and Laura sent him her best *Be patient* look, and he countered with his own *Don't tell me what to do* look—and there it was, they were married, this was what it came to sometimes, this is what the years can do. One day they're playing Vivaldi and releasing doves outside the cathedral for you, and the next day they're hiding behind barrels in the dusty center of town, watching the two lone gunslingers squaring off in the road. You draw your gun and I will. Don't and I won't. When it used to be so different. When you couldn't fit a piece of paper in between them.

Certain parts of this, they'd been told what to expect. At one point they were asked to be part of a study, with other parents who had suffered the loss of a child. Laura would have done it, but Pick refused, and they only wanted couples. Later it came out that two thirds of the volunteers were divorced or separated within twenty-four months of their child's death; the rest were, at best, in holding patterns.

Love isn't all, is what every one of those couples said.

"Tell me, Sweetheart."

"You're gonna miss her recital." Andy was answering for Molly. "She's the turtle this year."

Andy often spoke for his sister. Not the best thing and he knew he probably shouldn't. Still, it was touching to see him come to her aid. Even Laura had been struggling more and more, just to have the patience and the detachment to give Molly all the time she needed to get a whole sentence out. It hurt too much to remember when she didn't need help at all.

"Molly," Pick said. "Honey. I'm sorry. I didn't know I'd have to go away this time."

"Y-y-y-ou nev-nev—"

"Please honey. I came to your bunny one and I was there when you were a flower, and—"

She pushed back from the table and ran down the hall crying. Pick paused, looking at her empty chair, half expecting to see a cloud of smoke still holding her shape, as if the Road Runner had just whooshed off.

"She was never a flower, Dad. Liana was the flower."

Pick's face tightened. He looked down the hall. "I'll go talk to her," he decided.

"Don't," Laura advised; as many times as not, going in to make it better only made it worse. "Sometimes she just needs time to herself," she added, hoping that would soften him enough to let Molly be and keep the morning on schedule.

"Maybe you're right," Pick offered. "What'd that neuro-guy say?" he asked. Laura had told him about an appointment with another specialist, that Pick had missed due to the court case.

"Same as the rest. Be patient."

"That's what *we* can do. What about what *he* can do?"

"You asked what he said."

Pick looked down the hall again, in the direction of Molly's room. "He couldn't give ballpark? How long it can take?"

"For Molly, or for us to be patient?"

He looked at her; she was right. They were both equally worried and agitated about Molly's state—Pick was just more upfront about it. In this case, the truth was that Laura was in the same damn hurry he was in—even more, if possible—but she couldn't afford to admit it. She'd feel too guilty if she did.

"All right then," Pick said. "Gotta-gogotta go." He lifted up the suit bag. Rubbed Andy's head. "You're the man now."

Andy nodded, spooned up some more cereal as Pick walked past. He turned to Laura. "You all right?" he asked.

Laura nodded. "I'll take movies of the recital," she said. She remembered then that the camera was messed up—the coating on the lens had gone all streaky somehow. If the recital was that good, she'd buy the tape that the school always makes to sell afterward. They usually did a decent job.

She'd have taken still photos if she still did that. She'd put her camera down when Liana went to the hospital and hadn't picked it up since. Her studio/darkroom where the psychiatrists' office used to be, remained unvisited. The gallery showing her work had folded when the landlord quadrupled the rent, and the owner moved to Portugal. She hadn't bothered to look for someone new.

"I can stay, you know. I could do all this from the phone if I had to."

"He asked for you, Sandy. He might be dying. You don't want a phone call on your conscience."

Pick agreed; Laura's logic always had a way of cutting through. He asked her if she was okay again. She told him she was, and thanks. They kissed goodbye—somewhere between a routine kiss and a wish that it wasn't. And then he was gone; the vortex followed him into the garage. Laura heard him back the car out and into the street and then floor the thing, just to get to a corner stop sign. Pick only drove that way, she knew, when he felt he had no power of his own. Patience was never going to be his thing.

"Who's Stewart Goodman?"

Laura turned, looked at Andy. "Daddy knew him in high school," she said. "So did I." She watched him get up from the table. "Why?"

"I heard him on the phone this morning. You were in the shower. Dad was telling some guy it was gonna be his fat fuckin' ass if he didn't find Stewart Goodman."

"Excuse me?"

Andy shrugged. "He said it, not me."

He went to the refrigerator, drank some orange juice straight from the carton, then walked past Laura as if he hadn't just done that, and hadn't just sworn in front of her to boot. "I'll tell Molly she can come out now."

Laura watched him go. She looked at Andy's cereal bowl, at the floating bits he'd left behind. The cereal came in colors made in laboratories, and Laura wondered how this one had made it into the house. They must have slipped it past when her resistance was low, which wouldn't be all that difficult; there were times when they could have hosted game shows in the living room, and Laura wouldn't have noticed.

She saw the clock then and snapped out of it. There was a day ahead, after all, and days are to be gotten on with. Because no one knew more than she did, you only get them once.

8

Griffin

There was grey in his hair, and the stubble on his face showed white. His eyes, barely open, were glazed and distant. There wasn't a single vital function his body could perform for itself; machines crowded around him, hovering like apostles. His wife dabbed moistener on his lips.

"I made the mistake of telling him he looked 'distinguished,'" Mary told Pick. "Because of the hair. He said turning fifty was enough, I didn't have to throw fuel on the fire."

Pick grinned, but couldn't hold it for long. "Can he hear me?" he asked.

"No one knows," Mary answered. "The studies all disagree. I prefer to think he can."

Pick moved in a little closer. A thin trail of perspiration went down from Griffin's forehead and then behind his ear, pooling up in a nickel-sized cleft in the pillowcase. His breathing was slow, somnolent, narcotic. It sounded awful.

"Mr. Griffin. It's Sandy Piccolo. It's Pick, Mr. Griffin." He shrugged. "I called in a bunch of big shots. They're gonna take care of you . . ."

"It must be driving him mad," Mary said. "Imagine not even being able to say hello."

From a million miles away, Griffin heard that. He felt pulses going, in his brain—like downed power lines, damaged after a storm, whipping themselves on wet and tragic streets. Showers of sparks exploding as the wires tripped back and forth; convulsing, out of control. Trying to reconnect with whatever they can.

His first day in front of a classroom. His hundredth. His promotion to Dean. A long-ago September night, in his office.

"My name is Carmine Piccolo."

Griffin looked up from his desk. Every muscle he had went tight.

"You got a minute?"

Griffin nodded. Carmine nodded back, and then two more men walked into the room, flanking him. This is how they get you, Griffin thought. When you're working late—when you're alone. Only what were they getting him for? Why was Carmine Piccolo standing across from him, with bodyguards? What could they possibly want with the dean of a boarding school?

Carmine gestured, and then the kid slouched in, so dwarfed by his father standing there that it looked hard for him to breathe. "This is Santamo," Carmine said. "I want him to go to school here. I want him to live in the dormitory."

It was the third week of the term; enrollment was capped and there wasn't a single open spot. And a waiting list, twenty spots deep—all who'd gone, diligently, through every step of the process. There'd be trustees to deal with, and the board, and they each had their favorites on the list; Griffin had no appetite to do battle for a latecomer who'd sidestepped all the rules.

"He'll need to take a few tests," he heard himself say. "Placement exams. And we'll need his transcripts, from his current school."

Carmine nodded. "Work it out." He gestured to his bodyguards. They backed away and stood in the anteroom. He looked at Griffin again. "I've heard about you. You're tough. That's good—Santamo

needs tough." He turned and walked out of the room, without look-
ing at the boy, or saying goodbye. The bodyguards followed him and
closed the door.

Griffin sat still, listening to their footsteps going away. What
had just happened? What was he going to tell Mary when he went
home tonight? Let's see, the student council wants the dress code
repealed, which student councils want every year. Alumni Weekend
coming along as planned, three students have the flu already, another
might have mono—and oh yes, I nearly forgot—a crime lord stopped
by the office and left his son behind. And how was your day?

"Could you not call me Santamo?"

Griffin took him in. Thin, angry, dark, all coiled up and tight
as a wire. Offer a dollar for every ounce of meat on his bones, and
you'd still have your dollar.

"I'd rather be called Sandy. Or Pick—Pick would be even better."

Griffin waited. They could hear the car outside, leaving. The low
rumble of a heavy V-8.

"I hate the son of a bitch. I don't want him for a father. He doesn't
want me for a son. We only live a couple minutes from here, so why
do I gotta be a boarding student? You tell me. I hate him."

"Mr. Piccolo." That stopped him; with kids like this, it usually
did. "We try not to call our father a son of a bitch."

"Even if he is one?"

9

Pick

He turned the car off when he realized he'd been sitting there idling for too long. He looked up at the sign over the door; with the engine off now he could hear the little electric buzzes and neon snaps that came from old age and exposure to the elements.

Piccolo's—For Fine Dining.

Going to see his father was an ordeal Pick avoided whenever he could. Certainly theirs was not the Madison Avenue version of a family visit: car pulling up, kids bounding out, grandparents at the door, flinging their arms open wide, travel-weary parents happy to be back again. Happy to be home.

This was not that. The oceans would turn to Marmite first.

He tore off the visitor's pass from the hospital and crumpled it down to nothing. Left it on the seat and went inside.

"I got *shot* and you didn't come to see *me!*"

"You didn't get shot, Pop. You got shot *at.* And besides, you told me not to come."

"And that's the time you pick to listen to me?"

"That's the time," Pick answered.

Carmine rocked forward in his office chair. A metal walker waited by the side of his desk—but being Carmine's, even that looked like you'd better not give it any shit. He called out towards the kitchen. "Donato! Heat somethin' up! Somethin' for Santamo!"

"Don't call me Santamo, Pop . . ."

"What's wrong with Santamo? Santamo's your name."

"I changed it. Legally. Why do I have to tell you this every time?"

"Because it's bullshit."

He led Pick out to the dining room and sat down. Little by little, Donato brought plates out, while the staff hung back and watched from the kitchen door.

"You visit your mother yet?"

Pick shook his head; he hadn't gone to the cemetery. "I went to the hospital. After that I came here."

Carmine reached for the loaf of bread, broke some off. "Go see her," he said. "Take some flowers. Sweep up the grave."

"Pop—"

"Make it nice. Aunt Luisa too. She's two down and to the right. With that fuckface she married."

"I know where Aunt Luisa's buried."

"Then go there."

He dipped the bread into a dish of olive oil, then some fresh *arrabiatta*. Pick looked at the staff hanging back, watching. Carmine grinned. "Big time lawyer they're lookin' at. They see the news. They know."

Pick watched him stuff the bread in. Carmine used to say this was the only food he trusted, and the only kind he'd ever eat. The worst was back in the early days, when he had to go to foreign neighborhoods to shake people down house by house at dinnertime; they'd offer *pierogi*, and basement beer, in exchange for not pissing blood in the morning. Half the reason he rose so quickly, he'd tell you, was the cuisine. He liked what he liked and he didn't like anything else.

"So, Pop. Listen—"

"Finish your food. You'll hurt Donato's feelings." Carmine reached for the loaf of bread again. "Big time lawyer." He laughed, and looked over at Donato, who laughed along with him yet couldn't get over the sight of Pick coming back here—successful, on the news and everything. He snuck him a look of approval, which meant a lot; praise from Donato didn't come cheap.

They walked outside the restaurant, up to the lot nobody used anymore. Carmine shot a glance over at Pick's car—which meant, here it comes. Any minute now. Carmine missed nothing.

"What is it, Pop."

"What's what?"

"What you're thinking. 'It's not a Cadillac. It's not even a Lincoln—why's he gotta buy from Germany? What did they ever do for us?'"

"You're nuts. I didn't say nothin' about the car. Did I say a thing about the friggin' car?"

"Only because you get more out of not saying it."

Carmine shook his head. "Guy's fuckin' nuts." He pushed the walker up the rise, over crumbling macadam and thick weed roots. "If you're American you should drive American—that's all." He turned to Pick, following behind. "But you knew that."

"It was built in Tennessee, Pop."

"So? So where's the money go?"

"To people who live in Tennessee. So they can pay their taxes and put food on the table and send their kids to school."

"You think so, huh?"

"Yeah, Pop—I think so. You can buy a Ford built in Korea or a Toyota from Mississippi. It doesn't work like it used to anymore. Money doesn't carry a flag."

"Big shot," Carmine said.

Pick was surprised to find a chair already set up. An old lawn chair, but at least it meant his dad came out here sometimes.

He'd make the climb up to this spot, and he'd sit in his chair and he'd look out at the valley—and what? Think? And what would he think about if he did?

"Thirty million bucks, I heard. Not bad. What was the guy—a doctor, right?"

"He was a surgeon," Pick said. As if Carmine didn't know that, as if he hadn't been following the case all along. "Now he's done. The rest was arithmetic."

"What do you get, a third of that?"

"More or less."

Carmine shrugged it off. "I coulda got you more," he said. "And without goin' to court."

"Can you get him his hand back?" Pick asked, and knew that he shouldn't have, because what good would it do? He hadn't come here to fight—and even if he had, it wouldn't matter anyway. He could keep upping Carmine, and Carmine could keep upping him, and each was as stubborn as the other and there was nowhere good that this could go; whatever Carmine did to Pick as a kid, Pick did right back as an adult—by leaving, as soon as he could. By rejecting everything about him. By shutting him out of his life.

"I gotta find Goody, Pop. It's for Griffin. I need your help."

Carmine looked at Pick. "What'd you try?"

"Everything. Everything I could think of. So, I'm here."

Carmine thought some. Like going through old files. "Wasn't he into some kinda hippie shit?"

"Yes and no."

"The hell's that mean?"

"It means yes he was, but no it wasn't hippie shit. Some Buddhist monks picked him up the day he took off and he went out west with them and stayed at their temple. That's where he wrote that fuckin' book, and nailed Laura and me to the wall with it. Whatever the hell was Buddhist about that, somebody oughtta tell me someday."

"Well? Steal a guy's girlfriend, guy writes a book about it, I don't know—seems like a draw to me."

"It's not a draw, Pop. I loved her. What he did was revenge. It was almost a movie for Christ's sake. Can you imagine? Talk about telling the whole world."

Carmine was with him there; even he had gotten one of his people to read through Goody's book when it came out. You never know what the kid might have observed—and the movie people, you don't want them picking up on the wrong thing, the shiny thing, and running with it all out of proportion. Then you have to go around and break heads. "Ever find out what happened?" he asked.

Pick shook his head. "I don't look a gift horse. Enough that it all went away. And right after that, so did Goody. Again."

They were quiet. Pick looked down at the roof of the restaurant. There were leaves in the gutters, packed in deep and groaning—he remembered how Carmine used to force him up there to clean them out. There'd be nasty wet mush, and birdshit and worms. Stiff twigs that stabbed out and dragged scratch lines along his arm.

Still, he thought. In retrospect? Something like that would be easy. Give him a gutter to clean today and he'd thank you for it. Job like that'd be a dream.

"You never wanted my help before," Carmine said.

"I never wanted to need it."

A pair of wrens screeched overhead. Two more showed up and screeched back—suddenly lots of wings were flapping madly and all hell broke loose for a while, and then just as quickly it ended. There were no apparent winners; feathers hung in the air as if on strings.

"Maybe he don't want to be found," Carmine said.

"Too bad," Pick told him. "I gotta find him anyway."

Carmine shifted his walker a little like he was pretending to take in the view, but to Pick the man looked tired. The kind of tired where you can get twenty years older in the time it takes for a cloud to pass by. Pick wondered if he was the cloud this time.

"You look skinny, Santamo."

"I was always skinny."

"Well now you look it."

Pick clenched his jaw. He looked out, past the restaurant. He didn't know you could see the school from up here, but there it was: little blue dot of a bell tower in the distance. Unmistakable. He felt like the place was reeling him in now—slow and sure, like a kite, pulled by a hand that was as strong as it was unseen. Killing the lie that he was ever flying free in the first place.

"I lost a grandchild," Carmine said. "I find this out from your wife. The funeral, from your wife—*after* it happened. What kinda shit is that?"

"You wouldn't have come anyway," Pick said back, and as soon as he did he was sorry. Sorry for getting drawn in, for getting thrown off track, sorry his daughter died and sucker-punched their whole lives and he didn't call his father and tell him about it. He was sorry for so much shit right now that he didn't know where to start.

"I should've told you," Pick admitted. "I should have called, and told you, and left it up to you."

Carmine looked away. He sucked some air through his teeth. "Go visit your mother," he said. "I'm going back inside."

Pick watched him, but stayed back for a bit, before driving back into town. He knew he couldn't do what Carmine had told him; Liana's funeral was one cemetery too many. Standing there with Laura, choking back the taste of that grappa and wondering why they didn't just skip past drinking and score some morphine from the hospital instead. As if anything could keep out the cold dull hell of what that day was like.

He remembered this sad bunch of flowers somebody had handed him at the church—hyacinths, Laura told him later, and he'd hated those things ever since. When it was time to lay them down on Liana's grave he just couldn't do it; he left them in the crook of some tree roots, and huddled back to the limo. Squinting through streaks of rain at the rest of the cemetery—the jumbled rows of tombs planted there, big fat waterdrops bouncing off the headstones like marbles, pinging onto neighboring headstones before a final, mortal swan dive to the ground.

If you couldn't see the names, Pick thought, you could almost pretend that all of this was here for some other reason— any other reason. Someone dropping down from another planet, for instance. Give them a thousand guesses what's under those markers, and boxes full of bones would never cross their minds.

10

Laura

She got a shot glass and a bottle of vodka and took them to the kitchen table, where she'd brought the yearbook, dug out from the guest room closet. There was a solarized picture of the bell tower on the cover, with *The Clarion Call* embossed on it, and *The Past is Prologue* gilded underneath. As a student Laura never really understood what that meant; to her, *The Past is Prologue* was just one of those slogans yearbooks always have—the kind of thing grafted onto school crests when they don't have something in Latin instead.

Now, in this kitchen, alone at night, a wife and a mother and feeling a failure at both—now Laura got it. You don't start learning until you start remembering; it's the things that stay with you that become your guides. Just as the things you forget can become your demons.

The hard part, though, is when you want to forget things that won't stay forgotten. Like breaking Goody's heart—twice—that'd be a good place to start. All the way back to her original sin. And like any good sin, it followed her, and Pick, everywhere. Like the paint cans in the basement, the file cabinets in the

garage, the rusted push-mower in the shed off the porch—
Goody lived in the corners, the creases, the tucked-away parts
of their house and their lives. They never talked about it, but
they knew. To talk about it was to admit it was there.

Andy came in; Laura closed the book like it was contraband.
Sat up straight and wondered why she just did that. "What are
you doing up?"

"I forgot to check the locks."

"I already checked them."

"Dad wants me to do it anyway when he's gone." He walked
over to the cupboard and helped himself to another shot glass.
"Set me up."

"Aren't you taking this man of the house thing a little too far?"

"I can drink grape juice, and pretend."

"Pretend *what?*"

She watched him go to the refrigerator and get out the
Welch's. He brought the jar over and plunked down his shot
glass. "Start a tab."

Laura gave him a look and poured for him. They clinked
the glasses together and emptied them. Laura poured seconds,
while Andy started flipping through the yearbook. "So, who's
this Stewart guy anyway?" he asked.

"He was Daddy's best friend. In high school. They were very
close. But they had kind of a fight."

"Did Dad win the fight?"

"Nobody won the fight. Nobody wins any fight."

"Right, Mom."

She looked at him. "They haven't spoken to each other since."

Andy looked down at the yearbook. "So why's Dad trying
to find him?"

"Because they were close to Mr. Griffin. He was like a father.
And he asked for both of them."

"But Dad has a father."

"I know. But 'father' and 'like a father' are different sometimes."

He cocked an eyebrow at her. Already a lawyer. He turned the page, landed on the picture of the *Echo Review* staff. "Stewart Goodman," he pointed. "That's him?"

"That's him. I met him in tenth grade. But this was taken in twelfth."

Andy looked closer. There was a separate picture of Goody, accepting some kind of scroll. "You can win things for writing?"

Laura nodded. "He was good then, and he got better. He wrote a book."

"Yeah?" He looked again. "What kind of a book?"

Laura thought about how to answer that. *The kind he never should have had to write? The kind your mother drove him to? Your mother and your father—do you really want to know?* "It was a good book," she said finally. "It was really popular for a while. They were going to make a movie out of it."

"He must be rich," Andy figured.

Laura shook her head. "Everything he made," she said, "he gave away."

"What do you mean? Why would he do that?"

Laura wondered how little of this she could get by with and still get him to go to bed soon. "Stewart wrote the book from a monastery, out in the Northwest. A monastery is like a church, except there are people, called monks, who spend their whole lives praying there, and not just Sundays. They gave Stewart a job and let him live there. And then when his writing made money, he turned it over to them."

She hoped Andy would let her leave it there. When you got down to it, this is just how Goody was; for him, a vow of poverty would have been redundant—he never wanted money in the first place. If he didn't give it to the monastery he would have given it somewhere else. There'd be open palms anywhere he looked.

"Here he is again," Andy pointed. He was at the back of the yearbook, where all the candid shots were. "He's kissing someone."

"Give me that."

But Andy pressed down; leaned in closer for a better look. "Hey, that's—"

Laura swept the book out from under him. "It's late, young man. Let's go."

He argued the whole way back to his room. And when he wasn't arguing he was asking questions—about his dad and Stewart Goodman, about the fight they had, why they had the fight and why his dad seemed so extra uptight when he left that morning. But Laura held firm and didn't give in.

She made him brush his teeth a second time, for the grape juice. She turned out the light and kissed him on the forehead—eager to get back to having some time for herself, even more to get out of this bedroom before Andy picked up on that yearbook again and the things he'd seen inside. *I met Stewart first,* she could have said, *before I met Daddy. And things got a little tangled after that.* But then he'd want to know details, and Laura just wasn't up for that tonight. They were all in the book, that was for sure. Goody had laid it out like a road map. And she hoped her kids would never see it.

"Can you sing something?" Andy asked. So long since he'd made a request like that—simple and real, and actually doable. So she got on the bed next to him, and turned her head away so he wouldn't smell the drinking on her breath.

"The night we met, I knew I needed you so . . . And if I had the chance, I'd never let you go."

"I like that one," Andy said.

"So won't you say you love me? I'll make you so proud of me . . ."

"That's Darlene Love, right?"

Laura shook her head. "The Ronettes. Darlene Love sang with the Crystals." Andy nodded, banked that information, and didn't interrupt her anymore. He felt sleepy and cozy and didn't want his mother to stop.

"We'll make them turn their heads every place we go! So, won't you please be my, be my baby?"

He fell asleep before she got out of the second chorus. Laura finished the song anyway, and then sang it once again, just for herself, looking the whole time at a picture on the night table of her and Pick. A Polaroid Andy had taken, while they were on a car trip to Annapolis—where Pick had a client, where Laura could feel the snap of salt air on her skin again, and where Andy saw the Naval Academy and declared he wanted to go there, until he found out what time they make you get up in the morning, and how many hours you have to spend shining and polishing things that are already shiny and polished, and how much they yell at you, all the time it seemed, whether you did something wrong or not. He needed that, he said, like he needed a second butt.

That whole trip seemed so long ago, Laura thought. Eons. She was still a mother of three back then. She ran her life in reverse for a while; wondering where all the time went and thinking about what she had done with it. And what she hadn't done. And how in the world she might know what to do next.

"*So won't you please . . . so won't you please . . . so won't you please . . .*"

She listened to Andy's breathing. She thought about the yearbook downstairs, still on the kitchen table where she left it. It, and the vodka, could wait.

11

Pick

He looked down at Wilkes-Barre from his hotel room. His view wrapped around from Market Square to the river. But the place was the same to Pick in any direction: somewhere to get away from, and quick. He knew all along he was going to have to escape here, to put this valley and Carmine behind him if he would ever be able to survive. He didn't get out the way Goody did—just running the fuck away in a rainstorm— but he left here all the same, and there wasn't a single thing about it that he missed. He envied the ones who stayed in their hometowns, and built their lives there, and were happy with that. He wondered what it would be like to feel at home in the town you came from. To have it be a part of you that you would actually want to keep.

Immigrant families settled the place—Polish and Irish and Italian, miners and millworkers, union people. They had big hard knuckles and lots of kids, and they built their own churches and drove proud GM cars with heavy bags of road salt in the trunk, for traction in winter. They brought their old customs with them and passed them along, and from front porches and stoops and cellars they fed and fired the same blood feuds and rivalries that they'd carefully nurtured back home, over centuries. Growing up among them, Pick often wondered why they all bothered to leave the Old Country in the first place, since they always made it sound so great. He asked it out loud once, and got smacked for his efforts. No one liked a wise guy.

The river flooded when he was six. His mother had been dead less than a year. He remembered the chaos that came; the smell, the rescue sirens, the people who flocked to Carmine and said they'd lost everything, bringing soggy photographs of loved ones who'd drowned, and stories of houses washing away.

After Mass one day, Pick told Father Jerome he didn't believe in God anymore, because God sent that rainbow to Noah and swore to him there wouldn't be a flood like that ever again, and then there was—so God must either be lying or not God after all if He's not going to keep a simple promise. Father Jerome listened very thoughtfully, then went behind Pick's back and told Carmine everything he had said. When God didn't stay Carmine's hand, Pick stopped believing in priests. He couldn't remember the last time he prayed.

"How's it going?" he asked.

"Fine," Laura said. "How's it there? How's the hotel?"

"Pretty much the same. They're renovating. They're sorry for the disturbance."

"Do they still have the uniformed doormen?"

"They're gone. The barber shop's gone too."

"I didn't know there was a barber shop there."

"It was downstairs. Carmine used to take me. Something tells me he didn't pay." She sounded lighter, Pick thought. Off her guard. Drinking, probably; he knew she'd been hitting it lately. He wondered how much of that had to do with him.

"So, did you ask?" Laura was saying. She meant Carmine. She meant, did he throw himself prostrate and genuflect for help. Or maybe that's just the way he thought she meant it.

"Yeah," Pick said. "I went to see Griffin first. It doesn't look good."

"I'm sorry."

"You liked him, too."

"I said I was sorry."

Shit, he thought. *Here we go again. Not tonight. I cannot do Dodge City again tonight.* "I don't know what the old man's gonna do," he said. "Whether he's gonna help find Goody or not."

"Do you think he even could?"

"Maybe. Probably." He felt tired. Sapped. Carmine could find him all right—the day the Mob couldn't root a person out would be pretty sad all around. "Plus," Pick said, "I'm gonna see if they can move Griffin back to the house."

"Really? They can do that?"

Pick shrugged. "He's not any better and he's not any worse. Why shouldn't he be home someplace where it's not so depressing for everyone?"

"As long as the doctors are okay with it, I guess."

"We'll see what they say. Anyway, look. I'm gonna get some sleep. Kiss the kids."

"I did that. Hours ago."

Pick looked at the room clock. Christ. "Well then it's your turn now. Don't stay up all night."

"I won't."

He washed up and got into bed. He thought about how they always used to kiss goodnight, over the phone, the times when he was away, and how long it took for them to hang up. He didn't know when they stopped doing that, or if they officially had stopped, or when it was they drifted off. It probably happened, like a lot of things, when everything else did. When good nights themselves became a thing of the past.

He set the clock radio for morning and made sure it wasn't tuned to a religious station with the volume all the way up. Pick knew Andy liked to do that on purpose in hotels, as a courtesy prank for the next guest—but plenty enough other people did it for real; wherever you went, city or country or wilderness, somewhere on the dial there was a religious station. There was an endless market for faith it seemed. Or maybe they were spy stations, saying things in code—every fourth *Hallelujah* could mean the coup d'etat is one step closer; every *Amen* another reformer in shackles, being led down urinated hallways in the night.

He turned off the light. He thought about Andy, and how he was growing so much. Then about Molly and how hurt she must be, to not even be able to talk right anymore. Then, before he got to Liana, he stopped thinking at all. The only way he could think of her, was not to.

He listened to a tow truck outside, hoisting a car up and securing it with chains. Then, when things had finally gone quiet, he heard a bell from somewhere and he knew it had to be the school; in the quiet of the night it had no competition. If you closed your eyes, you could think you were right on campus, with homework due in the morning.

He hated being back here.

Where the fuck was Goody.

He flicked the cigarette out the window and looked across the room. At this galoof he had to live with now. So what if the kid had to live with him, too? Who was the injured party here? Try a brand-new school, in your last fucking year. Try sleeping in your own bed one night and then the next night you're in a lousy dormitory— surrounded by Beatles posters, with this freak from Hershey who knows every fucking word of every fucking song, and probably in the order they came out. Who the fuck is from Hershey, anyway? Who the fuck lives there—little candy people?

And on top of all that, he was Jewish.

"So?" Goody asked.

"I'm just sayin', I never met any Jews before. Two, maybe."

"S'no big deal. God is God."

Pick closed the window. There was a floodlight on the corner of the chapel vestry, and just enough of it was leaking in through the trees. He remembered driving by that building with friends not two weeks ago, throwing beer cans. "Religion's phony." Pick was sure of this. "Buncha grownups tryin' to make people jump through hoops. It's a scam."

Maybe now he gets it—coming here wasn't exactly a choice. Why would it be? With Carmine for a father you didn't get choices. You got commands.

"I think it's like a box," Goody said.

"What is?"

"Religion. It's like a big giant box, in the middle of a stadium. Each side is painted a different color. Everybody is in the stadium but from where they're sitting they can only see one side of the box. Only one color. And that's the color they believe in."

"So?"

"So, inside the box, is God."

Then he was quiet over there. Like he was thinking about it. Like he thought about shit like that all the time. This interested Pick, who never thought about it at all. "So how come you're here?" he asked.

"Here? At school? I wanted to be."

"You get beat up at home or something?"

Goody looked at him. "I just wanted to be away at school," he said. "What about you?"

"My old man dropped me off. The car was running the whole time." He could see Goody thinking about that. "Somebody told me your dad died," he added. "Like over the summer."

Goody didn't say anything; Pick took that as yes enough. "What happened?"

Again, Goody was quiet for a while. Normally Pick liked this; he smelled weakness. But strangely, he didn't do what he was used to doing when this happened—he didn't rub a thumb in it.

"He had a heart attack," Goody ended up saying.

"No shit."

Goody confirmed. "It was on a golf course. It was July."

"In Hershey?"

"Yeah, in Hershey—Hershey has golf courses. Listen I don't want to talk about this. I was supposed to have a single room this year—Mr. Griffin said there was a new kid and maybe I'd be a good roommate for him. It wasn't like I could say no or anything."

"Hey, this wasn't my idea either. Christ, Goody." Pick had heard guys in the hall calling him Goody before, so he gave it a shot.

"I didn't say it was anybody's idea. And I didn't say I didn't want you to be here. My dad had a heart attack and he died on a golf course and the golf course was in Hershey, and the rest of it I don't want to talk about—all right? That's all I said." Pick made a mental note about the part where Goody had said *"the rest of it."* Again he sensed a weak spot. *"Let's just talk about something else,"* Goody went on. *"Or maybe go to sleep. Sleep is a really popular thing here at the school—some people do it every night."*

Pick got a kick out of that. Just because this guy was some kind of deep thinker and all, didn't mean he was all soft and would just roll over. He looked around the room: the light from outside was laying a big pattern across Goody's bed and hitting this little rug he had, the kind you use to step out of the shower. The floor itself was made out of those big squares of thinnest-possible linoleum, many of them chipped and broken at the corners; all kinds of hair and shit got stuck down there and ground in over time. A paper clip, a trapezoid shard of an old broken light bulb, a flattened-out piece of gum from the Second World War. Pick made a vow never to go barefoot in this room.

"What about girls?" he asked.

"What about them?" Goody sounded tired; Pick was wearing him down. That was good—when people are worn down and off their guard, that's when they start to tell the truth. One helpful thing Carmine had passed along. One of the few.

"What are they like here."

"The girls? They're girls."

Pick nodded. *That could mean a lot of different things. "So how do I put this," he said.*

"How do you put what?"

"Let's say on a scale of one to ten, in the area of personal virtue."

"Yeah?"

"Well, where are they? Where would you say most of them fall?"

"For crying out loud, Santamo—"

"Pick," came the correction. "Call me Pick. And don't think I forgot the question."

"I didn't forget—you asked it five seconds ago—I just don't know how to answer. Everyone's different, I guess. When you like someone, you find out for yourself."

"Yeah but we're roommates," Pick said. "I thought that was the whole big sell job on putting kids in dorms together. We're supposed to tell each other this shit."

"Maybe not the first night," Goody said back, and he turned away in his bed. No surer sign to Pick that as far as Goody was concerned, this conversation was over.

"Then what about you?" he asked. "You got a girlfriend?"

"I do," Goody said. "But I don't want to talk about her."

"So, God's okay, you can talk about that. But not your girlfriend, and not your dad."

"Not the first night," Goody said again, and then he went cold. Pick could feel that, from across the room. And he guessed he'd have to accept it, and be quiet. So, he did.

But shit, man. It was his first night here. And he was wide awake and didn't want to be. He might have to resort to counting front doors again; he had this habit where he'd picture all the front doors on the houses along his street, and count them. And any time he got them in the wrong order, or left out a certain detail, he'd have to start all over again. Nights when it was really bad, he could go all the way to the light at Keezic Street; he was really hoping this wasn't one of those nights.

"Tell you what," Goody said, long after Pick figured he was in dreamland.

"What?"

"You see that poster by your bed? The Yellow Submarine one."

Of course Pick saw it; it was impossible not to see that thing. So fucking bright that even in the dark you couldn't get away from it. He heard once that you can see the Great Barrier Reef from outer space, with the naked eye. Add this poster, and Pick would believe it. "What about it?" he asked.

"The bottom left corner. Right behind Ringo—lift up the tape a little. I have a couple things of Percodan I keep back there."

"You're kidding me," Pick said.

They were his dad's, Goody explained, for a bad knee. And now that he wouldn't be having that earthly problem anymore, Goody availed himself. He said they helped with his writing sometimes, plus they made it easier to sleep on the nights when his mind wouldn't shut down on its own. "I'll split one with you," he offered. "We'll get a pretty good buzz for about half an hour, and then pass out. Tomorrow's Saturday—I have a service project but if they didn't assign you to anything yet, you'll be able to sleep in if you want."

"You are fucking kidding me," was all Pick could say back to that.

"Look behind Ringo," Goody told him, "and see."

12

Chip

He sat with his mother by his father's bed. There was a nurse there too, always—if not in the room every minute then damn nearby, and ready to blaze back in if any of those buzzers went off. But even though that part was pretty strange, Chip was glad to have his dad home. He wasn't sure how it happened, but he wasn't complaining; anything was better than that hospital.

His teachers had given him the morning off—to "acclimate," they said, but the truth was that they were worried about the way he looked, and decided as a group that a mental health day was in order—at least through lunch, and after that they were still leaving it up to him. Again, Chip wasn't complaining. Normally he didn't like missing class; it was too easy to fall behind when he did that, and he didn't like to mess with his rhythm. But things were seriously not normal right now, and they might not be getting that way for a while. So if they were offering, he was taking.

"What are all those black and blue marks?" he asked. His dad was pocked with bruises, up and down his body—misshapen lakes of purple and sickish discoloration, like he'd been roughed up by muggers and left on a doorstep.

"Those are from blood samples," Mary said. "The nurses have to take blood, and they can't keep using the same spot."

Chip looked again; it didn't seem like there'd be many spots left before long. He wondered what they'd do after that. If after that ever came.

The bell rang outside, and people started going to class. When it rang again they would change classes until it rang for lunch and then rang again before and after each of the afternoon classes and then for dinner and study hall and then the lights out warning bell and then the final bell that ended the day until seven in the morning when it started all over again.

It was supposed to be a big privilege to ring it. For the longest time it was the seniors' responsibility—back when the school was started, different members of the graduating class were tapped for the honor of going inside the bell tower and climbing halfway up its length so they could pull the rope up and down at scheduled times of the day, and the custom held for years. Then when the school had its Centennial they switched it to incoming freshmen, to make them feel like part of the place—until a few years ago when some mastermind in the Young Inventors' Club figured out how to run the whole operation through a Macintosh computer and a half dozen winches that could be triggered on a schedule, and they never went back after that—only for high level ceremonies and when special guests came, like a big time donor or some distinguished graduate who'd come back to get crowned or something, and then give a speech. Last year alone there was an astronaut, then someone who helped invent an even smaller microchip, and a woman who owned eight Pizza Huts, only she had to cancel. And for the first one this year they had a guy who sold more tires than anyone in the world. He had a mansion and a lake house, up near Duluth. Top of the country and top of the world, he told them. Top of the pile. Don't forget what they're teaching you here.

Chip saw Ellie two times since his dad got sick—and both times she had other people around. At some point though, she'd managed to slip an envelope through the mail slot at the house; it was more like a sympathy card than anything else. It sounded so formal, dry as a recipe—like she copied it out of an etiquette book and then had all her friends go over it with red pencils, checking to make sure nothing of any substance got said. The Ramification Squad.

"Who's paying for all this?" he asked.

It was as good a time as any to bring it up. The nurse had gone outside, and was knocking back whatever it was that she kept in that thermos. In a few more hours the next one would come and this one would bring her up to date, and then go home. There were seven of them in all, sometimes two at a time, sent by the same agency that came in with the bed and about a ton of other stuff. Round the clock, every day. Chip knew that took money.

"A friend of the family," his mother told him.

"Really," Chip said. "I didn't know the family had any rich friends."

Mary looked at him. "We're covered, but only to a degree. No one knows how long this might take. Health plans have their limits."

"My college money."

"That's a last resort. Let's not think that far."

The phone rang in the kitchen. Chip listened as the recording kicked in, and his father's voice floated down the hall through the speaker. He had a way of making the smallest little instruction—*Please leave a message*—sound like advice you could use all your life.

"So, who's the friend?" he asked.

Mary looked at him. Maybe she hoped he'd forgotten. "Sandy Piccolo," she said.

"Piccolo. You mean like Carmine Piccolo? The Mafia guy?"

"He owns a restaurant, Chip. Sandy is his son. He's a lawyer, in New York."

"I think you better have some coffee, Mom. And wake the heck up. If one is connected, so is the other. That's how they do it."

"Says who?"

"Says everybody."

"Everybody said the world was flat, too."

Chip couldn't believe this. He remembered Mrs. Levering saying the name, but he'd discounted it at the time—and now here it was again. He looked around the room, at all the medical gear sustaining his father. "You know what happens when you take money from these people? How do you even know them?"

"He was a student here."

"The father or the son?"

"The son," Mary said. "Sandy." Although the idea of Carmine attending Pocono Prep as a youth was an entertaining one.

"So, of the two guys Dad asked for," Chip said, "one of them is a New York lawyer, Mafia guy's son."

"He owns a restaurant," Mary repeated. "He's a restaurant owner's son."

"What about the other one?"

"He was a writer."

"Was—what's that mean, he's dead?"

Mary shook her head. "He gave it up," she told him. "He'd been living at a monastery at one point. He was training to become a monk."

"A monk . . . what kind of a monk?"

"A Buddhist monk. The people he lived with were Buddhist monks."

"No way," Chip said. "You mean like those guys that set themselves on fire, to protest wars and stuff?" He'd seen the photos in Mrs. Cacia's class. Her husband had been killed by a sniper at An Loc, when he stopped to pet a goat.

"There are other kinds," Mary said. Hoping that Goody was not one of the ones who set himself on fire, for anything. She couldn't get the pictures out of her head.

Chip thought of what he knew about monks, which was not very much—basically they seemed to swear off, through the ages, anything that seemed like fun to people who weren't monks. "Why would someone do that?" he asked.

"Do what?" His mother looked like she was ten topics away already.

"Become a monk. What's in it for them?"

Mary couldn't speak for everyone, she said; only what she knew already about Goody. "Stewart was always looking for something. He was thoughtful. He wrote beautifully. He was popular. But he was always unsettled, too. Unsatisfied. He always had to know why."

"Why what?"

"Why everything. Why are we here? How did it happen? Why are there so many people in pain in the world, while others have so many advantages? And what are we supposed to do about it?"

"He asked those things in high school?"

"He did. Stewart asked those questions. He wrote essays about them, in the *Echo Review*. Some won national awards."

Chip thought about that. A wealthy lawyer and a guy who wondered things, who might have turned into a monk. What kind of hold could his father have over these two people, from that far back, that they would jump out of their lives just because he asked—and what kind of hold did they have on him that they would be the ones?

"But he also might not be what you said," Chip said.

"You're right," Mary admitted. "He could be anything." She filled Chip in a little; Goody had been quite visible, for a while—newspapers, magazines, interviews with the explosive young author—the press loved the monastery angle, as much as Goody tried to downplay it at the time. But then, after that? Nothing. At his peak he disappeared.

"How come?" Chip asked.

"Nobody knows," Mary told him. Thinking about the speed of it all, how Goody had gone from obscurity to fame and then right back to obscurity—beyond it, actually—in such a short amount of time. He walked out on all of it, and just vanished. It was really quite a feat.

"What was it about?" Chip asked. "The book he wrote."

Mary looked at him. She heard the nurse coming back down the hall.

Angels, these people.

13

Laura

No one knew this, but since September she had started going into the city again. Now that Molly was in first grade and in the same school as Andy, there was time to do things like that; park the car somewhere safe, check out the photo galleries, quick little lunch somewhere and get back home before the bus dropped the kids off. She could have been a super hero, fighting crime during school hours, and they wouldn't have known. As long as she was home when they came in.

It wasn't just about having the time, though; after so many months, Laura was finally beginning to sense that there might be an end to this tunnel, and maybe even some light there— when any other time she'd have told you it wasn't possible. But you can't spend your life hiding and afraid, and Laura knew it. So, in baby steps or big ones, it was time for the land of the living. And if it wasn't, she'd push it till it was.

She'd start off with her gallery of choice at the moment, so she could see what they were shooting these days, and how they were printing it, and who had the hot hand when it came to sales. It seemed like decades since her own work was on similar walls; just cresting as a niche travel photographer, she'd cut back when Andy was born, when the allure of passports and dusty buses and crooked interpreters became no match for bath time and baby powder and bedtime stories. When the twins were born she'd cut back even more; then, when Liana died, Laura stopped completely. There was nothing left about life that interested her anymore—nothing worth taking pictures of, anyway—so she let her contracts expire, put her gear away and quickly drifted out of relevance. Even her old agent had become a footnote by now; word was he was living off widows, and speculating in wine. Gamblers will gamble on anything, Laura supposed.

She drove toward the kids' school on the way in; a detour that cost some time, but this was her ritual. There was something so comforting, just to know Andy and Molly were both behind those bricks and windows, where the lesson plans are all laid out, where time is marked, and words are spelled and numbers are counted and songs are sung, where drawings and paintings and colorings are made, where games are played and friendships and alliances are struck, and the answers to all problems are at the back of the book, and indexed for easy reference. Behind those bricks and windows, an orderly and judicious world. Where tales of fairness were told, their necessary lies planted like fertile rows of corn.

Laura pulled over and watched from the car: they were taking down pumpkin pictures and hanging up Thanksgiving ones, with turkeys and pilgrims in buckled hats. After that would come Christmas trees and menorahs, in the usual eighty/twenty split—and after that would come the snowflake cutouts, and the snowmen. Martin Luther King silhouettes would follow, then valentines, and Washington and Lincoln—then shamrocks, then spring tulips, and finally the annual banner with *Have A Great Summer!* and handprints smattered on.

And if you were lucky—if no one died, if there weren't any plagues, if the world wasn't invaded by aliens—another Labor

Day would roll around, and you'd do it all again. Another school year. All of it familiar, and all of it brand new.

Their singing could be heard from all the way across the quad. The joy in it felt eternal.

"Today I met the boy I'm gonna marry . . . He's all I've wanted all my life and even more!"

It was a Saturday morning, and students from Pocono Prep were sprinkled around the valley, doing service projects—sprucing up the roadbeds, visiting rest homes, painting over graffiti. Laura and Rosa and Dot stayed on campus; they'd pulled kitchen duty, which meant taking all the grease traps from the dining hall at Gemmell, and bringing them outside to hose them down and get them unclogged and cleaned up. It was gritty work—but it was still September and the day was nice and warm, so they could fool around with the hoses and get some practice in, too.

"He smiled at me, and then the music started playing . . ."

They were acting like the Crystals—or the Shirelles, or the Ronettes, all those venerated pre-Motown, pre-Supremes Phil Spector sensations; except in this case, one of them—Laura—was white.

"'Here Comes the Bride,' as he walked in the door . . ."

Rosa and Dot were Laura's best friends at the school, right from the beginning, although the matchup seemed unlikely: Laura was a Scotsman's daughter from a Finger Lakes Rotarian family that was so upright they could pass for spindle-back chairs; while Rosa and Dot were Deep South black girls, scholarship girls, who sang in their church choirs, and sure as hell didn't come all the way up here to learn how to clean grease traps. This kind of work was everything they were trying to escape in life.

Besides Laura, no one at the school really took the time to get to know these two. Certainly they were oddities—foreign bodies from kudzu country, plunked down in the land of coal and snow—which only intrigued Laura more, and she was rewarded to find out how full of life they were, and how sharp, and how fun.

"When we kissed I felt the sweet sensation . . . this time it wasn't just my imagination!"

Before long, the three of them discovered that they had a whole lot more in common than there'd be any reason to expect. Each one read books and then more books, and argued heavily for their favorites. They agreed that Italy was the first place they'd go to if they ever got the chance, and Venice was the first place they'd hit when they got there, with the Amalfi Coast and Capri right after. They liked and disliked the same movies for the same reasons and all three had learned early that cigarettes tasted horrible no matter who else looked cool smoking them. They had a thing for 60's girl groups which bordered on the insane, and they each had ideas about how their grownup lives would be that were so big and grand it made their hearts nearly burst just to think about them.

"Today I met the boy I'm gonna marry . . ."

Rosa was going to be the Governor of Virginia, and would start turning that place around from the minute she got to Richmond. Dot was going to solo at Carnegie Hall if it killed her, only it wouldn't, and she'd be great—and Laura was going to see the world through the lens of her camera, and have gallery shows that traveled from capital to capital, and she would be shy about doing interviews but would do them anyway, because it all comes with the job. Plus, they would all have families, and husbands who would know, without fail, that they were married to women of treasure—and God help them if they ever forgot it.

"He's all I wanted, all my life and even more . . ."

Only when Laura was with Goody was she not with these two. Rosa and Dot were all right about him; they could see how much he cared about her—he flat-out worshipped her—and while they liked their own men a little less cerebral perhaps, and a little more on the wild side, they wouldn't begrudge Laura the attention. They suspected that once he got out in the real world, Goody'd get eaten up, and pretty damn fast; some people are just too nice. They knew this already.

"When we kissed, I felt the sweet sensation . . ."

They laid off the grease traps for a while, and were using the hose nozzles for microphones, doing the dance steps that went with the song. They were vamping, but still singing very earnestly in that total pretend way where you just knew they were a million percent into it: they weren't in a concrete drainage basin now, but a packed arena—and they weren't wearing coveralls and gloves but slinky sequined dresses that were tight and sleek and slit up the thigh. They were glittery and laughing and their eyes looked like diamonds.

"He smiled at me, and the music started playing . . ."

Laura was the first to see Pick. She stopped mid-step—bumping into Rosa and then Dot who drilled looks at her like she was killing the act but then they saw him too—a new kid, standing there and looking not contrite enough at all to suit them.

"Who are you?" Dot wanted to know. Rosa took up the same tough posture, while Laura looked embarrassed; her cheeks flushed hot because she was the one he was staring at—the one who had Pick's brain so locked up that he could barely hear what they were asking.

"I'm looking for the field house," he managed to say. "I'm supposed to be there."

"Does this look like a field house?" Dot asked.

"No," was Pick's reply.

"Have you seen anything in the vicinity that looks like a field house?" Rosa joined in.

"No," Pick repeated. "Or I wouldn't be asking."

Laura's eye never left Pick, who looked at her whenever he could, in the spaces when he wasn't being grilled by her friends. He was tough, and dangerous and magnetic. He looked like everything that Laura, and all nice girls, had been told all their lives to forget.

"How come we never saw you before?"

"I just got here last night."

"From where?"

"I live nearby. I knew where the old one was. But it's not there anymore."

"That's because there's a new one."

"Oh," Pick said. And he waited, but nothing more came from them. "Look, I'll find the thing myself. Thanks a lot."

"What dorm you in?" Rosa asked.

"Huh?"

"She said what dorm you in?" Dot pressed.

Pick pointed: he was in Skipper. Some philanthropist had given a shit ton of money to the school on the condition that they rename the main boys' dorm after his childhood dog. The school couldn't afford to negotiate.

"What grade?"

"Twelfth."

Rosa and Dot looked at each other. "What the hell are you doing coming to a boarding school a few weeks into senior year when your house is so close to here?"

"What the hell difference does it make?" Pick asked back, and the southern girls grinned because now they could start to respect him.

"It's off campus," Laura said, meaning the field house. "About five blocks away. Someone should have told you."

He held up a slip of paper. "All I got was this. It says to go there and get stuff for PE."

"Come on," Laura said. "I'll show you." She said goodbye to the girls, who let her know right off how much ribbing she was in for later on; then she went over to Pick to start leading the way—while Rosa and Dot went back to the song and did it even louder, making the whole thing pretty darn obvious.

"Today I met the boy I'm gonna marry . . ."

Laura tried to ignore them. She asked Pick what floor he was on in Skipper, and he told her. She asked if he had a single and he said no, there weren't any left. "Who's your roommate then?" she asked, and he told her his name was Goodman, but people were calling him Goody. Laura coughed and excused herself, but then she coughed again. How likely was this? she wondered. Here was this new guy, and he was so different and interesting and look who they put him

*in a room with—her first and only boyfriend, in the same four walls
and none of this seemed fair.*

"What are they singing?" he asked her.

"Darlene Love," Laura said. "She sang with the Crystals. Please
ignore those two."

But Pick kept listening; Laura couldn't tell whether to enjoy this,
or be embarrassed.

"It sounds kinda old," Pick said.

"Not that far back. But we like it. People tease us, but then they
ask us to sing it at parties and talent shows. Maybe they just like to
laugh at us."

"Why?" Pick asked. "You guys are good."

Laura was about to defend her friends and herself, but then she
saw that he meant it. And the compliment felt nice. "What do you
like?" she asked him. "What kind of stuff do you listen to?"

"Italian death music," Pick answered. And then when she looked
at him strangely, he told her that he didn't really listen to music—
not music of his own, the way someone would have a collection and
favorites. "Italian death music" meant opera—his father played it a
lot, and his aunts and uncles, like it was in their blood cells, to listen to
opera or to always have it on—at the restaurant, especially, his father
had a restaurant and they had that stuff playing there around the
clock. Pick didn't understand a lick of it although he'd been hearing
it all his life. Possibly it came with age, he suggested—like dentures,
or mutual funds.

Laura laughed; Pick looked surprised by that, as if he'd never
been told he was funny before. And Laura liked that look of surprise.

They crossed Laurel Avenue, which wasn't much of an avenue—
and as far as Laura could tell, had nothing to do with laurels and she
always wondered why they gave it that name. Pick told her that a lot
of things were named Laurel around here, that the mountain laurel
was Pennsylvania's state flower—although he personally had never
actually seen one, as if he'd know what to look for anyway. They just
tell you this junk like in second grade or something and they do it

*in a way where you couldn't forget it if you tried. But all you have
to remember are the names of them, he said. Not how to find one.*

*Laura understood; she said the New York state flower was the
rose, which had always bugged her because it seemed so boring. Or
maybe not boring but just not real original. Although the state bird
was the bluebird and that wasn't so bad—still not all that original
but the bluebird was a pretty cool bird. A sign of happiness and all.*

*Pick told her she got off easy. "Our state bird's the ruffed grouse,"
he said.*

*"The what?" He looked dizzy when she looked at him; Laura
never would have guessed it was leftover haze from his half of
Goody's Percodan from the night before. "What the hell is a ruffed
grouse?" she asked.*

*"That's what I wanted to know," Pick told her. "And I got shit
for it because in grade school you're not supposed to ask 'what the hell'
is anything—especially in Catholic grade school, so they made my
dad come in for a meeting. Father Terry said I made inappropriate
comments about the state bird. He said what state bird. They told
him the ruffed grouse."*

"What'd he say?"

*Pick shrugged. "He said, 'What the hell is a ruffed grouse?' Then
he took me home and hit me with a fan belt."*

*Laura couldn't believe that something like that could be true,
but she could see that it was. "What about your mother?" she asked.*

*"She died," Pick said. "I was five. My dad got my aunt to take
over. But she's dead too, now."*

*Laura looked at him. The field house was a block ahead of them,
right there in plain sight. She wanted more than anything to take
Pick's hand and hold it, but she knew she couldn't, and it made her
mad that she couldn't, even if she could understand why. She wanted
to hold his hand. She wanted to know everything about him. And
those few blocks would never be enough—those, and a few hundred
more, would still leave her wanting.*

Goody or not; she was wishing for miles.

14

Chip

She spread soft margarine on two pieces of wheat bread. She put the first one in the pan; right away it started to sizzle, at just the right heat. She had only done this thousands of times: same spatula, same pan, same order of business. But this time felt different; Chip sensed there was more going on, beyond just a mom making yet another spot lunch for her son. As if all those other times were carried on train cars—and both of them knew, without either one saying, that every train has a last car before it rolls on out for good.

Like everything else. Sudden or slow, ready or not. Everything ends.

"Remember when you were younger, and you wanted to go to the White House for a steak dinner?"

Chip looked up from the table. He was drawing football plays on homework paper; originally, he'd been making lists of Ellie's name there, but he crossed those out and now he had Randy coming around left on the option, and it was time to either dish it off to him quick, or find a blocker to get behind and run like hell for the score. He'll know next Saturday, when Nihaminy shows up and he sees how quick he can break their scheme.

That is, if he still gets to play next Saturday. If his father is still alive.

"Dad and I were watching the news, and you came in during a story about the number of White House State Dinners that were coming up that month. You thought they said 'steak' dinners, and asked if we could go there."

Chip looked up again. Something was going on. It was a guaranteed clue when she started telling stories about when he was a kid.

"You went to school the next day, and told Mrs. Breimer and the whole first grade that you were going to be president. And you invited them all to the White House, for a big steak dinner."

"I don't remember that," Chip said. And he didn't. It took him out of everything else he was thinking about. "That's weird . . ."

"Wait till you get to be my age, and see what you forget."

"Well you're doing better than I am, if you can remember something I said in first grade."

"That's different. That's being a parent."

She flipped the sandwich. The first side was perfect. But the other side got violent when it hit the surface. She raised the pan off the burner and turned the heat down. "See, I forgot something already," she said. "I should have lowered the temperature first. You can't let the pan get too hot."

"Pan too hot: bad thing. Got it."

"But don't turn it too low, or that side gets all greasy."

"Pan too cool: also bad thing."

She looked at him; he was pretending to write it all down. "You laugh. But before you know it you'll be making these things for yourself."

Bingo. Now he knew what this was about. It was about college.

"How about this," he said. "You can just follow me around and keep making them for me. Then I'll never have to have a burned or greasy grilled cheese."

"Don't think I haven't considered it," Mary told him. She

turned the burner off, and scooped the sandwich onto a plate; brought it over to him with a smile that she couldn't quite sell. "I'll go see if the nurse wants one," she said, and left the room in a hurry.

Chip sat there. He took a bite of the sandwich and stopped, half chewing. *Something's going on,* he thought. *Underneath everything else that's going on, something's going on.* He tracked back through all that had happened since his father got sick. Everything looped around to the two guys he asked for. That was where all the underneath stuff was coming from, and all Chip knew about them came from things his mother had told him.

"Stewart was away for a weekend. Something happened to him, while he was gone."

He got up and went to the sink. Filled up a glass and drank half of it before getting some ice for the rest.

"And then something worse happened when he came back."

Chip had asked about some of this in the hospital, and in bits and pieces since then. Beyond the issue of who was footing the bill, and where his father's mind might have gotten stuck, nothing else about all this history seemed like such a big deal at the time. But maybe he'd been wrong. Or maybe he just hadn't been listening hard enough.

The two guys had gotten into a fight; he remembered her saying that. But it wasn't just them, she said. And when he asked her what she meant by that, she had this really strange look on her face, like she was watching on a movie screen and couldn't turn away.

"There was a girl," she told him. Praying, it looked like, that he'd leave it at that.

Chip finished the sandwich. He checked the kitchen clock. *Okay, so there was a girl. But that's not who he asked for. He asked for the two guys.*

When he heard the bell, he stayed where he was. He could feel the ground beneath him, rumbling from all the people who were getting up and moving somewhere now. He could hear the last chairs scraping the floor in the dining hall, the doors opening and the voices of the first people leaving. In another second his mother would come in, and ask him what he was still doing there.

It's not that there was a girl, he thought. *It's the way she looked when she said there was. It was the way everything was when she said that.*

He got up, and went out. He made it to class in time, but he didn't remember a thing about getting there. He was on automatic pilot, the rest of the afternoon.

"I still remember the rain," his mother had told him. *"It was raining so hard that day."* But the rain was a detail; Chip knew that wasn't the story.

There was a girl, was all he was thinking.

15

Pick

They ate at the Blue Knight Diner and walked to Kirby Park. Pick, and Goody, and Laura—Goody's dream girl who he never stopped talking about. And wouldn't you know it, wouldn't you just fucking know it, it was the same girl Pick saw that first Saturday morning, soul singing with the two black girls. It was the girl who walked him to the field house when he already knew where it was, but he couldn't think of anything else to say when he saw them all and his mind blew to pieces. He had never thought about any other girl this way.

Laura Appleby. Goody's girl.

And if it were anyone else, it wouldn't matter. But Goody was different than any other kid Pick had known. A kid who liked him right away, who accepted him without reserve, who let him talk bullshit and let him talk truth without keeping score, or judging which was which. Goody just liked him. And somehow, instinctively, Pick trusted Goody, and that was a total first. Also Goody ran interference for him, steering him through those first few days, until Pick got his land legs and started asserting himself in his own unique Piccolo way. Still, from the start, he was in there on Goody's coattails, and he didn't even mind being grateful for it.

Only problem was, the guy had the wrong girlfriend, and he wouldn't shut up about her. And he didn't just talk, it had to be all poetry, and loftiness—like it wasn't enough to like her, so he had to go and pour a gallon of syrup over everything and it drove Pick crazy. Girls were people—yes, even Laura—they breathed oxygen, were subject to gravity and went to the bathroom just like everyone else. But to Goody, they had to be more than that—he always had to raise them up, and make them all holy and sacred and shit. It went right to your stomach sometimes. Even if, in this case, Goody might be right.

And for the first time ever it gnawed at Pick that he didn't have the poetry in him—not the kind he'd be needing, for someone like Laura. Goody had the market on poetry. Goody had sensitive all locked up.

Also—and this one you just couldn't minimize too much—Goody met her first.

They walked past the Armory and in towards the center of the park. There were a couple pieces of old artillery, pointing skyward and fighting off rust. A torpedo, which was pretty cool, and an Army tank. And some big cannons, from older wars, whose barrels were plugged with cement. When he was younger, Pick had heard that a kid got stuck in one of them once and suffocated, and that the kid's parents sued people's brains out beyond all reason, and that's why the things were capped now.

He liked that. Teaching people a lesson, that was right up his alley.

Goody held Laura's hand; here and there Pick threw bottles, when he could find them, to hear what they sounded like when they hit the train tracks. It bugged him to have to see these two this way, and the only thing worse was not being around them at all—left alone to picture what they might be doing, Pick's mind would attack him with images so vivid they made his whole body hurt. This way at least he could keep an eye on them, even if it felt like the worst sometimes.

All the time.

"I'm gonna write a book," Goody was saying.

They were coming up to where there were benches under some pine trees. Laura had her camera out and had started taking pictures.

Pick looked around for more bottles; he knew Goody would be throwing them too, if Laura wasn't along. That's another thing Goody would do—he would change his behavior sometimes, depending on who he was with. Pick couldn't see the percentage in that—you were who you were, and if anybody didn't like it then fuck 'em. Right where they breathed.

"What kinda book?" Pick challenged.

Laura aimed the camera at him, and it was easy for Pick to smile now—at least those two weren't holding hands for a change. And, Laura was looking at him. He could pretend he was the boyfriend, when she did it that way.

"I don't know yet," Goody said. "It'll be about us. You. You guys. People write about their lives, and that's what I'm gonna do."

Pick shook his head. "People have to have lives first. Don't you think? And we're fuckin' kids."

"I didn't say I was gonna write it now. But I'm gonna write it. And it's gonna be good." He looked at Laura when he said that, and she saw the shine in his eye and knew that he meant this. "You two are very literary characters," Goody went on. "You just don't know it."

Pick blew that off. Literary. He threw another bottle—an empty pint of Richard's Wild Irish Rose that he found under their bench. It missed the tree he was aiming for, and when it hit the ground a rabbit raced off, looking freaked. Here's your poetry, Pick was thinking. Here's your hearts and flowers. Why can't she love me instead?

"Don't anyone laugh," Laura said. "But I used to read horse books. I still sort of do. I have some here at school."

Goody looked at her. Pick hated that look, hated how Goody so loved everything about her—Laura could vomit on his feet if she wanted, and Pick knew Goody would love that too. "I saw this book with pictures of horses once," Pick offered. "This princess or something was trying to get it on with one. They had to hoist the thing up in this gigantic sling to get it into position."

"I don't think that's the kind of book she means, Pick."

"So? You try fucking a horse. That's a book I'll read."

Goody looked at Laura, like he was trying to apologize for Pick's behavior. Laura smiled back at him, but it wasn't a real smile, it looked more like she was the one protecting Goody's feelings— something that was getting harder and harder to do these days; you can't have your father die over summer vacation and come back like nothing ever happened. Pick caught the exchange, somehow understanding right away what Laura was going through. It was like he already knew her, even the parts she wouldn't want anybody to know. But somehow it felt okay if he knew them, and that it wouldn't frighten her. Maybe it was even kind of a relief.

"I'm out of film," Laura announced. *"I have two pictures left. Who wants to be in them?"*

"Not me," Goody said. And it was true, he didn't like having his picture taken. He said it made him uncomfortable. Self-conscious, and stiff.

Pick didn't have the same problem; he started unbuttoning his shirt. *"Clothing optional?"*

Laura laughed. *"No,"* she said. *"Just like that. Just like you are right now."* And she pointed the camera at him and gave him her total full attention. Damning herself out loud, for not bringing another roll, just when things were getting interesting.

And now Pick knew what it was like, all those times in the movies, when music started playing, out of nowhere. And he knew what people meant when they'd talk about falling for someone, that perfect someone special, and they'd say things like *"sometimes you just know."* They just didn't say what you were supposed to do about it once you found out.

16

Chip

Spain was out of the question. There was no doubt in his mind that the class trip there was going to have to go on minus one Chip Griffin. It wasn't the money; over vacations and the summer, he'd earned enough to pay his share. And it had nothing to do with the language, because he was good at it—he had taken Spanish all three previous years, which meant he was eligible for Mrs. Wainscot's 4th year Practicum class, which was by invitation only and one of the rare truly fun courses Chip had—mainly because Mrs. Wainscot didn't treat you like a kid anymore, once you'd made it this far with her.

Plus, she talked about Spain in a way Chip hadn't heard anyone else talk about any other country, and every year she took a small group of seniors there, during spring break. She had been all around the country, in college and many times since, and she was trying to communicate to them—her selected ones—that there was more to the place than cathedrals and tapestries and old drafty castles. A lot more.

Chip had a feeling that there were all kinds of things that Mrs. Wainscot would have liked to come out and say, but couldn't do it directly—maybe in case the walls had ears or something. But it seemed like she was trying to pass along, in a *carpe diem* sort of a way, that Spain, if you went at the right time in your life, was a place you could *carpe diem* your head off. And everyone, except Sussman, would know what she meant.

But he couldn't go to Spain, even after all the semesters it took just to qualify—because Ellie had also qualified, and she was going too. And if sitting in a class with her was every kind of torture, then what would a trip across the ocean be like? How could they be on the same airplane together? The same halls in the *Prado*, the same hostel in Sevilla, the same beaches at Santander? The bike trip through Basque country—God knows what else, but he just couldn't do it.

"Mrs. Wainscot? *Señora?*"

"Chip. Come on in."

Chip was glad she didn't pull rank and make him have this whole conversation in Spanish. That was another cool thing about Mrs. Wainscot: all the other language teachers, no matter what you came in to talk about, they wouldn't let you do it in English. Your ass could be on fire, and if you didn't know how to say, "My ass is on fire" in the language they were teaching, then you were out of luck. While Mrs. Wainscot was the only one who made you actually want to learn something, by specifically not shoving it down your throat.

"How's your father?"

"No one seems to know. But he's home and all. He's got nurses there all the time."

"I hope things get better for him. For all of you."

"Thanks. I do too."

"Tell your mom I said so, will you?"

"Sure. Thanks. I'll tell her when I get home."

She nodded, watching him. "You can also tell her that you're doing fine in this class, and there's no way under the sun that I'm going to let you drop it."

"What?"

"That's what you came in for, isn't it?" She gave him a look that told him to please cut the crap with her. "Just admit it, Chip—and then we can get on with what there really is to talk about."

"What do you mean?"

"What do *you* mean, *muchacho?* Think before you answer."

Chip thought he *had* thought about it, but now she had him confused. "I didn't come in here to ask you to drop the class. But I wanted to talk about the trip to Spain."

"Well there you go," she said. "You surprised me."

She signed him out to go off campus, and took him to Greenberg's Delicatessen, where she said she ate twice a week. She had a pastrami sandwich with coleslaw, and mushroom barley soup and a strawberry yogurt. Chip didn't want anything; the smell of pickles and bacon smoke put him off, which was confusing to him—for a place that was supposed to be serving Jewish food, Greenberg's smelled more like burned bacon than anything else. Yet from all he knew, things like bacon were way off limits in that religion. He decided to ask Mrs. Wainscot about that, some other time.

"And now, I'm going to tell you why you're the luckiest young man in the world," she said.

"Huh?" was all the captain of the debating team (fourth place in the state) could say.

She pushed the sandwich aside and started in on the soup. "You're seventeen, right? Almost eighteen? You're a senior in high school—and the love of your life has broken your heart. Because that's what this is about, isn't it?"

Chip could only watch her. This was amazing. How could she just sit there and chow down on food like that, and say this stuff?

"For this conversation to be effective, Chip, she really has to have been the love of your life. Are you sure this was the one?"

"What do you mean? Of course, she was. I mean she *is.* We've been going out since ninth grade."

"All right then. I'm just making sure. Otherwise you might not be so lucky."

"Lucky. How in the world am I lucky?"

"Here's how you're lucky: because no one in your life, from here on in, will ever break your heart like Ellie's doing right now. And because as impossible as it seems, your heart will heal, and you will feel better in time—and when your heart does heal, it'll come back stronger. And no one, Chip—no one will ever get to you this way again. You may have other broken hearts, but they'll never be as bad as this one. Because they won't be your first love."

"And that's lucky?"

She nodded. Scooped up some yogurt. Chip saw little pink streaks on the bottom of the spoon. Slivers of pearl onion on the rim of her soup bowl. "It's lucky because sooner or later it happens to everybody. Everybody who's alive, anyway. Are you alive, Chip?"

Chip stared at her. He didn't know how to answer that.

"I think you're alive," she went on. "Sick in the stomach, that's alive. Heart weighs a ton, that's alive. Want to dig a hole somewhere, and hide forever—love isn't all about jumping for joy, you know. It's the other side, too—and the good news is, you're getting it out of the way, *now.* You're getting stronger, *now.* You know how many great authors wrote some of their finest works about a love that broke them to pieces? She did you a favor, *mi amigo.* She put a novel in you."

"But I don't care if there's a novel in me. I just don't want to go to Spain. I really don't think I can."

Mrs. Wainscot ordered a lemonade from Mrs. Greenberg behind the counter, smiled a thank you when she brought it, then drank the first half of it down in one long sip. Chip started to catalog, in his head, the variety of unrelated things he had just watched this woman eat and drink in the space of the last ten minutes.

"I'm going to tell you a story," she said, "and I'll try and be quick about it because I know we need to get back. But when I was twenty years old, I was in love. I was in love so bad it was silly."

"Really?"

She held up her hand, to make him not interrupt. "And the boy I loved had committed to join the Peace Corps, in Kenya, which was one of the things I adored about him. So, on my Christmas vacation from Antioch, I went to Kenya. And let me tell you, I won't say what year this was, but it wasn't easy to get from western Ohio to the other side of Africa. It wasn't like you strapped on a jetpack and sailed on over."

She finished the rest of the lemonade, and Mrs. Greenberg automatically brought more. "Reykjavik, Iceland," she said, crunching on an ice cube. "Cheapest flight you could get. I had to go from Dayton to Pittsburgh, Pittsburgh to Newark, Newark to Reykjavik, Reykjavik to Dublin, then to Frankfurt, then Athens, then Cairo where I wasn't allowed to get off the plane because I had a prior stamp from Israel on my passport—until finally Nairobi. And then it was seven more hours inland, away from civilization, and you went there by something resembling a bus—except it didn't have a roof on it, or seat cushions or shock absorbers, and they drove it on something resembling a road, except it was giant ruts of mud broken up by the occasional six-foot boulder. Are you getting that it was a hard trip to make, Chip?"

She waited for Chip to nod. "Now comes the good part. I am nearly two full days out of my nice cushy co-ed suite at my nice progressive little college. I am in the middle of an extremely foreign country. I have come to see my love. I get to this not-quite-charming African village and I manage a few questions and before long I am standing outside a tattered little hut where my heart of hearts has been staying, and living, and returning all my passionate letters with heated ones of his own. So I step inside, and I pull back five layers of mosquito netting, and that is when I meet Shona."

"Shona?"

She winked at him. She cracked another ice cube. "Shona was from Arlington, Virginia, and she had thick red hair, and absolutely beautiful skin, and I'll bet she even had a gorgeous singing voice. But I didn't stay long enough to find that out."

She gulped down the rest of the lemonade and asked Mrs. Greenberg for the check. "They're a big power couple now, down in Washington. I've seen their pictures in magazines. She's still got it."

"Wait a minute," Chip said. "He married her?"

"Of course, he married her. What'd you think the story was about?"

"But—where'd *your* husband come from?"

"Pensacola, Florida. He was a flight instructor at the time. We met in Key West while everyone else was watching the sunset. And every day I thank God and Moses and Abraham that I took that trip to Kenya. And that's why I can say that this is the best thing that ever happened to you."

He followed her to the cash register. Watched her pull a Snickers bar off the rack and pay for that too. "Menopause," she said. "Some people get flashes—I get hungry."

Chip looked at her. She dropped the Snickers in her pocketbook and zipped up her ski jacket. Then she zipped up his for him. Like a mom would.

"You're a lucky young man, Chip Griffin. And you're going to love seeing Spain."

17

Griffin

He captured the smell of a wet basement—lingering water problems that were never really solved. He remembered building the French drain outside, on the north part of the yard where the ground was higher, so the rain water would siphon off away from the house, instead of into the ground right next to it, and through the walls and under the foundation where it would never let you forget it—because no matter what you tried to do, that damp musty thickness would always be there—a hint on the best days, a slug to the senses on the worst.

Everyone in the valley knew the smell. It was resident, permanent, like an unwelcome house guest who never leaves. The only defense was to prepare your home and belongings for the next event. And since the river, at its fullest, could never be held back, there would always be a next event. Even the best of engineers, they could only do so much—when you put a city in a flood plain, you tie their hands from the start.

Griffin was proud of his French drain. He had read up on how to construct one, he'd talked to the groundskeepers at the school extensively—he even went to Shea Stadium once, just to take the tour so he could talk to the groundskeepers there. How to keep rain off a baseball field was a subject as old as baseball fields themselves, and Griffin wanted to learn from the masters.

"Mr. Griffin?"

He felt movement underneath him. Wheels, like someone was pushing him on wheels. He thought of a shopping cart, but why would there be one of those? And why did he smell a damp basement? But then, just as quickly, the smell had gone, and the feeling of being wheeled went with it.

Replaced by the sound of a bell. He knew that bell, from somewhere. It was light years away, and as close as his own breathing.

"Mr. Griffin?"

"Yes, Mrs. La Fave."

Mrs. La Fave stood in the office doorway. A crisp, bitter woman whose family had lost their fortune buying land around the airport thinking there'd be hotels there one day. She was young at the time, and never thought she'd have to work for someone; she was brought up to believe that other people did that.

Griffin's predecessor had hired her as a favor to the family—and now Griffin had inherited Mrs. La Fave and there was nothing he could do about it; on top of being sour, and diffident, she was barely efficient and would blame anything, even a spent roll of masking tape, on someone or something else. He looked forward to her retirement more than his own.

"Mr. Griffin, it's about the bell."

"What about it?"

She hesitated. As if delivering any kind of message, was beneath her. "Well it doesn't work," she said.

"The school bell?"

She nodded. That's the one.

Griffin looked at his watch; come to think of it, he hadn't heard the noon bell, which would have gone off by now. "How can the school bell not work?" he asked her. "You pull a rope, and it rings."

"But there has to be a rope to pull. And there isn't one."

"Mrs. La Fave. What do you mean, there isn't a rope?"

"I think you'd better come out and see for yourself."

There was a small group of students milling about underneath the bell tower—the way people stand around and look at a crime scene, only this one was up above their heads. When Griffin showed up they backed off and gave him room; watched him start to take command of a situation where everyone else seemed to know what was going on—including, and he knew this—his own secretary, who could easily have tipped him off ahead of time, if she'd wanted to. Thank you, Mrs. La Fave. Where would I be without you?

He reached the top of the belfry and saw Goody sitting there. Next to him was the rope he'd pulled up, the rope that rang the bell— the bell that was silent because he'd climbed up here and brought the rope with him so no one else could ring it, because a teacher was getting fired for having adult magazines behind his radiator, and Stewart Goodman did not think that was fair. In fact, he knew it wasn't, and if this was the way it occurred to him to protest, then here they were, and Griffin could detention him until they grew cantaloupes on Neptune but it still wouldn't make it right to let a good teacher go—unless there was some other reason, something more, and they just weren't telling anybody about it.

"No, Stewart. There is no other reason. There was a maintenance person in Mr. Weavodau's apartment in the dorm, and he had to remove the radiator cover and when he did, he found the magazines."

"With pictures of other men in them. So, you're firing him."

"Ordinarily, Stewart, I would not be climbing up to the top of a bell tower to discuss a morality issue with a student. The trustees of the school have made their decision. It was their right to make it and their right to follow through on it."

"A moral decision? What's moral about it?"

"Moral as the parents would want us to define it."

"Did anybody ask them?"

"Who, the parents?"

Goody nodded: did anybody ask the parents? And Griffin did have to concede that no one had been called and polled on their opinions about whether a teacher in Eddie Weavodau's predicament should be removed, or retained, or maybe just reprimanded and let go with a warning. So he explained that it isn't the job of the board of trustees to do that, that the nature of the fiduciary responsibility the Board takes on includes the handling of matters just like this one.

"Well it's wrong. I mean I get it about the trust thing and not bothering the parents every time a decision has to be made. But this time the decision was wrong. You don't fire a teacher for having magazines."

"They weren't just magazines, Stewart, and you know it."

"Were there kids in them? Were the pictures of kids or adults?"

"As far as I know, there were only photographs of adults in the magazines."

"Adult males."

Griffin was beginning to get impatient here—but yes, he answered. The pictures were of adult males, and that was enough, in the higher circles, to conclude that Mr. Weavodau wasn't a fit role model for the students he taught.

"Why?" the boy wanted to know. "Do they think he'll come into our rooms and do something to us?"

"I'm not sure anyone even got that far, Stewart. In the board's opinion, Mr. Weavodau's behavior compromised the standards of the school to the point where they determined he should be removed."

"Because he likes men."

"Stewart—"

"Because that's what this is about, right? The part that nobody's saying? Would they fire him if the pictures were of women? Do they think he would be a danger to the girls of the school if he had pictures of women behind his radiator?"

Griffin looked at him. "I think, Stewart, that there is a good possibility they would."

"I don't believe you," Goody said. And he looked at Griffin with all the righteous ferocity of youth, at just the moment when innocence *and belief are up before the firing squad. Griffin's choice was either to lie—which wasn't really a choice—or to explain the stone walls and sinkholes of real life out there, to the last person in the world who needed to be disillusioned right now. The poor sod had been through enough this year.*

"Well I can see that we're at an impasse," Griffin told him. And Goody looked at him almost reverently, as if that were the last thing he ever expected the man to say—because to be at an impasse suggested that these were two equals talking, and not one person with a lot of power, just waiting to use it on another person who had none. "So what do you think we should do?" Griffin asked. He was bringing Goody in on the solution, and he wasn't kidding about it—not what you expect when you openly defy the authority of the school.

"I don't know," Goody answered. "I just know that firing Mr. Weavodau is wrong, and that I had to do something about it."

"Well now you've done so. I would say you've done a very good job of it. And thus, we have our impasse."

"Because it's time for lunch and there's no bell?"

Griffin held back a grin. "Because you've come up here, Stewart, and you've brought that rope along with you. And now I've come up, to talk to you, and listen to you—which I hope I have adequately done."

Goody waited. Like he was being told a story—a campfire tale that had him on the edge of his seat—only this time he was one of the characters in the story.

"The difference is," Griffin continued, "I have to go back down there, and you don't. And when I do that I'm going to need to present some kind of result."

Goody nodded, as if he saw Griffin's point, that he couldn't afford to come off as ineffective; added to that, his surprise that he wasn't making Goody come down with him.

"This is your protest, Stewart. Nobody is questioning the integrity of what you are doing. You can understand, though, that the school has to go on." He got up and dusted off his trousers, feeling a kink in his back from sitting like that. "We can work something out with

the public address system, to cover for the bell not being in use." He looked around the belfry, like a parent summing up his child's first apartment. "There's no food or water up here, and no bathroom. And I can't let anyone bring anything, or help you out. But other than that—stay as long as you like."

"But what about Mr. Weavodau?"

Griffin turned, where the stairway began, and looked back at Goody. Sitting with his knees up, his back against the tower wall, holding on to the end of that rope; Griffin realized he had never let go of it, the whole time they'd been speaking. "Mr. Weavodau has been fired, Stewart. That decision will not be reversed. He'll move on, and he'll find a new job—maybe at another school, though likely not. Either way, he won't be working at this one again. I'm sorry. Your protest is noted, but it won't bring him back here."

He had one foot on the stairway when the shouting began from down below; one person then a few people then many. They were alternating between chanting support for Goody and calling for Mr. Griffin—and the one whose voice rang the loudest was all too familiar. Griffin looked out through the eaves and sighed.

"You might want to see this," he said. And he watched Goody get up and actually wonder what to do with the rope—bring it over, or leave it unguarded? In the end he left it, joining Griffin and they looked out there together, hearing their names called out now, and in something close to unison—someone was taking charge down there, and gaining waves of support.

"I never told him to do this," Goody said. "Mr. Griffin, I swear."

"I believe you," Griffin told him. And he did; the scene below them was not a Stewart Goodman scene, but pure Sandy Piccolo. Down on the ground, at the base of the bell tower—point man in a large and growing semicircle bringing in just about every boy who lived in the dorms. And they were all holding magazines— adult magazines—Playboys and Penthouses and others even worse. Some had a stack of them. They must have raided every drugstore within reach.

"*We have naked pictures, too,*" *came the challenge.* "*Kick us all out, or bring back Mr. Weavodau!*"

They were each standing up, in their own unique ways. Griffin wondered where these two had possibly come from. And where it was they might be going. And how far, if there even was a limit, could they reach.

But all that was later; right now, it was time to get ready for a long afternoon.

18

Laura

"I tell a guy to fly up here," Pick was saying. "The number one guy in the country on strokes and the shit they can do to someone. But he gets on the phone instead and does a consult, decides when he's done that 'his presence isn't necessary.' Lazy *scaffone*, I'll kill him."

Laura listened from the edge of the tub, while the water filled up. She had the cordless with her, the one the catalog said was perfect for around the pool or other wet conditions. It was the one Andy made off with the most—he had this thing for taking telephones lately—he'd hide them, and days later they'd show up in some completely unpredictable place. She found this one in the downstairs laundry hamper; before that it was in a pile of grass clippings, outside.

No one got on him for this—they knew what he was doing. Liana died and they each had their own way of reacting. Where Molly stuttered, Andy snatched phones. Pick went into hyper-drive, concentrating on work—saving the people he could actually save, while Laura watched all of them; knowing why they were doing it all, unable to stop them when she was barely holding on herself. She'd keep the house running and make sure the kids had clothes the right size, and got to all their appointments and events on time, with all the props and playthings they needed for each different activity they had. And for the times that Pick couldn't make it to something, she would go and represent them both—every single minute, screaming inside. Hoping to God that she wouldn't fall apart. Praying for anything that could save her.

"So I called back and got the service. They said, 'the doctor is at the symphony.' I said I didn't care if he was at the symphony, I didn't care if he was the fuckin' *conductor*, I wanted him up here. So, we'll see."

Laura was sure of that; bet your money they'd see. If Pick wanted a doctor to fly, drive, bus, or camel his way up to Wilkes-Barre, from wherever, then eventually that doctor would report. Pick was relentless if it meant coming through for somebody—anyone who, in his mind, wasn't an asshole. If he thought you were genuine though, he'd move mountains. Like the surgeon—Pick had any number of cases to choose from, and this was the one he wanted. *That guy got screwed*, he'd say. *The company fucked up, and the company should pay. You don't go around electrocuting people.*

Laura admired him for that. Always did. The leopard is a ferocious protector.

They said their goodbyes and Laura clicked off—already thinking ahead about where she might leave the phone this time, so that Andy wouldn't find it and hide it again; finally, she lit on the idea of putting it back right where it was, and that way he could think she hadn't found it yet, and might not take it somewhere else. The best defense and all.

She went over to get the loofa sponge from the shelf, and some Advil from the medicine cabinet. She caught her image in the mirror and stopped to study it. The lines around the mouth, that was her mother—tightening, pulling in, from years and years of things not said, feelings pursed and held in tight. Not so much of Andy in her, but plenty of the twins; the eyes set wide—curious, careful, a sense of play—and even at their age, already the decorum. Generations of Scottish breeding.

And then she saw the face of her youth: Laura Appleby, at the edge of the lake, buried in a horse book at nine. At twelve, getting a speech from her mother about the changes in her body and the secrets of being a woman. And then at eighteen, in her waitress getup, staring past the water off Chincoteague during a break. Her plans for the future, completely derailed.

It was too young to be wondering what had happened to your life. It was too young to have ruined everything already. Yet you did, yet you did, yet you did . . .

She remembered how Goody had told her once that she "didn't look at you, but out at you." Laura really didn't know what he meant at the time. But here and now, in front of this mirror, she saw it—she *was* looking out from somewhere. Separate, a refugee, watching life go by from behind a spike iron gate between her and the world. Going through her whole life seeing, but never feeling seen.

For a while she thought Goody saw her; but soon she realized this couldn't be true—not really. The light he shined on her was just too bright; she could never live up to the way he thought about her. She was human, guilty, eminently fallible—capable of all the things she would do to him one day, and more. He was bound to find out, and it would crush him. It would only come down to when.

The label said Harvest Bouquet, but the shampoo inside smelled more like soapy peaches than anything else. Still, it was free, it came with the room, and she had forgotten to bring her own shampoo from the dorm. Beggars can't be choosers, Laura thought.

She turned and saw Goody come in, wrestling with a wine bottle. He had pants on but no shirt; she had a big, long loose shirt on but no pants. She watched him use a keychain knife to start digging away at the cork.

"I told Pick to get the kind that had a cap instead," he said.

"Maybe he was being thoughtful. The wines with the corks are generally better."

"Not if you can't open the bottle."

She watched him keep trying, could feel his frustration because he wanted so much to get this right. "It's okay," she said. "I've seen people have trouble even who do it all the time."

He looked at her, gaining reassurance. God, he needed so much. He reminded her of this kid from grade school, Jimmy Lamm. No one ever wanted to get behind him in the water fountain line, because he took so long to drink it and then there'd never be enough time for anyone else. He was the sweatiest kid in the class and he'd drape himself over the fountain like he'd just crossed the Continental Divide, instead of playing kickball, or four square. And the rest of the kids would wait forever, while he drank, and drank, and drank.

"Do you want to do the water and I'll try the cork?"

Goody didn't answer; his attention was somewhere else. "What's that sound?"

Laura listened. "I don't hear any sound."

"Turn off the water."

"But I just got it—"

He reached around her and turned off the tap. They didn't have to wait long. The bell from Pocono Prep. Two miles off if it was an inch.

"God," Laura said. "Is there anywhere in this valley where you don't hear that thing?"

"That's lunch," Goody reported. He looked at Laura as if he'd heard a tornado warning and not a school bell. Then he walked out past her, to the middle of the room, where he stood trancelike between the TV and the two double beds. One was covered with the clothes they brought, with schoolbooks and some music, and a bag from the grocery where they bought Hershey bars and orange juice, magazines, and the condoms they were hoping to learn how to use.

That was where the other bed came in.

The pillows were out, on top of the bedspread, which was all rumpled from when they were fooling around—before Laura had gotten her idea about a shower together. Now, because a bell had rung, Goody was staring at the empty bed. Like a soldier hearing gunfire in the distance.

"It's all right, Stewart. We don't have to be anywhere. We're signed out." She watched him; intense, alert. "Unless you're nervous about something else . . ."

Goody stopped and looked at her. She was not wild about herself for saying that, but it just made her mad to see him standing there listening to that stinking damn bell when it didn't have anything to do with them today, when they could be in the shower together right now, and after that get on with what they came here to do. Or finished already, because she wasn't sure how long it was supposed to take. Laura had heard stories about it taking too long, and stories about it not taking long enough. What she hadn't heard, was where the middle ground was, and how much time and practice it took before you got there—all she knew was that they had to start somewhere, and today was supposed to be the day.

"I'm not nervous," Goody said. And to prove it he walked past her again, but this time into the bathroom and not out, and this time he was pulling her by the hand and taking her with him. He lowered the lid on the toilet and sat her down on it while he turned the water back on. Then he reached around behind her to get the wine bottle and the pen knife, chipping away at more and more of the cork while the water heated up again.

Laura felt lifted to see him act with such determination. She felt like she mattered to him, more than the things he was afraid of. Like getting caught? he would say, and she'd have to admit that he had a point there. There was a lot to be concerned about in terms of getting caught.

So when they heard the pounding on the door outside, she was just as alarmed as he was. Goody went out to see, and then Pick was there; rasping and out of breath.

"Your mom called the school," he said. "Griffin talked to her."

Goody looked like he'd been clubbed. Pick was looking past him, into the room where Laura was standing. She saw him and she blushed so hard she had to cover her cheeks with her hands, her shirt pulling up and showing her legs while she looked out over her fingertips at the two of them by the door.

"What'd she want?" Goody had to ask him twice—jogging Pick's attention without realizing why he had to.

"Who cares what she wanted—you're signed out to go home this weekend, and your mom thinks you're still at school! Griffin flagged me down and I had to lie to him and I'm pretty sure he fuckin' knows it."

Goody looked at Laura. This was the end of the world. Nothing less.

"You don't have to go, Stewart," she said.

"Are you crazy?"

"Stewart, you don't have to go!"

"I'll be back!"

And that was it; he was gone. Laura stood there in the silence he left behind. She looked at Pick, in the threshold, poised between his highest and lowest instincts. "I better go, too," he said. He gave her one last look and then she was alone.

Laura sat down on the bed; not knowing if or when they'd come back, or which one might if only one did. Till then she had candy, homework, and a box of condoms, worthless at present and she didn't know how long they'd keep. Were there expiration dates on these things?

She thought about Pick, watching her from the doorway like that. Strangely, though, she felt as if he were still there. His eyes at least, lingering on her legs, following them up to where they disappeared under the shirt tails.

What she wanted there, God help her, were his hands. What she wanted was all of him.

19

Chip

He looked at Pick in the doorway. "You're the lawyer," he figured. "I'm Chip." He stepped back, and shifted the laundry basket he was holding so the guy could get in past him. "My mom's out," he said. "The nurse is in there doing something, so you probably oughtta chill." He nodded towards the kitchen for a place to wait—then stepped around Pick and went down to the basement, where he changed over the laundry and took out the stuff of his that was dry enough for now. There was a pair of jeans that had gotten mixed in there, left behind from some earlier washing—an old pair of his father's work jeans. Chip remembered seeing him outside doing repairs on the steps, just days ago; he wondered if that was an activity Henry Griffin would ever be engaging in again. That, or anything.

When he came up he found Pick at the table, in his dad's chair, reading a newspaper and looking way too comfortable about it—as if he sat at that table every damn day of his life, and read the paper like he belonged there. But what the hell; in the end, Chip figured the guy didn't know whose chair it was and just sat down where he felt like it. Or maybe all alpha dogs just know where they like to plant, and it's as simple as that.

"I'm supposed to ask if you want something," Chip offered. He stepped back from the refrigerator, so Pick could see what they had. "A lot of people've been bringing stuff."

"No. No thanks." Pick looked down at the laundry basket Chip had brought in; a frayed jersey top, sweatpants, and a jockstrap—and all of it a dull monochrome grey now, from being washed together so many times. "You play ball?" he asked.

"Yeah," Chip said.

"What kind?"

"Whatever's the season."

Pick grinned. "My kid's like that."

Chip nodded; sent some credibility Pick's way. "What school's he play for?"

"He's nine."

"Oh." He shrugged. "My parents started old, too."

Pick looked surprised by that; as if he'd been called just about everything in his life, but never *old*. And this kid wasn't even *calling* him old; he was *assuming* it. Which made it even worse. "Is that Genoa salami?" he asked.

"Yeah."

Pick watched him put the sandwich together. "A lot of people think Genoa's too strong," he said. "It's not an entry level cold cut."

Chip shrugged. "I like it." He closed the door with his foot and sat down. With any luck, the guy would stop asking questions. With any luck, the world would finally produce a grownup who would know how to stay out of people's faces. Chip swore that when his turn came he'd be different.

"Baseball," Pick said. "Andy likes baseball."

"Cool," Chip chewed. He got back up and took a banana out of the freezer; when he brought it to the table it sounded like a gun being placed there.

"Basketball too," Pick went on. "But baseball more I think. He likes third base. Even at nine, he can make that throw to first from the corner. And he hates it when anything gets past him."

"That's what it takes, to play third," Chip said. "You gotta be tenacious and you gotta have the speed. Where's he hit?"

"Seventh."

Chip winced: seventh? He couldn't remember one team in his life where he had batted any lower than cleanup—even T-ball, where they tried to put on that it didn't matter. But it did, and every kid knew it. Anyone who batted after sixth, all they wanted to do was get it over with. They'd go back to the dugout with their heads kept low, so they wouldn't have to see their fathers, and feel their disappointment that they came all the way out here, took off work and everything, and their kid didn't even make it to base again.

"They have cages where you live?" he asked Pick.

"Batting cages?"

Chip swallowed. He added some barbecue sauce to the sandwich; it pushed out some mustard that was already there. "It's not the same as having a real person throw at you," Chip told him, "and it's not like being in a game—but it's good practice. If he's comfortable in the batting cage, he'll probably do better at the plate."

Pick agreed. "Sometimes he goes there with the team, but all he'll get are one or two chances. He asks me to take him, but it's tough. Weekends are short."

"Yeah I know. Time's a bitch," Chip said. He got up from the table. "I got practice coming."

He put half the sandwich back in the refrigerator, and picked up the laundry basket on the way out—and just like that, he was gone. Like he had nothing more to say to a dad who'd let his kid bat seventh, and possibly ruin the boy, for life.

20

Griffin

*H*e was in the middle of the boat, pushing off from the dock. Goodman was at the bow, Piccolo in the stern where Griffin was facing. It was a silent spring morning; only the wooden oars, pushing through the water, and the occasional splash and drip of a minnow breaking the surface, trying to escape being some bigger fish's breakfast. Things would be different soon—in summer, with constant crowds and powerboats, adding the grind of their engines and the shouts of jacked-up water skiers to the music from a hundred different sources, bouncing back and forth across the lake from the back yards and screen porches and the private docks of the houses lining the shore.

But that was summer. And this was now.

The first crack of sunlight from over the treetops lit up a layer of mist that covered the water like a soft gray quilt. Watching dawn crease the lake this way filled Griffin with a deep sense of reverence, and holiness, and connection; he couldn't understand why the science people and the religion people couldn't quit fighting over who should get the credit for all this—when to Griffin they were two sides of the same coin. On one side, everything you can see; on the other, everything you can't.

They talked about God that morning; considering all that was around them, and on a Sunday, it was a natural topic—and Griffin took the opportunity to open up the floor. Piccolo's point of view, burned into him by circumstance, was that religion was a big giant trick—just another way to get all these people to march in step, by pinning every hope on some ultimate Grand Prize they'd get, if they'll just make sure to cool their behavior—while everyone else is laughing their asses off and running away with all the plunder.

Then Goodman told this story about puppies. He said what if there were all these puppies in a kennel, and every day when the caretaker came in, certain puppies ran over to him and certain ones didn't, and every time it was the same ones behaving each way. But then if one day there was a fire in the kennel and the caretaker could only save a few of the puppies, wouldn't he pick the ones who had sought him out? The ones he recognized, and already had a special thing with? And that's how he imagined God, he said. You have to keep seeking Him, so that He'll know who you are when there's trouble. To which Piccolo said, What kind of God is worth believing in if he can only get some of the puppies? And Goodman had no answer, save the look on his face.

Griffin was moved by both of them: Goodman, the searcher—and Piccolo, the hardened cynic already, who was searching more desperately than he could ever admit to himself. Together, the two of them, they lifted his heart and they made it pound with hurting, all at the same time. He wanted his own, dammit. He wanted his own kids to raise and it wasn't happening and sometimes he and Mary thought the yearning alone might just do them in. Nothing wears down on a soul like unmet desire.

"I read somewhere, about parents and children," he said. It must have seemed roundabout and unconnected to them, to suddenly be talking about this. But no one was complaining, so he kept on going. "That the child is the arrow, and parents are the bow—and that their job in life, is to prepare their children to leave them."

"Only my dad left first," Goodman said.

"And mine's a thug," Piccolo added.

Griffin raised the oars and rested them. Water dripped off the blades and plinked into the ripples as the boat continued to glide. He looked out over the mist and considered which direction to take them, depending on whether actual fishing was the goal here or just the excuse to get out in the boat. But first—for now—just let the lake take over. Let the water roll, let the grasses sway by the banks. Let nature furl out the full morning, in her own sweet time—do just that, and God can speak for Himself.

Goodman broke the quiet. "I ran away," he said. And when they looked at him to see what he might have meant by that, he swallowed hard and went on. "My dad, after he died, I took off. I snuck away from the funeral, and I was gone for three days. I worried them really bad."

Griffin nodded as if to say yes, he should think people might be worried in a situation like that. He could have added that Goodman's family had called the school, looking to see if Stewart had found his way there—but he felt no need to mention it right now. He thought of an old Quaker phrase taught to him as a child: "Be very sure," it went, "that what you have to say is more important than silence." Every time Griffin remembered that, he was glad.

"We were on the golf course when it happened. I never went out there with him before. I don't know why I did that day, or why he even asked me to."

Griffin let the boat glide some more. The current had changed, which meant a harder time rowing back—but a little extra effort would be worth it if it got this kid to open up.

"At one point he wanted to sit down on this bench that was over by the tee. So he started walking there but then he didn't make it all the way. He just sort of folded down next to it, on to the grass, but was still trying to stay sitting up. He said there were some pills in his golf bag, and they were for his heart, and I said what's the matter with your heart, and he said will you just get the pills? So, I looked but there weren't any, there were only extra golf balls. And he said look again because there had to be, and I looked again but still there

weren't any pills in there. Then he started yelling and he said to bring the golf bag over to him and he'd find them himself."

This was making Piccolo uncomfortable; he started looking here and there, the way someone smelling danger instinctively starts checking the exits. Griffin hadn't seen this in him before.

"And I thought fine, go find them yourself, and I took the golf bag over to him but when I saw how bad he looked I dropped the bag and ran for help—I headed for the locker room because I was thinking that's where he had the pills, in his locker, and he just forgot to put them in the bag. But before I got there, Maizie Cohen saw me crossing the parking lot and asked me what was wrong. And when I told her what happened, she got a couple lifeguards from the pool and we all ran out to where he was, but it was too late. My dad was dead. With a thing of pills in his hand, that he wasn't able to open."

"Jesus," Piccolo said. Griffin looked at him, then back at Goodman. "Stewart . . ."

Goodman shook his head; he had to get this out. "They were in some other extra compartment I didn't know about—some zipper behind the thing I had already unzipped and he was holding them in his hand and one of the lifeguards had to bend down and take them away. He said it was nitro-glycerin. And then he looked at me and said, 'This could have saved his life.'"

"That guy was an asshole," Piccolo declared, and immediately looked at Griffin, and said he was sorry, he knew he shouldn't use language like that but come on, what kind of person stands there and tells a teenage kid that he basically just killed his own father?

"But he was right," Goodman said. "If the pills were there, and if the pills would have saved him, then the lifeguard was right."

"Stewart," Griffin told him. "You didn't know your father had a heart problem. And no one knows how they're going to react in a situation like that. I know you did your best. And anyone who'd even hint at something different—" he looked at Piccolo before he finished—"is an asshole."

Piccolo grinned; it felt good, getting validated like that.

Goodman, however, was too far gone. "But then I ran away," he said. "I couldn't face them—I couldn't face any of them." He shook his head and held off tears for a long as he could. "They canceled sitting Shiva because they were so worried about me—I didn't say Kaddish for him, and that was my job, I was his son and I was supposed to say the Kaddish for my dad. And I never got to say goodbye, or tell him that I was sorry, for not believing him about the pills and letting him die there by himself . . . "

Griffin locked the oars in place and balanced his way over to where Goodman was sitting. He made room next to him and drew him in. Holding him as the sobs came now. The quaking heaves that came with bearing such a burden and finally letting it out. Not letting it go; Griffin wondered if Goodman—if anyone—could ever let go of a thing like that.

"It's all right, Stewart," he told him. "It's all right." He patted Goodman's shoulder, telling him it was the pain that made his father yell like that, nothing else. He saw Piccolo looking at him—staring, for some reason, at his hands. Griffin looked at them himself; beefy, red and chapped, holding onto a heart so tender it could barely hold onto itself.

And how could these hands ever be big enough, he was thinking, to hold all the life that he wanted for them?

Griffin's eyes moistened. He stared up from the pillow. He could hear them: Piccolo, and a nurse. He could know that they were there; there just wasn't any way to pass that on—that, and everything else there was to say. He was locked. Silent and still, haunted by events and motives he might never get a chance to explain. When everyone was together, he knew, the answers would come. Nobody knew everything, but each one knew something. And they all had to be there for the picture to be complete.

"Fully grown kid," he heard Piccolo say. And, "Jesus Christ." And then the nurse's voice, that he still couldn't quite get; the sound was like talking through sea foam, or pillows. Then Piccolo again. "Makes you wonder what else you don't know," he said.

Then, once more, the name of the Lamb of God.

21

Mary

Later, when they were alone again, Chip told Mary that he'd met him now, at least one of the famous two blasts from the past, and he still couldn't figure out what the deal was. Why did his father ask for them?

"I know it's hard to understand, Chip." She was looking for something in the cupboard, and reorganizing it along the way. Chip watched her go about this—automatically, efficiently, in a groove. "Just try not to resent them. And try not to resent Dad. He needs you—and he needs to feel your love. You can't know how important that is."

"But if he needs me so much, why didn't he ask for me?"

"If you'll remember, Chip—he didn't ask for me either." She gave him a grim smile and moved on. Henry hadn't asked for either of them, and that was that.

"What's going to happen, Mom?"

Mary stopped. She had an unopened box of loose tea in her hand. She had no recollection of buying it, and she knew she didn't have the little contraption you need to make loose tea; she'd gotten rid of it a long time ago, when she decided it was too much trouble to clean out. She wondered who'd brought the tea, then, and if she had remembered to send them a note—people went crazy when you didn't send notes sometimes, and you could never tell which people because they would never come out and say it. There was a lot more mileage in resentment.

Then she heard Chip ask again. Straight out. *What's going to happen?* And why not; he was on his way to eighteen, a legal adult and he had the right to not be protected all the time, from things in life that might hurt—even the ones that are guaranteed to.

"Mom."

Looking at him, Mary remembered being eleven years old and ice skating on the pond that the Dewberrys had behind their barn. They skated hard that day, and the sun turned warmer than they'd realized. Standing at the northern bank, already deep in shade, Mary could see a chain of different wet spots, and realized she was going to have to chart her way back very carefully if she wanted to get across without falling in. And this, right now, wasn't much different.

"When Stewart came to school here, and then Sandy," she paused; Chip waited. "Dad and I wanted children. There were problems, and then more problems, and we'd about given up. But then, after getting to know them—the two of them—we didn't. We wanted one even more. A lot more. So, we started talking about adopting."

"And then you got me. I knew that. So what?"

"Well, there were some complications."

"What do you mean?" Chip asked. "What kind of complications?"

Mary looked at him. *The thick patches*, she thought. *And the thin.*

22

Pick

He left Griffin's house on the premise that there was work to do, back at the hotel. But something made him stop along the way, and park the car and get out and start walking. He needed time to think, and driving would get him there too quickly. Also, he knew that if he stayed in the car, anything was possible. Six hours north and he's in Montreal. *Steak frites* and a goblet of red and leave this shit behind.

When the thoughts finally did start, Pick considered the collision he felt coming. He had always liked to live his life according to compartments—and lately, these compartments had not been cooperating at all. They were supposed to stay separate and distinct, and allow only him to move from one to another freely, the way a ghost can pass through solid walls when no one else can.

Home and work compartments would mix sometimes, but he had a pretty good handle on keeping that to a minimum. The occasional business event where he'd promise Laura they would leave as soon as socially possible, and then do that, to both of their relief; his was never Laura's crowd to begin with, and the last people Pick felt like hanging out with on a Friday night were the same ones he'd been doing business with all week. He kept his weekends separate—doing the same amount of work, but from home—where, theoretically, he could at least be more relaxed.

He remembered Goody telling him once how the Jews invented the weekend—that by consecrating the Sabbath, and by locking it into the rhythm of the week, they were setting a pattern of living and making it a rule for life. Take a good look, Goody would say, it really was written in stone. Says so right on the tablets.

"Religion. I think it's like a box."

Then there was the Carmine Compartment; on instinct alone, Pick kept that one quarantined and heavily guarded. Carmine set the tone early on, and Pick merely kept the practice going. If Carmine had no use for Pick during his childhood, then Pick had no use for Carmine once he grew up. It was simple; nice little thing called quid pro quo. Maybe not written in stone but a damn fine arrangement just the same.

"And each side of the box is painted a different color."

Before he knew it, Pick had reached the bridge to Wilkes-Barre. The Sterling was right across there; he could go in and get some work done if he wanted. Call Iris, have her pull up some files, stay tuned in and tuned up, build on the momentum of the settlement they had just won. The iron's hot, Team. You snooze, you lose.

Although suddenly he didn't give a damn. It wasn't like him, and he knew it. But standing by this riverbank, his past creeping up on him like a dense noxious vapor, with Griffin down and maybe for the count, and Goody out there, somewhere, teasing with his whereabouts while Laura's sadness curled off her like peeling layers of paint—like it or not, staying tuned and hot irons and momentum were the last things on Pick's mind.

Precious minutes then, to be by himself. Sentries at every compartment, locked and loaded, waiting to see which way he'd go next.

He stood on the bridge, and listened to the slap of the river on the limestone piers below.

They found the right bus to Hershey and watched Goody climb on. He made his way to a window seat and sat down. He looked out at them and waved. Laura and Pick waved back.

"You think he'll be okay?" she asked.

Pick shrugged. "It sounds like a pretty heavy deal. Like they're having the funeral all over again. What a thing."

It was a memorial service, Goody had told them, for his father, and it went with the unveiling of the headstone. This was a standard Jewish tradition, and the family was crystal clear on having him be there; they were counting on him to not repeat his performance from the funeral. No vanishing act this time.

Laura had tried to get down to Hershey to be with Goody during the summer, back when his dad died, but her parents wouldn't take her and wouldn't let her go all that way alone—so she had to wait until school started again to see him. And no one could deny, it was a different Goody who came back that fall. He was sadder, sapped—the light that was always there, you could only see occasionally now— and never for very long.

Then, when Pick showed up, things got better. Griffin knew what he was doing; what both of these guys needed, more than any-thing else, was a friend. They sparked each other, and each seemed to come much more to life when the other was around. Proof that unlikely pairings can be the best sometimes.

The bus pulled away, and Laura said she guessed she and Pick should probably go back to the school. Pick agreed but didn't want to; he wished Laura wouldn't want to either, but she'd already said she did. Otherwise why would she bring it up?

"You want to see something?" he asked.

"Sure," was Laura's answer, and it spiked Pick's hopes that she said it so quickly. He switched directions, and not long after, they were at his house—a place Pick took no one. Not even Goody had seen this house.

"What are those lights?" Laura asked. She pointed to some fixtures in the row of tall maples framing the driveway. High up, in the branches.

"Security," Pick said. "At nighttime they can white out the whole place if they have to."

She asked why they'd have to do that, and Pick gave her about a tenth of the reason. Burglars, he told her. Once in a while they'd been hit by burglars. So, his dad had floodlights put in, among other things, to make people think twice next time.

"Wow," Laura said. She told him about Oneida, and how people would just leave their doors open there, and not even think about it. "What did they take?"

"I don't know. Nothing of mine." Pick left out that sometimes they didn't take anything—that people just as often brought things in, and planted them there. Microphones, for instance. Once he saw his father get so mad that he punched a bare-fisted hole through three sheets of standing drywall; that was how Carmine Piccolo felt about federal snooping motherfuckers coming into his fucking house and leaving their motherfucking shit behind.

"My father sells Buicks," Laura offered. "'More Buicks Than Anyone from Nyack to Niagara Falls'!" she chimed, and she told Pick that if he lived anywhere within those bounds, then that phrase would have been engraved on his cortex, for all the times it was on radio and TV and in the newspaper. It was on billboards, too; once her dad even dropped leaflets from a crop duster. A restored bi-plane that crashed into a Purina factory, the very next week.

"I didn't know a lot of people bought Buicks anymore," Pick said.

"Watch out, or he'll put you in one."

Pick laughed out loud, and he hardly ever did that. It struck him funny, this image of some Dale Carnegie Sales Guy in upstate New York slapping him on the back and trying to put him in a Buick.

Laura told him not to worry—Pick's laugh had a great sound, she said. It sounded real—and she wouldn't say so if she didn't think it.

Pick's skin felt like fireworks; he couldn't begin to tell Laura what he liked about her. For starters, he didn't know how she would take it—and if she didn't take it well, then all this feeling he had right now would just zap itself away. And he would hate it if that happened.

But if she did take it well . . . well, what if?

They went the long way back, along the river. For a while they dropped sticks in the water, and made bets on whose would float faster. They watched a train cross the railroad bridge, about a quarter mile downstream; Pick told Laura everything he knew about the valley they were in—about the coal still buried in the hills around them, and how the trains used to run twenty-four hours a day. He talked about floods, and levees, and how the Susquehanna got its name, and when he was finished he said he didn't even know he knew that stuff, or how it had gotten into his head the way it did— and he knew he was only talking about it because he was nervous about running out of things to say.

They switched into talking about Goody, mostly because they thought they ought to. Laura told Pick how they met as sophomores, and how Goody was a lot more outgoing then. She said he got her into all kinds of things: the film club, where you got credit for watching movies, if you took part in the discussions. The listening booths at the library downtown, where you could hear almost any record you wanted, for free—vinyl records, not cassettes, with all the cracks and pops that came with being authentic. Also, Goody found a photo lab that would print Laura's pictures for next to nothing, as long as she'd come in on Saturday afternoons and answer the phones. And he turned her on to bagels and lox, which she thought were delicious— and since Oneida, apparently, didn't see a market for that, Goody had treated Laura to her first. "Judaism on a plate," he called it.

She admitted that he got pretty intense sometimes; Goody told her he loved her before they'd known each other even a week, although she didn't see how he could. But she wasn't against it, she felt good around him; she liked feeling needed, and Goody gave her a whole lot of that. He needed her, and he wanted her, and all of that was very, very new to Laura.

Pick *was confused: "Who wouldn't want you?" he wondered out loud, and Laura told him he could start with her parents. Exhibit A was boarding school; Exhibit B was that she was given no choice about Exhibit A.*

Pick *was surprised to hear this. "I thought I was the only one," he said.*

"If you were," Laura assured him, "we'd be at a very tiny school."

The rest of the way back, Pick's *mind would not stop once. He wanted to tell her everything—and not about coal trains, and the Susquehanna. He wanted to say things he knew he couldn't say, going all the way back to September, to the day he found her cleaning those grease traps, singing Darlene Love.*

But for the first time in Pick's *short life, right and wrong were things he suddenly cared about. And he was going to have to do the right thing here—no matter how much it hurt him, no matter how much he wanted it or how right it might be in the end. Because you don't make a move on your best friend's girl. You just don't. Even Carmine Piccolo's boy knew that one.*

23

Chip

He took off his gear and put it in the usual places; wet stuff where the wet stuff goes, dry stuff where the dry stuff goes. Up and down the aisles, the rest of the guys were doing the same. Everything looked the way it always looked, sounded the way it always sounded.

Usual. But different.

He had an idea, and went around to the next aisle where Silva's locker was. A good pass catcher, reliable, the first guy Chip would look for whenever Randy was double-teamed and couldn't get open.

"Hey."

"What's up?" Silva was stuffing his towel and his wet warm-up shirt back into his locker. They were going to *cook* in there.

"You know, you gotta clean that stuff," Chip pointed. "You're gonna have germs the size of lobsters, walking out of there on their own."

"Thanks, Mom," Silva said.

Chip realized Silva was right; what did he care if the guy's gear was disgusting? "Listen, you work on the yearbook, right?"

"Hell no. I just went in a couple of times when Krissy did. Then we got caught in there alone, so I stopped." He looked at Chip. "How come?"

"Nothing. I was just wondering where all the old ones were. The old yearbooks. They keep them, right? At least one copy of each, they'd have to."

"I didn't see any around. 'Course I wasn't looking." He shrugged. Silva's needs were simple: food and sex, using football as a means to get both. "What do you want with old yearbooks?"

"I just wanted to check something out. Who's head of it this year?"

"Ellie."

"Ellie? Since when?"

"What's-her-name got anorexia."

"Oh." What's-her-name was Melinda Pelfrey. Chip had noticed her getting thinner, but it didn't seem anything drastic. That stuff must come on pretty quick, he thought. "Anyway, thanks," he told Silva.

"No problemo."

Chip couldn't stand it when people said *no problemo*. But he let it ride this time, and turned to go.

"How's your dad?" Silva asked.

"He's okay." It was an automatic answer to an automatic question; the way Silva made it sound, Chip's dad could be napping on the couch with a fishing show on TV, instead of tucked in between bed rails and fighting for his life. Still, you couldn't blame anyone for asking that way. Nobody knew what to say. If things were the other way around, Chip wouldn't know either. And now, with his dad being in the house, it all seemed even more unreal. Or too real to be real. Or something.

"Try the library," Silva said. "If there were old yearbooks, they might be in the library. You know—year by year. Like with the encyclopedias or something."

"Why didn't I think of that?" Chip said.

"Maybe you're thinkin' about other shit."

"Yeah. Maybe. Thanks." Chip looked at Silva. He felt good enough to handle another *no problemo* at this point.

"Plus, you won't have to deal with Ellie."

Chip tensed. "Who says I don't want to deal with Ellie?"

"I don't know. I just thought. Take it easy."

"I am taking it easy."

On the way to the library it occurred to Chip that there was one teacher, Mrs. Vanderlip, who had been at the school forever. She was older than half of the trees on campus, Chip's dad would say—which could mean that on a good day she might know and remember who Piccolo and Goodman were. Plus, there were two others who might have been around that long—Miss Hauge, the school registrar, and Mr. Ronci, who came in a couple times a week to teach a math practicum that only about four people a year qualified for; Chip never minded not having the grades for Mr. Ronci.

Still, asking any of these people was way down the list—especially, if he could help it, not Mrs. Vanderlip. Lately she'd been prone to blurting things out at unfortunate times, along with other signs that she just wasn't up to the job anymore. Mostly the stuff she did was harmless, and no one had the nerve to fire her anyway—they just kept giving her less to do, and making it sound like more. And every year at graduation they gave her new awards for lifetime service, hoping she'd get the message; if she did, she wasn't saying.

Chip had heard his parents talking about her, just recently. Mrs. Vanderlip had spent thirty minutes delaying a delivery man by swearing he had been one of her students, when actually he was from Senegal and had only been in the country for six months. Slips like this were on the increase, and everybody knew what it was, although no one wanted to say.

There were plenty of times when she was sharp as a tack, Chip's dad had said. And his mom had replied, it might be better to ease her out now while they can still be graceful about it—until his dad responded, there's nothing graceful about losing your faculties, and if they take this job from Mrs. Vanderlip, then they might as well just go ahead and take her reason to be alive. So they eased up on the gas instead, and did things like moving her from Gemmell over to Critchley, where she could have a nicer apartment and where the older girls were, who were a little more responsible for themselves. Let her roam the halls over there and be a presence. And people could hint all they wanted—but as long as Henry Griffin had a say in this, unless the signs got a lot more disturbing than they'd been so far, no one was making any final moves. Firing Mrs. Vanderlip was not on the table.

Chip was proud of his dad for saying that. And proud of his parents for how they'd sit down and talk things out. Like partners—thoughtful, respecting each other's opinions, even when they disagreed—when too many of his friends' folks seemed to communicate through attorneys and flying dinnerware instead. These were the times Chip knew that he'd been blessed with exactly the right family. And he knew how rare that was.

The librarian was temporary—a grad student from Wilkes College across the river—so she was pretty excited about a chance to be helpful. But Chip blew her off as politely as he could manage, telling her he just needed to look through some encyclopedias, and he knew where they were, and that if he couldn't find what he needed, he'd come back. She said okay, and smiled like she meant it.

Silva was right—there was a whole lineup of yearbooks, right about where he had predicted. But the bell rang just as Chip found them and he didn't have time to dive in; at least next time he'd know where to look. Maybe he'd bring somebody, to help him. Twice the work in half the time, and they wouldn't have to know why he was looking. You pick the right person, you get the right help. He'd think about it.

The Wilkes girl smiled at him again on the way out, said her name was Reesha if he ever needed anything, and waved. Chip waved back, awkwardly, thinking that this Reesha from Wilkes was sort of a looker, which surprised him—up until that moment, the only girl he wasn't blind to was Ellie; other girls just didn't show up on the dial for him. Randy, in particular, was concerned about this. Maybe there were vitamins, or some other treatments Chip should look into, to cure his affliction. Chip put up with the teasing, but he did notice the Wilkes girl, and he noticed that he noticed her—and that he could do that without any stress on his conscience. So this was either the beginning of a cure, or an anomaly. Time would tell, he guessed.

He hustled to the chapel for the mandatory weekly assembly, wondering if "anomaly" was the right word. It was just the kind of thing Ellie would know, too. Unfortunately, she wasn't talking.

24

Laura

Pick called her from the Blue Knight Diner, and in her memory she could see the whole place: swivel stools around a U-shaped counter topped with some kind of cheap dark laminate that was wearing thin even back then. She wondered what another generation's worth of elbows leaning on it would have done to the thing.

The phone Pick was calling from would be against a wall next to an electric Hires Root Beer sign. There were some tired wooden booths along the other walls. A cigarette machine crowded the doorway, which grated on the school officials who didn't want it any easier than it already was for students to get their hands on the Luckies and the Kents and Winstons in there. There was a jukebox squeezed in between two booths and underneath the corner window, where Bill the owner had tacked up a row of Pocono Valley Prep Blue Knight pennants, so that their points hung down, and that way they'd pass for curtains.

"So how'd the thing go?"

Laura knew what he meant. "Great. Molly stole the show."

"Come on."

"No really—you should have seen her, Sandy. And I don't mean—"

"I know." She hoped he knew she wasn't trying to make him feel guilty; just trying to share what it was like to be there.

"It's just—this quiet little kid. Even before anything happened, she was always the quiet one. But put some kind of costume on her, put on a little makeup, turn on the lights and she just—turns *into* something. I mean there's only so much you can do with a turtle, but don't tell Molly that. Before we know it, she'll be Lady Macbeth."

They had talked about her before this way: the quiet ones. All they needed sometimes was the right thing to spark them. With Molly, apparently, it took lights and a part to play—and it didn't even have to be the part of a human. Molly would play a shoelace if someone cast her that way, and she'd find a way to make it a shoelace you'd never forget.

"Anyway what about Henry?" Laura asked.

"Henry? You call him Henry?"

"We're in our thirties now, Sandy. Somehow calling him 'Mr. Griffin' feels weird."

"Calling him 'Henry' seems weirder, if you ask me."

Laura nodded; she knew Pick couldn't see her but would know that's what she was doing anyway. They'd been married long enough to be on different galaxies and still know each other's pauses and gaps. A good thing, until it became a bad thing. Was everyone's marriage this way? And was it even a bad thing, to know someone that well? *We marry for life*, Laura found herself thinking, *without knowing at all what those words really mean.*

"I've been trying to hook up Howland and Imboden on a conference call," Pick was telling her, "and get them to talk doctor to each other, so I can listen in and figure out what's going on and make some decisions. You wouldn't think that would be so hard."

"So what's the problem?" Laura asked, and regretted right away having put it like that. All you had to do was inflect a question a certain way sometimes, and Pick could shut you right out. There had been some hope, back when the phone call started, of some positive flow between them. She could hear in his voice that he was open, and it was nice to be off all the eggshells and walking on solid ground for a bit.

But she blew it, Laura felt. She blew it, and she could tell by his tone from the minute she said that. It was his office tone, his go down the list and get things done routine.

"Look. If Howland calls the house, tell him where to find me. Tell him to leave a message at the hotel. You got the number? The Sterling."

"I know what hotel. I know where you're staying." She wished it didn't bother her the way it did. Pick didn't mean it the way it sounded; he knew the difference between a wife and an employee, and Laura knew that.

But still.

"Tell me something about the diner," she asked.

"What about it?"

"I don't know. What's different?"

"Far as I can tell, nothing. Bill's still here. Wearing the same damn apron, I think. Still looks pissed off at the world."

"Is 'Whiter Shade of Pale' still on the jukebox?"

"I don't know. I didn't get over there yet. It wasn't exactly on the plan or anything."

"Would you check? And would you play it if it is?"

"Jesus, Laura. It's a song. On a jukebox."

"I know it's a song on a jukebox."

"Plus you're not even here."

I can fix that, Laura thought, and had to cover her mouth to stop herself. "We probably have it here some place anyway," she said instead. "Forget I asked."

"Done," Pick answered. "And Laura."

"What?"

"Nothing," he said eventually. "Forget it."

"Done," Laura echoed.

"All right look. I gotta go. This place is making me hungry. Not for anything here though."

Laura agreed—even as kids, they risked a lot by eating there. Bill's single affirming feature was that his was the closest food from the campus; he had location, and that was it. Throw in his relaxed attitude towards teenagers buying cigarettes, and he had all the edge he needed—not one other thing could possibly recommend the place.

"Laura, can I ask you something?"

"Sure," she said.

"Am I as bad as I sound sometimes?"

Laura listened to him waiting. "I don't know how to answer that," she told him.

"Well let's say we're out at dinner and there's some loud guy at the next table over and he's saying the kind of stuff I say sometimes. Would I be telling you what an asshole the guy is?"

"Well, I don't know," Laura said. "You have a lot of different categories and criteria covering assholes at the next table over."

"Have I been fitting into any of them lately?"

"Lately you have been fitting into six."

Pick nodded. "So, there's work to do."

Laura grinned. "Just by asking, you got rid of four."

They hung up, and suddenly Laura had an appetite, too. She went into the pantry and came out with a can of chicken noodle soup. Not a standard menu item in the house, but she usually had a couple cans around, to give to the kids when they were sick and home from school and she wanted to get something in them in a hurry. And that's what they'd have at Bill's all the time, at the Blue Knight Diner on stinging cold days with a low still cloud of smoke in the air and "Whiter Shade of Pale" on the jukebox time after time after time until Goody ran out of quarters or everyone else ran out of patience. Still, you couldn't blame that on the song—it was a good one, it put you in a mood, it brought other moods back like long lost friends—it was like a signature, and it floated over Laura's memory of that place and all the time she spent inside there. Every moment of it, in hindsight, priceless.

"We skipped the light fandango . . .turned cartwheels across the floor . . ."

She sang what she knew from memory, pouring the can out and then filling it with water to add in. Out of habit she looked at the label and the ingredients before rinsing it out to recycle it. She recoiled at the amount of sodium, and thought maybe she'd start making her own again, and freezing it for just the right times.

"I was feeling kind of seasick . . .but the crowd called out for more . . ."

The song made her feel good, as it always had—before she'd met the two of them, before she even left Oneida, she knew the song and liked it. It was the song that was playing in her head the day her parents drove her down to the school, to drop her off. It was the song she was thinking of when she got out of the car and stepped onto the campus for the first time—her own personal moon landing, with Henry Griffin coming down the steps of Foyle, to greet them officially. Deacon Rotarian George and his Cheerful Other Half.

"And though my eyes were opened wide . . .they might have just as well been closed . . ."

It was the song in her head the day she met Goody, when a Frisbee skipped to a stop at her feet and there he was—his frayed army jacket, his John Lennon haircut and the way he smiled down at her, from a whole other world, extending a hand and inviting her to join him there. Like an emcee plucking a volunteer from the audience.

And once they discovered they liked the same song, it was the one Goody played every time they went to Bill's, even over the Beatles—and they'd sit in their booth and talk about everything there was to talk about. Then, when Pick came aboard, the subject often had to do with why Goody couldn't seem to find any other buttons on the jukebox; Goody would say there's beauty in ritual, and Pick would say that variety could be a ritual too, so why don't you try some of *that* once in a while? Mix it up a little, give the rest of us a break, is that a fuckin' crime? Laura would listen and laugh and take pictures and only when she got the pictures back and studied them did she see it in such plain sharp relief: two different heartbeats, battling for space and waiting for her to tell the truth to herself. She knew she was in trouble.

"That her face, at first just ghostly . . . turned a whiter shade of pale."

She went and found some Saltines to crumble into the soup. Adding sodium to sodium. No wonder we were doing cartwheels.

Irony, she thought. The shit can make you crazy.

"Four hundred and fifty thousand dollars?" Pick asked. "Goody you gotta be kidding me."

They were sitting in front of Foyle, opening their mail. Laura and Goody had letters from home, plus Goody had gotten something official in a legal envelope. Pick had a book he'd ordered, on how to count cards at blackjack—all they had to do was get to Reno where he had a contact who'd sell them fake ID's, and get them into the casinos. Goody wondered out loud whether there was a directory in the back, listing Bail Bond Services for smartass underage amateurs who think they can beat the House.

"Look at this," Pick said. He had snatched Goody's envelope away and was reading the title page. "It's got like fifty lawyers' names across the top."

Laura wasn't paying attention; she was busy skimming through the letter she got from her folks. Not too much going on up in Oneida, but it sure took a lot of pages to say so.

"Four hundred and fifty . . ." Pick repeated. He searched the rest of the envelope. "Where's the check?"

"There isn't any check. I have to sign the papers first."

"So, when do you get it?"

"I'm not exactly sure, Pick. Maybe if I had the chance to read that far." He gestured to get the papers back. But Pick wasn't finished; he scanned through them again, businesslike. "This is insurance money," he said. "This pays off right away . . ."

Laura looked up from her letter: right away?

"It's how it happened with my Aunt Luisa," Pick explained, "only with her it was like eleven hundred dollars—not half a fucking million."

Goody took in the information but didn't seem real excited. "It's okay," he told them. "I'm not gonna have it for long."

Pick looked at him like he had just dropped some dreadful medical news on them. "What do you mean?"

"I mean I'm giving it away," Goody told him. "I don't want it."

"All of it?" Laura asked—even faster than Pick, who was choking on the whole idea. Then Goody confirmed: he wasn't going to keep the money no matter how much it was. He couldn't feel right holding onto something like that.

Pick turned to Laura. "Can you believe this?" Then he lit back on Goody. "You know something? You're nuts. You're fuckin' nuts. You know what I would do with that kind of money?"

"I'd be scared to find out," Goody said, and he took the papers back, so he could put them away.

Pick looked at Laura; torn herself, between admiration for something she could never do, and full blown-out sex appeal, like Pick's, for the money. "Well who're you gonna give it to?" Pick wanted to know.

Goody thought for a minute; after all, the thing had just gotten here. "Churches," he said.

"Churches?" This was a word Pick knew, just not in this context. "What the hell do you mean churches?"

"I was talking to Dot and Rosa before. After Rosa gave that

report on all those church burnings in the South. Money like this could go a long way down there."

They looked at him, stunned. "Yeah but—" Pick started to say. He turned to Laura, who didn't know what to say either. "Listen," he went on. "Goody. Don't be so quick about making up your mind here."

Goody shook that off. "People don't have a place to pray, they might stop praying. And if someone's going to burn a church down, they have to know that someone else'll put it right back up."

"But it doesn't have to be you!" Pick said. "I mean come on—there are people who already do this shit. Charities—not high school kids blowing their fuckin' inheritance."

"The government too," Laura added, and Pick was glad to have the backup. There were all kinds of places, private and public, whose only job was to see that people like this got help.

But Goody shook his head. "Could take years," he said. "According to Rosa. And what'll they do in the meantime?"

Pick and Laura shared a look. Exasperated; like parents of the next Pavarotti, who had just announced he was leaving music forever, to take a job at a toothpick factory in Idaho.

"Goody, listen," Pick said. "Nobody's father leaves money to their kid if they think they're gonna do what you're doing. If Carmine died and did this? And found out I just handed it over like that? He'd kill me. He'd have people waiting by the time I got home. He'd put out a contract from beyond the fuckin' afterlife."

Goody grinned, at the image. But the reasoning washed over him.

"How about this," Pick tried. "You just give some of it—most of it. Give away maybe three-fifty. It still makes you out like some kind of saint, to do something like that. Plus, you get to keep a hundred for yourself."

"So which churches don't get built so that I can have a hundred thousand dollars?"

"But what about college?" Laura asked. "You have to have money for college, right?"

"Scholarship, I guess. Work my way through."

"No school'll take a guy this stupid," Pick said.

Goody shrugged that off too. *"Could be it for college then,"* he said. *"Listen are you two finished with this? Because I sort of am."*

"No, we're not finished with this! We're not going to fucking sit here and let you just hand off four hundred and fifty thousand dollars!"

"Then you'll have to sit there and do something else," Goody said. *"I'm going."* And he meant it, he was getting up to leave.

"Stewart?"

Goody turned. If anyone could talk reason to him, Laura'd be the one.

"Do you really think this is what your father wanted?"

He stood there, looking at her. At both of them, with an expression that neither one had ever seen before. He looked haunted. This whole thing was out of their league, and they knew it.

"I don't know what he wanted," Goody said. *"Only thing in here's the money."* He gave a sad little look, and walked down the steps. The envelope in his hand like it had nothing more than confetti in it.

Pick turned to Laura. *"Do you understand what happened just now?"*

Laura looked at him uncomfortably. *"Sometimes he's just— beyond me,"* she admitted. *"I don't understand him at all sometimes."* She was quick to add that she loved him though—a little too quick, maybe—and Pick was just as quick to acknowledge that. Then they went on to agree, wholeheartedly, that there was probably no one at the school, no matter who they were, who didn't love Goody somehow.

But understand him? That might be asking just a little too much. To understand Goody called for more time and inclination than most people had. While, for Laura, understanding Pick was easy; no assembly required. Being with him felt like being with herself, only better—Laura knew that Pick saw all of her, unblemished, and not just the good parts. When for all of Goody's love for her, he only saw Laura in the light; either he ignored her faults and flaws, *or he somehow just didn't see them to begin with. But Pick saw everything—he recognized Laura's shadows, and knew them for what they were—so easily he could almost give them names.*

And not because he had any special talent for this. But because Laura's shadows, every unmapped one of them, were exactly the same as his own. And that felt safer, to both of them, than anything.

25

Chip

One part of the answer wasn't any further than the Yellow Pages. He stood there, looking at the listing, almost forgetting why he had opened the book in the first place: his athlete's foot had gotten out of hand again, more than any of the over-the-counter stuff was going to help. He had to call the drug store where they had his prescription on file, but when he found *Drug Stores*, it made him go to *Pharmacies*—and when he overshot the P listings and went into the R's, he saw the ad in the Restaurant section.

Piccolo's. For Fine Dining.

Piccolo, the crime guy. The guy he'd heard about, the guy that everybody had heard about. And Piccolo the lawyer, who'd been calling in the infantry, the special ops, to come and save the day for Chip's dad—who somehow knew, in a case like this, that this was the right guy to go to. So far, anyway—because it didn't take a genius, that's when the money showed up. Along with the nurses, and the home care, and the specialists that the Griffins could never afford on their own. And if the other one ever turned up, whatever he might bring to the party was still an open question—but this guy Piccolo was coming through, and big.

For Fine Dining. Authentic Italian. From Intimate Occasions to Family Celebrations.

Right, Chip thought. *Family my ass. We all know about that.* But what did he know about it? There was an Italian restaurant up in the hills. He'd been there only once, with Randy and his family back when Randy first came to school and they'd started being friends. And he knew that Cindi Lindberg went there with her parents sometimes, when the folks weren't shooting off to Manhattan for the weekend, and trusting the house to Cindi—which was an epic miscalculation, for all the times the fiesta flag went up the minute they were gone.

The parties at her house were legendary. Always restricted to couples and only inner circle. There was a ping pong table, and a hot tub, and a pool they could use in the warmer months. There was a whole hierarchy of bedrooms, from the basement to the master, where people could go off and be alone. No alcohol was allowed, but weed was okay if you smoked it outside. The difference, according to Cindi, was self-evident: people who drank too much got boisterous, uncooperative, and sometimes destructive, to friends and furnishings—while the ones who got too baked would just philosophize each other until the last one passed out. No harm, no foul.

Finally, no matter what, everybody had to spend the whole last hour diligently removing any and all traces that they'd been there. And if you goofed up, even once, you couldn't come back; some other couple would eagerly take your place.

Chip was never really crazy about Cindi. First, there was the way she spelled her name—he was generally not big on girls doing tricks with their names, like putting a letter *i* at the end instead of the *y* that's supposed to be there. He remembered griping to Randy about it, on the walk back from one of Cindi's parties. Chip told Randy he should do the same thing, and call himself Randi—and Randy said he would, if Chip started going by "Chippe." They tried it for a full three blocks—and only then because they were stoned—and nothing came of it after that.

But this went beyond how Cindi spelled her name. There was something Chip didn't like about the way she let her parents think she was trustworthy, when she routinely broke their rules whenever they weren't around. She did it carefully—responsibly, if you looked at it a certain way—but still she did it. Although it didn't, even once, keep Chip from having any problem with going over there when they went out of town without her, which happened a lot—and he was as grateful as anyone to have Cindi's place to escape to.

It was where he went with Ellie, which hurt to think about now: he knew which bed they used (the master), and what the room looked like (like successful people lived there), and what it felt like to splay out on those unbelievable sheets and pretend they were older now, and this was their place and everything was taken care of and they didn't have to go anywhere and they could have real life honeymoon sex whenever they wanted, even one more time right then and there.

The first time he was with her, or with anyone, it was at Cindi's house. As freshmen, they started in the basement, with other rookie pairings just like them, who were scared and clumsy and trying to figure out what to do and how to do it. Sophomores took a number and used the pool house, and once you had gone all the way with someone you were promoted to a bedroom. Chip and Ellie were no different in that respect—yet by the end of junior year they had made their way unchallenged to the master bedroom, the top of the heap.

There were chenille ruffles around the bed frame. Chip remembered Ellie saying that; the phrase came back to him on his way over to Cindi's to ask her if she minded driving him out to Bear Creek. He knew she'd probably say yes, because: a) she loved to drive and her parents had just gotten her a killer

Miata, a two-seat convertible with a CD player and a stick shift; and b) he knew Cindi liked coming through for people whenever she got the chance—especially the boarding students, who didn't have their own basements to hook up in, and guys like Chip, who lived on campus because their parents worked there. It was too much of a fishbowl to do anything questionable on home turf.

That kind of generosity, Chip liked about Cindi. Also, there was this thing she did with overalls and a white cotton top, that she wore on weekends because you couldn't dress like that for school. And when people came over she looked like she had always just washed her hair, and Chip was now aware that he really liked the look of that—with her still-drying hair all clean and feathering out onto her shoulders so that you could see parts of her neck, parts of the white cotton top, and the straps from those overalls, all mixed together and it all looked great. Chip found himself picturing what it would be like to be over there on a day when no one else was around, and go up the stairs behind Cindi while she slipped out of that outfit piece by piece, and then kept on going right down the hall to the big master bed.

That was the one with the chenille ruffles, and the first time Chip heard Ellie say the words he laughed so hard he got the hiccups. He and Randy had just been out in the yard, smoking some freshly scored hydroponic, while Ellie and Cindi and Janet Pardini and some of the other girls were trying to figure out how to get the rice cooker to work because they had decided to make sushi that day but they didn't have any fish so they decided just to make the rice and slap other things from the refrigerator on it. The girls were pretty wasted too, and eventually they ditched the idea altogether and Ellie went looking for Chip and asked him if he wanted to go upstairs—which to Chip was the sweetest sound in the world, her asking that.

And then when they got up there, she said the thing about chenille ruffles because for some reason she had just noticed them, which was strange because she could swear they weren't new or anything, she just hadn't seen them before. And Chip couldn't get over how funny those words sounded together, *chenille ruffles*, and he told her they probably weren't even real words—especially coming from a girl who moments ago was too far gone to find the on/off switch on a modern rice cooker, which had only the one switch to begin with. And Ellie said it wasn't the *switch*, it was the *measurements* that got everyone confused because there were two different bags of rice in the cabinet and the instructions on each said different things, and neither one matched the directions on the rice cooker—and yes there *were* such words as "chenille ruffles," because that's what those things were on the bottom of the bed and on the matching chair and ottoman across the room, and if Chip didn't believe her he could go into any decorating store and ask for them and they wouldn't bat an eye, they'd just ask what color.

Chip was sure this was a trick; what else could it be? He'd walk into a decorating store—as if he'd even do *that*—and say "chenille ruffles" and they'd laugh at him harder than he was laughing right now, which got Ellie all righteously steamed and she climbed on top of him, pinning him down and ordering him to admit it right this minute that she was right, that they really were real things, and it *is* hard to make rice whether it's a fool-proof cooker or not—because anyone will tell you, perfect rice is really tricky, even with all of Williams-Sonoma on your side.

But Chip kept laughing and hiccupping and it only made Ellie madder until the next thing they knew they were throwing their clothes off and having the best sex either one of them had ever dreamed could be possible. Sex like in the movies, it was that good and both of them knew it.

Only now it was over. It was over it was over it was over—and the thought of never being with Ellie again like that spread through Chip's insides, and ate away at him like an acid.

It was over.

And instead he was walking to Cindi Lindberg's, to ask her for a ride up to this restaurant in the hills so he could check something out. On any other day, Ellie would be with him and they would go over there as a couple and Cindi would take the bigger car and drive them up to Bear Creek together, like they were all on some kind of mission. Which they were; only this way it would be a mission of two, because Ellie was dodging him—and it was finally drilling through this time that she might really mean it, and mean it for good.

He rang Cindi's bell and there she was. Let her spell her name any damn way she wants, Chip decided. At least she had the goodness in her to say hello.

26

Laura

S he set the kids up with a video, so she could get some time in the attic undisturbed. She had gotten out the carton labeled *Clothing Misc.*, which had just enough miscellaneous clothing under the lid to camouflage the real contents inside: her old journals, some of her textbooks from high school, and one box so private that she'd put a false bottom in the bigger box to protect it even more.

She leafed through a couple pages of US history. Then a little ancient civ—Plato, Sophocles, the Greek tragedies—and after that, a few of her English texts. The fat book of anthologies, where she first read Poe, and Hawthorne, and Mark Twain. She found *Walden,* and Emerson, and wished she had the time now to read them again and really dig in when maybe she could understand it all a little better than she did at sixteen. She found a quote she'd written, on the inside flap of a notebook. *No man steps in the same river twice,* it said, in her earnest eleventh-grade handwriting. It was from Heraclitus—something Laura was proud to remember, although she also remembered there was a second part to it, that tied the whole thing together, but for some

forgotten reason she'd neglected to write down. Distracted, probably. It was hard to keep your attention on anything sometimes.

Finally, she was ready. She lifted the false panel and took
out the box she'd hidden there. First came the scrapbook; sitting
back Laura opened it and fanned out the pages—there were
articles and photos pressed behind clear sheets of cell material,
crackly now and amber with age. Newspapers, magazines, the
reviews and the cover pieces, all charting young S.A. Goodman's burst onto the literary scene—the press loved the angle
where he was a teenage runaway who ended up at a Buddhist
temple and worked for the monks, and how a writing teacher
at a community college brought this book out of him and then
found a publisher for it; you couldn't ask for a better pitch than
that. And as soon as people read it, they knew: this wasn't just a
gimmick, this was the real thing. The kid could write.

There was a bidding war for the movie rights; Goody was
flooded with job offers. A famous script doctor was hired to
teach him the peculiar language and form of the professional
movie screenplay, and Goody was a quick and prolific learner.
In a very short time he was writing for everyone, it seemed.
Everyone who mattered. Names you read about. He went from a
one-room cabin at Mt. Raymond to a four-bedroom in Malibu
Colony, with a saltwater pool and a private gym and a screening
room, all on the studio's dime.

And then one day he left. His movie was being prepped,
he had three other scripts under contract and backup offers for
more. No warning, no explanation, breaching agreements with
places you just don't do that to. The project shut down and the
book drifted off the charts and out of the discussion. But Goody
was long gone by then. The other jobs he'd signed for went to
other writers who were happy to snap up the work; if they knew
where to find him they'd have sent cards saying thanks.

Laura shook her head at the speed of it all, at how rap-
idly Goody went from anonymous to sensation to *persona non*

grata—as suddenly as he'd arrived, he was gone—and there were enough people involved with enough long memories, to make it plain and clear that he needn't bother to ever come back. *If they gave out Oscars for burning all your bridges,* one article said, *Goodman would win in a landslide.* Maybe the kid could write, but he sure didn't know how to play ball. And there were others who could do both.

She put the scrapbook aside and turned to the main event. *The Bell Tower,* by S.A. Goodman. First edition, first page. There was his handwriting. There was his note to her.

To Laura. I wish I knew how to fight for you. From Stewart.

She put the book down and closed her eyes. Maybe, downstairs, they'd watch the movie twice.

She had never been to Malibu before. So far, the only beaches she knew were the ones down along Chincoteague, and further south: low lying Atlantic strands that went on for miles, with grassy dunes at your back and not wild mountains like they had out here—and of course, Laura's beaches didn't have record albums written about them, and teen movies and an entire subculture of cars and bikinis and surfboards, of endless summers and California Girls.

But it was pretty, Laura thought. It sure was pretty. The ocean did things with shades of blue that she'd never seen before. And there were flowers blossoming, everywhere. Languid exotic splashes of hibiscus and bougainvillea, spilling over walls and balconies and stairways wherever she looked.

And it was winter. When she and Pick left New York, their plane was delayed by ice. Were they in the same country?

"This is for you," Goody said, while he wrote something in the book he'd brought for her—just like that, as if it were a birthday card, or a modest check to some charity and not a successful, published novel. And she knew that if there were such a thing as the first book off the first press, like the inaugural ceremonial car off an assembly line, this would be it. Goody would do that; that's how he was.

She had already read it of course—her friend Tris's copy because she wouldn't dare bring one into the house—but this was different. This was from Stewart's hand to hers, his own bare and unbleached account of what had happened between them, back when they were in school. It was beautifully written, popular from the start and now it was going to be a movie; there was guessing in the papers out here about who would be in it. Frantic, breathless guessing—and all from Stewart's words. Incredible.

She read the inscription he wrote for her, with sunlight hitting the water and dolphins outside—real dolphins!—and mountainous green salads getting delivered that very moment and Laura thought she just might faint.

Of course, there were other reasons for that.

"So, you guys are driving up the coast after this?" Goody was asking.

Laura tuned back in. She said yes, that she and Pick hadn't had a vacation in a while, and were taking advantage of one of his occasional business trips out here to tack on a few extra days for themselves.

Goody told her he'd taken that drive before, but in the other direction, when he first came down from Mt. Raymond. And he confirmed: the route is as beautiful as everyone says it is.

He asked how often Pick came out this way; Laura told him it wasn't that often and nothing regular or anything, just that a few of his New York clients had work that crossed over into some aspect of show business or other, and that Pick always came home glad that he didn't pick entertainment law to go into. Smoke and mirrors, he'd tell her, didn't come close to explaining it. It was insane.

"Does he know you came out here today?" Goody asked.

"Probably," Laura said. "He didn't exactly ask, and I didn't exactly say."

Goody nodded. He looked across at her hands. Her diamond was substantial. "I tried calling him," he said, "a bunch of times. I called at work, so it wouldn't mess things up at home. I'd leave a message, then here and there I'd try again. At some point I just stopped."

Laura looked down in her lap. Her napkin had anchors on it—linen napkins, in the afternoon, not bad—with little blue anchors, and the faded red stencil of the company that did the cleaning. "You run away from school," she started. "You get picked up hitchhiking by a van full of monks who take you out to a mountain in Oregon. You write a book about what happened with the three of us. And people figured it out, Stewart. Neighbors. People at Sandy's firm, and it's embarrassing. Even our friends, they'll steer their wives away from him at a party. As if he's going to run off with them, if anyone turns away for two seconds. So, if he hasn't been sending you valentines—I mean you're not exactly surprised, are you?"

Goody looked at her. She was serious. There'd been damage.

"That's not why I did it," he told her. "You know that, right?"

"I don't know what I know," Laura said. "I just know what happened."

Because the papers had covered that, too: how Goody resisted all the offers at first, stressing over and over that he had only been writing the book for himself, for his own healing process. But at the same time, the temple was having financial difficulties that peaked when a major donor died, and her executors cut off the payments. And when the situation got critical, Goody knew what he had to do. The place had been good to him and now it was his turn to pay them back.

"But are you sure that's all?" Laura asked. "There wasn't even a part of you that wanted to hurt us back? Can you really say that?"

Goody met her look. "Not to hurt you," he said. Leaving it open that there might be another reason, maybe even an obvious one, and all she had to do was ask. Hoping, that she would.

"He could have sued you, Stewart. For God's sake you used our same first names. You, and the publisher, and now the studio? But he knew it would only make him look even worse. It's the only time I've ever seen him walk away from a fight."

A waitress came by, saw right away this wasn't a good time, and left. "He wanted to stop the movie?" Goody asked.

"In its tracks," was Laura's answer.

Goody looked stunned. Pick was that angry, that hurt. He could have taken Goody down, and didn't. Was it worth any of this, to have caused that? Would it have been worth it if it brought Laura back?

"I just never thought anybody would read the thing," he told Laura. "I really didn't."

"Surprise," Laura said.

After lunch they walked on the beach. They were barefoot, carrying their shoes. Goody told her that he did this as often as he could now; that walking barefoot along beaches was the best thing about being a writer down here, the only thing about the whole experience that really made any sense.

"You hear about it all your life," Laura said, "the movie business." She asked how much was real and how much was myth, when it came to people's behavior and all. Goody said he could only speak from his own experience, that he'd met some people whose behavior was not just admirable, but often inspiring—while others were capable of doing things you couldn't even imagine, until you saw it for yourself. And you still might not believe it.

Laura wondered how it all might be affecting him—far away like this, in a world that couldn't be more opposite than where he'd been before. From a place of quiet reflection, to a place so loud it can't be heard over the sound of its own celebration; where "prayer" is what happens when you want your rival's movie to tank, and "service to others" is what the judge gives you for aggravated assault with intent. Yet as far as Laura could observe, Goody seemed to be handling it all just fine. And she was relieved to see it; she knew that success often brings distance, and there was already enough of that between them as it was. But she needn't have worried; after all these years of not seeing Goody, and of seeing him for the last time as he was running away in pieces, Laura found it surprisingly easy to talk to him—maybe, she thought, because she had never really stopped. She was always talking to him; he just wasn't ever around to listen. But even that didn't feel true—because in the strangest way, she felt like he was.

"So, our waitress—she was an actress?" Laura asked.

"The one who took over was," Goody told her. "Not the one who started out."

Laura had seen them trading table assignments; she wondered if Goody was the reason. "And that's why we got all that extra fruit?"

"That wasn't extra—they just give out a lot of fruit here. It comes with everything."

"In the hotel room there was a bowl of oranges. They were like basketballs. Sandy said a client sent them."

"Everybody sends things to people. Fruit baskets, rare books, box seats for the Dodgers—you can get a whole new Ferrari out here, if you make enough money for someone."

"You wouldn't know what to do with a Ferrari."

Goody grinned; maybe, maybe not.

Laura watched him while they walked. She remembered him in that park, years ago, full of fire and telling her and Pick he would do this very thing; she felt his determination that day.

"This'll probably sound—I don't know, but I'm proud of you," she told him. "I really am."

"Proud?"

Laura confirmed. It still wasn't the right word, but she stayed with it. "You did something," she said. "Something real. You went through something terrible, and you came out the other side. And with a beautiful book—really, for all the ways it shook things up at home, it is still just beautiful. And I can see it making a great movie. Everything seems to be falling right in place for you."

"Not everything," Goody said. "But why split hairs."

They stepped around a thatch of dried-out seaweed; tangled and brittle, with sandflies zipping around like electrons. "Anyway," he went on, "it could also just be nothing. It could all go away in a second. Things disappear into thin air out here."

"It won't go away. And it isn't nothing—it's something. It's a huge something. It's more than most people even get to dream of. I hope you realize that."

Goody said he wasn't so sure. He told Laura what they'd say at

Mt. Raymond—there's nothing wrong with achieving things, but being attached to accomplishments leads to suffering. Yet everywhere Laura looked in this place, attachment to accomplishments seemed to be working out just fine for a whole lot of people, and seemed to be what drove the whole machine. A system that'll give you a new car or even valuable pieces of art, for giving them a hit, a system that'll put you up in a beach house, just so you can write? She saw it more clearly now, why so many people go so damn crazy when someone hits the jackpot.

"I was just thinking," Goody started to say, "how this spot right here could become known forever as the place where you decided to tell me that you've been thinking real hard, and you've made a phenomenally colossal mistake—and that you are overcome with regret about marrying Pick and not me, and that you're looking for the best conceivable way to turn this whole sad and mistaken episode around and finally make it right."

The abruptness of that caught Laura short; almost more than the thing he had actually just said. She watched while Goody pointed out a circle around them on the ground. "It happened right here, the sign would say. There'd be souvenirs. Tour buses, lining up. The locals would complain about the added traffic and noise."

Laura looked away; she was afraid of what would happen if she didn't. "You've put some thought into this," she said.

"There are ten good scenarios, all ready to go. I ranked them in order of risk and reward. But in every single one of them, the reward is really worth it."

Laura smiled; she remembered how sweet he could be, and glad to see how much of that had remained. In her opinion, it was Goody's inborn sweetness that made his book what it was—when other hands might turn out a vengeful litany of biting recollection, and nothing more.

"I can't say yes," she answered. "You know that, right?"

Goody looked out at the water. Screeching seagulls following a trawler. Panicked schools of fish, underneath. "Tell me you haven't thought about this too. Because it feels like you have."

Laura looked down. She didn't want him to see how right he was. Of course, she had thought about it. She wasn't especially proud of it, but it was true. "The thing is," she started to say, but Goody stopped her—he knew what that meant. She wouldn't need to elaborate.

"Just remember I asked," he told her. "Just always remember that. Because every day, I'm ready to ask again. That'll never change."

Laura shook her head; she had to get this out now, before she lost her nerve. "The thing is I'm going to have a baby," she said. She watched Goody take some time to absorb that. "Out of pure common sense you're the last person I should be telling. Instead, somehow you're the first."

Goody looked at her. He took a breath. "Well—thanks—I guess. And congratulations."

Laura asked if he was okay—knowing he wasn't, knowing he'd just laid his heart out on a platter, yet again, only to stand there and have to take it back.

"Things are clear," Goody told her, leaving out how cold and dead and wrong a clarity like that can feel. "I can start with that."

Laura smiled, and took his arm. "You're a classy guy, Stewart Goodman. You're a hell of a writer, with a whole lot of class."

Goody shrugged. "Everyone from Hershey's got class," he answered.

They walked through tidepools on the way back to the restaurant, where Laura could ransom her rental car from the valet. Water got on their feet, around their ankles. Some beach tar too; Goody told Laura the best way to get rid of it was with paper towels and baby oil and some good hard rubbing. Laura attempted a joke about how she didn't quite have baby oil in stock, nothing with the word "baby" in it yet, and Goody laughed with her, because he knew that lightness was what she needed.

And then Laura told him how sorry she was, and how terrible she felt for everything she ever did that hurt him, and she meant it from the heart. She asked him if he thought they would ever see each other again, and Goody said he didn't know. You never know what's on the next page, he told her—if there's one thing he'd learned, it was that. And Laura agreed: books or life, the next page is a blank until it's written.

"There's one more thing though," she said. "Something I have to tell you. And then I'm going to need your advice."

"My advice?"

Suddenly she didn't like the sound of that. "Scratch the advice. And change it to just listen—if it's at all possible, because you're not going to like this, and I need your friendship anyway. You're the only one I can tell."

Goody looked at her. Whatever this was, it was big. It was why she had come to see him. "Is it about the baby?" he asked.

Laura nodded. "But not this one," she said.

Laura put the book down. She caught one last wisp of the title page, with Goody's inscription, before the cover came down on it. She put it back in the space she had carved out, and put the false bottom back in place. She heard the kids downstairs, and hurried now, so that she'd get to them before they got to her. And when they asked if they could watch the movie yet again, Laura thought, *hell fucking yes*. She'd join them this time—she'd get out more blankets, and the big pillows from the guest room, and they could all make tents.

Popcorn too—and not the kind for the microwave. They had a stovetop thing, the old-fashioned kind, with the handle and crank, that popped the stuff up for real.

27

Chip

"If you knew how many people had abortions in this school," Cindi told him, "you'd be shocked."

"Bullshit."

"Oh yeah?"

They were in Cindi's Miata. She had the top down and the windows up and the heat on full blast and she had a CD playing loud reggae that Chip didn't think he liked until now. And she was wearing shorts—carpenter shorts with big wide pockets, and loops to hang tools on—and a thick Blue Knights sweat-shirt with a hood. If other people were dressing this way, Chip hadn't noticed. He just knew that she had nicer looking legs than he had noticed before this. And it knocked him out that she would have the top down but still use the heat. Combining the two like that, he never would have thought of it before now.

"So, who had them? Who had abortions."

"Now that would be gossip. I'll pass."

"Come on. You can't just tell me half a thing like that and then hold back the other half."

"Sure I can."

She shifted the car down to third. They had just gotten off 309, and were on the road now that climbed up to Bear Creek and the restaurant—to Piccolo's, For Fine Family Dining, where Chip didn't know what he would find. He was glad not to be doing this alone.

"Okay so tell me this," he said.

"No," came Cindi's answer.

He looked at her; she meant it. "How can you say no? You don't even know what I was going to say."

"Okay, so say it. But the answer's still no."

"Then what's the point of asking?"

"Because you want to so bad you can't stand it. Even my saying no—you're going to ask anyway."

"Okay then. And fuck you, by the way."

"Fuck you too, Chip." And the way she smiled when she said that made him almost forget what they were talking about, and what it was that he was trying to find out.

Almost.

"Was Janet Pardini," he asked, "one of the ones who had one?"

"You know I can't answer that."

"I wouldn't tell Randy—I swear."

Cindi grinned. She told him to forget it. She looked great, doing that.

"What about you then?" Chip asked.

"What about me."

"Are you one of the ones who had an abortion?"

"I'm one of the ones, Chip. Who had two."

Chip was quiet for a second. "No shit," he said.

"I beg to differ," Cindi told him. "It was total shit."

The restaurant was different in the daylight. The one time Chip was here, with Randy, it was night, and warmer, and Chip remembered unfamiliar music and the smell of grilled meat. Randy's family was big into steaks; they listened politely to a long list of authentic Italian specialties, and then went ahead and all ordered the Porterhouse instead—no wine, not even coffee afterwards. *This is what Randy's up against,* Chip remembered thinking, *when he tells his family of Mormons and sports worshipers that BYU—and football—were not in his plans. Wait'll they hear that their golden boy wants to go to art school, in Rhode Island. Could sell that one on pay-per-view.*

"Yum," Cindi said. "Smells good." She threaded her arm through Chip's and walked beside him to the entrance. He gave her a strange look but didn't pull away. "You know, what I told you before, Chip. About the two things I did?"

"Oh." He had forgotten. Except that he hadn't. He had just forgotten *now.*

"Well no one else really knows that. I don't even know why I told you."

"Because I asked?"

"That's one reason. There might be more."

He looked at her. She was different from Ellie, that was for sure. And Chip was starting to discover a real bright side to that. "Did the guy at least go to the place with you?" he asked.

She shook her head. "I went alone. Both times." Then she shrugged. "I wanted to." She put on a brave face about it, but Chip could see the cracks.

"I wouldn't have let you go there," he said. "Not alone."

"I know."

"I mean, even if I wasn't—"

"I know what you mean, Chip. And thanks."

She went on to say, with all proper respect, and casting no aspersions, that from her point of view Ellie was a lunatic for dropping him. Not every guy opens a door, not every guy says he'd go with you to get an abortion, whether he's the responsible party or not—just so you wouldn't have to go through it all alone.

Chip couldn't speak to that. He stood aside and waited for her. But suddenly he looked so pale.

"What should we do," he asked, "when we go in there. What should we tell them?"

"Why don't we tell them we want lunch," Cindi said.

She gave him a little grin. Then, by the arm, she guided him through the door.

28

Pick

His walk brought him back around to the Sterling, so he decided to go up to the room and lay out for a bit—but then saw his message light on, and there went that idea. There was a fax waiting at Reception—from Iris most likely, although the desk guy didn't say. Pick put the phone down, and went and splashed cold water on his face for a long as he could stand it.

Down in the lobby, the manager was dealing with a lady who swore there were bedbugs, based on a report she'd seen on the news: *treat all hotels suspiciously*, was the expert's advice. Further away, three nuns looked over a rack display of tourist brochures. The nuns were from Asia—Vietnamese, Pick determined. And by the way they fawned over those brochures, you'd think they'd stumbled onto the Land of Oz—when for the life of him, Pick couldn't imagine what possible attractions this place could have that would make people want to go visit them. Or maybe it's all just relative, like a lot of things; there were plenty out there who'd call this a paradise.

He caught himself wishing Goody was there. The Goody he knew before anything happened—because who the fuck knew what the guy was into now, or what he was thinking, or even where he was. But the Old Goody; the Old Goody would take a scene like this—a nothing moment in a hotel lobby—and make it sound like something you couldn't possibly think up on the spot. He'd nail every detail straight to the wall—who each person was, where they lived, what was in their refrigerators, whether they were lonely or sad or the life of the party, or maybe even all three. He could tell you what they did for hobbies and who'd be the first one they'd call if they had good news—and if there was an emergency, and they had to evacuate their homes, Goody would be able to tell you exactly what things they'd grab hold of if they had twenty minutes to get out of there with the items that mattered the most. And by the time he was finished, you'd actually feel like you knew them. You'd care about them. That's the kind of thing Goody could do. Standing right there, he could do it.

"And every side of the box is painted a different color . . ."

Instead it was Pick, alone, waiting for a fax, aggravated that he came down here at all, when for the cost of a two-dollar tip they would have brought it to his door. Without Goody here, this lobby was just what it was: a slow-motion mausoleum, under archways that pretended grandeur—with a paranoid bedbug lady and happy little nuns across the way, from a country we used to level with napalm. You need a generous heart to look at people, and see past the surface—and then maybe past a few other surfaces, to get to who they really were. And that was Goody, right there; the son of a bitch had a more generous heart than anyone. The Old Goody, at least. The New Goody could be anything by now. A mercenary. A trader in slaves. A politician.

"And that's the color they believe in."

The kid came back with the fax. "Thanks," Pick told him, and he started to walk away—but when he tore open the envelope and read what was inside, he stopped.

Jesus H. Jesus Fucking H.

He had to go to the gift shop and buy a packet of aspirin. Then he went to a chair nearby, and sat down to read the fax again.

They found him. They found Goody.

Carmine had made the arrangements. He was already on his way.

His head was starting to hurt from thinking so hard; from the wine he'd been drinking, alone in the dorm room, to help himself get a grip on things—or to forget it all, or maybe at least to see it from a different angle. Whichever came first would be fine with him.

But all Pick could think of was Laura, and everything that had happened the day before—from the moment they dropped Goody off at the bus station, to the walk to Pick's house, then back to the school for dinnertime, when they had to check back in at the dorms because that's all they'd thought to sign out for in advance.

That was yesterday, and Pick had spent the whole day today avoiding her because he didn't know what else to do—yet even while he avoided her, he hoped they'd cross paths somehow, and be together again. It had never been so easy for him, so completely easy to be around a girl, especially when they were alone. And that was why he had to stay away.

It was killing him though, not to know if it was easy like that for her too—if she was thinking about him even one little bit in the way he was thinking about her. And while he couldn't stand not knowing, he also couldn't bring himself to ask—and that was what was killing him, because there wasn't any good answer. If she said no, she was sorry he'd got that in his head somehow, he was a nice guy and all, but this was the limit of it, and she never meant to mislead him, then he knew he'd be destroyed. And yet if it went the other way, that she liked him—holy fucking hell if she really liked him—then there'd be Goody to deal with, and that was just as bad. Well maybe not as bad. But bad enough. A deal breaker.

He had to get out of the room, he felt, and quickly—even though it was after lights out and everyone was supposed to be locked down and tucked in for the night. So he stole down to the basement, past the TV lounge to the alcove where the laundry machines were, for kids whose parents didn't sign up for the outside service company that came in once a week and took everybody's stuff. No one really used these machines though; maybe at the girls' dorm, things were different—but most guys who didn't get the service would just wait, and hold out for a school vacation or something, or a weekend at home, or a sympathetic day student's family who'd let them do their dirty clothes over at their house for free. Which made the basement laundry room the perfect place to go, when you had a mild wine thing going and a lot of stuff to deal with and couldn't stand to be alone in your own allotted space.

He must have fallen asleep, he concluded, because he only thought he'd been gone a few minutes—yet when he got back up to the room it was almost two in the morning, and he remembered going down there a little before eleven. And this time his room didn't seem so bad; it was a refuge again, like any kid's bedroom is supposed to be.

"*Hi.*"

"*Holy—*"

She was in Goody's bed—Laura, sitting up, with the covers all wrapped around her. She waited for Pick to close the door, but still she spoke in a whisper. "We snuck out," she said. "Rosa and Dot had this whole plan worked out, with Kenny and Chase. They asked me to come, too, so I did. I thought Stewart would be back from Hershey by now."

Pick couldn't stop looking at her. Was she naked under there? Could something like that be possible? "I thought so, too. Maybe the thing ran late—he might have just decided to stay over."

That didn't sound like Goody, to either one of them. He wouldn't spend one more minute down there than he had to. "Did he call?" Laura asked.

Pick shook his head. "He wouldn't have gotten through if he tried—fuckin' Korchinski was hogging the floor phone all night. What about over there?"

"*It was Amelia that Korch was talking to. People wanted to kill them both.*"

They looked at each other. That about settled the issue; if Goody didn't call, and if he wasn't back yet, it was looking like tomorrow for him.

"*When are Rosa and Dot leaving?*" *Pick asked. He looked nervous.*

"*We synchronized our watches for five,*" *she said.* "*But I guess I wouldn't have to wait for them. I mean if you wanted me to go.*"

Hell no, he didn't want her to go. This was his favorite person in the world—his favorite person ever, and she was right here in his room. Inches away from the bed he wanted her in, but still—she was here. Angelic, serene, almost unreal in the moonlight.

He wobbled a little bit and then he burped—flying in the face of all the manners he knew about not doing that in front of girls. Instead of being put off though, Laura grinned at him. "*Have you been drinking?*" *she asked.*

Pick nodded. "*Some wine. I took it from the restaurant.*"

She grinned again. "*How's it taste?*"

Pick shrugged. "*It tastes like wine. You want some?*"

"*I don't know. Why not I guess. If they get me for being over here I might as well have a buzz while we're at it.*"

"*That's great reasoning,*" *Pick said.* "*You might live to be twenty with a system like that.*"

He dug back to the far corner of his closet and brought out a bottle and two paper cups. He poured for both of them, and sat down on the edge of the opposite bed. They reached across the small space between them, clinked cups and swallowed some.

Laura's face puckered tight until she got it under control. "*What's in here?*" *she asked.*

"*Chianti, mostly,*" *Pick told her.* "*But I threw in some other kinds to bring it up to full.*"

"*Well then it'll probably go well with anything,*" *Laura joked. She held out her cup and he filled it again. Then two more refills for each of them after that. They made wine comments, pretending to be connoisseurs. They would remember and then forget to keep their voices and laughter down.*

Pick started feeling strange though, and out of place. He got up and went to the window; clouds were covering the moon now, when it was clear as a mirror before. From farther away they heard thunder. Like the low growl of an animal, who didn't want to be bothered.

"Did he tell you what happened? On the golf course and everything."

Laura nodded; Goody had told her—once, and that was it. Heavy stuff.

"He told me and Griffin," Pick went on. "Some doofus lifeguard as much as blamed him for killing his dad. Fuckin' imagine."

"I can't. I can't imagine," Laura said. "What a situation. No wonder he takes all those pills."

Pick looked at her; he didn't know she knew about Goody's thing with pills. He closed the window and came back. Laura was shivering under the blankets. "Where are your clothes?" he asked.

"They're in here. With me."

"Are they on you?"

"Don't even ask me that."

He didn't know what to make of this. He checked the wine bottle, but it was empty. He took their cups over to the trash, and crumpled them, then forced them inside an empty Pringles tube and put the cap back on—then he sprayed the whole thing with deodorant to finish the job.

The thunder was closer now; the first of the raindrops started hitting the window, and the trees started twitching out there. The girls would have a much harder time getting back—it would be fine with Pick if they never had to.

"You know what I wish?" he asked.

"What," Laura said. But Pick didn't answer right away. He stayed with his back to her, so she wouldn't have to see him in case this all blew up on him.

"Maybe you shouldn't tell me," she offered. She was giving him a way out, and nicely. But Pick shook his head: he was alone with

her, loosened up from alcohol, in plenty of trouble with his conscience anyway, not to mention his priorities—so what was there to lose?

"I wish that I was the one you came here to see," he told her. "And not Goody."

Laura didn't say anything. And Pick didn't turn around. This was not a place he had ever been before; he had never risked being stripped clean like this in front of someone. Let alone a girl, let alone one he felt this way about. Up till now he didn't know you could feel this way at all, about anything.

He was fucked.

"You want to talk about it?" Laura asked.

"No," Pick shot, and then he wondered how that had jumped out of him so quick—and why he even said the thing he said before. It was like a different person was in control inside, making him do things without asking his opinion—because the truth was that he did want to talk to her, desperately. He wanted to talk to her all the time about it—and in between the talking, he wanted to love her in ways he didn't even know about yet.

But then, under all that, there was something else that was true—even more true—and that was the thing that was really at the bottom of all this for Pick, which was exactly what made everything so damn fucked. Because they tell you on one hand that you're not supposed to hide your light under a bushel, and how you're supposed to Go For It and Seize The Day and all that crap. But on the other hand, you don't do shit that you know from the outset is going to hurt a person if they don't have it coming. And you don't make best friends with a guy, especially a guy like Goody, and then plain out fuck him over. Nobody should even have to tell you that.

And then it dawned on Pick that he had spent the whole year almost, actively not fucking Goody over, because he'd felt this way about Laura since that very first day—since Darlene Love, when he didn't even know she was spoken for. Which meant, to Pick, that under the policy of not fucking Goody over, he had just spent from September to now, fucking himself over instead—and how could that be any good either?

"*Sandy.*"

"*Yo.*"

She waited a second. "Well first turn around, all right?"

"Okay," Pick said. And he had every intention of doing that, but his arms and legs stayed locked. He tried saying "Okay" again, as if that might be the flint that lit the ignition that would get his body to listen to his brain and do what he was trying to tell it to do. But it didn't work. He couldn't move.

He heard bedsprings creak; he heard Laura crossing the distance between them. He felt her hands on his shoulders, and the gentleness that helped unfreeze him, and make it so he could turn around and finally face her. She was wearing a big fuzzy sweater, and jeans with thick white socks poking out. She looked like everything he would ever want to come home to—she looked like home itself—something he never would have known until now.

"Hi," she said. And she smiled at him, in a way he always dreamed someone would. Someone just like her. Her, in fact.

"If we both go at the same time," Laura told him, "then neither one has to go first."

Pick knew what she meant; their next action was mutual. And whatever became of this, from this moment forward, would also be mutual. And that was fine—in fact it was perfect. Love and guilt and shame were no longer the same agreement—and Pick's mistake all along was to think that to deny his feelings towards Laura would all be in the name of loyalty, and stuffing his own happiness for the sake of something bigger—when in fact there was nothing bigger, anywhere, and there never would be.

They kissed—it worked, no one went first—and somehow they made their way to Pick's bed, and under the covers, and they took off their clothes that way, fumbling and bumping and holding and hugging and hungering while trying to keep it all within the confines of where they were—as if an elbow that might protrude, or someone's heel exposed to the atmosphere might cause it to disintegrate, and take both of them with it. And yet in the dark of that room, and

*the even darker world they had created among blankets, Pick felt he
could see her. He could see her as if she were standing right in front
of him, at fingertip distance, wearing nothing and all his. He had
memorized her, over months; yet at the same time he felt that he
didn't need to see anything at all, if he could live in the sound and
the smell and the feel of her—her hands and her mouth and her face
and body. Her skin pressed in with his, the way it felt when they
were inside and outside and over and under each other, with the sly
and triumphant awareness that nobody had to tell them what to do
here—that nobody has to tell anybody what to do or how to do it,
when the right two people come together, at the perfect time, in the
perfect place and the perfect way.*

All with the perfect person. All with Laura.

*And as they found each other, as they erupted and reverberated
and erupted again, Pick realized in one crystalline burst that
everything that he ever thought he knew, he now knew was wrong.
Everything he had ever seen and heard, everything anyone had ever
told him, in his life, was wrong—and everything that no one had
told him yet, when they ever did tell him, those things would be
wrong too. Because now he knew that there were things that no
one could possibly tell him—things so right they can't be described.
No book, no song, no movie or painting or poem could ever bring
off what this was like. This was communion; what the angels sing
about, right here. This is why the angels were born singing. And in
every way, this was their song.*

*And even when the door opened, when Goody's silhouette filled
the threshold, it took Pick and Laura a minute to remember: there
was, in fact, a world out there. The world that had those other rules in
it. And Pick knew that everything beautiful, everything sensational,
everything that was ever worthwhile, was all about to crash.*

29

Chip

"This is good spaghetti. It's different."

"It's angel hair," Cindi told him.

"Oh." He twirled some more on his fork. Scooped a mussel out of its shell and ate it, then poked around at his plate like a prospector sifting through pebbles. "What's this?"

"Tell me if you like it first."

Chip shrugged and took a bite. "Kinda rubbery. What is it?"

"Calamari."

"Which is Italian for . . ."

"Squid."

Cindi looked surprised, even relieved, that Chip didn't make a face. Or make a display of pushing the rest of it all to the side.

"The Griffins don't get out a whole lot," he said. Then he dug in and had some more. "You're pretty good at all this. You guys must be regulars here."

"From time to time," Cindi explained. "But I go to the city a lot, with my parents." Chip knew that by "the city" Cindi meant New York. That's what you were supposed to call it if you were all up on things—and usually it bothered him when people did that. But not with Cindi. At least not today.

"There's this place in Little Italy that we always have to pil-grimize," she was saying, "or my father'll start taking hostages." She watched Chip noodling with the calamari some more. "I like that you didn't say it was gross."

Chip shrugged again. "It's just a little rubbery. That's all. But it tastes really good."

Cindi grinned, watching him. She pointed a few tables away. "That's what my dad always gets—the Osso Bucco. I sort of draw the line at that."

"Why, what is it?"

"It's a braised veal shank. So first of all there's veal, which is not exactly a good thing to eat if you're at all concerned about karma. The rest of it, I just never liked the taste. And it would always stay with me, for days. My mouth would feel all furry."

Chip thought about that, Cindi's mouth feeling furry; he'd never taken much notice of her mouth until now—just like he'd never thought about her legs until before, in the car—and he felt a little embarrassed about it. He looked around to see the Osso Bucco guy. He was in his fifties somewhere, grossly overweight, sucking on a bone and making a lot of racket. "So, loud slurping noises, that's part of it?"

"If you want to get the good stuff inside," Cindi said.

Chip looked at her. She started to smile. He wondered if she was trying to slip a double meaning in there. The thing was, he could never tell with girls. Ellie was the only one he had any real experience with, and she was always—until lately, anyway—completely straightforward. As a rule, whatever Ellie had to say, you got it right between the eyes. Good or bad, there it was.

"Anyway, I'm working on this theory, Chip. That at some point, you'll tell me why we're here."

"I did tell you."

"You said to see if someone might be here. But you didn't say who."

"The owner," Chip said.

"Carmine Piccolo? You know him?" Cindi looked impressed, which Chip knew he didn't deserve. Suddenly he was sorry now, to be in this place—sorry to have come here at all, and he couldn't wait to leave. He wanted to go back to the moment he had the idea, and then not have it this time.

"So how you two enjoyin' yourselves?"

Chip turned so quick he banged his elbow on the old guy's walker. Here was Carmine Piccolo—no one else it could be—yet he was friendly, expansive. Like, say, a guy who owned a restaurant.

"I see you got the *capellini*," he said to Chip. "Good choice."

"Actually, I think this is angel hair."

Chip saw Cindi grinning, and knew right away what he had done. In its own way it was worse than the elbow.

"And you, you like the *puttanesca?*"

"I do," Cindi said. "I like it a lot. Thank you."

Chip was amazed, watching her. Cindi wasn't fazed at all by this man. The more he thought about it, Cindi was one of those people who just seemed friendly with anyone, without ever seeming phony, or put on. He wondered why it took so long to discover this.

"How 'bout some dessert," Carmine offered. "Some *spumoni, tortoni?*"

"Actually," Chip started to say.

"We make it ourselves back there."

"No thanks, sir. I mean that's really—"

"*Ecco*, Donato," Carmine called out. "Bring some dessert for these two. *Spumoni*, some *fragole—e due piatti, per favore!*"

Cindi leaned forward a little to translate for Chip. *Spumoni* she didn't know—but *fragole* meant strawberries, and *piatti* meant plates.

Carmine got a kick out of that. "You look familiar," he said. "You been here before?"

Cindi nodded. "With my parents. Gus and Lillie Lindberg."

"Lindberg. Radio, right?"

"That's him." Cindi's dad owned a bunch of AM stations—mostly in Pennsylvania, but some in Maryland and New Jersey too. From the way things looked around the Lindberg house, there was very good money in radio.

"Okay, I'm gonna do something now," Carmine said, and he sat down at the table. You'd never have known the guy was using a walker, the way he pulled off the move. "I'm gonna tell you a story about your old man. Lunch is on me, by the way."

"Sir, I can't let you—"

Carmine waved Chip off like a moth; then turned back to Cindi. "Your father—when things were rough around here, when the last frippin' recession hit this place, this whole area—he walks in for dinner one night. And he saw that there were, what, five or six tables full out of forty-some. And he asked me what was goin' on, and I told him—look around, you can see what's goin' on, there's a bad economy out there, and no one's comin' in. And he said—your father said—that you can beat a bad economy, because even in down times, people still have a need to go out and do things. Sometimes even more so, he said. Now, I'm thinking, this is a very smart man."

Donato appeared from the kitchen; the *spumoni* turned out to be ice cream with flecks of other stuff in it. Dried fruit maybe, and a few scattered nuts cut into cross sections. And the strawberries he brought were huge.

"*Un'espresso per me. Per favore.*"

"*Prego,*" Donato nodded. When he left, Carmine turned back to Cindi. "Next thing I know," he said, "your dad is talkin' to me about commercials on the radio—and he spins out this whole campaign, right on the spot there but like he's been thinkin' about nothin' else for the last half a year. He said I should advertise out of state. He said the New York and Jersey places advertise to people out here, so why wouldn't it work the other way—the highway goes in both directions, right? So let 'em know you're here, give 'em a reason to stop, and they'll stop.

And I'm listening, because I know this is a smart man. But it was still a bad economy. So where was the money for commercials gonna come from?"

"You mean you didn't have it?" Chip asked.

Carmine turned to him. "You know sources of money that I don't know about?"

"No, sir."

"—So, my dad said not to worry," Cindi jumped in, smiling at Carmine, deflecting his attention and convincing Chip that he owed this girl his life now. "About the commercials, and the money. He'd do it on spec for the time being, and if you didn't like the results then you wouldn't have to pay him."

"He told you this story?"

Cindi shook her head: not this one, but others. "What's important," she went on, "above everything else is a relationship. And in tough times, people in a community have to stick together—because that's what community is about."

"That's exactly what he said. How'd you know that?"

"I eat at the man's table, Mr. Piccolo. It rubs off."

Why didn't I ever notice that smile of hers? Chip thought. *It's like how the Eskimos have all these different words for snow—Cindi's got so many different smiles and they all seem real and they're all so pretty—where was I, to only see this now?*

"You're from down at the school," Carmine said. "Pocono, right?" They answered that they were, and that they were seniors, and a little bit nervous about college, and the future and all. "You're good kids, I can tell. Both of you. You make a nice couple. You two bein' careful?"

Chip gulped on a bite of *spumoni*, turning colors while Cindi handled the question: they weren't really a couple *that* way. Carmine nodded as if he only half believed them, repeated that they'd be smart to watch themselves with the you-know-what and got up to say goodbye. Reminding them, as he left, that lunch was on the house.

In the car Chip was kissing Cindi before she could even get her seat belt on. He was more surprised than she was. He wanted every bit of her.

"Chip."

"What."

"Not that I mind what we're doing. But do you think we could get out of this parking lot?"

Chip stopped, and looked around. Yes, they were in a parking lot. In a convertible, in daylight.

"I mean, there are other places to go," Cindi said.

"Where?"

"Well how's my house?"

"Your house."

"You know? Where I live?" She watched Chip think about it; saw a grin escape. "What?" she asked.

"You'll laugh," he said.

"So? I like to laugh."

He shook his head, then decided to run with it. "Well I was thinking about chenille ruffles. You know, when you said your house."

"Chenille ruffles?"

"On your parents' bed."

She looked at him, like something was off here. "I don't think so, Chip. I don't think there'd be chenille ruffles on *any-body's* bed. Chenille's not something you'd use for that."

"It's not?"

"Whoever told you it was?" she asked, and then as soon as she did she knew the answer. And didn't like it. "Tell you what—we'll go to my house. I've got a blue pullover, like a sweater, which is guaranteed made of chenille. And you'll see why it wouldn't be used for a bed ruffle."

She started the car. "I'll put it on and show you. After that it's your move."

Chip looked at her. Thirty different smiles, a Mob Boss at their table with a very weird vibe about him. Calamari, slurping bones, Angel Hair and radio spots, shorts in October with the heat full on, and now chenille that wasn't chenille. What was anything anymore?

"Why would anybody even *have* bed ruffles," he asked.

"To keep things hidden," Cindi said.

——— 30 ———

Pick

"Welcome to the Zen Center at the University of Delaware! This booklet should explain some of what you need to know about who we are, the way we do things, and why. Or stay and observe, although we ask that you maintain respectful silence in the meditation hall if there is a session going on. Our rituals and routines are described and explained in this booklet beginning on Page 3, right after the weekly schedule. Please note there are special sessions for beginners, every Monday night at 8. Sunday Dharma talks are at 5pm, and open to the community.

   Our director and head dharma teacher is Shindo Stewart Goodman. Shindo Stewart is an ordained Zen priest. He was the personal assistant to Hataka Sudo Roshi, at the Mt. Raymond Monastery in Oregon, then later followed him to Japan where he received his ordination and direct transmission. This is his fourth year as director of the UZC. We are happy to say he has revitalized our community, where his honesty, directness and humor are very much appreciated."

Put Pick under oath and he wouldn't be able to tell you how he got there. One minute he was in the lobby of the Sterling with a fax in his hand, and the next minute that same hand was on Griffin's doorbell and Mary was there, and Pick was asking if there was anything she needed him to help her do around the house—like a kid from the neighborhood, looking to make a little extra spending money doing chores on the side. He saw how she looked at him, with the pure understanding of a mother; having gone his whole life without one, Pick had a fleeting but sour awareness of just how much he had missed. And how glad, and grateful he was, that his own children had Laura to look at them that way. He couldn't remember ever telling her that.

Shit.

Mary said there was laundry to finish, and led the way down to the basement, where they turned on all the lights and folded every clean thing there was to fold. It was warm down there, rebelliously cheerful for a wet and gloomy day, with so much hard reality going on, right above their heads.

"Have you told Laura?" she asked him.

Pick nodded, but looked off—as if he'd done some distasteful but necessary task, like burying a kid's dead hamster in a shoe-box in the yard. He'd told Laura the broad strokes of what he'd learned so far; Carmine's people had found out a good bit in a short amount of time, and Iris was able to fill in a lot of the rest from there. All of it, swimming in Pick's head like eels in a barrel.

"She wasn't surprised," he told Mary. "She said she wasn't surprised."

"Were you?"

"I don't know," Pick admitted. "I'm trying not to think."

"I'm not sure I believe that," Mary answered.

"Desperate times," Pick said.

Mary watched him with the laundry, and said she was impressed with his pace and efficiency. It was all the traveling, Pick told her, the packing and unpacking—this was just one of the many road skills he'd taken on as part of the job. Plus there was Carmine's influence: if there was anything his father taught him, and stood there to make sure he mastered, it was how to properly fold a dress shirt. This was maniacally important to Carmine—an interesting selection for something to teach your child, when you'd left out nearly everything else.

"Delaware," he said. "What Buddhists are in Delaware?"

"Universities," Mary supposed. "College towns. Even Wilkes has a group. Every now and then they're in Market Square. I'm always sorry when I don't go talk to them."

Pick wasn't convinced. "You go to Delaware when you want to register your corporation—and you don't even have to go there to do it, you just fill out a bunch of forms and pay the fees. I've done it a hundred times, for clients." He shook out a towel, loving the *whap* it made: something sharp, and definite.

Not that Pick, if pushed, could tell you the *right* thing Goody could have been doing all this time. Only that this—running a campus Zen center out of a converted one-story bungalow—felt particularly not right. A normal street in a normal town. Shopping malls and gas stations. Teaching courses, giving talks. Community pot lucks and donations at the door. Probably doesn't even own the bed he sleeps in.

"What's the matter with Japan?" Pick asked. "What happened to going off into the mountains and meditating in caves?"

"From what I read," Mary told him, "he did that too."

It was true—the research had it covered. Once Goody's movie had fallen apart, there was a short period of time that couldn't be accounted for; after that, Goody didn't just leave Los Angeles but had skipped the country entirely and made his way to Japan, where Roshi had returned after the temple at Mt. Raymond had gone under—largely because Goody's earnings couldn't help them keep the lights on, now that he suddenly wasn't earning anymore. Roshi had gone back to the monastery where he'd gotten his own training, where his parents had dropped him off at the age of seven when they could no longer afford to feed him. Goody found him there, handed over his passport, and said he was ready now: he had nothing to gain, nothing to lose, nowhere to go, and nowhere to be gone from. There was nothing to remember and nothing to forget. There were only the vows, and he was ready to take them.

And so he took them.

"Last night I had this dream," Pick said. "I was driving here, from the city. And Goody was with me."

He started separating some towels according to which ones had the braided designs going down the borders and which didn't. In his own house, he wouldn't have noticed the distinction; Laura would, and now Pick wondered if he had been taking her for granted for that. And not just towels, but all the other stuff—*tons* of other stuff, the invisible routine things that people do, things that so rarely get affirmed. Pick got all the headlines in the family, that was for sure. But Laura was the story. And the story, that's what lasts.

"I was the way I am now," he went on. "But he was the Goody from back then—on a good day, on a day that he felt really on it. And he's trying to tell me some bizarre theory kind of thing and we're both laughing like crazy, but I can't hear what he's saying because it's the dream—you know? You can hear but you can't hear?"

Mary nodded; she knew. Everyone knows. "You miss him," she said.

Pick shrugged. "He was really funny. He didn't always come off that way, but he was. And he gave a damn about things. About me," he said, "he gave a damn about me. I didn't know what that was even like until then."

"And yet you dread him coming here," Mary said. She looked surprised at herself, for being that blunt.

Pick met her look, felt her encouragement to speak freely. "It's like in *High Noon*," he said finally. "All these bad guys are coming, and they're gunning for Gary Cooper, and he knows it—where they're coming from, when they're going to get there, and what they're going to do to him. He's the loneliest guy in the world, knowing this." He picked up a clump of socks; little static crackles while he separated them and sorted them out. "Only in this case, I'm not Gary Cooper. I'm still the guy they're coming to get—but somehow, I'm the bad guy too—and they're not. All of a sudden they're the Magnificent Seven now, and I'm the evil sheriff."

Mary shook her head. "You're not any bad guy—for heaven's sake Sandy. And nobody's coming to get you—especially Stewart. You or anybody else."

"So why do you think he's coming here?" Pick wanted to know.

"Same as you," Mary told him. "Because he was asked." She watched him take that in. "Why, do you think there's another reason?"

Pick shrugged. "I don't know. All these years. You'd think we'd be off his radar for good by now."

"Was he ever off yours?" Mary asked.

Pick looked down at the shirt he'd half-folded. He could feel her eyes on him. "This should be on a hanger," he said.

Mary pointed over to an improvised coat rack, made from a dowel hung down between two ceiling beams. Pick took the shirt over, unfolding it along the way. Then, looking at it, it came to him that the next place Griffin might be wearing a shirt like this could be his own coffin. It sent a chill that Pick never wanted to feel again.

"Thank you," Mary said. "You're right. I don't know why I've been folding them. The cleaner always returns them on hangers."

Pick was about to ask why they didn't go to the cleaners this time, but before he did it came to him: Mary was cutting back; circling the wagons around a future that was beginning to look pretty grim. This was the time of year to be thinking of Thanksgiving coming up, the whole holiday season; now she had a brand-new situation at hand. A long convalescence, at best—but widowhood was just as possible, and single motherhood, and middle age without the partner to whom she had pledged her life—so of course, why not, let's just top it all off with money problems. And Pick knew—he'd dealt with insurance companies—no matter how you're fixed, medical costs will run through a family like shit through a goose. And the Griffins, he suspected, were not braced for any of it. Few people were.

They were quiet for a while. A couple of car horns sounded outside, but the school itself was still; all the kids were hunkered down in classes. Pick found it hard to believe that he had once been one of them. He wondered what he'd have thought if somebody back then had told him what he'd be doing as an adult—took him by the hand, whisked him to the future, gave him a snapshot glimpse of his life right now—and then whisked him right back, before he even noticed he'd been gone. He knew that on the face of things he'd be proud. Hell, he'd built a life. A career, a family, a name in the community. In very many ways he'd become the guy in that movie he saw, and that was nothing to be ashamed of.

Underneath though. As a kid he would never have imagined how much could really be underneath. How could he? There are layers of things under layers of things under layers of things; all the stuff he'd pushed down and away, so he wouldn't have to feel it. It was enough to scare the hell out of anyone, and that's probably why they never let you know in advance. Nobody would ever sign up for that.

"I looked it up," he said. "The kind of monk he is, they can marry. They don't have to swear off relationships. They can have regular lives, and just be monks while they're doing it."

"So?" Mary asked.

"Come on—you read the book. I stole her, years later he steals her back. You couldn't set the stage any better."

Mary looked at him. "First of all, you can't steal a person. Laura's not a stereo. Also, keep in mind—you're the one she married."

"That's the thing. Maybe I'm not so sure she'd go the same way today."

"If you have to wonder that," Mary told him, "then I'm not the one you should be talking to."

31

Laura

She didn't tell Pick she'd decided to come; he could persuade her right out of it, and she didn't want to run the risk. This was her past too, and her future—and there wasn't any way Laura could watch it unfold from the wings. Anyone who didn't think so, would just have to think again.

She packed comfortable pants and comfortable shoes; clothes to wait around in. She figured on two days maybe, three at most, because she couldn't see leaving Andy and Molly behind for any longer than that. All she knew was she had to go there—enough to call her parents and ask them to come down from upstate and take care of things. Another in a series of olive branches; bygones would never be bygones all by themselves, Laura figured—even if she had to be the one forgiving them for not forgiving her. Somebody had to keep the ball rolling.

She was almost finished with the List: what to do, who to call, where the medicines were, where the Ipecac was if they took something poisonous, what doctors to page for which catastrophes, what friends to line up for play dates, what detergents to use for which kinds of clothing, who liked what cereal and in

what combinations, who got whole milk and who got the aci-
dophilus, where the extra keys were, where the gas cutoff was,
what to do if the raccoon showed up behind the garage, how to
get to the all-night drugstore, how to get to the other all-night
drugstore if the closer one didn't have what you needed, detailed
instructions about which pizza place to call for deliveries, what
to order and where the coupons were, detailed instructions
about which Chinese place *not* to call, even though Andy will
bargain for it and tell you it's all right when it plainly is not all
right, the only reason he likes it is they shovel so much MSG
on everything to make it taste better, but then he's high as a kite
for the next two days, which he thinks is funny when it isn't, it's
dangerous and unhealthy, and here are reprints of three recent
articles on MSG that back up everything she is saying but above
all do not let Andy sway you when it comes to Chinese food.

There was more: about the movies they can watch and the
ones they can't. About the channels they can watch and the
ones they can't. About the computer games that, again, Andy
must not be permitted to play for more than an hour at a sitting,
because he plays them too long and loses his sense of passing
time and he will deny it until he's blue in the face, but the games
give him nightmares and when he has nightmares he will try
and convince you that chocolate chip cookies and milk are the
only things that will calm him down, and they do except for
the caffeine in the chocolate and the corn syrup in the cookies
and then he will be up all night anyway and he will be good for
nothing in the morning, he will be one sleep-deprived sugar
crash all the next day and that is not pleasant, not pleasant at all.

And you have to be patient with Molly, you mustn't make
her feel that there is something wrong with her even though it
can take her five minutes or longer to tell you something simple,
like it's raining outside, when you can very easily see that for
yourself—and just in case it does rain, you have to step carefully
with her, because the rain freaks her out—you have to be calm

and patient about going out there because she will want two layers of raincoats and her Very Special Hat, and backup pairs of boots and gloves because to this day she is still convinced that *not* having all those precautions is what killed her sister, because it was raining the day they took her to the hospital. And it's no use trying to tell her any different; it was the weather and that was that.

And if Liana's name does come up, don't quash it, don't sweep it under the rug, let Molly know it's okay to talk about her. More kids are screwed up from things that grownups hide from them than they are from the things they come out and say, and here are some reprints that back up and confirm that. So, level with her, don't be more scared than she is because she's plenty scared enough. The poor thing lost her sister, her twin, she *knows* she stutters and she knows she didn't always. So can you imagine how fractured she must feel inside?

"Mom! They're here!"

And there it was, out the window, pulling up in the drive. This year's big, green, brand-new Regal sedan—hot off the floor, with the immaculate, faux-leather interior and the cruise control and the matching hounds-tooth suitcases in the spotless, cavernous trunk and the clear-eyed, upstanding grandparents in front. Her dad would get out and stride up the path, proud of his mileage while her mom would toddle up behind him, closing her purse because she would have just touched up her makeup in the car and he never waits for her—once Good Old George Appleby is ready, he's ready by God—and if the rest of the world isn't ready when Good Old George Appleby is, well then, the rest of the world can just find its own darn way to the door.

As long as Laura could remember, it had been this way. Deacon Rotarian George thrusting onward, Better Half Alexandra trailing with all the details. Her mother had to possess something magical, Laura thought, to live with him all this time, and not have her soul melt away, like silent pools of wax.

And now the chime was going and she was racing down the stairs with her list unfinished so she could be there to open the door for them because that's what she was brought up to do. Her parents would never think of affording themselves entry into another person's house—even their own daughter's, with their grandchildren inside. "That's what doorbells are for," Good Old George would say. That's what doorbells are for.

They had some quick coffee cake together, from Laura's favorite, the Finger Lakes Bakery back home. They talked about the best way to get to the airport, which her father knew nothing about but there was no sense arguing; then, careful about the time, Laura got up to go. She put her bags at the front door and turned around to run down the list with them—an overview, bullet points, not the whole thing. She looked at the four of them. And kept looking.

"Laura?" her mother said.

"I changed my mind," Laura announced. "I can't leave them."

"What?" said everyone.

"I just can't—I'm sorry. Mom, Dad, I really am. But they're coming with me."

Molly looked relieved. Andy looked at his mom like she was crazy; he'd just gotten used to the idea of spending a few days with his grandparents, and had a fully detailed agenda, already plotted out.

Item Number One, was intercept that list.

32

Chip

It was the kind of thing that could get you kicked out of school, but he didn't care at this point. He ducked in the side door of Critchley Hall, then ran like a shot to the back steps behind the common rooms. He had taken this chance before, times when Ellie knew ahead that he'd be coming—only now he was flying blind; reckless and unannounced and unconcerned with consequence. But he had to talk to her, and he'd had enough of waiting and being dodged, and he didn't want to risk cornering her on campus somewhere only to have her cut and run and have it happen in front of people—and just basically he couldn't stand it anymore, not being able to talk to her and especially now that he had a concrete reason he could hang it on.

So it was up three flights and down two long hallways, whizzing past doors with posters on them—cartoon characters, fluffy animals with big soulful eyes, shirtless heartthrob guys with impossible stomach muscles and faraway looks—then around a tight hairpin corner, where traction was always key, past Janet Pardini's room with a classic Audrey Hepburn glamour shot that boldly told the world that Janet knew of such things as Audrey Hepburn and glamour—until finally there it was: Ellie's door, neatly laid out with quadrants of info sheets covering just about every environmental nightmare and nearly-extinct species she could fit on there to rally for.

"Chip!"

He closed the door behind him. He was barely even winded; say what you want about Coach Milpitas, but the man knew how to condition his players. "Hi," he said.

"*Hi?*"

Chip nodded. Gulped down some air and steadied himself. "Listen—you're really good at mysteries, right?"

"Mysteries?"

He nodded again. "Silva had this idea and I was following through on it, but the bell rang. So, I thought maybe you could help. It's at the library."

"*What's* at the library?"

"Yearbooks."

"Yearbooks?"

Chip confirmed. "They're in the reference section but they don't let you take those out."

"Oh, but *this* you can do. And by the way, hello? Did someone in the room just get out of the shower here?"

He stopped and took her in. She was in her bathrobe, with her hair wrapped in a towel in that turban way that only girls can do. She had tried to show him once, back in happier times, but he couldn't get his towel to stay on. On the other hand, he couldn't teach her how to skateboard more than eight or nine yards without endangering the hemisphere. So in a strange way, they were even.

"Just come to the library," he said. "It's not a trick. I'm asking for your help."

There was a knock on the door. "Ellie?"

Chip froze. Ellie went over, cracked it open just enough to answer someone's question on the other side; then came back to Chip looking freshly annoyed. "That was Foster Devlin, who is absolutely who you don't want knowing you're up here. She's pushing for head proctor next year, and this would thoroughly clinch the deal."

"I don't care about Foster Devlin."

"Well maybe I do."

"Well maybe you shouldn't."

They looked at each other. "Listen," Chip said. "Please. Just come to the library with me. They went here in the seventies."

"*Who* did. Who the hell are you talking about?"

"*Ellie?*" Another knock, and this time both of them froze. "*Ellie, are you in there?*"

Mrs. Vanderlip. Shit. The glory days of when it was only Foster Devlin were starting to look nostalgic by comparison.

"Ellie? Are you all right in there? Are you alone?"

"Just a minute!" Ellie said. Then she flung open her closet door and shoved Chip like a car was coming; right away he tripped on some exercise gadget and lost his balance. He grabbed for a towel hanging over the top of the door, but it pulled down like an avalanche and sent him tumbling into the foreign regions of Ellie's closet—stamping over shoeboxes like landmines and bouncing off both door jams before he finally fell back into a thick nest of coat hangers—wooden, wired and plastic and all of them loud as a pep rally—while Chip flailed around in there, looking for anything he could hold onto that would *just stay still.*

"All right, Ellie." Definitely Vanderlip out there. "I think it's time you let me in now."

"Please," Chip heard Ellie say back to her. "Give me a minute."

He came to rest on a crushed shoebox with a pair of something formal inside—hard as hell and no doubt shiny, and stabbing at him so hard it made his eyes water. He clenched his whole body, waiting, while he listened to Ellie opening the door so Mrs. Vanderlip could come into her room.

"Now, what's going on in here."

"Nothing," Ellie said.

Inside the closet a long cotton sleepshirt slipped off its hanger, floating down and covering Chip like a shroud. Somewhere in the back of his mind—way back—he had the feeling that from certain points of view, this might be pretty comical. Randy, for one, would have a blast with it. But nothing about it seemed funny right now. There was going to be serious hell to pay, from a hundred and eight directions.

"All right," he heard Mrs. Vanderlip say. "I'm pretty certain someone's in there, and I'm pretty certain I know who it is. So, I'm going to step back out into the hall now, and wait a moment, and then I'll knock again—and when I do, things had better be proper."

Chip heard her step out. He had his instructions. He was struggling to pull himself up when Ellie opened the closet door, blinding him with light from the windows across the room.

"My God," she said. "A herd of reindeer would have been more delicate in here."

"We've been out of practice." Chip reminded her. And it was true: they had drilled for this. They had signals set up, and everything. Except to make the thing work, Ellie had to know he was coming. That was the part Chip had left out today.

"So, do you want to call my parents, or should I?" Ellie asked.

She was not being dramatic; they were in truly deep trouble here. People did not send their daughters to Pocono Valley so they could learn to hang around in bathrobes while football players paid illegal visits to their dorm rooms. The school would have to come down hard on this, just to show an example. And for Chip, who'd committed the bigger crime here, coming down hard could only mean one thing: the Nihaminy game. Homecoming. A classic way to show they meant business.

He was sure of it.

33

Laura

"Why are we driving?" Andy wanted to know. He was fidgeting in the front seat. They were on Route 80, the Interstate, where the road rides the high hip of the Poconos, heading west. Molly was asleep in the back; Laura could hear the clogged breathing of someone who might be getting a cold.

"Because once it became the three of us, flying didn't make sense."

"Driving doesn't make sense."

"Why doesn't it?" Laura asked.

"Why does it?" Andy asked back.

"Okay—it's more comfortable. We don't have to pack the same way. We can spread out more, don't have to deal with headaches and security, and waiting in lines—we can just go." She looked over at him. "What's your way?"

"My way, we get to fly."

Laura grinned; he had her. Because of course—from a kid's point of view, the airport's an exciting place—all that movement of people, the signs and announcements, the food stands and souvenirs—every new moment its own separate adventure. And next thing you know you're up in the clouds, looking down.

A kid's point of view. Now there's a luxury.

"When Dad and I first got married, we traveled a lot. I would take pictures of the arrival and departure boards at all the different airports and train stations—in Europe especially, the train stations. I couldn't get over how you could go to so many places, that were all so different from each other, in such a short amount of time. But there they were, right on the list."

"So you took pictures of names of places?"

Laura nodded. "When you look at them later, out of context, it's almost a kind of poetry."

"Sounds pretty out there, Mom."

"Possibly," Laura admitted. "But you'd be amazed at how many things we take for normal every single day, but they sounded out there when someone first thought of them. And how ordinary things that people can walk past all the time, when someone looks at them a certain way they can be art."

"Whatever."

Whatever. Nothing came off more dismissive than that word. Laura felt deflated, but tried not to lean into it all that far; this was her nine-year-old son, not an honest conversation partner. And to Andy's credit, he was probably doing everything he could to hang in as long as he did. How could she expect him to care about pictures of departure boards? Who else *would* care about a thing like that?

She knew right away who would. She shooed away the thought like a cat on a countertop.

"How about this," she asked Andy, "next time we'll fly somewhere. But for now, let's enjoy being just us."

"It's always just us," Andy said back. "That's the thing."

Laura bit down on her lip. "There's a thing?"

"No, Mom," Andy said, but he knew it was already too late for that. She had her Concern Face on.

"Well there has to be a thing, or you wouldn't have said that. And if there's a thing, we should talk about it."

"I have homework."

She gave him a look. "Andy. Sweetheart. Things happen to us in life. Good things and bad. And when bad things happen, if we don't face up to them, they get worse. And the best way to face up to things is to talk about them."

"I don't want to talk about them."

"It doesn't have to be with me. Or Dad, even."

"Please, Mom. Not Dr. Taubman again."

Laura looked over. Her Concern Face kicked up a notch. "What's the matter with Dr. Taubman?"

"Nothing," Andy said. "He wears those stupid t-shirts like he's trying to be young. And he has coffee breath and he's always saying stuff like 'it's all good' no matter what I say to him. So if everything's so all good all the time, why do I have to go there?"

Laura held back a smile. "All right," she concluded, "no Dr. Taubman. But Honey—think of it this way—think of it like shoveling snow."

"Like what?"

"Well when it snows, you know? What happens when we don't shovel the walk the first day?"

"It melts."

"Okay what if it doesn't melt but then it snows again the next day. And that doesn't melt either."

"It stays there."

"And the next day, when it snows again, but instead of shoveling like we ought to, we just walk over our own footprints from the other days before—and if we keep doing that, and it keeps snowing, after a while what we get is this big thick layer of ice under everything—and by then it's all packed down and harder than ever to shovel it. Do you know what I'm saying?"

"I think so."

"And it's sort of the same way with your feelings. If you let them pile up—they only get harder that way." She looked over at him. "Will you think about that?"

Andy shrugged okay. "Can I listen to music now?"

"Sure," Laura said. Letting herself down easy while Andy dug into his backpack and came out with the Discman that Pick gave him for his last birthday. He popped in a CD, popped the earphones on, snapped the top off a Gatorade—then sat back and within seconds he had completely tuned her out—with such alacrity, Laura thought, that it might just be genetic.

She heard the volume leaking out, speculated on the damage to Andy's ears and then felt like somebody's square spinster aunt for thinking that way. She turned her attention to Molly, and listened to her breathing; made a note to call Amy Coleman, the homeopath—whatever the ailment, Amy's orders were to catch it early and call her right away. Kill the monster while it's small, she'd say.

Laura wondered if there'd ever be a day when the monsters would be small again—when a kid's sore throat would be just that, and not a funeral in the making. When a raspy cough wouldn't set off alarm bells, with visions of hospitals and the latest techniques, and "sometimes people just draw a bad number"—all leading to that long walk down the hallway, when you just know what the doctor is going to say. Like war mothers, going about their day when they see the government car coming up the drive. No one can ever put a name on a stone-cold terror like that.

She drove between high hard walls of black jagged slate, where they'd blasted through a hill to make way. The deep rock crevices already had frost on the north side; before long there'd be icicles as big as tollbooths there. A family in a minivan passed her on the right, and caught a shear of wind that nearly spun it around. Laura shook her head at the carelessness of some people. With kids in the car no less.

"M-m-mama?"

Laura looked in the mirror. "Hi, Sweetie. You sleep okay?"

"I'm th-th-th—"

"Thirsty," Andy said.

There was a sign for a pullover up ahead; coming out from between the walls the road opened up, and curved north—and there it was, the whole valley, spread out below as if a grand curtain had been drawn back to reveal it. A wide, rolling expanse dotted with crookety industrial towns with singular, timeworn names—Avoca, Moosic, Forty-Fort—listing and weathered, their clusters of homes and shops and churches huddled together like drinkers at a bar.

"Is that it?" Andy asked. They were eating sandwiches Laura had made ahead of time, while her parents looked on, still in shock that they'd come down from upstate and weren't even needed now.

"That's Wilkes-Barre," Laura pointed out. "And that's the river, and across the river is Kirby, where the school is."

"L-l-l-et . . . let m-me—"

"Want to see?" Laura boosted Molly up on the picnic table, so she could get a good view. "You can't see the campus, but it's somewhere on the other side of that bend."

"What's the deal with boarding schools anyway?" Andy asked. "What do people do that they'd get sent there?"

"Boarding schools are different—it's a different way of learning, and living. And not everybody was 'sent' there. A lot of the kids really wanted to go."

"Did Dad?"

"No."

"Did you?"

Laura took a minute. Maybe once in his life he could let her get away without answering.

She sat in the back seat, as always. She should have been home, starting school with her friends, where she belonged. And yet the whole year before, plus a full summer's worth of pleading, did her no bit of good—like an arranged marriage, Pocono Prep was an Appleby family standard. She had been opposed to the idea from the moment she'd first heard of it—and for all the times they'd been flexible when she was deeply against something, this time they were firm as steel.

They came to a bridge that led out of downtown and over the Susquehanna. There were two mammoth columns, big grand gateway-to-somewhere-columns, with stately carved eagles on top and a bunch of Latin writing—as if Julius Caesar had conquered the place, instead of coal miners. As if Caesar would even want to.

"Here we are, Princess! Kirby, Pennsylvania!"

The cars all seemed to have old people in them. A page of newspaper was caught in a wind spiral in front of the Armory her dad had been going on about. There were donut shops, tire stores, discount clothing outlets, pizza joints, little first-floor places where you got your nails done, bars that were all dark inside in the middle of the day—and every one of them seemed to have the same exact sign, with the word COCKTAILS *in neon under a tipping martini glass with little crooked straws in it, and bubbles that blinked on and off. Laura had never had a cocktail in her life, but was beginning to feel the urge.*

"Maybe this is the back way," her mother said.

"Nope!" chimed Good Old George Appleby.

Laura closed her eyes and kept them that way, wishing that she could open them and be home again, where there was a deep blue lake and not this brown, unfamiliar river—and as long as she was dreaming, she thought, why not throw in a set of parents who'd let her stay where she was, where she knew people and had a history? Everything that was important to her was back at home, and she wasn't even given a choice. Why couldn't all those other generations finally be enough and let the legacy stop with her? How could they do this?

"I think we should turn around," she said.

"Nonsense!" said Good Old George. No doubt he was already timing the trip back to Oneida. There was a special Rotary meeting that night; he'd have to push that Buick for all it was worth.

"Mom. Please."

"You're not even giving it a chance," her mother said.

They pulled up to the school. The name of the street was Foyle, her dad was saying, and so was the main building, and so was the field house. Laura opened her eyes: here, it was a slightly different picture. Trees, at least. People, and energy. Something, but not enough. What could be enough?

"Let's look lively, Princess!" Her dad had gotten out and now he was opening her door for her. Laura noticed a spot on the windshield where a bird had made its mark, and wondered how long it would take him to get out his handkerchief and wipe it off, in front of everyone. Nobody carried handkerchiefs anymore, only him. Just like nobody called their daughter "Princess" out loud in public, after the age of about four and a half.

"If you just let yourself, I think you could like it here," said her mother, popping her head in the other window. "Good things can reveal themselves over time." She looked like she was trying really hard to believe her own words.

"I want to go to school at home," Laura said. "Please don't make me do this."

"It's really for the best," her mother answered. "You'll see."

Laura shook her head. "Please, Mom." She turned to her father, as if one more reasoned approach, one more plea from his daughter, his Princess, would be enough to bring down the pillars of Appleby tradition.

"Well, look at that," said Good Old George. "There's Mrs. Vanderlip. Is she still here?"

34

Mary

"Hi, Mrs. Griffin. Remember me?"
"Remember us, Mrs. G?"

As a career faculty wife at a boarding school, Mary Griffin knew that she could open her front door at any time of day and see someone standing there saying some variation of those words. Former students of Henry's were always showing up; it was a losing campaign to stay up to date on all of them.

"Hi, Mrs. Griffin!"

"Look how big Chip is getting!"

Mary handled each of them, as gracefully as she could. And now, since her husband had gotten sick, a few more were coming around personally; she would resist whatever gifts they brought, be unsuccessful at it, and thank them from inside the doorway. The only visitors he's getting, she thought, have already been invited.

"I'm Laura Piccolo," this one said. "Laura Appleby? I really should have called . . ."

Mary stood there with her hand on the doorknob, letting the draft from outside curl off the porch and swoop into the house like a spirit. This wasn't your typical former student with her children in tow.

"I should have called," Laura repeated. "I know it was rude to just—"

"It's all right—believe me. I've actually expected you."

"You did?"

Mary nodded, opened the door all the way now and stepped back. "You haven't changed at all, really. I can see it now—you're even more beautiful."

"That's very generous, and massively untrue, and thank you very much." Laura grinned.

"Same shy smile," Mary added.

It was raining so hard that day. I'll never forget the rain.

"Where's Dad?" Andy wanted to know. He turned around and looked at the street, scanning for his father's car.

"This is Andy," Laura explained. "And Molly's our daughter."

Mary looked down at Andy, who still wanted his question answered. "Your dad called from the hotel," she told him, and Laura remembered what was great about this woman: when Mary talked to a kid, even when the kid's parent was there, she made sure she talked to the kid. Directly. "He had just gotten off the phone with a doctor he'd been trying to reach, from Los Angeles."

"L.A.? Sweet," Andy said.

Someone else must have been the one who ushered them in, Mary thought. Someone else must have stooped down to that quiet little girl's eye level to say hello to her. Someone else must have told her brother where the TV was, and watched as he took his sister—was she stuttering?—down the hall by the hand. Someone else must have praised them, and brought their mother out of the hallway into a room where they could sit ... if you showed her a movie with the part where Laura Appleby Piccolo came to her door, Mary would only shake her head, and tell you that she didn't remember a single thing about it.

Because you can only have so much room in your mind at any given time, she'd say. And right now, crammed to capacity, Mary's mind held only one thought.

And any minute now, he'd be home.

35

Chip

"Why won't you talk to me."

"What do you mean?"

"I mean you haven't been talking to me."

Ellie looked at him from across three chairs and an end table with magazines on it. They were outside the headmaster's office, where Dr. Scotchmeyer was getting briefed by Mrs. Vanderlip, who nearly had to be taken to the hospital with palpitations, and also Foster Devlin—Critchley Hall's new Golden Girl, in every meaningful way except she'd have not one single friend now, after what she did. It would look just splendid on Foster's college applications though—Senior Proctor—and that's what she was in this for. You get the edge in this world or you lose it. Success doesn't come on a platter; it takes the bold to get the gold.

"Just because I haven't been talking to you, doesn't mean I'm not talking to you. I haven't *seen* you."

"Because you've been avoiding me."

Ellie met his look. Chip's knee was brushing up against the latest issue of *World Tennis*. Scotchmeyer was a nut for the sport; hell or high water, he caught Wimbledon every year.

"And don't tell me you want to be friends if you don't," he went on. "Everybody who ever does that should just do the world a favor and give it up, because it doesn't help anyone. If you want to break up, make it clean—so people will know what they have to deal with. It's hard enough without being confused."

"Look, I'm confused too. Don't think you're the only one."

"Good—now we're both confused. All we have to do is flip that around and both be not confused. Then we can put everything back," he said.

Ellie shook her head. "I can't."

Chip knew that look—that *Sorry, We're Closed* look, one of Ellie's classics. He picked up the magazine and chucked it back on the table but it fell off the edge, and a bunch of subscription cards splayed out and slid across the floor. He got up to get them, sliding past her on his way to the trash can.

"You should recycle those," Ellie said.

"They shouldn't print them in the first place," Chip answered. "The people who make these things should be shot. There ought to be a law. Instant fucking death. No appeal and no reprieve."

"Except you can't exactly kill people for wasting paper."

"You can shoot them in the leg," Chip said. He saw Ellie, looking at him; admittedly, until this moment, he'd had no idea what his stand was on magazine subscription cards. He'd heard this saying once, about how you're never really upset about the thing you think you're upset about, because it's always something else, hiding behind the thing you thought. Maybe that applied here. Or, maybe he just really hated those fucking subscription cards, and it was as simple as that.

"Didn't your dad talk to you?" Ellie asked.

"When?"

"Before his—thing happened."

Chip shook his head. "What would he have talked to me about?"

"Well I told him something. In confidence. The night just before."

"About what?"

"He was going to tell you. I can't." She looked down; thinking, collecting herself. "I was scared to tell you, so I went to tell your mom but she wasn't home, so your dad said it was okay to come in and he was the one I told. And now I'm even more scared, because I think I might have caused all this."

"Caused all what—you mean my dad?"

"Well, when you tell somebody something kinda big one night, and the next day he's in the hospital. I couldn't live with myself if I did that."

"I don't think it works that way, Ellie. I think this stuff builds up as it goes. You don't just have a stroke. At least I don't think so."

"You're not just saying that, right?"

"Ellie, what the hell? You're saying you told him something so big his brain burned up, but you can't tell me?"

"He was going to tell you," Ellie repeated.

"Well he can't now, can he—so why don't you?"

"Because I can't!" she said, in a whisper that came out like growling.

Chip closed his eyes. He rubbed his temples, the way Randy told him some girl had showed him would work for stress headaches. She was a cheerleader from a school they played up in Binghamton; Randy had spent forty-five minutes trying to set records with her, then he drove everyone crazy demonstrating this headache technique on the bus back home to school. At the time, Chip didn't believe it would work—but he was counting on it now.

"So, what were you trying to find out?" Ellie asked. Feeling a little better about things, now that she hadn't nearly killed the dean of the school.

"I wanted to know about these two guys," Chip said. There were noises from the Headmaster's office. Vanderlip was starting to sound real animated in there; a boy in Critchley Hall was more than an old-schooler like that could take. And Foster must be just loving it. She was evil. She was cursed. And she was going to succeed, like crazy.

"What about them?" Ellie wanted to know.

"They used to go here. The last thing my dad did was to tell Mrs. Levering to find them. One of them is some kind of religious guy. And the other's this big lawyer—he's the one trying to get all these new tests and doctors. His father is Carmine Piccolo."

"You're kidding me."

Chip shook his head: not kidding. "So I went up to his restaurant."

"I heard," she said. "And I heard who you went with."

"She had a car, Ellie. And you would have been welcome to come, by the way."

"Oh, right—like I'm going to go up to a mob guy's restaurant. A guy who's *killed* people. What the hell were you doing?"

"Eating squid."

"With Cindi Lindberg."

"She had the *puttanesca*. With olives, and anchovies." Chip smiled inside; suddenly he was thinking about Cindi now—about cotton tops and overalls, and hair washed fresh. And facts about ruffles that could stand up to scrutiny.

"So what did you expect to find in yearbooks?"

"I wanted to find out who they were. And who they were to my dad, that he would ask for them."

"How would that be in a yearbook?"

Chip looked at her. "I don't even know anymore," he told her. He felt drained. "I guess I just had this instinct to start there."

"You wanted to see that they were real," Ellie suggested.

"Maybe," Chip said. "Or maybe I don't. I just don't know."

The door opened then, and Foster Devlin stepped out. "Whew," she said. "It's pretty bad in there . . ." She smiled at them, like they were all in this together and on the same side. Mentally she was decorating her dorm room at Cornell already, and ruling out paisley. "I'm sorry about your dad, Chip. I sure hope he's okay." She drenched the room with sympathy, then turned and walked out.

"Chip. Ellie."

They turned. It was Dr. Scotchmeyer. Behind him, they could see Sheldon Rinehimer, a pompous and wormy alumnus who owned the Valley Bank & Trust, and was on the school's Board of Trustees; next to him were Mrs. Levering and Mrs. Vanderlip, who had a lace handkerchief in her liver-spotted fist and she was choking the living shit out of it. If it had been up to her, boarding schools would never have been coed in the first place. *And this was why!*

"I'd like to see you one at a time," Scotchmeyer told them.

36

Laura

She sat with Mary, on opposite sides of Griffin's bed; his thin breathing monitored and displayed on screens, along with every other function that mattered—except moving, and talking, and laughing, and eating, and enjoying any semblance of the life he knew before it all changed.

They talked about Goody and Pick, the way two mothers talk about their boys—the one who took the traveled path, and the one who didn't; who couldn't take the traveled path if he tried. And how unique it was, to have affected each other's lives to such a thorough and consuming degree—even with all the miles and the years between them. And how both of them were coming home to a place they'd run from.

"It's amazing, you know?" Laura wondered. "When you think about it—the people who picked Stewart up that day—they could have been anybody. Jehovah's Witness. Survivalists. He was seventeen, for God's sake—if they were hockey players, he'd be skating backwards and having fistfights on tv. If they were hustlers he'd be fleecing old people out of their nest eggs."

Mary had her doubts about the fleecing, but agreed it was lucky that the people who picked Stewart up were the ones who did.

"And yet," Laura went on, "part of me wonders if that's how it works sometimes. And it wasn't really luck at all."

"What do you mean?" Mary asked. "Fate?"

Laura shook her head. "Fate would be too convenient," she answered. "Fate gets me off the hook."

"For what?" Mary wondered.

How about everything? Laura thought. *I would like to get off the hook for everything.*

"Mom?"

They turned. Andy was in the doorway, with Molly just behind him. "Molly's hungry," he said. Laura saw him grab a peek at Griffin, with that leery fascination that kids get, when they see something in real life that they'd only seen in pictures before.

"Do you know where the kitchen is?" Mary asked.

"Yeah, it's that way. We passed it coming in."

"That's the one," Mary nodded. "Knock yourselves out. If you need any help, come get me."

"Cool," Andy said. "Thanks."

They were quick to slip away but Laura stopped them. "Excuse me? Doesn't anyone have something to say to Mrs. Griffin?"

Molly turned and came back a few steps. She looked at Mary. "Th-th-thaaan-k. Yyyyou," she said. Then she spun around and caught up with Andy. As if they'd been bouncing down that hallway since the day they were born.

"She's been that way since her twin died," Laura said. "I'm surprised that she can do anything sometimes." She tilted her head towards the hallway, where the kids went. "And it's not just the stuttering. She's afraid of the rain. She's afraid of a lot of things. She told me once she was scared that God was going to take her away, too. What can you do when you know they're thinking these things? And who knows what she isn't even telling me? *I* don't have the words for it, how could she?"

"I wish there was enough sympathy," Mary said, and Laura knew she was sincere: you could fill the Grand Canyon with sympathy and it wouldn't be enough. But she thanked her for saying so and she meant it—somehow out of all the times people tried to say something comforting and couldn't come close, what Mary said actually found a home inside Laura, and helped her feel a little better. Never say no to possibility, after all.

Mary's gaze drifted out the window, before it drifted again and finally fell on Henry, like an extra blanket to cover him. "They're talking about moving him back to the hospital," she informed Laura.

"Oh, no. I'm sorry . . ."

Mary shrugged, philosophically; it looked like some of the fight might be draining out of her. "Sometimes they wake up after years. Other times they never do. But they're saying he should be back there."

Laura looked at her; feeling now that maybe less was more in this case and it wasn't such a good idea to come up here. She was just about to pull the troops together and leave, tossing apologies over how inappropriate it had been to just arrive like this, when they heard footsteps outside and the front door banging open. To see the way Mary tensed up at the sound, it could be storm troopers coming in.

"I've been wondering where he's been," Mary said.

"Who?"

"Chip."

"Chip?"

Mary nodded, listening; first stop would be the kitchen, maybe the bathroom next but not this time—just the refrigerator door and then that tilted lumbering gait of his, down the hallway where he'd first learned to walk.

"Hi Mom," he said.

"Did something happen at practice? I thought you'd be home earlier."

"We gotta talk about that." Chip took a bite out of a sandwich he'd brought from the kitchen; a piece of salami escaped and hit the floor. He bent down to get it, and on his way up Laura noticed maple syrup on his breath. "Did Dr. Scotchmeyer call?"

"Why would Dr. Scotchmeyer call?"

"We gotta talk about that."

Mary watched him. "Chip, we have company. This is Mrs.—"

"Laura. Laura's fine. Hi, Chip."

"Hi. Is that your kid in the kitchen with the nurse?"

"You mean kids, right?"

"Looked like just one to me. He was eating string cheese."

Laura shot straight up. "You mean there wasn't a girl?" She was past Chip and out of the room already.

Chip looked at Mary. "What's wrong?"

"Get the nurse," she said. "Tell the nurse to come back here with your father and you stay with the boy."

"What's going on?"

"Stay with him!"

She was down the hall and out of the house like a hard wind across the prairie. Taking with it all she had intended to say.

37

Griffin

He was aware when there were people in the room, and of their movements in and out. But he wasn't aware of time: how it accumulated, and passed, how it was structured or organized—or why it mattered, or was even invented. For Griffin, presence and memory were now the same thing. Time was spatial, no longer linear. A rocket launch, a World Series, a visit from a troubled girl. Moments would squeeze in, and separate, and rearrange and squeeze and separate again. A summer job, a factory tour, the one time he ever milked a cow—he watched his history like you'd stand and watch a motorcade, only propped up, mummified, powerless to react or respond to each passing sight. Like numbers in a lottery, painted on ping pong balls and popping up at random; whichever memory came, Henry Griffin was at its mercy. A silent witness, unable to look away.

She had waited till night to come to see him. He remembered the porch light, and how she stood just outside it and he didn't know who she was at first. Like before—like before? Did this happen before or was it only this once? She asked to see Mrs. Griffin, and Mrs. Griffin wasn't around at the moment—did that also happen before?—so he invited her in to bring it to him instead. Whatever she had come to talk about, whatever burden she had, maybe he wasn't as good as his wife at this, but he still knew how to listen, and to understand, and to keep it between the two of them.

He remembered the taste of a soft pretzel, from a vendor on the boardwalk on a trip to Asbury Park. The caramel apples his mother made every October, with real New Hampshire apples, that he could see from the window in his room. The first time he'd ever had buttered popcorn, and a hot dog off the grill. And he remembered the broccoli and cheese they served in the dining hall, and the time he went through the kitchen at Gemmell and saw the wholesale containers of liquid cheddar, the eight-gallon cans of it, that Mrs. Ricciatti would glop like shellac over any vegetable that could handle it—broccoli, cauliflower, brussel sprouts—the continuing battle to get greens into teenagers who need to eat them, even if it means covering everything up until it glows.

Industrial buckets of cheese. Whatever it takes. He remembered.

"Is Mrs. Griffin here?"

"No, I'm sorry. She's out for the evening. Is there something I can help you with?"

She was standing in the shadows, just outside the porch light. It didn't take him too long, to finally talk her inside.

It was both girls, he remembered, that came to him this way. That same look, of trial and trembling. Different faces, years apart. And Mary wasn't home, either time.

It was both of them.

Griffin's eyes watered. He blinked to make it go away. The nurse, reading a book about raising Golden Retrievers, didn't see. He blinked again; found himself on a humid evening in spring, long ago and right this minute.

He missed the sign for Bear Creek and had to double back. He'd left the rehearsal early, saying he had business off-campus. He'd been to enough May Day Celebrations to know where to stand and what to say; he had an abbreviated version of his speech ready, in case it was too hot outside that day. Or too cold, or too rainy, or too anything—the weather this time of year was unpredictable to say the least. It was the mountains, he knew; the Poconos took normal weather patterns and made jokes out of them. Same as New Hampshire—the smartest thing his parents ever did was say goodbye to their life in the north and buy that tackle shop on Cape Hatteras. There was a year-round population down there; you could be open twelve months and still get some good time on the water for yourself once in a while. There were lots of little inland creeks where you could keep on using your flies like you were used to. And once you got switched over to the saltwater life, you could do pretty well just standing in the surf. Most people did.

It was a good deal, Griffin thought. His parents were content. His dad would call him up during the winters, just giddy about the snow he wasn't shoveling, the ice he wasn't hacking off his windshield. And his mom was happy behind the counter, and thrilled that her husband had other people besides her to talk fishing with. She thanked her customers every day.

"Try this," Carmine said. He handed Griffin a cherry tomato. "We got two boxes in just this morning. Friday they were droppin' off a vine in Sardinia."

Griffin bit into the tomato. It tasted like sunlight. "This is delicious," he said. "This is remarkable."

Carmine took a handful, like they were beer nuts. "When I was a boy we couldn't get ridda these things. We used to throw them at each other. Now you should see what I gotta pay for 'em." He held

one up, turned it this way and that like it was a rare polished gem.
"That's what time does," he said. "It puts a value on things."
    Griffin nodded. Carmine pushed another tomato on him.
"Mr. Piccolo. We have to talk."
"It's about Santamo?"
"I'm afraid it is."
"What'd he do. He flunk out? Not doing his work?"
"Your son's a bright young man, Mr. Piccolo. I'm not sure you
know how bright he really is."
"But you didn't drive out here to tell me my son was bright."
"No sir, I didn't. That's not what I came here to say."
"This about that friend a his? Kid ran away or somethin'?"
"Indirectly. But, also, yes—directly."
    Carmine paused; popped another tomato, looking at Griffin.
"Have a little dinner. Va bene mangiare.*"*
    "I appreciate the offer, Mr. Piccolo. But I ate back at the school."
    "We got orrechiette tonight. Donato made some fresh. Ten
grandmothers couldn't make it better."
    "Mr. Piccolo. Your son's in a bit of trouble."
    "Well you already said it wasn't school trouble. So, what'd he do,
get some girl knocked up?"
    Griffin nodded; maybe not how he would have put it, but yes.
    Carmine looked at him. Griffin met his eye but said nothing
more; the two men sat in silence until the cook came over, with a
big serving bowl and two pasta plates. He put them down and left.
    "You never had orrechiette before."
    "No, sir, I haven't."
    Carmine spooned enough out for both of them. "Little ears," he
said. "That's what orrechiette means. Because of the shape." Then he
tucked his napkin, and dug in. "When Santamo was young I used
to tell him it was the ears they cut off, from the kids who wouldn't
listen to their parents. Maybe that wasn't such a smart thing to do."
    Donato came back with a wine bottle and put it down. Carmine
poured for both of them, then sat back to let his breathe.

"So how much do I need to know about this girl?"

Griffin slid his plate aside and leaned in closer to the table. He started with some background; the relationships between Carmine's son and Stewart Goodman, between Stewart Goodman and Laura Appleby, and then added some of the personal observations he'd made over the course of the year. All leading up to just a few nights ago, when Laura showed up at his door—drawn in and desperate for help.

"And now we've got a situation," Griffin said.

Carmine agreed. "You talk to the parents? The girl's?"

Griffin nodded. "They were emphatic—they can't have her at home. I wish I could tell you this is the only time I've seen this."

"Jesus," said Carmine. "That's even worse than me."

Griffin wasn't going to argue that either way. "Additionally—and unfortunately—she can't remain at Pocono Valley, either. I haven't spoken to anyone on the board yet, but I'm sure they'd be resolute. Every student knows the rules."

Carmine studied him. "Listen. She wants a procedure, I got nothin' to say. So, if that's what you came here for—"

Griffin interrupted. "She wants to have the baby. She's leaving school on her own. She's made up her mind." He watched Carmine take this in. "She's willing to give it up once it's born. But she wants to see it through. Which makes your son—legally speaking—the father."

Carmine snorted. "And how did Santamo take the news?"

"He doesn't know yet. The girl asked me not to tell him. And, because he's a minor, I thought it was time to bring the matter to you."

He watched Carmine think this through. "She wants to have a baby, that's her life. But Santamo's still a kid and that means I'm in charge. And if he don't know now I say he never finds out."

Griffin nodded. "It's possible you won't always feel that way."

"Like hell it is."

Carmine forked some pasta around on his plate. Griffin watched him. "If you're interested, Mr. Piccolo, I believe there's an option worth considering."

"I'm interested. Go ahead."

Griffin sipped some water. "Well, this is pretty sensitive. But you're the child's grandfather. And the grandparents on the girl's side have removed themselves. So a lot depends on how concerned you are with where this baby ends up."

Carmine looked impressed; Griffin had walked him right up to the ticket window, and that wasn't an easy thing to do. "Anybody you had in mind," he told Griffin, "would have to have a place for the girl to stay, and stay healthy, until she has this baby."

"I believe I have such a place in mind."

Carmine watched Griffin closely. "And anybody you had in mind to be the parents," he continued, "would have to promise—on their souls they'd have to promise—that no one alive would ever know how all this came about."

"I think the parents could make that promise."

"You think?"

"The parents can make that promise."

Carmine eyed him. "They have any kids of their own?"

"They've tried. It's been ruled out."

Carmine thought some more; he stabbed at an olive on the edge of his plate, pointed it at Griffin. "The girl can never know where this baby ended up. And Santamo, I don't want him to know there was ever a kid in the first place. At all—never."

Griffin nodded. Carmine liked his resolve. "Also—he stays at the school. Santamo graduates—you said he was smart, so he sees out the year. Tu capisci?"

"I don't see how we could remove him from the school, sir, without addressing why. And that would negate the agreement we just made."

Carmine looked even more impressed. "So it's you and me and that's it—tutto, si? The knowledge dies when we do. Nobody knows where this baby came from."

"Mr. Piccolo. With all due respect. The mother who adopts—my wife—she should know. It's only right."

"Then we got no deal."

He meant it. Griffin considered this: in their whole life together, there would be one secret he would have to keep from Mary. There's no better indicator, he thought, of how badly we can want something, than what we're willing to do to get it. And we can't know what our limits are until we're tested. Really tested.

"I'm sorry," he told Carmine. "I can't do that. I can't start a family on that foundation. If you can't trust us both then you can't trust me—and if you can't trust me, then someone else should raise your grandchild."

Carmine leaned back, looking hard; finally, he nodded. "Then she better not talk," he said.

Outside, they shook hands. Carmine took in the evening air. He walked Griffin to the school maintenance van—realizing only then that the man didn't have a car of his own. "There'll be some money now and then," Carmine told him. "A little anonymous assistance. Don't stand on pride."

"Mr. Piccolo. I'm sure I can't accept—"

"You don't want to see me angry, Paesan. I've been good tonight. Trust me."

Griffin nodded, and opened the door. He watched Carmine make his way to the restaurant. Then he backed out of the lot and drove down the curving mountain roads and finally into town, and the campus. He returned the van to Maintenance, where he found the overtime crew assembling extra bleachers for May Day. He had paperwork remaining at the office, and calls to schedule for morning; after all, he had cut out early tonight to go and make his visit. So even half an hour at his desk, would make tomorrow go a whole lot better.

But all he wanted to do was see Mary. And talk to her, and hold on to her. He had just brokered their baby, from a gangster, over a plate of little ears.

38

Chip

"So, your dad is Sandy Piccolo?"

Andy nodded. "People call him Pick though. Except my mom." He took another bite of cold chicken.

Chip was pulling different bowls from the refrigerator, bending back the layers of tinfoil to see what was underneath. Between the food in the dining hall and everything people kept bringing, it would be a while before anybody cooked up something from scratch around here.

"His real name is Santamo," Andy said. "That's what it used to be."

"Santamo, huh. Not one you hear every day." Chip found something he liked—cold mashed potatoes—and sat down with Andy. "It's Italian, right?"

Andy confirmed. "His dad still calls him that name. They don't talk to each other. Can I have some of those potatoes?"

"Sure." Chip slid the bowl to the middle, so they could share. He found two forks. "You want them heated up?"

"No, they're good this way."

They dug in together like that, saying nothing for a while. Andy spoke first. "Think they'll find my sister?"

"Yeah, don't worry. It's pretty hard to get lost around here. You worried?"

"My mom's worried."

"Yeah, mine is too."

Andy took another bite. "Your dad's pretty sick, isn't he? Do they think he's gonna live?"

"No one's real sure yet. Your dad, though, he's been pretty cool about this. He's got all these specialists calling in. And my mom says he's paying for it—because we sure never could."

Andy shrugged that off. "He's loaded."

"Yeah?"

"Yeah," Andy nodded. "He's a lawyer."

Chip already knew that. "What kind?" he asked.

"I don't know what it's called," Andy told him. "But he's on TV sometimes. Can I have something to drink?"

Chip told him to go see what he wanted. This was a pretty cool kid, he thought. He felt like calling Randy up and telling him that he ought to come over and check this guy out. *His father's a lawyer and he's on TV sometimes, and his grandfather's Carmine Piccolo and I had lunch with the dude, and dessert with Cindi Lindberg, and oh man did I learn a lot about her but here's the real news, I am DOA for the Nihaminy game and maybe the rest of the season because I was up in Ellie's room and that bitch-fuck Foster Devlin tipped off Vanderlip and we all had to go see Scotchmeyer today. And now I'm here with this fourth-grader while everybody's looking for his sister who took off, and he's a really cool little kid, Carmine Fucking Piccolo is his grandfather, you really gotta see this.*

Andy brought a jug of Tropicana to the table. Definitely a gift from someone; the Griffins bought their O.J. from the school and it sucked.

"You know what I did one time?"

"What," Chip said.

"When we have leftover mashed potatoes like this, my mom'll make patties out of them, and fry them like hamburgers, and they're really, really good. So once when she wasn't there I tried to do that."

"What happened?"

"I couldn't get them to come out the way she did, and I ruined a couple things. Some pans, and part of the countertop, because I put a hot pan right down on it and it melted through, and then there was smoke damage to the wall."

"Smoke damage?"

"When the counter burned it made everything all black. My dad lost his temper when he saw it. He said I couldn't cook anything ever again until I'm forty."

Chip had to laugh; he really liked this kid.

"Go ahead," Andy told him. "If you ever got in trouble like that, you wouldn't think it was so funny."

"Oh yeah? Well try this—I might be getting kicked off the football team."

"Really? How come?"

Chip debated, then told him. He was careful with his words; as cool as this kid might be, he still wasn't even ten. But Andy didn't look the least bit surprised.

"That's what happened to my dad," he said.

"What."

"Except in reverse. The girl was in his room. It happened when they went here."

"No way."

Andy glugged some of the juice. "I heard him talking to some guy at the country club. The guy was asking him if the stuff he heard about was true. But when they found out I was listening they shut up about it. Hang on." He stopped talking, and then sat up straight and very still, like he'd just seen something. Then he let go with a burp—deep, rumbling, a classic Adirondack summer camp tuba blast, well worth the money it took to send him there. "That felt good," he pronounced, and scooped up some more of the potatoes. "Is it okay if I finish these?"

Chip nodded. "But wait a minute. Tell me this from the beginning. About the dorm."

"I don't know it from the beginning."

Chip had to think about this. "My dad asked for two guys," he said. "One of them was your dad."

"And Stewart Goodman."

"Right. What do you know about them?"

"They were best friends. And they had a fight."

"Over what."

"I don't know. I asked my mom that before, and she wouldn't say."

"My mom said there was a girl," Chip said. "And your mom went here too. So, she was your dad's girlfriend while they were here."

Andy waved no to that. "She was Stewart's girlfriend."

"What? How do you know that?"

"I saw them kissing—there was a picture in the yearbook, of the two of them kissing. When I asked my mom about it she got all weird and made me go to bed."

"Hold on. You said she was in your father's room in the dorm. She told you that?"

Andy shook his head. "That's what my dad and that guy at the club were talking about," he said. "Plus, it's in a book."

"Say that again?"

"I remember the guy asking my dad that. It was like he was teasing him. He wanted to know if all the stuff in that book was true."

"What's the name of it?" Chip asked.

"I don't know. I told you, they shut up because I was there."

"Fuck!" Chip slapped the table so hard their forks danced in the potato bowl. He remembered his mom saying something about the book Goody wrote; at the time he didn't think there'd be any connection to what was going on here and now. It pissed him off that now he'd have to go and find out something he could have already known. "Fuck fucking fuck!"

Andy looked at him. "Now you sound like my dad," he said.

39

Pick

"**D**on't make me look, Pop!"

He's five. His aunts and uncles are there. They've all been up to the front of the room but they're back at their seats again and his aunts are crying pretty hard and now they want him to go up there too. He knows the thing they were looking at is called a casket, but he doesn't want to go see it even though they keep saying he should. Even with his father taking him.

"You gotta come see the casket," Carmine is saying. "Come on." And his aunts and uncles are nodding but he still doesn't want to go. He already said two times he could see it from here but they all made awful faces and his Aunt Luisa asked "What kind of boy doesn't want to say goodbye to his mother?" and Pick said "My mother isn't here, she's in the hospital," and something about the way they look at him and each other this time makes him finally realize what's been going on—that caskets are for putting people in, dead people, and that's what his mother was now, a dead person, and she was actually in there, that's the box she's in and that's why everyone's here and they all seem so upset.

He feels like crying but knows he can't because men don't do that, that's what they told him in the car and they're telling him again, *they're saying he has to be a man now, and the one who says it the most is his father.*

"Look at her!"

"No!"

His arm hurts. He sees his father's hand wrapped around it. He jiggles his feet and can't feel the floor under him anymore and now he knows he's up off the ground and rising, his father is lifting him, so he can see down into the box.

"No! Don't make me look!"

"They're gonna put her in the ground after this!"

"But I don't want them to!"

He squeezes his eyes closed and it makes his father madder. He tries to stop crying but every time his father shakes him he only gets worse.

"Santamo, you gotta be tough!"

"I want Mama!"

He feels the sting on his cheek and it takes away the place he was saving, where his mother kissed him in the hospital and promised she would see him tomorrow. He feels the sting again and through his tears he sees his father's red face, his hand reaching back and now he knows the sting means he's getting smacked.

"Be tough!"

But all he can do is cry harder.

He sat on a stone bench facing her grave. He had flowers that he bought at a strip mall on the way out. The place was dark and stuffy and hard to breathe in—so he grabbed the closest arrangement he could find and dropped a fifty on the counter, so he could get out of there without having to wait for the couple ahead of him at the register. The pair of them might have been the only other customers all week.

He looked at the marker. DEVOTED WIFE AND MOTHER, it said, and Pick figured he'd have to take both claims at face value. He had very little memory of what she was like as a mother; a vague feeling of safety, perhaps, a sense of comfort and peace that he'd never known since. As far as a devoted wife, he didn't really think having a husband like Carmine would leave her any options.

"*I'm scared!*"

"*Be tough!*"

It started to drizzle. Pick watched a few drops hit the top of the headstone, and slide down the sides of it like tears. He wanted to get up and leave but he didn't; forcing himself to stay, when his usual thing was to get as far away as he could, and as fast, from anything that made him feel the way he was starting to feel right now. *There must be some kind of way outta here,* the song went, and Pick's specialty was finding that way, and taking it, at warp speed times ten, and never looking back.

But then, he thought, this also meant he never stayed with the place that the song was talking about. The place called Here. Pick was never Here; he was always on the way to There. And the space in between had no value of its own—it was just the thing you had to cross. If you did it fast enough you could make believe it didn't even exist.

He remembered from business trips to London, how on the Underground they'd have signs everywhere, and announcements saying *Mind the Gap*—a courteous, civic reminder of the small bit of distance between the station platform and the train doors, and to be careful that you don't hurt yourself. In America it would all be about lawsuits, and Pick knew he was as much a part of that as anyone—but the way they worded it in England, and the way they flavored it, it just felt different. The polite, educated voice on the recording, the simple clean logo that over the years had grown far beyond its original intention and into a national and cultural identity. There were coffee mugs and t-shirts and dish towels and decals that all said *Mind the Gap* on them—a simple fact of engineering, spun into a national identity and cottage business in souvenirs—and, if you looked at it a certain way, a possible if unintended lesson in mindful living overall.

Pick, who never looked at things that way, now found something personal in all this—that there was a gap that he wasn't minding, that he was doing everything he could to ignore. And now he knew why: because the gap was where the pain was. It's the thing you step over, where you don't look down, because that's where things are scary. And he wasn't allowed to be scared. He'd learned early; scared was not a choice. So to even think about minding the gap, then, would mean admitting in the first place that there is one.

And there was just no way. There wasn't.

The trips to London he had taken alone. Short trips, taxing and compacted, half the time he never made it out of Heathrow, where the meeting he'd have flown in for would take place in a conference room in the luxury lounge at British Air, and then as soon as it was over he'd turn right around and fly straight back. But other times he did make it out of the airport and into town, and it was still all business, but it wasn't *all* business—he could have brought Laura, they could have gotten away a little, even if they didn't see each other till eight or nine at night—which now that he thought of it, wasn't much different than things were at home. It would be different enough for Laura though, who could have had a few days over there to play with; there were galleries and museums and all kinds of other places to just walk around and lose herself in, or find herself in, or just stop and do nothing. London, for Christ's sake. Dickens, and Holmes. Buckingham, Kensington, the National Theatre. Charing Cross Road, the Albert Hall, Fortnum & Mason serving high tea. Covent Garden and the Thames. Chelsea playing Tottenham, the pubs filled with fans.

Yet Pick had never asked her. Compartments again maybe, work versus personal and all—but still. They had a solid core of friends who'd take the kids, and everybody would have loved it. And after Pick's business was finished for the day he and Laura could have met up, and stayed out, they could have built some extra time into the trip—either plan something out or just get on a train and go anywhere—the whole fucking continent is thoroughly connected, with a clean and modern rail system that puts the one we have to shame. Laura had pictures, Pick remembered. All those train boards. She was so adorable doing that. And no one could have guessed what some of those prints would sell for one day.

But he never brought her with him. He went alone, every time, and at once he knew what a mistake that was. Multiply that times all the getaways they could have taken, and now he had a problem. Or now he saw the problem—because he'd had it for a while. If he'd been minding the gap, he'd have known.

He looked down at the bouquet he'd brought, because Carmine had told him to—*Bring some flowers, sweep up the grave*—but he changed his mind about leaving them. The flowers looked even worse in daylight. Rotting in that shop was probably a highlight for them; leaving them here would only make things worse.

They were hyacinths, it turned out. What the fuck was it with hyacinths.

40

Laura

She sent Mary in the direction of the chapel, and the gym, and the boys' dorms—while Laura would cover Foyle, and Critchley, and Gemmell. It didn't surprise her that she could pull up these names right away, from instant recall—it was half her lifetime ago, and she still had the map of the campus imprinted on her memory. Major routes and shortcuts, too. What did surprise her was how familiar it all felt, and how strangely good—considering the way everything had fallen apart before she ever got to finish.

All she knew, arriving here, was that she'd had no joy inside. She needed someone to help pull her out of the depths—and the first person to do that was Stewart. His roadhouse laugh and his same color shirt every day and his notebook with pages covered in writing and his join the film club and get extra credit. His parabolic dreams about the future and all the things he was going to do with it.

And oh yes. His friend. Do not forget the best friend. You fell twice as hard for the Leopard.

She asked some girls in front of Critchley if they'd seen a six-year-old, in a raincoat and a floppy hat; they said no, and went back to what they were doing. She turned the corner to go around behind the dorm but stopped to look back at them first. They were normal everyday kids—sophomores, juniors at most—their afternoon interrupted by a nonentity that they'd already wiped clean from their experience.

But even if she'd been of no consequence to them, Laura felt she knew these girls by heart: this one played music, that one was an athlete, this one would be printing up flyers all night because something was unjust, and something needed to be done about it. That one would use her father's credit card and do something stupid with it, and get caught, and because she's basically a good kid, would never do it again.

All standard stuff. But what Laura also noticed was that none of them looked the way she remembered feeling back when she was in their shoes. These girls looked tethered to the world; if they felt as wobbly and unsure as she had, then they were doing a wonderful job of masking it—and if they weren't feeling that way, then she wondered what their secret was. When at their age, Laura's young life was already out of control—skidding hard toward the guard rail, and no hands on the wheel.

She stepped back off the porch and waited, just outside the lamplight. Hoping she had knocked loud enough, praying this door would open, soon, and sweep her in. Holding back the panic that things had come down to a choice like this.

"Laura?" He stepped outside, partway, holding the door behind him.

"I need to see Mrs. Griffin," Laura said. She felt wilted, helpless.

"Mrs. Griffin isn't here tonight—she went to see a play, at the college. Is there something I can help you with?"

"I don't know if anyone can help me," she said.

"Well, come on in," Griffin told her. "Let's see if we can't give it a try."

She remembered the car ride. They'd left around four in the afternoon, on a Friday, and she fell asleep soon after. She remembered overhearing the Griffins talking about how rarely they managed to get away together—and now here they were, what do you know, doing just that. They had borrowed the car from Dr. Imboden, the school MD, who wouldn't be using it over the weekend anyway, due to some minor foot surgery he'd been putting off. It was a Chevy, a Caprice Classic, top of the line—a much better car, they were remarking, than any they could ever see buying for themselves, and Laura could tell that part of this made them feel a little giddy with luxury. She felt like she was intruding, but also doing them a favor somehow; she didn't really understand what they meant about why it was better to go at night than in the morning—not right away, anyway. She wouldn't start getting sick in the mornings until she'd been down there a few days—but they couldn't have known that. They were just doing their best to anticipate.

She remembered the dream she had, in the car that night. A horse was involved, naturally, since a strong majority of Laura's dreams had horses in them—one horse in particular, a paint mare named Sierra, who lived on a small farm out near one of her father's dealerships. Laura had spent entire days dreaming about this horse, so it was only natural to be dreaming about her at night too. In every single one of the dreams, Laura was Sierra's owner, keeper, and absolute best friend. And in every single one of the dreams, Laura had a secret to tell, to the only one in the world who would listen and never repeat it. Laura rarely remembered what the secrets were, just that Sierra was always there and would always listen.

This night, in the car, Sierra was also in Laura's dream—but things were reversed now, the mare had the secret and Laura couldn't figure out what it was. She couldn't understand her language, and Sierra lost her temper from that, from all the times she had had to hear Laura's side of life but now she couldn't communicate one damn item to her, and now this very large animal was angry and flaring and kicking the walls of the stall, and throwing hay around—which shook Laura into crying in her dream and screaming finally, piercing her awake to realize where she was again—in the back of Dr. Imboden's Chevrolet which the Griffins had borrowed, to take her to her new home, since the one her parents raised her in was no longer open to her now. Not with the way she had behaved. No one brings shame on the Appleby house; in times of trouble one brings cover stories instead, and George and Alexandra had thought up a good one and were quickly pushing on with their lives. Whatever pain they felt—whatever feelings they had at all, about what their daughter had done and what it meant in the larger scheme of things—they kept it all to themselves.

Part of Laura had already forgiven them, even that night on the way to North Carolina. Part of her understood. And at that point, truth be known, she wouldn't have been real jazzed about going home anyway—especially in the role of someone's scandalized daughter. This would be a new start, in a new location. Plus, Griffin's parents sounded just fine. If they set the bar as high as these people did, mother and baby would do all right.

She passed the far side of Critchley and went down along where the parlor rooms were. Something in one of the windows caught Laura's eye, and she stopped. A boy and a girl, all braided up on a couch in there. Kissing, deepening, shutting off the world outside until everything around them was gone.

Laura closed her eyes. She felt like rapping on the glass—smash a rock through it, if she had to—so she could warn them, for the future's sake, to stop. To go against their very nature right now, every screaming hormone, and jam on the brakes and turn their lives around and get the hell out of there.

Because look what happened to me, she would say.

And ask us if we care, they would say back. And so, in the end, Laura moved on and let them be.

She had her own children to save.

41

Goody

He sat on the bench and narrowed his eyes. He could feel the cold through his coat and clothes—and then, just as soon, he didn't. He breathed deep, studied the flow in and out, then released his attention to anything—to everything—and remained there; sitting, gone.

No different than a leaf. No different than a breeze. The cells from each, the same as his. Molecules, floating about, until there weren't even molecules. Until there was emptiness. Which was all there was, anyway. Enough of it to contain all that is.

In silence he chanted the Heart Sutra for the ten thousandth time.

Form is Emptiness
Emptiness is Form . . .
This Body itself is Emptiness
and Emptiness itself is this Body . . .

When they first got to Mt. Raymond, the monks brought him to see Hataka Sudo Roshi. Roshi took him in with a glance and told him to go home. Goody said he couldn't. Roshi turned to the monks; the rest happened in Japanese, but it wasn't that hard to get the gist of it—the man was not real happy with them for bringing him here. Goody felt awful to see them being scolded, just for being good to him. He would never have brought them this trouble. He was sorry, for their sake, that they ever picked him up.

When Roshi finished with the monks, he turned back to Goody and said again, *Go*. Goody said please, he wanted to stay. He said he couldn't go back and he told him why. He poured the whole thing out—right up to why he was out on that highway where the monks found him and took him in. He told Roshi they shouldn't be blamed for anything, if that's what was happening, that he was out of his mind that day and they might have saved him from something much worse, and that he couldn't see how that could be bad. And that he never knew anyone to just be that out and out *kind*, or at least not to someone they didn't even know. And that being kind like that shouldn't get them in trouble. If that's what was happening.

He went on like this for a good ten minutes. When he stopped, the silence made him dizzy. He woke up two weeks later.

Therefore, in the void there are no forms and no feelings,
conceptions, impulses and no consciousness.

It was the flu, a bad one, possibly pneumonia. Roshi stayed with him the whole time. The monks had never seen this before. The master dropped everything. The daily schedule carried on without him. Two retreat weekends where other senior monks subbed in and gave the dharma talks, when everyone who came to the retreats did so just to hear Roshi. One of them muttered something about "understudies," then left the mountain entirely to go have a spa weekend in Vancouver instead. Hearing that, Roshi entered the meditation hall one night, startling a session in progress. He said to the group, "*Too much attach!*"—then walked out again, to go tend to Goody, who was still too out of it to even know where he was. Nobody complained after that.

There is no eye, ear, nose, tongue, body or mind;
there is no form, sound, smell, taste, touch or idea.

The fever broke the third week. Roshi would have this horrible tea brought in, and by the end of another week Goody could drink it without throwing up. There was a painter's palette of herbs and pastes that were equally repulsive whether they were topical or oral. There was one that went on the temples and burned like dry ice; Goody would see it coming with dread, but he wouldn't put up a fight. Roshi still scared the shit out of him, but Goody trusted him completely.

As he began to get stronger, they'd talk. When Goody said that his father's company had made screen doors, Roshi asked, "In a screen door, which is more important—the frame, the pattern of the screen, or the space in between the pattern?"

"I want to be a monk," was Goody's answer.

Roshi laughed, loud, boisterous, deep as though it came from the center of the earth. "*Not ready!*" he said. "*Answer phones! Good English!*" Then he left, for the first time in nearly a month. And Goody went to work for him.

There is no wisdom, and there is no attainment whatsoever.
Because there is nothing to be attained.

When Goody would ask again, and then again, to take formal training, Roshi would again and again deny him. "Not ready!" he'd repeat. "Too much attach!" He didn't have to say it, and Goody didn't have to ask: he meant Laura. "But how do I stop being attached?" Goody would ask. And invariably Roshi would just laugh again, and give him more work to do.

Because there is no obstruction he has no fear,
and he passes far beyond all confused imagination.

The bell rang; students came out of doorways, hurried across sidewalks and worn-down paths over lawns, threw balls at each other, shouted plans, laughed at jokes, popped soda cans and drank the sodas and threw the cans in trash bins, and went back inside into different buildings and hallways and classrooms as the bell rang a second time, and the doors closed behind them, and all was quiet again. Just more molecules: racing, exchanging, combining into different patterns. While Goody sat there, not there. They hadn't even noticed him.

Whoever can see this

No longer needs anything to attain.

He wasn't sure when the girl had joined him on the bench. Just that, at some point, he felt an added presence. He smelled wool, and peanuts, and sweaty shampoo. Then the girl put her hand over his and let it rest there—and the exchange of molecules, and the information they brought, caused Goody to open his eyes and look at her.

The girl smiled up at him. Goody smiled back. A micro tuft of dandelion drifted by. The girl let it dance, right in front of her nose, then whooshed out at it and watched it twirl away. There was nothing more beautiful than this.

"I h-have a s-s-sister," she said.

Goody looked down at her. Her feet swung back and forth under the bench.

"Sh-sh-she's in H-heaven," the girl added. "She l-l-looks just like mm-me."

She swung her feet some more. This time she scooted forward a little, experimentally, just enough to have them barely scrape the ground. "Her n-name is Liana. My d-d-dad is Daddy a-and m-my mother is Mama and my b-brother is A-An-Andy and m-my si-sister is Liana and I'm M-Molly. Liana died. It was raining, and she died."

She looked up at Goody earnestly. He was listening—with all the time in the world, and she could have as much of it as she wanted. No one had ever been this untiring with her.

A few feet behind them, Goody sensed something; molecules of tension and concern came his way. He breathed them in, exchanged them for molecules of comfort and reassurance, and sent them back. Behind him, after a moment, he sensed patience, and relief.

"It is not dark in heaven," the girl said. "And there are moons, and lots of stars." She squeezed Goody's hand, closing her eyes the whole way to see it all up near again. "And I waved goodbye to Liana, with both hands."

Then, when the image was complete, the girl looked up at him. "She's my sister," she reminded. And when Goody nodded his understanding, she smiled and beamed out rainbows at him.

"Molly?" came the voice behind them. "Sweetie?"

"Mama!"

The girl skipped off the bench and ran around behind it and hugged her mother tight. "I was worried about you," Laura said, planting kisses. "It's not good to run off like that."

"I'm sorry Mama," Molly said, and nuzzled her face in Laura's neck. She was fully in her embrace now, and life in the world was perfect.

Laura looked out over the top of Molly's head. Goody was standing by the bench. "Stewart," she said. "I just—thank you. Thank you."

Goody shook off that there was anything to be thanked for. "She looks just like you. I should have guessed."

And then Molly piped in, telling her mother all that had just happened, starting from back at that lady's house where she saw a squirrel out the window and it looked like it was hurt and so she went outside to help it—and how the squirrel would go under some leaves and she would come up to it really carefully but then it would scurry out and go under some more leaves, and how there were *lots* of little piles of leaves around and so she kept following it, from one little pile to another, knowing she wasn't supposed to touch it but happy just to be up so near to it that she was able to look and see—until the squirrel went up a tree and started jumping from branch to branch, and she wondered if maybe it wasn't hurt that badly after all.

And she told Laura how she didn't know where she was after that, and she started to get scared but that's when she saw this bench with a man sitting on it, and she thought she'd go over and ask him if he knew where the lady's house was—but when she got there, he looked like he was asleep, like he was sitting straight up asleep, and she didn't want to bother him so she just thought she'd sit there for a while until he woke up or until something else happened and then she'd know what she should do.

Laura listened, to every gushing word of it, astounded. "She used to stutter," she said. She looked at Goody. "Up until—I don't."

"I'm cold, Mama," Molly said.

Laura put her coat around the girl and said they should probably go inside. She looked over at Goody—as if they'd both been standing right here, just yesterday—as if Goody had always been here, was never not here, had never gone and thus had never returned. And yet he had gone, he had returned. *And how is Molly talking again?*

"No driver's license," they heard. Turning, they saw Pick leaning against a tree. Never with his eyes off Goody.

"No car," Goody said.

"And no credit cards."

Goody shook his head. "I get offers, though," he grinned. "All at attractive rates."

"And 'Shindo,'" Pick went on. "Is that a name, or a title—like Doctor, or Rabbi? Do we call you that?"

Goody grinned. "Call me 'Rabbi' and my mother'll die happy," he told them. And when Pick said that they'd tried Goody's mother and couldn't find her either, Goody said she was in Phoenix now, married to an osteopath.

"She took his name," Goody added. "Old school. She's Sylvia Hoffman now."

"Hoffman," Pick said, nodding as if now it all made sense. He looked at a loss over what to say next.

"We were over at the house," Laura jumped in. "Molly got away."

"I was following a squirrel, Daddy!"

"I heard that," Pick said. "We're lucky the squirrel didn't cross any streets." He looked at Laura, as if accusing her that the world had streets in it. As if accusing her of everything.

"Mama you said he'd be wearing robes," Molly asked. "Those are just clothes." She pointed to Goody's outfit: sneakers and corduroy, an aging fleece parka from LL Bean over a cable sweater that looked like it was hand-made by a girlfriend on a commune. Whatever else Goody had brought was bundled in a tired canvas satchel by his feet. Clearly fashion had remained unimportant to him over the years.

"We keep the robes at the *zendo*," Goody said to Molly. "Kind of like a church, except it's a big empty room. We wear the robes in there."

"Where's Andy?" Pick interrupted. As if all this normalcy was just too much right now.

"At the house," Laura replied. She gestured in the area of the Griffin house, to clarify.

Pick nodded. He looked at Laura and Goody. "Well then. Who wants to go first?" he asked. Casually, as though they might be choosing sides for a few friendly games of canasta. "The two of you? Me and him? Me and you? Or should we just all three of us go down to Bunty's and get cheeseburgers. We can talk about old times—first one who can look back on all this and laugh gets to eat for free."

Laura looked at Pick—as if she knew this wasn't him, it was the anger and the hurt that coiled around him like a snake that nothing could shake loose. She stood there with her arms draped around Molly. Ever protecting her.

"Buntyburger Supreme, hold the tomato," Goody said. "Bunty special with Swiss and mushrooms, and plain with extra pickles."

Molly looked up at Laura. "What's he talking about?"

"Bunty's," Laura told her. "He's talking about where we used to go and get cheeseburgers. When we were teenagers."

"He can remember that?" Molly asked.

Goody looked at her and smiled. Of course he remembered. He remembered everything.

42

The Bell Tower

Excerpt from the novel, by S.A. Goodman.
The Unveiling

The bus broke down ten miles outside of Hershey—too far to consider walking back. Everyone had to get off and wait in the frost, while Trailways scrambled a bunch of 12-seaters to come and get us—they said it would be under an hour, but nobody believed that. I already knew that I'd get to Harrisburg too late now to connect to the express bus back to Wilkes-Barre, and I'd end up on a local—that meant stopping off in two hundred scattered little towns nobody ever heard of, on narrow back roads that were never made for buses—and if you were asleep you got jolted awake with every pitch and roll, until the brakes finally stopped hissing and the driver swung the doors open and made his announcement about where we were. And in half of the places you stopped, there'd be no one getting off the bus anyway, and no one to pick up—yet you always had to go there, hell or high water, because the towns were on the schedule and you had to stop at every single one. It was the law.

On a good day the local took over five hours, once you connected in Harrisburg, while the express took two. That's three extra hours that I could have been with Laura—plus the one we'd lost already, which made four. Before the unveiling that day, before the cemetery, I had the goal of getting back up at school by dinnertime; now it was looking like a push just to get there before lights out, and even that might be hard to pull off.

Then when we did get to Harrisburg there was another delay. Something was going on that took up all the buses they had on hand—they never really said what it was—and everybody traveling north had to wait for two more replacement buses to show up from Pittsburgh, where there was a late season ice storm which they said was moving our way. That could mean midnight—if we were lucky—and then I wouldn't be seeing Laura until morning. And face it, we hadn't been all that lucky up till now, so things didn't look real rosy at that point.

I didn't like connecting in Harrisburg—it wasn't like Hershey, where you could wait at the counter in the drugstore if the weather was bad, or outside under this huge old sycamore tree if it was nice. The drug store was on Chocolate Avenue, and that's where the Trailways picked you up. It was actually and officially called that— Chocolate Avenue—though no one I told this to at school would ever believe me. And if they didn't swallow that, there was no use telling them that the other main street was named Cocoa, and that the streetlights in town were in the shape of big foil Kisses, complete with the white wavy label that stuck out that said HERSHEY *on it. That was the kind of thing people had to see for themselves, so they wouldn't think you were just making shit up.*

Inside the store I bought two bricks of Hershey's Original to take up to school. Five-pound chunks of solid milk chocolate, one with and one without almonds, that came right from the factory and that they only sold at the main drugstore there and nowhere else in the world. One I would split into thirds, with Laura and Pick, and the one with the almonds would go to the Griffins, because a five-pound hunk of chocolate wasn't something they would ever get for themselves—even if the company started selling them in stores all over the place. Even at a discount.

The weekend itself was horrible; the unveiling was even worse. Everybody went out to the cemetery, where my dad's headstone was covered up in burlap, and we stood around forever while the rabbi had all these remarks to make, and the cantor sang a long trail of prayers—as though he had to stretch out every ancient syllable for as long as it could go, so the people who were sad enough already could feel even worse. And the ones who weren't quite with it yet could pick up some speed and get in sync with everyone else.

I used the time to calculate bus schedules—the only actual prayers I said at the service had to do with Please Make This Thing Be Over, so we could go back to the house and do that part, and then someone could drop me off at the drugstore, so I could get the soonest bus I could and finally go see Laura. Not one of them understood what it was like not to be able to see her—none of them understood the ache all over, that only got better when she was around. They would have laughed at me—condescending, patronizing, telling me it was impossible to love like that while I was still so young. And what they didn't say to my face they would whisper to each other, worried about me. "Poor kid," they'd say. "Says he knows what love is. Just wait till he really finds out . . ."

The service peaked when they took the burlap off—and everybody who wasn't crying up to that point got a royal invitation. With a flourish that seemed just evil to me, the rabbi pulled the string—and like a sorcerer's cape the whole thing dropped away, and there was the word GOODMAN, chiseled deep in speckled granite. There was my father's name, and there was my father buried underneath it—but the thing I noticed, that I wished to God my eye could've skipped, was that the grave itself was off center, and didn't line up with the headstone at all. Plainly someone had made a mistake—but I couldn't point it out while the cantor was singing, and while all those people were crying. And I couldn't bring it up back at the house because that would be too cold, too rude, to get everyone started again when they were only just beginning to calm down.

So I did what my dad used to tell me: that before you open your mouth to ask a question, you should open your eyes and your ears first—because that's how you teach yourself to learn things. Observe, and notice whatever you can. Don't make snap judgments, but come to your own conclusions and test them. And of course, if you really tried hard and got nowhere with it, you should never be afraid to ask—only now he wasn't around to answer, and there wasn't anybody else I wanted to bring it up with.

It was when the bus got to Pottsville, three hours out of Harrisburg with two more long ones to go, that I figured it out. The bus stop was on the central street going through town—but before you got there, there was a brand new development on the outskirts where a whole bunch of modular houses were being built. I always took a head count at this point, guessing how many more houses there'd be, compared to the last time I missed the express and found myself here.

This trip, the big sign of progress was a long row of brand new mailboxes—rural boxes, all lined up next to each other, on wooden posts driven into the ground. But they weren't finished being installed yet, so only about a third of the posts had mailboxes on them, and the rest were headless and bare and waiting. And that's when I put it together about the cemetery, and why my father wasn't centered like he should be—it was because he wasn't going to be the only one there, just the first one—and eventually, my mom would be there, and then eventually me. I had just spent the better part of the morning, standing at my own future grave.

It sent me over the edge, realizing that, and suddenly my throat and chest and head hurt like vise grips and I couldn't breathe and I was on the bus crying and gulping for air to the point where they had to take me off, and call someone from home once they got a name out of me—any name, of anyone who could be responsible and who could drive up and get me, while they covered me with a blanket and gave me some soup from a beat up thermos with Johnny Cash on it, that the lady running the magazine stand had brought from home for her dinner. I didn't want it, I didn't want to take it from her, but she insisted, she'd 'call my Carl' and he'd show up with more, it was no big deal. There was always more soup, they told me—it was a cold day in Pottsville and every stove in town had a family-size kettle going. I knew that was meant to be soothing, but it only set me off crying even more, and then I couldn't breathe again. My dad was dead and one day my mom would be too and so would I and we would all be dead together, and living right there. Soup and Johnny Cash would never change that.

Meanwhile the bus had gone ahead now, with my other clothes and schoolbooks still on board, and the two bricks of chocolate—and now I had no choice, I'd have to sit there and wait for my Uncle Jacob to come up, so he could bring me down to Hershey—not back to school because they would have all discussed it and concluded that Stewart Needed Rest—they were convinced about this, I was having some kind of a breakdown. A delayed reaction to my father's death and now I needed help. They would have decided that school could wait, but now it was time for some serious attention—the last thing I wanted.

My uncle coming to get me was a doctor. My mother's older brother, and he'd be bringing some valium along, like he did over the summer while we had breakfast before the funeral—he passed them out like M&M's back then, so the family could all get through the ordeal. Just to take the edge off, he told us, giving everyone each their own pink pill with half of one to Yours Truly, who kept his eye on every move of that bottle, before I snagged the whole thing. Then we all put our clothes on and got into town cars that smelled like spoiled cologne, and people drove us to the cemetery where we sat through the service like ghosts, watching Eli Gershon Goodman get lowered into the ground—right before Eli's son Stewart disappeared, and medicated himself through three days and nights at the Turkey Hill Turnpike Inn, using cash I stole from a half-dozen pocketbooks, right after I lifted those pills. It was easy to slip away; in their grief and distraction, everybody just assumed I'd gone home in someone else's car.

I knew there'd be valium again this time, or whatever my uncle had in his arsenal that would tranquilize me, and keep me in bed so they could all fret over me until I got better, only by their definition and not mine. They'd set me up with Dr. Herman, so I could talk about my problems. I could see right away where all this was going, and I wanted no part of it—my problem was that I wanted to get to school, damn it, and not back to Hershey. My problem was my dad was dead—really dead, it was almost a year now and you can't make up stories to yourself about this being just another business trip because nobody goes on business trips that last for ten months. He was dead, and so would I be and so would we all and I wanted to see Laura and it had already taken much too long now and there was no way they were dragging me back home and keeping me there for days, which could be weeks or even longer, long enough for them to call off all this boarding school business. You didn't have to be a genius to know ahead that this would be their plan, and the only thing I knew I could do to stop it was to not be in Pottsville when my uncle showed up.

I finished the soup and told them I wanted to call home again, and then I left the blanket on the bus station bench and called a cab instead—and when the cab came I slipped out the door and asked the driver to take me to whatever the next town was that had bus service, which turned out to be Reisterstown, another local and Greyhound this time, with a layover in Hazleton—which would put me in Wilkes-Barre around one in the morning and I'd have to walk across the bridge and all the way down Memorial to the school, because there wouldn't be any cabs at that time of night—and even if there were, there'd be no money left to pay with because I'd spent what I had on this one.

But the Top Story here was this: I wasn't going home. I was going to see Laura, and nothing was going to stop me. Not my mom, not Uncle Jacob with his tranquilizers, not Dr. Herman so we could talk about things. Laura was who I needed, and if nothing else went wrong I'd be there in the morning. I sat in the cab and thought about that, while we came down the last hill into Reisterstown. I would see the girl I loved when the sun came up. Throw a pebble at her window to get her attention. Throw a hundred if the first ninety-nine didn't do it.

Then I decided I should probably try and get some sleep. There was a lot coming up, and I'd want my wits. I was glad I'd had that soup, I thought—it'd have to last me for a while now. Those were nice people back there. Way to go Pottsville.

43

Mary

She stood in the doorway behind Goody and watched him. This wasn't like anyone else who'd come in to examine Henry since his stroke—efficient but sealed off, like scientists constantly checking data. Only this data was her husband. They'd shine a light in his eyes but never see his face.

"Is it strange to be here again?" she asked him.

"In every way," Goody told her, and she was relieved to see him grin when he said it. She didn't want this to be painful, for anyone.

She watched Goody's hands; starting at Henry's feet and working their way up, he'd either press or probe or give a little massage at each place he stopped. Pressure points, he told her. Meridians. Just like arteries and veins. They were mapped out ages ago—thousands of years—and Goody was tracing them, like highways, up and down and across Henry's body.

"I like this," Mary pronounced. "He's gone from being a pin cushion to a Ouija Board. It's an improvement."

"Ouija Boards," Goody said. "I forgot all about those." He paused his hands, and looked at her. "You want to know if he'll ask you to the prom?"

Mary laughed. How good did that feel. A most unexpected gift. And damn if she didn't sense something shift just then. Or thought she felt a shift—or wanted to feel a shift so badly that she conjured one up all the same. Which, when she thought about it, was in fact an actual shift. Wasn't it?

Goody asked if he could look at Griffin's tongue; Mary told him he could, and just had to trust there was a reason why, since no other doctor did that. Then he asked her to come closer, and when she did he showed her how to massage her husband's ears, guiding her hands to the right spots and pressing just so. She forgot what he said it stimulated, but she liked the idea of doing it, and when he showed her how to do the same with his feet, she eagerly took that on as well. Moves the *chi*, he told her. The animating force of the universe. It doesn't like to stay still. He said she could do these things as often and for as long as she wanted. Keep those pathways open. And Mary thought, why not?

Why not.

"There's something I need to tell you, Stewart. Unless now's not the—"

Goody turned, looked over his shoulder. "Sure," he said.

She thought about it one more time. Nodded to herself. "The morning you left," she said eventually. "I was here."

She pointed behind her, out towards the hallway, towards the front of the house. "I'd been up in the night with a headache. I was coming down the steps to get something for it, when I heard this commotion outside. I saw you with that duffel bag. I saw them following, and arguing, I saw Laura crying and Sandy caught between you. I couldn't hear anything over the rain."

They both agreed, it wasn't just rain that day. It was biblical.

"What I think about," Mary went on, "every time I go back to that—is how I never really thought you would step off that curb and keep going. And that even when you did, and I could have done something—I didn't."

Goody told her it was okay, that he didn't think he'd do it either, that he only went ahead because it scared him more to think about going back. But to keep going was scary too, and he had been considering turning around when he saw the lights ahead, the taillights of the VW with the monks in it. And that seeing how messed up he was, and hungry, they pulled over at the first exit that had food and ended up at an International House of Pancakes—that they'd never been to one before seemed pretty clear, and they enjoyed it thoroughly, Goody said; laminated menus, pictures of pancakes stacked high as their faces, four kinds of syrup when they'd never seen any until just then. They went crazy over that stuff, Goody told her. He described their sense of real delight, in the smallest things.

Mary marveled at how simple he had made it all sound: Buddhist monks, taking a soaked and frightened boy out for breakfast, and all the things after that came from that. We have such a loose hold, she thought; what we think are our choices might be nothing more than gigantic detours away from ourselves. And what we think are our detours, might have been the real path all along. Scared, lonely, completely torn apart, at an interstate rest stop with strangers, miles from home—and in that episode was the origin of what was happening here, right now. And all of it because a bus broke down in Hershey. When Goody couldn't get back to school until late.

None of this was a detour, Mary thought. *And there was no good or bad about it—it was just this way, and this was why. It all had to happen so that all of it could happen.*

She remembered her seventh-grade science teacher, Mr. Vogler. He told the class once, that if you go far enough fast enough, you can catch up with things that were said even hundreds of years ago—the Gettysburg Address was the example he used. That fascinated Mary; she tried to picture the rocket ship that could take her to hear Lincoln. Next stop, the Sermon on the Mount. And on the way back, what the heck—stop off and catch *West Side Story*, opening night on Broadway. Sharks and Jets and Officer Krupke. Bernstein takes his ovation; the papers rave.

Or leave all that to history, and just take me back to hear Henry say, "I do" again. And again, and again. Forever and ever, our wedding day.

When he was finished, Goody came out and asked if there was a room he could go to privately. Mary said there was a bedroom on the third floor that nobody used, and except that it might be chilly up there, he was free to use it. Also, if he wanted to, he was welcome to stay at the house overnight, or for as long as he needed; she knew he wouldn't have the kind of money for hotels. And even if he did, even if he could get rich as a sheik at all this, he wouldn't keep any of the money for himself. As far as Mary knew, he never did.

Meantime, her house was alive: the kids were in one room watching TV, Goody was up on the third floor in the shower, while Pick and Laura would drift from TV room to kitchen to the front living room. And with all this activity, Mary had the never-before sense of having a bustling family in a house that was designed for it, but hadn't been put to the test; it actually seemed to be happy to have the chance. Her house could strut now.

If only Henry. If only Henry.

If only.

44

Pick

They were down in the Griffins' basement, waiting for Goody's clothes to finish in the dryer. A kid next to him on the bus had thrown up on Goody's original outfit, which he'd changed out of and stuffed into a plastic bag, and now it just made sense to clean everything and start from scratch.

"I gotta admit," Pick said, "I thought you'd be talking like Yoda. All wise and all. It's a relief."

Goody shook his head. "They don't teach you that stuff until you're fifty," he told him. "Otherwise it's just silly."

Pick looked at him. It was a Goody thing to say. Whatever had gone on, monk-wise, it was still Goody in there. Part of that was reassuring, and part felt like a threat.

"He's sick, man," Pick said. "He's really fuckin' sick."

The tips of Goody's hair were still wet from the shower. He was wearing a borrowed bathrobe that Chip had gotten last Christmas, from an aunt who clearly didn't know him at all. He looked strong, but not muscular—as if the total amount of strength he had was spread out evenly from head to toe, where he had access to all of it at any time. Solid, yet entirely flexible.

"Mary said you were doing some kinda hocus-pocus shit, checking him out. I didn't know you were a doctor too."

"Not a doctor," Goody specified, though the way he said it made Pick think that in some shape or form, he probably really was. He'd gotten training, he explained, in a lot of different areas—'a little of this and a little of that,' he called it— although it sounded to Pick like a lot more than a little, whatever it was. Goody said he'd seen some of his teachers do things you wouldn't believe if you weren't standing right there yourself. Things that can take your whole life to learn.

"So what's your diagnosis?" Pick asked.

Goody shrugged, and looked at him. "He's really fuckin' sick," he concurred.

"Jesus," Pick said.

"Yeah."

There were footsteps on the ceiling above them—the bend and creak of different floorboards, the kind of sounds people will memorize when they've lived in a place long enough. There was lots of crossing, this way and that—then people settled in again up there, and the house went still. Where for Pick, being still and doing nothing came about as naturally as chewing through aluminum.

"So, help me out here?" he asked.

"Okay," Goody agreed.

Pick looked over at him. "You go to this place out in Oregon. You write that damn book there, suddenly it's going to be a movie so you're down in LA, and then suddenly it isn't and you're gone. You end up on a mountain in Japan for a couple years, you travel the world with this guy and now you're in Delaware, teaching meditation to college kids." Pick tried to picture Andy, the future Andy, heading off to college at five figures a year, so someone like Goody could show him how to sit still and count his breathing. "I'm saying, it doesn't add up."

"Does it have to add up?" Goody asked.

"Yeah," Pick said. "It does. In my world things have to add up. It's like with accountants—at the end of the day, the column on the left has to match the column on the right. Otherwise you're fucked."

Goody nodded, looking thoughtful, again in a way that both reassured and agitated Pick. "So, let's add things up," he offered.

Pick checked to see if the offer was legit. "How'd you get to Delaware?" he asked. "Let's start with that."

"Tokyo to Chicago," Goody recalled. "Chicago to Philadelphia, and someone picked me up."

"Fuck you," Pick said. "You don't get to be funny yet. I need to know."

Goody nodded. "The guy who started the Zen center at the school was one of Roshi's first students when he came to the States. When he retired, Roshi sent me."

"So, you went."

Again Goody nodded.

"Can you leave if you want?"

"I can. I might."

Pick didn't like the sound of that. Having barely absorbed what he'd learned about Goody's current situation, he was also not at all ready for it to turn into something else. Truth be told, he'd been surprised to learn that Goody wasn't up to much grander things with his life—as if, by design, he was meant for a hell of a lot more than the small potatoes world of a college town. More likely—by a lot—was that Goody was not under-achieving but under-reporting, and that running that center was the least of what he was up to. That made much better sense. Which made it more unnerving.

"Ever think of it yourself?" Goody asked.

Leaving the business, he meant. Leaving the law. Or, maybe, more than that. "Too much at stake," Pick told him. "Too much to unravel."

Goody grinned, softly. "*Too much attach!*" he said—a phrase he told Pick was a favorite of Roshi's; that his teacher's guiding philosophy was that every care in life could be summed up in those three words. There were volumes and volumes of text, going back millennia, all pretty much saying just that.

"You just had a big case happen," he said. "Did I hear that right?"

Pick nodded. "Fuckin' surgeon. Gets electrocuted by a peanut butter machine. People came from all over the world to get operated on by this guy. He was the best." He shook his head; the dreadful absurdity, the wrongness of it all. "Now he gets to give lectures. Or just cash out and buy an island. And buy his own jet to fly there. What he can't do is operate."

"Peanut butter," Goody said.

"Can you fuckin' believe it," Pick confirmed.

They looked through the porthole of the dryer; Goody's clothes thrashing in there. Pick had an urge right then, to just fuck it all and open up—no editing, just let it spill. To tell Goody how mad at him he was, but also how much he missed him, dammit, how much it sucked to not have a friend like him anymore, how much it sucked to have had things end so badly, to have had so much time go by. That he was sorry for the shit he did, that he still thought Goody should be sorry for the shit *he* did—none of that had changed.

But Mary was right. He missed him. Bottom line.

The dryer buzzed. Pick watched Goody go over and get his clothes out; watching him fold, Pick heard Carmine's voice inside him, criticizing Goody's technique.

"You were ninety miles away, man."

Goody stopped. Something had been building and now here it was.

"I mean I know, all right?" Pick continued. "You tried a long time ago, and I didn't take your calls. You were about to splash my life in public again, only in cinerama this time, and I wasn't feeling all soft and gooey. But for Christ's sake, Goody. You're gone without a word—the last four years you're right down the frickin' Jersey Turnpike, and we don't know it. Alive or dead, we don't know. You know what that's like?"

"I thought it was best to stay out of your way," Goody explained. "I thought I owed you that."

"But you were never out of the way," Pick corrected. "Not for a minute—not knowing where you were made you never out of the way. That was the problem."

It was the first time Pick had said, out loud, that there was a problem. The words like they'd been fired off a battleship. He and Laura had a problem. There it was. Right away, he regretted revealing it. Right away.

"I'll go change now," Goody said. He went over to where a shower curtain had been hung, to screen off a small utility bathroom. Pick watched him slip inside and pull the curtain closed behind him.

45

Chip

He ran it all by Randy first. They were in the parking lot next to maintenance, on a golf cart that the buildings and grounds guys always drove around. In the winter they kept it parked over where the laundry vents were, so the thing wouldn't be so cold every time they needed to use it. It suddenly reminded Chip of Cindi's convertible, out there with the top down and the heat on like that. A brand new memory, and a good one.

"Here's the part I don't get," Randy said.

"What?"

Randy shrugged. "Situation like this," he wondered. "Disciplinary, you know? The chain of command. Your dad'd be the one to get into it."

"I know," Chip said.

They gave it a little more thought. "Neat problem, though—kicking your own kid out of school?"

Chip agreed. "Especially when you can't even wake up."

They chewed on that point, and talked about it some more. After a few minutes they got off the cart and started throwing a football around, that Randy had brought along. They had only thrown a ball between them a million times like this. Any ball, any season—whether there was importance to discuss, or nothing at all.

"You tell your mom yet?"

Chip shook his head. "There's always someone around."

"Well when's a good time anyway?" Randy wondered, and you couldn't argue that: there would never be a good time to do this. When you could pick your moment, you did—and when you couldn't, you went with the best that was available. And when nothing good was available, sometimes Mother Nature would step in and create the situation for you—a flood, a fire, a crisis of health—and the best you could do was just assume, somehow, that this was all for your own good. Just like regular mothers; your own good almost never felt like it.

They were on the way back to Chip's house when Randy begged off. He saw Janet Pardini coming out of the library, and no way did he have the energy to run into her right then. "Long story," he told Chip, although he didn't have to. Then he darted behind a holly hedge until he could make it past the chapel, and then he'd be free. While Chip—because there was nowhere else to go now—went home.

"What do you mean, you might get suspended?" Mary asked him. "From the school or from the team?"

"I think they want to do both—but they don't know how to do it."

"I don't think they *can* do that. Your father's the one who does that."

"That's what I mean."

Mary thought a minute. It felt like shaking flies in her head. "Well what did you do?"

Chip stopped, thought about what to say. His mind was all twisted up. All he knew was that there was way too much going on, and that he wanted the whole world to just stop, even for a second, so everyone would have a chance to catch their breath and try to make sense out of things. He wanted everything to drop into place and settle there, and be quiet. He craved that moment, however brief, of pure completion. *Ashes, ashes, all fall down.*

"Chip?" his mother asked. He looked up at her, trying again to sort it all out and think of what to say. He could have started with Ellie, and Vanderlip, and Foster Devlin; he could have thrown in Randy, and Cindi Lindberg, and carpenter shorts and chenille, or Piccolo and Goodman and hospitals and strokes and doctors, and yearbooks in the library and tripping over shoes in a closet, or maybe the nurses in his house and his black and blue father who'd run out of places for them to take blood samples.

But all that came to him was a nursery rhyme. Where children, linked together, would go in circles until they were blurry, then stop on a heartbeat and drop down in place—queasy and jumbled and bursting with excitement, for no other reason than they had just, collectively, all fallen down. Because that was the way the game was played.

Ashes, ashes, Chip thought. But he couldn't tell his mother that—he couldn't tell her any of it. When even one word, he knew, could bust open the floodgates; once that happened, he might not be able to stop. And if that was the case, he couldn't afford to start.

So he buried his head and said nothing.

46

Goody

Excerpt from National Public Radio, August, 1989.

*N*PR's *Eugenia Griggs talks to Shindo Stewart Goodman, a protégé of Hataka Sudo Roshi, the revered Zen master who was one of the first to bring the Rinzai tradition to America. Shindo Stewart received his ordination in Japan directly from Sudo Roshi, and has just arrived in the States, where he's currently giving a series of talks up and down the east coast, prior to taking up a residency at the University of Delaware. We caught up with him in Philadelphia. He was kind enough to sit for a short interview, before leaving for Norfolk, for his talk the next day.*

Eugenia Griggs: First of all—is "protégé" the right word?

Shindo Stewart: (laughs) Definitely not!

Eugenia Griggs: Is there something more accurate? You worked very closely with him, for years.

Shindo Stewart: As his student, yes. If I thought I was his protégé, it would mean I'd learned nothing.

Eugenia Griggs: Moving on then. Your talk tonight was packed. And it was a very varied audience—some I spoke to were brand new and curious, and others were there specifically to hear you. Common to all of them though, was this sense of hunger. A restlessness. Is that what you're finding too?

Shindo Stewart: That's a pretty good description. When everything's working, we don't go looking for what it all means.

Eugenia Griggs: But sooner or later, something changes.

Shindo Stewart: Sooner or later everything changes. That's where we start.

Eugenia Griggs: The law of impermanence.

Shindo Stewart: Can't escape it.

Eugenia Griggs: We want a sense of control . . .

Shindo Stewart: And it's not going to happen. We will never control events. The best we can do is manage our response. That's what a lot of this is about. Day in and day out.

Eugenia Griggs: I wrote in my notes: "The Buddha taught that the cause of all suffering, is grasping. And the cure for all suffering is to let go of grasping."

Shindo Stewart: It's the difference between wanting something and having to have it. Everybody has desires, we're human. But then when something we want becomes something we have to have . . . that's where we get caught. We start doing things.

Eugenia Griggs: You told a personal story. Someone you wanted in your life very badly.

Shindo Stewart: More than you can imagine.

Eugenia Griggs: And when it didn't turn out the way you wanted—

Shindo Stewart: Repeatedly. When it repeatedly didn't turn out—

Eugenia Griggs:—when it repeatedly didn't turn out. Your life went into a tailspin.

Shindo Stewart: Again—more than you can imagine.

Eugenia Griggs: And what about now? You've trained with some of the great masters. You're a teacher yourself. Have you been able to get over her? Is there hope for the rest of us, who need to learn to let go?

Shindo Stewart: Of course, there's hope. There's always hope. And, yes—I've let go of the grasping on that one.

Eugenia Griggs: But the wanting. Have you gotten over that?

Shindo Stewart: Well. We're all a work in progress, aren't we?

47

Pick

"Fuckin' cold," he said. "Fuckin' mountain cold."

They were headed down Memorial, toward the river, where Pick had left his car. It was Pick's idea—not so much from feeling amiable, as wanting to put off seeing Laura and Goody in the same room together, for as long as he could. That wouldn't work forever, Pick knew—but for now, he and Goody were out of the house, and Laura was back there in it. He'd take care of later when it came.

He jammed his hands deep in his coat, as far down as he could get them. "I forgot how quick it happens around here."

Goody agreed. This valley was just plain harsh.

They walked past a firehouse that had doubled in size since last time. Past a drive-up photo kiosk that they'd had to hide behind once, on the way back from sneaking into a jazz club, when they were smoking a joint and saw a police car coming. It was October then too, Pick remembered—just like now. He remembered a time in winter when he and Goody made it the whole way to the bridge from here, kicking the same chunk of ice back and forth like a hockey puck. The thing started out about the size of a grapefruit and ended up smaller than a quarter. But they made it the whole way—they felt like champions.

"So, what'd you do back there?" he asked Goody.

"Where?"

"Before, on that bench, with Molly. What'd you do?"

Goody thought about it. "I didn't do anything," he said.

"Come on. A girl with a major stuttering problem plops down next to you, few minutes later she gets up only now there's no problem anymore. You're gonna tell me that just happens?"

"Sometimes," Goody told him. "Sometimes it just happens."

"Or was there some kind of cosmic goofball mystical wizard shit going on."

Goody grinned. "Sometimes that happens too," he said.

Pick looked away. Across the street there was a used car lot with four cars on it; the rest was vacant gravel. There was a high post, with big sign on it, with removable letters like movie theaters have. "THE PIZZA PARTY IS CANCELLD," the sign said; Pick thought of cars going by, and kids getting all broken up over the news, and parents having to explain how these things happen sometimes, and it isn't fair, and maybe next time—in the history of parents saying that, Pick doubted that it ever made one single kid feel better. Nothing makes anything feel better when something you've been hoping for gets taken from you.

Plus. Guys. Spell the fucking sign right. Set an example for Christ's sake.

"She tell you about her sister?" he asked.

"Only the part you heard," Goody told him.

This was not technically the first time Pick had spoken up about Liana. The first was to a stranger, next to him on a flight to Milwaukee for a deposition he didn't think he might ever arrive at; crosswinds from a violent storm shook the plane around like a snow globe. Pick never got around to finishing the story on the flight anyway—like most of the other people aboard, he was too busy heaving. Come to think of it, he didn't feel all that differently this time.

"It was one of those freak things," he said eventually. He remembered that first night, back in the dorm, when Goody wouldn't talk about his dad; the memory bubbled up in him like tar from under his feet. "Molly woke us up one night and said Liana's throat closed up and she couldn't breathe. She was in the hospital for a week. They did everything—believe me, I was watching. But nothing worked. She had to die from it before they knew what it was that killed her."

He clenched his fist inside his pocket—a technique they taught in trial class, for concealing body language. He wished now that he hadn't gotten started on all this; thinking about Liana, about anything from back then, just ruined him.

"I gotta tell you man—it was fucked. You never want this. My worst fuckin' enemy, I wouldn't want them to lose their kid."

Goody nodded, sympathetically, but it wasn't the same sympathetic nod Pick was used to getting from everyone else. Not that their sentiments weren't sincere; people tried, and hard, yet all you saw was the trying. But something about Goody's sympathy rang true. You could feel how much he cared about you. He was the same that way with everyone. It was effortless and instinctive.

They got to Pick's car. Pick took his keys out but didn't open the door. "Where do they get that, anyway?" he asked. "Where does a kid come up with 'it's not dark in heaven?'"

Goody gave it some thought. "Maybe it's not," he offered.

"Not what?"

"Dark in heaven. Maybe it's bright, like she described it. Moons, and lots of stars." He looked at Pick. "That'd be a pretty good place to go."

Pick considered that. It would be great to believe what Goody had just told him. As of now though, as much as he might want to, he couldn't bring it off.

A sudden wind came up, blowing dust and grit. They heard the bell, from the campus—carried from roof to roof, bouncing off the shale and slate shingles until somehow the sound and its own repeat reached them at the same time. They listened like it was a sermon.

"You know, they used to say to us," Pick said. "About the school, about the history of everything. And how it was all supposed to mean something one day—Griffin especially, he'd say that one day we'd come back here and look at the bell tower or something and get all choked up about it. I swore I would never believe him."

"I remember that," Goody told him. "He said it a lot."

Pick shook his head. The last timbre of the bell had traveled past them now, and left them behind. "But he was right, you know? I gotta say the man was right. It calls you home ..."

He could actually feel something tangible when Goody looked over at him this time: it was empathic, like ribbons, banding out to protect him. Anchored in something substantial, and eternal, and true.

He wasn't ready for this. Not yet, not at all. He didn't know if he'd ever be.

48

Mary

They put their winter coats on and went outside. It was cold enough to see their breath while they talked, and from a distance those dioxide clouds could have made it look like they had gone out to sneak a cigarette together. *And wouldn't that be something,* Mary thought. *The Dean's wife and the valedictorian, lighting one up on the Dean's back steps. Just try and live it down.*

"I almost don't know where to start," Ellie said. "I mean—I really don't."

"How about you start with Chip. And what's been going on with you two. And, to the best of your knowledge—why."

"That's the tough part."

"Which part?"

"All of it. Everything you said."

"Well, that's what we're here for then, isn't it? The tough parts. How about you tell me whatever comes to you, and later we'll worry about what order to arrange things."

Ellie looked at her; it almost seemed easy this way. She started with July, with the visit Chip made, to Ellie's summer family home in Maine. And how Chip had hitchhiked there, even though he'd told his parents something else, and it took eleven different rides until he got up to Rockland, where the ferry to Vinalhaven was, and that Ellie hadn't known he was actually doing this until he came walking up her path and proved it to her.

"He didn't think you'd let him visit me if you knew he had no real way of getting there."

"That's correct. We wouldn't have let him go."

"And you also wouldn't have let him go if you knew my parents wouldn't be there, like he might have said they would."

"Actually, if I'm remembering this right, I would have just assumed they'd be there. I would have assumed that Chip wouldn't even think of asking if he knew that wouldn't be so."

She looked at Ellie; the girl's ears were beginning to glow red. "So now we have him hitchhiking up to Maine, to see you at your parents' summer home, at a time when you would have been there alone."

Ellie nodded.

"And what you two were doing, were things you can only do when there's no one else around."

Ellie knew that tone. It was a parent's tone. And she knew she'd been fooling herself if she thought this could play out any other way. "If it makes you feel any better, Mrs. Griffin, it was mutual. Everything that happened was mutual. I mean, Chip was a good guy about it. He didn't push anything on me. He would never do that."

"That's good to know," Mary said. "It's good to know my son is a gentleman. So how pregnant are you?"

The bluntness of that question slammed into Ellie like a blast of hard air. "I'm not," she replied.

Mary looked at her. "I'm sorry, Ellie. I must have missed something. See, when you start with an unannounced visit to an unsupervised home and my son who was a gentleman who didn't push anything on you, I just thought this whole story was leading to a certain inevitable conclusion. Plus, let's face it, I haven't heard the word 'protection' yet. So, forgive me. I shouldn't have leapt like that."

"But you were right," Ellie said. "I mean, I wish you weren't, but you were. That's what happened."

"You mean, in terms of you and he . . ."

Ellie nodded; *that* happened. Her ears were crimson by now. "And we did use protection. Just—not enough."

Mary looked at her. "Ellie, I'm confused. When I asked if you were pregnant, you said no. So I thought I could assume—"

Ellie shook her head. "I meant—now," she told her.

"Now what?"

"Now is when I'm not pregnant," Ellie said. "But I was."

49

The Bell Tower

Excerpt from the novel, by S. A. Goodman

The Sign Said West

"Sandy, he's leaving!"
"He's not leaving."
"Stop him!"

They tried to talk to me, but I couldn't say anything—I couldn't even look at them, not after what I saw when I opened that door: my empty bed, and two people in Pick's. I was already stuffing whatever I could grab into a duffel bag I'd brought up from home, that I bought at the Army-Navy surplus store last time I was back there. It had the name P. Valentine, USN *stenciled on and I liked to make up stories about who this P. Valentine was and where he had served, how many ports of call he had known. One thing was for sure, he had to know what it was like to ship out in a hurry—and I would be continuing that storied practice right here and now.*

"Will you listen?" they asked me. "Will you just stop for a minute and listen?"

I left the room, and the dorm and started walking down Foyle as fast as I could. They followed me out, but I had a good head start and I was determined not to slow down. And every time they got close to me I shook them off and kept going.

"Sandy, he's leaving!"

"He's not leaving, Laura. He's gonna blow off some steam and come back. Trust me."

I got to the end of Foyle, and stopped; they stopped too, a little bit back, in front of the Griffin house. The rain was falling in sheets now. I unzipped my duffel bag and took out a white gym towel. I covered my head with it, and waited to cross the street. Two identical Ford pickups went by, each with a dead deer in back, and then a van for the Methodist church, which I thought was just perfect.

"Come on," I heard Pick say to her. "We have to get inside. We're not supposed to be out here this early."

Then Laura said she didn't care. "Fuck The Rules," was how she put it, and I had never heard her use that word before. Pick tried to get her to go anyway. He offered an arm to support her, but Laura wouldn't have it; she was staying right where she was. "Laura, he has to come back. There's no way he's really going. Where's he gonna go?"

When the coast was clear I started across the street. They came as far as the corner and kept calling me, but it didn't matter. Nothing mattered. Nothing might ever matter again.

"Go ahead and run!" Pick yelled at me. "Just run away, you're good at it aren't you, you chickenshit!"

I stopped, and turned around, and looked at him. I meant to say something, anything back, but I had no words anymore. So I turned again and crossed the rest of the way. The rain was hitting like fists.

"Sandy, he's leaving!"

"Good. Then let him go." He called me chickenshit again, the last thing I ever heard him say.

On Memorial a milk truck stopped and gave me a ride all the way out to 81. When the driver let me off it was pouring even harder, flooding my eyes now, stinging my cheeks, and now I was coughing—bringing up so much phlegm and snot that it laid a slick the whole way along the arm of my jacket when I used the sleeve to wipe off my face.

I lifted up my duffel bag and shifted its weight. A trailer full of frozen tv dinners came by and splashed a tidal wave coming right at me, and there wasn't any avoiding it, so I just let it hit me and soak on through. I shook my head back and forth, like a dog after a bath. There was wet hair whipping across my eyes. My skin felt like it was burning.

"Stewart, will you listen?" Laura had said. But hadn't she said enough, just by being there? They had both said enough—more than enough, and then more than that.

I turned and saw up ahead where someone had pulled over and parked—a minibus, an old VW—strange, because I didn't remember seeing it pass by. Still I started running. Pulled forward towards those blinking red lights, where I imagined it might be warm inside. When I got closer I could tell it was pretty crowded in there. I hesitated, for a second; but all it took was the thought of the two of them, in that bed—the smell of wine, and sex, and deodorant spray, and those looks on their faces. My blood vessels pulsing like they wanted to break through my skin.

I let the duffel bag drop away, leaving it behind with everything in it so I could run that much faster. Sooner or later, somebody would find it and realize it didn't belong to P. Valentine USN anymore, and then they'd get the police. I thought about that, and decided I would call my mom, first chance I got; I didn't want anyone looking for me, didn't want her losing her mind over someone finding all my stuff on the side of a highway, then not being able to tell her where her son was. I had already put her through enough. No need to have her think I'd been kidnapped or anything.

What I'd do was get a good bit away first, far enough to mean it that I wasn't coming back. Then, if I could lay low for just another month, I'd be eighteen. Nothing they can do after that.

"Sandy, he's leaving!"

I said hi to the people inside, and thanks. I was surprised at how easygoing I sounded about it, like hitchhiking in a pounding April deluge was something I did all the time, just for kicks.

There were four of them, including the driver. All men, Asian men, wearing heavy dark robes, with shaved bald heads—each one smiling at me with expressions that gave me this oddball feeling that they knew everything I was going through, even though they couldn't possibly. I told them my name was Stewart, and they all nodded and said "Stewart" a couple times, like they were working out an unusual new sound. Then they were silent.

The driver reversed the van and drove backwards along the shoulder until we got to where my duffel was. One of the other guys up front went out and got it, and then they were off again. I thanked them, but they didn't answer. They just said "Stewart" again, and the van rolled along.

"Then he's crazy," Pick had told Laura. "Let him go."

And so she did; they both did. Either one of them could have stopped me, if they really wanted—they could have teamed up easily. But they didn't. Which told me everything.

I looked out the window, as they connected onto 80. The sign said West. And that was plenty, for now.

50

Laura

They followed the train tracks toward the levee on the Kirby side. Weeds and age and corrosion had taken over almost everywhere. Overhead there were geese, in a tight V formation, following the course of the river. "Kinda late for those," Laura said. "They're usually gone by now."

She watched Goody tracking the birds. Following along, staying with them, cocking his head—as if nothing else existed but those birds right now. "Everything all right?" she asked. Meaning, without saying it, how did things go with Pick before.

"He doesn't like the cold," Goody said, and Laura told him she knew what he meant.

"He's big on Hawaii," she said. "It's his pressure valve, to talk about going there. If he meant it, we'd go."

"Does he know that?"

"Hawaii? You kidding me? I'm the one who gets out the real estate ads."

Two college kids jogged past, talking about which fraternity Nietzsche would pledge if he went to their school. Their voices trailed off, with the sound of athletic shoes over mounds of packed wet leaves. To Laura there was something comforting, and intimate about that sound. Or maybe that's just the way she felt right now anyway, and a police chase through the park couldn't spoil this mood. She was relieved to find it this easy to be with Goody—so different, and so much the same. How many times had she thought about what it would be like just to walk somewhere together again? And talk, and listen, as if nothing had happened—or maybe as if everything had happened but it just didn't matter as much. Not enough to drive a stake into the three of them, the way it did.

"So," she said. "Delaware."

"The Blue Hens," Goody confirmed.

"Sorry?"

"That's what their teams are called," Goody told her. "The Fightin' Blue Hens."

"Oh," Laura said. She wrestled the impulse to reach for Goody's arm and link it up with hers. "Are blue hens especially good at fighting?"

"I'm not sure they're even good at being blue. I've never seen one."

Laura laughed. It felt like parts of her, returning. She could almost begin to understand how Molly could feel better, just being around him. Something about him unlocked you.

The college kids came back the other way—this time they noticed Goody, gave him a quizzical look, and pressed on; he entered their discussion for a while, and then they were gone again. He had that ability, Laura thought. Goody just had an effect on people; he didn't even have to try.

"That's where you told us about your book," Laura remembered. She pointed up ahead—there were some benches, under a familiar, but much taller, grove of pine trees. Everything else looked exactly the same. She could even call back the clothes they wore that day. Pick, unbuttoning his shirt. What Goody must have felt when Laura killed that roll of film while his best friend performed for her. "It wasn't the way things were supposed to happen, was it?"

Goody told her he wasn't so sure about that; that the way it happened might have been exactly the way it was supposed to. He talked about Joseph, from the Torah. How he thought his life was over when his brothers threw him in the pit—and then twenty years later, second only to the Pharaoh, he'd be able to save his family and his people from starving. So, lesson learned. Nobody ever knows. Things will connect in ways you can't imagine.

"I think about Malibu sometimes," Laura said. "About the day we spent there. I think about it a lot." She hesitated, wondering if she should go on; wondering about the Ten Good Scenarios— were they still in effect? Does he think about it all anymore? She knew he remembered—hell, if the guy could remember twelfth grade and what they had at Bunty's—but there was no window into how much it might even matter to him now. Unlike Pick, who might never leave this behind, and who wouldn't believe Goody would ever be able to either. "Can I ask you something?"

"Sure," Goody told her. "Of course."

Laura took a second. "After we saw each other that day. What happened there?"

Goody paused. "I went a little crazy," he told her. "And then I went away."

She watched him. "What kind of crazy?"

"Every kind of crazy," Goody answered. And they both knew, by the way that he said it, that nothing would be gained if he said any more.

They walked toward the grove, and they talked. About circularity, about the world of possibility, about how life can do the things that life does, regardless of who might be left standing, and where, when the day is finally done. They talked about hope, and regret, and the plans people make and what happens to them when life has other plans. Laura spoke freely, openly;

nothing censored, nothing held back. And Goody listened, with the same quiet attention, no matter what she said—same as he did with Molly, Laura thought—and she began to understand her daughter's experience, and the liberation that can come from speaking to someone who hears you.

Really hears you.

"He still doesn't know," Laura went on. "Sandy. I never told him. And I'm not just talking about Malibu—I haven't told him anything. I couldn't. And every day that I didn't turned into another day that made it even harder—I've had to falsify our entire lives together, just to keep us going." She snuck a look at Goody, expecting him to be disappointed in her—half as much, at least, as she was with herself. But he seemed to understand. That part of him had never changed.

"Anyway, what am I supposed to say to him? 'Oh, hi Honey, how was your day? By the way, we had a baby that you don't know about, and I gave it up and swore off all rights to it, including the right to tell you—so I've been keeping it a secret from you, against every impulse not to. I didn't go to college, I lost my parents over it, and I've only recently gotten them back—oh yes, and the daughter we lost? Now you know why—because she was the payment. Somewhere along the line I was going to have to pay for what I did. I knew that. And Liana was the bill. Payback, right? Cause and effect—isn't that like the textbook case?'"

Again, Goody told her you can't be too sure; there was always a bigger picture than the one we're seeing, and we shouldn't be too shocked to find out that we're not always in the center of it. And he smiled, gently, in just the way she needed. Not a flicker of the judgment she'd been ready to endure. Just Goody, still listening.

"I mean everybody goes through a lot, don't they?" she asked. "All you have to do is participate—get up in the morning and put in the time—and things are going to happen. Can't be helped. You drive a car, and the tires wear down. You drive a marriage . . ."

She thought back, years back, flipping calendar leaves in her head. "And I don't know where it turned," she concluded. "But somewhere, at some point, it did."

She considered that: life, turning. Being on the move and thinking you're watching and alert but then still losing your way somehow. Those crucial times, landmark occasions where the fork in the road is laid out in front of you, and you stand there knowing that the rest of everything is going to turn on whatever you do next. And then, if you're lucky, one day you might finally get it: that it's not that the road shouldn't have forks in it—but that it really shouldn't matter if you know where you're meant to go.

"Well then," she summed up. "That's how *my* life turned out—how's yours?"

Goody grinned. "I teach meditation to college kids," he told her. Like some kind of sly confession, and they laughed at the randomness and the weirdness and the rightness of that. It was only a fraction, Laura knew, of all that Goody did and all that he'd become; no one she'd ever known would lead with that, and leave out all the rest. No one.

They left the tracks and got off the roadbed. Goody offered his hand and Laura took it as they went down the embankment. And when they were back on level ground, when it was time to let go, Laura looked at Goody and didn't let go, and when Goody looked down at their hands and then back up at Laura, she kissed him. Surprising herself just as much as Goody, who looked like he was about to say something, but before he could, she stopped him and kissed him again—and soon they were past their surprise and pulling close, in the witness of those same taller trees, they held each other and kissed and held and kissed some more; eyes wide open so they could see, so they wouldn't miss this or mistake it, the sensations shooting up and down their bodies like lightning, embracing and encircling them both—until eventually, finally, the charge dissolved, the world came back, and here they were, standing in Kirby Park, aware of nothing else but who they were and the thing that had just happened between them right now.

"Whoa," Laura said.

They looked at each other. They heard sirens, heading down Memorial. Up above them, another squadron of geese. Their precision was amazing.

"Whoa," Laura said again. Knowing how inadequate that was. But it was all she could think of to say.

51

Mary

They stood at the same spot where Carmine had brought Pick earlier; cracked macadam and weeds and an old lawn chair.

"You like the Pontiac?" he asked.

Mary looked down at the lower lot, where she'd parked the car. "Henry likes it," she said. "His father had an old Bonneville. He makes sentimental choices sometimes."

"The father?"

Mary shook her head. "Henry. He'll only get a Pontiac. I'm not sure they're even built here anymore. All the steel's overseas now."

"Even so," Carmine said.

Mary nodded. "Even so."

Carmine nodded, agreeing. "Money doesn't carry a flag," he said.

"Excuse me?"

"Something Santamo said," Carmine explained. He filled her in on the exchange he'd had with Pick before. "Toyotas in Tennessee," he recalled. "I tried to tell him he was full of it. I'm not so sure he is."

"But you couldn't tell him that."

"Hell no," Carmine grinned, and Mary grinned back. The politics of being parents.

"I think it's funny almost, that we've never spoken," Mary said. "When you consider everything. This is not a metropolis here. And it's been a long time."

"All my dealings were with him," Carmine pointed out. Wistfully, almost, as if he'd enjoyed his times with Henry; no doubt Carmine's other transactions in life were less sanguine and lofty than those with a school dean, who could afford to deal in terms of principle and integrity.

"If he were here," Mary started, "if it were me with the stroke instead of him—I think he'd be doing the same thing."

"Coming to see me."

Mary nodded. "And to tell you he thinks it's time we had a talk about some things. To take a look at some decisions that were made, and see if they're still right for today."

She knew that Carmine knew what decisions she meant— and that they weren't really decisions, but conditions; Mary just didn't use the word.

"And to let go of this secret," she went on. "He'd want to tell you why he thinks it's time to do that now, and to ask you to agree."

Carmine looked out over the valley. "He asks for not easy things."

"Well he used to say that if you don't ask, then you know the answer's no. And even a one percent chance is still better than zero."

Carmine grinned; just to be reminded of Griffin seemed to have an effect on him. "And so you've come to tell me—"

"—that it's time," Mary interrupted.

That put Carmine back a little; he was used to being heard, all the way through.

"To tell you that I think that whatever value it had to keep this situation a secret, that value has expired, and now there's a new value in telling it. In letting go. I know Henry would think so, too, or he wouldn't have set all this in motion."

"And what's that new value?" Carmine wanted to know.

Mary took a breath; later she would consider whether she was being courageous right now, or outrageously naive. "You kept this information from your son when he was seventeen. He was a minor, and I know you had your reasons—but he's thirty-five now. He and Laura are married. They have children. He's been to college, and law school, he's got his own firm, he's taken on real dragons and beaten them. I think he can handle the news. I think he deserves to."

"You might be right," Carmine said, "if that was the only reason."

"His marriage has been strained by this," Mary added. "His family. A wife shouldn't have to keep secrets from her husband. The same as the other way around—you were married, did you keep secrets from your wife?"

"Every thing I did was a secret to her."

His look showed no choice in that, and Mary understood. This wasn't ever going to be a normal conversation, where two concerned parents meet and talk on common ground. "Well—all marriages are different, and I shouldn't have assumed. But as far as I'm concerned, to have a fundamental dishonesty built into a lifelong partnership doesn't help things."

"Except when you got people to protect."

Mary looked at him. A low-flying plane crossed the valley lengthwise. Then the nose pointed up and the plane went with it, almost straight up it seemed, until the thing went into a stall. Student pilot, she supposed. Practicing for calamity so you'll know what to do if it ever comes for real.

"If you want to tell Santamo about what happened back then, go ahead. Because you're right about that. If it'll help their family, if it'll help his life, he should know. But he still can't know the rest. Not where the boy went. Nobody can."

"Can I ask why not?"

"Same reason as always."

Mary paused, to let herself think. "I'm sorry, Mr. Piccolo. I don't see what reason there could be anymore. Chip's going to be eighteen. Henry might be dying. If he used that moment to call out for your son, I think we both know why."

"Doesn't matter," Carmine told her. "He still needs protection."

"From what?"

"Accidents." He was watching the plane too—it was doing about the worst job possible of going into a loop. The engine strained. Staccato bursts that sounded like gunfire. "Santamo cannot know. His wife can't know. Only you two. That's it."

Mary looked out where he was looking. She tried to imagine what it must have been like for Henry, the night this deal was made. And here was the other half of that, right now. She couldn't let him down. "I'm going to just go ahead and say this, Mr. Piccolo, and I hope it comes out all right. But—"

"You know that his mother died young. Santamo's mother."

"Well, yes. I mean of course. An accident, he told us."

Carmine turned from watching the plane, and looked at Mary; there was something in his face that made her teeth clatter. "People find out I have a grandson. I don't want more accidents."

Mary felt her color drain; he was telling her his wife had been killed. Because of him. And now it's Chip? Someone would hurt or kill her boy to get to Carmine Piccolo? This was his reason? "Is it all right if I sit down?" she asked.

Carmine apologized, and held on to the back of the lawn chair, as if he were seating her inside the restaurant and the wine list was about to come.

"Does he know?" she asked him. "Your son?"

Carmine shook his head; he hadn't, and wouldn't ever, tell Pick.

Mary couldn't argue, couldn't judge. She wanted to run straight home and protect Chip, right now and forever. Faster than any car could get her there. "But you already have—you have two grandchildren right now. They have the same last name. They have an address."

"You think I don't know that?" Carmine asked. "You think I sleep at night? Not once. Not one night through, since the day they were born."

"That's terrible," Mary said. "That's just—"

Carmine waved her down. "I got things in place," he told her. "But you never know. I can't be everywhere."

Mary knew—the wish to be everywhere. Like a falcon, circling high over the field of your children's lives. Ready to bullet down where there's danger and take out its eyes. But Mary also knew that she lived in a world where accidents were usually just that, and the numbers are still generally in your favor. And Carmine's world . . . she'd never considered what a prison it could be to be powerful. Now she knew otherwise.

"Ask you something?"

"Of course," Mary said. "Anything."

"Something about him. Tell me something about him."

The question surprised her. It was a grandfather question, and she supposed it was her own shortcoming not to ever let herself think of Carmine that way. He had taken himself out of the equation completely—at least visibly, she knew now— and that was for everyone's good. Mary knew, if the roles were switched, she'd never have the strength to stay away.

"Well he loves football," she started, "but he got suspended from the team. He loves his girlfriend, but she's been avoiding him for weeks, and today I found out why. He loves his father, but might never hear his voice again, and I guarantee he's panicked but he won't discuss it. So as far as I'm concerned, any day he doesn't rob a bank and fly off to Rio, that's a good day. I know I sure feel like it lately."

Carmine watched her; his admiration was plain, but so were its limits. "Anything I can do?"

"Only the thing you can't," Mary told him.

"But now you know why. The sins of the father. It's a shame."

"It is a shame," Mary agreed. "He could use a dad right now."

She politely turned down a glass of brandy before driving home. She felt drunk enough, just from what had happened, to be unsure of her driving. She let Carmine walk her to her car, and open the door for her and wait till she was in.

The plane made more sounds. A poorly executed turn, and again the throttling bursts. This was not a good day up there. "Some people shouldn't be pilots," Carmine pointed out. "Right there is one."

Mary, watching, completely agreed. Some things would never be the way you want them, some things would always be out of reach; it was just the way it was. She started the car, and drove down the hill. She thought about Henry, years ago, doing the same thing. About how he looked when he came into the house that night. About how she must look right now.

She thought about Chip, and the invisible hand that had been at it his whole life, protecting him from behind the scenes. About why she might never be able to tell him what she still thought he needed to know. She thought about how people carry around the things that they've done, and how the hardest things to carry are the ones you were given no choice but to hold—like curses from old stories, played on the unsuspecting, who might never see the larger scheme they were stumbling around in.

He could use a dad, she'd told Carmine. Well couldn't we all.

52

Pick

*H*e balanced the plastic tub insert around the rim of the kitchen sink. Laura held the baby while Pick ran the water to get it to just the right amount of warm. Then he took Andy from her—gingerly—more like he was defusing a bomb than giving an infant its first bath at home. Laura was still recovering from the hospital and wasn't allowed to lift anything; she could hold the baby, she could tickle and nurse him—but all of Andy's transport needs, for now and the near future, would have to be met by Pick. In and out of the crib, over and back to Laura, watching her coo and sing to him, and cradle him with affection. In and out of the stroller too, though that was just for practice; neither one of them was keen to take the boy outside just yet.

"Has it cooled off too much?" she asked, and Pick told her no, the water was maintaining its temperature, it was only slightly less warm than it was twenty seconds ago when he first lowered Andy in there. They knew they were overdoing the caution here. They knew they were falling into every cliché there was that covered newborn children and first-time parents. And they could honestly say, that they didn't care one bit.

"Look at him." Pick turned just enough to the side, while still holding Andy and supporting his head, so Laura would be able to see how well they were doing. The wet mat of baby hair, the skin all pink from attention, the droop of suds on a perfect ear lobe. Pick saw a spot of shampoo threatening Andy's eye, and got to it in plenty of time: just because the label said No Tears, was still no reason take chances. Watching him show such concern like this made Laura feel so warm and safe that she thought she might be the one getting the bath instead.

"He's amazing," Pick said, as if he hadn't been saying it every ten minutes since they first got Andy sprung from neonatal. He was holding him upright, taking in every detail like he was trying to memorize it all for a midterm exam. *"I would never have bet you could love something this much."*

"Well don't forget about me over here. Don't forget the fat lady."

"The fat lady? Come on."

"Okay I'm not fat. But I'm not Joanie Solomon either—Jake was born two days before Andy, and Joanie sailed out of that place looking like her tummy got tucked, and not just had a baby."

"Because she did. She did both."

"How do you know?"

"Joel told me, in the cafeteria. They'd discussed it ahead of time." He reached for a little hooded terrycloth, and put that around Andy's head and shoulders while he got him from the water over to the counter, where a bed of towels was waiting. Patting him dry, reaching all the creases, wrapping him snug back up the way the nurses had shown him at the hospital.

"I don't know when I'll be pretty again," Laura said.

"You're pretty now."

"I'm not Joanie Solomon."

"Who gives a damn about Joanie Solomon?"

"She's more your type."

"I don't have a type."

"Everyone has a type."

"They do? What's yours?"

"Mine is you."

"Well then mine is you, too."

Laura shook her head. "You can't use that answer."

"Why not? You just did."

"I have leeway."

Pick looked at her. He had Andy all cozied up now, warm in the towel, using his free hand to tip the plastic tub and drain the water out. He took the baby over to Laura, placed him in her arms just so, and watched her peel back enough of her robe to get him started nursing. Watching her take over like that, watching the two of them hit their groove, Pick felt like he ought to revise his observation from earlier, because now he already did love something more than he did just a few minutes ago.

"He's doing that like a champ," he said.

"Because he is one," Laura told him, in her nursing voice—the softest, quietest, most gentle sound Pick had ever heard. The curve of her breast a more beautiful sight than anything he could dream of.

"Someone I'm crazy about," Pick said, "who wants me to kiss her a lot."

"What?" Laura looked up at him. Pretty enough to melt Norway.

"My type," he reminded her. "You asked, and that's it. It covers everything."

"Anyone I know?" Laura asked.

"Hope so," Pick told her.

"Always?"

Pick nodded: always.

"Then kiss me," Laura said. "A lot."

And so he did.

He watched the bartender hunt down a container with some cream. Someone pulled the stool out next to him, when the place was almost empty. Pick turned, irritated, until he saw who it was. And the two guys with him, waiting by the door.

"Pop. What are you doing here?"

"I called up to your room," Carmine told him. "Then I checked the front desk. They said to try the bar."

Pick nodded. "I needed coffee." He nodded at an open case file on the bar. "Guy calls into the office. He spent the afternoon drinking fogcutters at his country club and then he went out and tripped over one of those ceramic lawn jockeys. Now he wants to sue the club. I told him to go fuck himself, I'd rather represent the lawn jockey."

"Tough guy."

"That's what you wanted, right?"

Carmine let that pass; he looked uncomfortable enough just being there. "So—Griffin. How's he doin'? How's the patient?"

"Not good. The guy from LA flew in. Didn't like it at all that we moved him to the house."

"What do they know."

"A lot, Pop. They know a lot. These guys aren't punks."

Carmine watched him. He looked at the notes Pick had spread out along the bar, along with the phone they were letting him use.

"What's the matter, you don't have your own? Big shot like you?"

"Andy took it. I'm gonna kill him for it later." He gave Carmine a look, as if to say, *Kids.* But then Pick remembered who he was talking to; his father knew less about kids than a goldfish would know about the Rose Parade. "I see you're still checking all the mirrors. Who's tailing you this time?"

"Don't worry about it."

Pick looked at him. He wondered what his own life would be like, having rivals like that. He knew he'd pissed a lot of people off—making enemies came with the job—but he never had to worry about starting the car in the morning. And if he wanted to go somewhere, by himself, he could.

"So Pop. This is important?"

"No. I came down here for my health. I wanted to see if they still had that drink named after me."

"The Carmine," Pick remembered. "Two shots and you're dead."

They went out and walked across the street, to some benches along the riverbank. The ground was hard, from a winter that wasn't even official yet; but the sun was still out, and the light felt good. Still, Carmine shifted uncomfortably. Usually he had no trouble starting a meeting—it wasn't like him not to jump right in.

"You shoulda been to the restaurant before," he said. "This couple a kids came in, turns out they were from the school."

"Pocono?" Pick asked.

Carmine nodded. "Guy came off all earnest and all, but the girl looked hot to trot—her old man and me did business together. Radio stations. Good solid guy."

He looked across the street; a bus went by with a full-size ad panel along the side, pushing the Ice Capades. "All that innocent shit," he said. "All that bein' young. Anyway, it got me thinking."

Pick looked at him. Not used to seeing his father in a reflective mood. Or hesitant, or the least bit unsure—especially with his people nearby. "What do you want, Pop. *Cosa vuoi.*"

Carmine tapped his foot. Another bus went by, going the other way—this one was selling ladies' maxi-pads. He shook his head, as if here was one more sign that the world he knew was gone—where things that a man like him would never see even in private, are now plastered along the side of a bus.

"Listen," he said. "Santamo."

"I'm listening."

"There's some things you don't know. I mean I know you know everything. But there's some things that you don't know."

"Like what?"

"First lemme ask you something."

"Shoot."

Carmine looked at him. "Tell me how you met your wife," he asked.

"What are you talking about? I met her in high school. What's this about?"

Carmine stopped him. "Not school. After that. How'd the two of you meet later on. How'd you get married. How'd that happen?"

"Jesus, Pop. This is a hell of a time to go dancing through the family album."

"You didn't tell me then. You weren't talkin' to me then. So tell me now."

Pick looked out over the water, an endless coffee-milk brown. The Indians called the Susquehanna "Muddy River;" nothing could describe it better. "She got sick or something and her parents pulled her out. I called her house a bunch of times, but they were all uptight about it. They wouldn't let me talk to her, or tell me where she was."

"So, how'd you meet her?"

"Five years later. At the school reunion. She came to the city with me after that."

Carmine thought about that. "She tell you what she did in the meantime? Those five years?"

"She was a waitress. Down off the Chesapeake somewhere."

Carmine nodded. "And in all this time you been married, you never asked her any more than that?"

Pick shook his head. "Let her have her life before then. The more I don't know, the more I don't have to forget."

"Interesting way to be lookin' at things."

"Hey Pop. Listen, you know? It's getting really cold out—and I hate the fuckin' cold, half the time I don't know what I'm doing not practicing law in Hawaii somewhere, where I wouldn't have to put up with this shit anymore."

"Try this, Counselor. Maybe her parents didn't tell you where she was because her parents didn't *know* where she was."

"Why not?"

"Use your fuckin' head, willya? Use your fuckin' head for a change. Why would a girl not finish school like that? Why would her parents not know where she was? But before you answer that, think about what happened before she left. Anything that comes to mind."

Pick thought about it. He looked down at the river. Used the current to slow his thinking.

"Pop."

"Merry fuckin' Christmas. The light goes on."

53

Mary

*H*enry came in late, looking spent. She thought that maybe something had gone wrong at the rehearsals, some detail about May Day that had been overlooked but might have brought the whole thing to a halt until someone could fix it. Every year there was something unique and untimely that always reared its head—best to anticipate, during these early stages, before all the families and guests arrived.

But this wasn't about May Day. He asked her to sit down. Something had come up, he said, and they needed to talk. He looked like someone who had just gotten back from the doctor, with grim news. And it was true, they'd been waiting for some test results—the latest in a long line—to see if they should try again, or just live with it and give up on ever having children of their own. But Henry said no, he hadn't been to the doctor, and that this was pretty late to be doing that anyway—certainly no doctor he knew kept hours at this time of night.

Instead, he said he'd just been to see Carmine Piccolo. And it was time to talk about being parents.

There were terms he needed to explain, he added—and they might not all be agreeable to her. But for his part, his mind was made *up; all she had to do was hear him out, and think it through. And if she agreed, then come next winter they'd be a family.*

February, he told her. Come February, they could have their baby.

Cops and soldiers, yes. Firefighters, race car drivers, mineworkers, bridge builders. They go out the door in the morning and you have it in your mind that they might not come back. Every day they challenge life, and every day their loved ones challenge death; willing it to keep its distance and not touch them. Not today and not ever.

Even though. Even though.

But schoolteachers? Deans of Students? There was no Widow's Walk for the wives of academics. They're suppossed to just come home. They're supposed to just walk in the door.

Mary Rangely met Henry Griffin when he came out to Cedar Rapids to interview for a teaching position. He didn't get the job, but he stayed around anyway, to be with her; he didn't want to court her by telephone, he'd said. If she wanted to know the truth, he preferred to fast-forward the whole courting process entirely, and skip on past it. To his relief, and Mary's own surprise, she agreed. So he found work in town and sent out applications, and waited. They got married, outside, by the Dewberrys' pond where Mary had skated as a girl; from there they started a life that was tempered with waiting. And finally, when a boarding school called from Pennsylvania and offered a classroom and a chance for advancement, Griffin put the phone on hold and asked his new wife if going that far from Iowa was okay with her. When Mary said yes, so did he. And he did advance, and they made the place their home.

And now here they were, taking him out of the house, where his footsteps might never again be heard. They were getting him ready. All the equipment and supplies that had been brought here, were being packed and put away. The back room would be converted back to what it was, and there wouldn't be nurses in the house; there'd be silence, and awfulness, the spoils of stolen time.

There would be Chip, but only till school's out—and maybe sooner than that—because you never know how a kid is going to take it when one more thing goes wrong. She knew that in Chip's wildest dreams he would never have guessed why all these forces had really been assembled like this, over miles and years, because of a few desperate syllables his father had forced himself to push through—just as she knew Chip's own best interests were caught between two impossible outcomes: the one where he needed to know what she wasn't allowed to tell him, and the one that could happen if she did. Because now she knew why.

She asked the crew to give her a moment alone with him. They all traded looks—*people, with their damn requests*—and then finally backed off. Mary closed the door as best as she could; there were equipment boxes in the way, and a stack of coiled cables. So she stepped back over it all and sat by his bed: wheels locked, patient strapped in, professionals outside waiting to get on with it.

"Henry," she said. "They're moving you out of here. They're taking you back to the hospital. The doctors think that's best."

She watched him to see if he'd blink. To see if he could do anything. "And I just want you to know, Henry, that people care about you. So many people. The whole school is concerned, and people have heard from everywhere, and they're still calling in. Stewart's here, and Sandy—and if your memory's still here, then you know. And Laura came, too. And Chip, of course, and Ellie—Ellie came to see me, Henry, and now I know the final piece. I know why you wanted them here. And now they're here and I'll do my best. You know that. You know I'll do my best."

The ambulance driver knocked, cleared his throat. Mary looked around at him and he left the room again. She sandwiched her husband's hand between hers. She leaned in close, until her face was right up along his.

"There hasn't been one single minute since the day we met that I haven't loved you. I have never known the word regret. And if you don't come out of it in this life," she kissed him, and touched his brow. "I'll see you in the next."

She stroked his forehead, kissed him again, and told the EMTs it was all clear to do their job now. She asked to slip past them and go on ahead, so she wouldn't have to see the empty room.

54

Laura

They walked past Geno's Pizza; endless Friday nights paraded before Laura's memory. How they'd sit at the same table, always, she and Goody across from Pick, watching Pick demonstrate the "authentic Italian method" of holding a slice in one hand and curling it just enough to have it fit into your mouth. How Pick was so horrified, in the beginning, to see the two of them jabbing at their pizza with a knife and fork and eating that way. Good thing he came along to save them, he'd say—nick of time, too. And then Goody would tell them about Jewish food; about kishkas, and kasha varnishkes, about how bagels and lox were just the beginning—the mere doorway to true Jewish eating. And they would argue, and laugh, and make bets. Laura would watch and love them. She shot rolls and rolls of film at Geno's.

You need to think about what you want. What you really want.

They had talked about it. They had actually talked about it. From the park to Geno's, and on toward the campus, she and Goody had talked about what they had just done, and what might happen now that it had happened. Laura knew what was at stake; scenes from her future played out like the preview of a movie. *Logistics, custody, lawyers.* Things you never want in your life were suddenly the only things on her mind.

Either we never do that again, he had said, *or we never stop.* The way it looked, the way it felt, when he said that. Was it true, or just exciting?

Think about what you want.

"I want to kiss you again," she told him. *Affidavits, alternating weekends, Daddy's two bedroom in the city.*

The way he grinned. "Anything else?"

The way she knew right away. "I want to feel like this."

The way that pleased him. "Anything else?" he grinned again.

"Everything else," Laura told him.

The way the grin turned thoughtful.

The way he said, "Okay."

Trading off at holidays. Summers with the new girlfriend. George and Alexandra, shaking their heads, yet again.

They were at the corner of Memorial and Foyle. Laura looked at Goody while they waited for the light to change. Rays of light broke through rainclouds and split off into multiple, heavenly shafts.

"I don't suppose you remember Heraclitus," Laura asked.

Goody looked at her. "Was he a day student, or boarding?" And from his grin, his easy grin, she knew he remembered. She told him about the quote she'd found, about how no man steps into the same river twice, and how she knew there was a second half to it, but she couldn't remember what it was and had neglected to write it down at the time.

"Because it's not the same river," Goody recalled. "And he's not the same man."

"That's it," Laura said. "That's what it was." She thought about it, now that she had both pieces of the quote. Through the filter of time and experience, grasping today what was out of her reach when she was younger. "Although he could have just said 'things change,'" she went on. "It wouldn't have killed him, and I might have done better in Western Civ."

"Philosophers," Goody told her.

"Philosophers," Laura agreed.

Sitting down with their teachers. There's been trouble at home, they might show changes, they might act out. Please have an extra look.

"Although he did kinda nail it," Laura had to admit. "And his way, it's a lot more poetic."

"That's why they got the big money," Goody guessed.

The bank accounts, the credit cards. Have to untangle.

They crossed the street and didn't say anything the rest of the way to the Griffins' house. They rang at the door, but no one came. "There ought to at least be a nurse," Laura said. "They were covered round the clock. Sandy made sure."

Goody stepped off the porch to have a look around. Laura knocked again. Realizing, standing there, that she'd been in this spot before; she was young, and it was night, and she was terrified. She was standing on the banks of the same damn river.

Moments don't repeat themselves, she thought. *But even if they do. Same river or not, you step in or you don't.*

A student rode past on a bicycle, hands-free, playing drumsticks on the handlebars. Laura flagged him down and asked him if he knew where the Griffins were. He said he didn't know but he thought he saw an ambulance before.

Laura thanked him, and they watched him ride away. For a while it seemed like all they could hear was the sound of those drumsticks—no cars, no conversations, not even their own thoughts. Then they saw Chip, racing down Foyle, his backpack whipping like a kite tail behind him as he ran like a streak toward home. Someone had tipped him off and he needed a ride to the hospital, he told them; he flew inside, flew back out with the keys to the Pontiac and lobbed them in the air between Goody and Laura. Laura caught them, and Chip led the way to the car.

We'll have to mediate. Can't let it go to the lawyers. If Sandy stays mad he'll destroy us all. Plus, he knows every lawyer in town. I'll be ground into chum.

The utter oddness of driving down Memorial, looking like any normal family, wasn't lost on Laura: she didn't live here, this wasn't her car, the man sitting next to her was not her husband, and the passenger in back had years on her own kids. He had gym socks as big as Molly's sweaters, and ate turkey sandwiches, with—among other things—maple syrup on them. Yet to the uninformed observer, here they were. A family car with a family in it.

We'll need to find a support group. Sandy won't have a choice this time. It's for the good of all, he'll see that. It's for the family.

"Don't you have your license yet?" she asked.

"No," Chip answered. Then, "I mean I know how to drive. I learned. But I never took the test. The insurance is pretty bad."

"I guess so," she said. "But boy—it must be hard being sixteen and not being able to drive places."

"I'm seventeen," Chip told her. "I'll be eighteen in February."

"Whoops. My apologies."

The first Christmas without them all. The fifth, the tenth.

"So, I guess you like the water then," Laura tried.

"Not especially."

"No kidding. Because Pisces, you know, that's the fish sign."

"Pisces is later in the month. I'm Aquarius."

"Oh." *Plus—Stewart in Westchester? Shindo Stewart? Coming to soccer games? Just imagine.*

"My dad likes the water though. He likes to fish."

"That's right, I remember that," Laura said. "He used to talk about fishing a lot. He'd bring in all the kinds of flies he had, and show us how to tie different knots."

Chip shrugged. "His parents have a tackle shop. They sell some of his flies to collectors."

"Right, I remember."

"You remember?"

Something got trapped in Laura's throat. "Well he talked about that too. It's by the ocean, right?"

He nodded back there. "North Carolina. Cape Hatteras. I was born there."

Laura's cheeks drained. She was gripping the steering wheel hard enough to snap it.

"Laura?" Goody was looking at her.

Eighteen. February. Tackle shop. The ocean.

"I have to pull over," she said. "I think I'm going to be sick."

They held her steady while she threw up. She apologized, then threw up again and apologized some more. She didn't know what was coming over her, she said, and she felt terrible about holding them up.

You kissed him goodbye in that tackle shop. You signed the papers at the front counter. There was a sale on surf rods that day. He had a runny nose.

Chip said there were beach towels in the trunk of the car, left over from the summer but still clean and all, and asked if Laura wanted one, if maybe that would make her more comfortable somehow. Then Goody took Laura's shoulders and kept her hair pulled back and nursed her through the next round. She was on her hands and knees now, with towels underneath.

"I just need . . ." she started to say, but didn't get a chance to finish because here came more. *Like having contractions,* she thought. *Like delivering a baby.*

"She looks like she's sorta through," Chip said. They waited a little extra to see if that was true. Laura handed the keys over to Chip and they helped her to the back of the car. Goody got in on the other side, next to her. She looked like someone who'd been plucked out of a riptide, when one more deepwater tug would have done her in.

Aquarius, not Pisces, and he was going to be eighteen. Now she could see the similarities everywhere: his hair is thick and hard to contain, just like Sandy's—but the skin is Appleby all the way. He plays sports, which must mean he's competitive; score one for Piccolo. He's got a brother and a sister he doesn't know about—*good God, he's already met them and they don't know!*—and, of course, a father who doesn't know about him.

Born in February, conceived in spring, with the boyfriend's best friend in a dorm room before dawn. His father's hair and his mother's skin. Driving now, without a license. Ten minutes away and then we have the Leopard.

"You okay back there?" Chip asked.

"I think so. Thanks." That's the Appleby in him, she thought, because an Appleby would absolutely ask. But a Griffin would, too. And after all—above all—he's a Griffin. A good and loving home, that's what she was promised. And it looks like they delivered.

They just didn't elaborate.

"Damn," Chip said. "That's a one-way street. I gotta go around now." Goody nodded, like a driving instructor schooled in patience. Laura closed her eyes and tried deep breaths.

What's in a kiss? they ask. This is what's in a kiss.

She had to ask them to stop the car again.

55

Pick

" *Today I met the boy I'm gonna marry*
    He's all I wanted, all my life and even more."
    He kept the invitation in his briefcase for a full three weeks before
he opened it. The Pocono Alumni Office had been calling, repeatedly,
leaving messages to see if he'd gotten it. And they weren't crazy to per-
sist—second year at Columbia Law coming up and already the biggest
firms were closing tight. He had Future Benefactor written all over
him. Come to the Reunion! Catch up on old friends and memories!
    Five years. It had been five years already. Christ. It all went by
like a Sunday morning.
    The invitation had a list of people from Pick's class who had
confirmed so far; the two names he looked for weren't there. But when
he turned to the second page, he saw a note at the bottom. Personal,
handwritten, from the pen of Henry Griffin: "You might want to
consider attending," it said. "Unfortunately, I won't be there—but
you never know who might. HG."
    Pick put the letter down. He went to town on himself with the
possibilities:
    Laura could be there, but not Goody.
    Goody could be there, but not Laura.

Neither one of them could be there.

They could both be there, but separately.

They could both be there—but together.

Worst case, by a landslide, was the last one; seeing them there together, all sweet and reunited, that wasn't something Pick thought he needed to do. He hadn't spoken with Goody since the day Goody left and didn't come back. He hadn't spoken with Laura since she left the school too, not long after. Pick graduated while they didn't, so they could both be mad at him for that as well. They could have found each other in the meantime somehow—they could be married, and maybe they asked Griffin to intervene on their behalf and ask Pick to come so they could settle things up. And Griffin would've been able to use a little influence and invite them as his guests. As honorary, if not factual, members of the same senior class.

Something had to be up though, for sure—or the man wouldn't have written at all.

"He smiled at me, and the music started playing . . ."

He'd been wanting to get out of the city anyway; not that Kirby would be his first choice, or his tenth or ten thousandth. And he sorely didn't want to take the time off and drive back up to that place just to get fucked over by something he'd been trying to forget all this time—which was laughable because he would never forget, he would never even get close.

"Here Comes the Bride,' as he walked through the door."

And then there was Carmine. You pretty much couldn't go up there without a forced march to the restaurant, so you could kiss the bastard's ring. All in all, a real treat in the making.

So he had to be honest with himself: the odds were not good that anything desirable was likely to happen from this. He comes into a school where the two of them have already been thriving just fine without him, and next thing you know they're gone and he's the one who graduates. He wouldn't blame Griffin if he were setting him up for a tribunal.

"When we kissed, I felt the sweet sensation . . ."

But Griffin wouldn't do that—he wasn't the kind of guy who pulls something on you unless it's something you're going to like. And that's what gave Pick any hope at all.

"This time it wasn't just my imagination. . ."

When he walked into the ballroom and saw her on the stage his heart almost stopped and died. She saw him too and they locked that way; each one seemed to be challenging the other to tip their hand first and show how they felt about this. While also on the stage, Rosa and Dot—lively as the day they left the place—were trying to nudge Laura to get her act together here. Laura blushed and looked at Pick again; then jumped back in, just in time for the change into the medley.

"The night we met I knew I—needed you so
and if I had the chance I'd—never let you go."

Pick couldn't take his eyes off her. She beamed out light. She was beautiful. And Goody, so far at least, was nowhere to be found.

This was very good news.

Pick was alone with her in the waiting room. Everyone else had gone down to the cafeteria. The kids wanted Cokes, but Laura said no. They didn't need more sugar, they didn't need more carbonation leeching the calcium out of their bones. She'd read an article about that too, about kids as young as twelve turning up with osteoporosis, from all the soda they drank—only no one was in the mood to hear about it. They asked if fruit juice was okay, and she told them which kinds, and make sure it was real juice and not corn syrup. They knew not to get her started on corn syrup.

Pick asked them to bring up a black coffee. Laura asked for tea if they had it. And if they had chamomile, if that was even possible, then even better. Perfect for an upset stomach.

"You couldn't tell me?" Pick asked Laura. "What the hell does that mean?"

"I wasn't allowed. I had to swear to that. It was part of the arrangement."

"With Carmine."

"Carmine was the grandfather. We were minors. He had all the say."

"What about your parents?"

"They were finished with me as soon as they found out."

Pick saw her expression. Must have been horrible for her, but he couldn't focus on that now. "He finds me in town today and he lays this megaton bomb on me, and what am I supposed to do with it? There's a kid out there somewhere, and it came from that night, and he never wanted me to know about it because then it wouldn't be safe. But suddenly today he wants me to know about it, but he won't tell me the rest and he doesn't want me trying to find out myself."

"But if he won't tell you, how can I?"

"Because we're married, Laura! And married people are supposed to *tell* each other certain things—like if one of them has a baby and gives it away, and keeps it to herself the whole time!"

"Because I had to! Do you understand 'had to?' I was pregnant with no options and nowhere to go!"

"What do you mean you had nowhere to go—you had me!"

"*I wasn't allowed to tell you!* Those were his *terms*, Sandy! I wanted to have the baby, but I knew I couldn't keep it. He promised a safe home!"

"All right! All right. Just—we gotta calm down, all right?"

"Oh sure. You can get as upset as you want about things. Fuck this and fuck that. But I have to calm down."

Pick looked at her. She was really holding her own here. Ordinarily it was something he'd admire. "Where the hell is that coffee," he said. "I'm getting dizzy from this."

Laura shrugged; she didn't know any more about the coffee than he did, and she said so. They both seemed to agree, silently, that it wasn't just the coffee they were anticipating. It was the one who was bringing it.

They were out in the parking lot, leaning against Pick's car. Next to it was an actual pink limousine that the old homecoming gang had rented for the reunion; the smell of spilled alcohol and stale perfume seeped out from the moon roof.

Music was still going strong from the hotel. A lot of hard laughter cracked the night; anxious bursts of loud spontaneous cheering. People were forcing the crap out of themselves to have a good time in there.

Laura and Pick had some champagne with them, but they weren't drunk. Just loose enough to be able to speak a little more openly, and a little bit sooner, than they might have without it.

"Here's my idea," Pick said.

"What?" Laura asked.

Pick held out his watch. He tilted it towards the light and pointed to what time it was. "From here to here is ten minutes," he marked. "Then I'll check again."

"Why?"

"Because let's see if we can go that long without mentioning Goody."

"We haven't yet, have we. Except for just now."

Pick shook his head; no, they hadn't. And just now was a technicality. Laura considered it. "What happens if we can?" she asked.

Pick shrugged, matter-of-factly. "Then we shoot for twenty."

Laura nodded; first, ten minutes. Then twenty. "And what happens if we get past twenty?"

"Then I ask you to come back to New York with me."

"Tonight?" She looked at Pick and yes, he meant tonight. "And what do I say back when that happens? If we get to where you ask."

"You say yes."

Laura thought this through. "That's a good answer," she said. "That's exactly the answer that I, personally, would really like to give."

"Really?"

Laura nodded. Really.

"I'll tell you what," Laura offered. "We'll call him. We'll call Carmine and explain. We'll get him to change his mind."

"Screw that," Pick answered. "And screw Carmine. He has no fucking business having any say in this ever again. I mean it."

Laura pressed. "We'll call him, and we'll tell him how much it matters. Maybe that's all he wants. Maybe he just wants to be asked."

Pick shook her off. He was finished asking Carmine. "I'm going to find out anyway, Laura. You know that, right?"

He watched Laura nod. Damn right she knew.

They had just crossed into Port Jervis from Pennsylvania and thought they'd celebrate by finding a restaurant somewhere, but there weren't any open. So they went to an A&W, got burgers and fries and shakes, and ate them in Pick's car. Laura had never been in an Alfa-Romeo, or any kind of Italian car at all. And her luggage, had never been in the back of one.

"Remember the Ford Pinto?"

Laura thought back. "They exploded or something."

Pick nodded. "It was one of our case studies. It would have cost the company one dollar per car, at the factory, for a plastic device that would prevent the Ford Pinto from bursting into flames if you hit one from behind in a certain way. Instead they spent millions of dollars on lawyers and lobbyists, trying to get out of being responsible. A one dollar part and the families got to go fuck themselves."

She looked at him strangely; that sort of came by surprise. "I don't remember how it ended," she said. "Did they ever have to pay?"

"Not enough. It'll never be enough." He reached into the A&W bag between them and took out some fries. "But that's what I want to do," he added.

"What?"

"People get stepped on, by companies that don't care at all about them. And the companies don't think they should ever have to answer to anybody for what they do to people. They just pay their lawyers to make it go away."

"So you're going to stop them?"

Pick was dead certain. "Places like that, they're going to wish they never breathed. That's what I'm going to do."

Laura looked at him. "I like that," she said. "You want to protect people."

"I'd do it for free," Pick told her. He took a long drink of his milkshake. The cold in it hurt his chest. Laura watched him.

"Will you have to?" she asked. "You know, for free?"

Pick grinned. "Not if I'm any good," he said.

The door opened, and Andy and Molly came in. Andy said that Mary and Chip had gone in to see Griffin, and that the weird guy should be right behind them with the drinks.

Laura and Pick said fine, and thanks for telling them. They put on their best strained smiles and listened to what the kids both had to eat downstairs; trying to look engaged, for the sake of not going crazy on the spot. Then Goody came in, with two takeout cups in a white paper bag.

Tea for her, coffee for him. Pick would drink some right away and burn himself, because it was always too hot, and he never had the patience to wait. But Laura watched him do it anyway.

"There's a bottom to this," he promised. "There's a place where this kid can be found."

"I know," Laura said.

Pick nodded. Damn fucking right.

~~~ 56 ~~~
The Bell Tower

Epilogue to the Second Edition
by S.A. Goodman

Only a Fool

I *watched from a coffee shop across the street. I had been to New York just the one time before, back when I met the agent who'd sold my manuscript—this manuscript—and the publisher he'd sold it to. They took me to lunch, at the Oak Room at the Plaza—to impress me, I supposed. But I was nervous and improperly dressed and had little appetite for the food there; everything was much too showy, much too elaborate for me, and it made me uncomfortable. Plus, these men, these book people, they were polished, they had their latest deals and their inside stories to hash around over drinks; then, once they'd all ordered, they swung it around to talking about me, and around me, and at me sometimes, and I was sure that they thought they were doing a right thorough job charming me up when in all honesty I felt utterly alone and unprotected.*

So I listened to them laying out their deal points and spinoff sales and first option film rights, and I watched them bat percentages around like it was racquetball—yet strangely missing was any talk about the actual book I had written, the words on the pages, and whether either of them had liked it, whether it had touched them and whether they thought it would touch other people. On one hand, I knew, they must have—obviously, or they wouldn't be sitting there dissecting the Latin American paperback market, because only a fool would think about Latin America as all this one giant place, rather than several distinct yet also interconnected territories. Only a fool, and these men weren't fools.

Somewhere between dessert and the bill, which the two of them theatrically fought over, I had also acquired a business manager, whose card I had in my pocket now, and who would be calling me on Monday—which would be a neat trick, since I couldn't know how to tell her where I'd be by then, or what kind of business there could ever possibly be for her to manage.

When the lunch was over and we all shook hands, I went for a walk and thought about things. I had a check in my pocket which I'd have to wait until I got back out west to cash. Most of it would go to Mt. Raymond, as planned. And some I'd send to my mom—not that she needed it, she was married again, and they were doing all right—but just so she'd know I was making my way out in the world, and that I was amounting to something in a way that she could put a number on, and maybe understand. You never know.

I had to go back to the Oak Room because I forgot about the necktie the maitre d' made me borrow. I saw the same agent and publisher, only with a different author—a woman, this time, and again they were talking about Latin America and not being fools. Out on the street, away from that place, I started to feel different; more than anything I noticed I was hungry, since I'd passed on most of that lunch. So I found a coffee shop, where I ordered up a bottomless breakfast, even though it was four in the afternoon. I had cereal and eggs and a bagel—things I hadn't had in so long—and after I was finished with those plates, I ordered a big bowl of oatmeal and ate that too. When in Rome, I figured, so I did what the

Romans would do, if the Romans usually ate three weeks' worth of food at a time.

After my third cup of coffee I asked for the menu again, and then it hit me that when I'd had that bagel before, it was with butter and jelly and not lox and cream cheese, and here I was a nice Jewish boy in the city of bagels and lox—so I ordered that too, and ate it along with a second milkshake, like I hadn't already scarfed a ton and half of food already by then. I had more than impressed everyone there, and when they asked me what my secret was, I said I'd just sold a book; one of them said, Well, you must have gotten a lot of money for it, and I said that was true, that I did. I hadn't thought much about it—really—but yes, they gave me a lot of money back there. They don't take you to the Oak Room unless they mean it.

Now here I was, one year later to the day: back in the city, back in the same booth of the same coffee shop, staring out the same exact window at a cathedral across the street. There was a wedding going on in there—and it was incredible to me, about New York, that there could be such a pageant happening inside, such a holy event, while just beyond the doors there were trucks and cabs going by, and bike messengers weaving through, and none of the people walking past the place would stop walking, or walk any slower just because two people are making their vows in there. Just because Pick is marrying Laura.

Just because everything.

I imagined their honeymoon coming up; goring myself with a list of places they could go. Scotland, where Laura would search for ancestors, where she'd hold close to Pick to protect her from the chill. Or Martinique, in the heat, where she'd hold his hand and walk in the surf, wearing one of those long wraparounds that she'd hike up to keep from getting soaked by the foam. These were the kind of places Laura would like; she'd have her camera along, and she would want scenery around her that spoke of passion, and permanence.

If it were up to Pick, he'd likely opt for Las Vegas, or Atlantic City if he didn't feel like flying, and the top suite on the top floor— where they could screw like turbines, call downstairs for whatever they wanted, and maybe throw some clothes on and see a show if there was anything good going on. And if Laura wanted to take pictures, if she wanted scenery, that's what the top floor was for: you could see forever from those windows.

The point was, she chose him. Whatever happened last time, this time was a clear and sober choice. We were kids back then, and this time we weren't. And soon now, it would all be over: the big doors would open, and Laura would come out, with her brand-new No One Put Asunder husband, Pick. The limos would take off and be gone, the parking lanes would be reclaimed, the sawhorses removed and the detectives watching for Carmine Piccolo would get all the look they needed if it turned out he was there. Laura and Pick would drink champagne—and at some point, among all their gifts, they would find a single small envelope, with a note inside—which said, simply, Congratulations.

They'd know who it was from.

— 57 —

Chip

"**M**om."
"Yes, Chip."

"I need to ask you something."

They weren't exactly private. Besides the guest of honor, there were nurses back and forth, and the occasional intern, and some kind of attendant—the hospital version of a busboy, Mary supposed—who kept coming in with different sized connector plugs for one of the monitors, and then leaving while muttering about never having the right size for the right jacks and who are the brain dead stupid clowns who designed this garbage.

Back in the hospital. Out of the house. No matter how they explained it, it felt like failure. And the crack about brain dead, that didn't help things at all.

"But before I ask you. You have to promise up front that you'll give me an honest answer—even if you want to duck out when you hear it, you're locked in. Otherwise I'm not asking."

"I won't duck out. It's a promise."

"Honestly? The total truth?"

"If I know the answer, Chip, I'll tell you the truth."

"Okay. Here we go. Ready?"

She looked at him. She was ready.

"First question. What's my name?"

"What?"

"What's my name, Mom. My full name."

"Charles Rangely Griffin. Charles after dad's father, Rangely because it's my family's name, and Griffin goes back so far, I don't even know. Vikings, probably."

Chip nodded. Debate team, fourth in the state. "And that's the name you gave me? You and Dad."

"Well the school had a contest. You were sort of a mascot. But in the end, we chose for ourselves."

"And that's what's it says on my birth certificate? Charles Rangely Griffin."

"You've seen your birth certificate, Chip. Was this your question?"

He shook his head. "What was my name before that?"

"Baby Boy Griffin. You were Baby Boy Griffin for about a week, before we made it official."

"And the bit before I was Baby Boy Griffin. What about that?"

"I can't answer that, Chip."

"Because you don't know?"

"Because that's the way adoptions work."

"You mean, you go through this agency and there are confidential files and they keep everything secret, so no one gets hurt?"

"That's how they're done. Yes."

He looked at her, and nodded. "But if you don't go through an agency, you can skip all that. Like a private adoption."

"You were the private kind," Mary acknowledged, as if she hoped that would be enough.

Chip leaned back a little—like a senator would, or the chairman at a board meeting. He looked composed, reflective. "On the way over here," he said. "In the car. Your friend was driving. I said something about Grandma and Grandpa's tackle shop, and she looked like she choked on a pretzel or something."

"What did you say?"

"That I was born there." He watched her react to that. "So she's not just a friend of yours, visiting with her kids. Is she?"

Mary closed her eyes, briefly, then looked straight at Chip. "She was never supposed to know where you went. Nobody was."

"Just you and Dad."

Mary nodded. "Just me and Dad."

Chip took that in. He had only wondered about this all his life, from the time he learned he was adopted. He had never pursued it, although he knew lots of people did and that different things at different times of people's lives triggered them to want to find out. And now that his own story was revealed to him, he thought that maybe there should be earthquakes or something. Righteous shockwaves of power, unleashed, over what he had just been told here. Buildings crumble; in the country, livestock fly past like gum wrappers.

Maybe that stuff comes later, he guessed. It might be that he was just in the eye of it now, and the full fury might rise up and blow through him at some other point. Or it could be shock; he'd read about how that kind of thing can happen. Right now though, more than anything else, he felt tranquil somehow, and strangely composed.

"And your friend—"

"Laura," Mary corrected. "Her name is Laura, Chip."

Chip noted that. "Laura was the girl you told me about, that came between those two guys?"

"That's right."

"And she went to bed with one of them, in the dorm one night. And the other one walked in. And he lost it and ran away."

Mary nodded.

"And then he hooked up with a bunch of Buddhist monks who just happened to be passing by when he was hitchhiking.

And he went out west with them, so he could try and forget her. But because she was the first great love of his life, he never did."

"How'd you know *that*?" Mary asked. Then, reflexively, she covered her mouth.

Chip shook his head. "Don't ever be a spy, Mom. You'd crack in a minute." He got his backpack out from under the chair, and started digging around inside. "When you went looking for that girl before, and you told me to stay with her brother? He told me about this book."

He watched her, like a poker player looking for a tell. "The temp librarian at school is pretty good," he went on. "She's from over at Wilkes. She found an S.A. Goodman and a book called *The Bell Tower*, but the school didn't have it anymore. But then the girl remembered seeing it at her parents' house. She still lives with them. So she took me there and we found it."

Mary fanned the pages, and handed it back. "You're right," she agreed. "That's a good librarian."

Chip nodded. "It's funny we don't have a copy at the house," he wondered.

"We do. We just don't have it out."

"I can see why," Chip said.

Mary looked at him. "The only thing in his life, Chip, that Dad ever regretted, was not being able to tell you. But he never regretted promising that he wouldn't."

Chip took that in. "So the lawyer one's my father. And not the writer."

Mary said yes. "And they were more in the dark than anyone. It wasn't so much kept from you, as it was kept from them and everyone else."

"How come?"

"Because those were the conditions. And that's how much we wanted you."

Chip thought about this. Methodically, because that's how he worked things. He looked at his dad, in the bed. "Something tells me there's more," he said to Mary. "Isn't there."

His mother's expression left him no doubt. "For now," she told him, "let this be enough."

For now. He was happy to.

58

Goody

*T*hey sat in the next to last row while the school chaplain labored through a speech that showed every sign of being watered down bit by bit by a committee of overseers whose main job was to keep anyone in attendance from being offended. No one would be inspired, either, but their bigger concern was the first one.

Emmett Vossedek taught Comparative Religion, which was required school-wide, plus separate Old and New Testament classes you could take by elective. He did his better work in the classroom, more suited to a simple ring of desks than rows and rows of seats; not everyone in the clergy had the same exact gifts, and large-scale public speaking was sadly not one of Emmett's.

Pick elbowed Goody, who was doing his best to listen. "Check it out," he said. "He says one thing about Jesus, and then right away he backs off twice as far."

Goody asked, without turning, "What do you care?"

"Hey man I like Vossedek. He's a good guy. But he lets these people rattle him." Pick pointed down at the front of the chapel; the clean necks and trimmed hairs of the officials who ran the school. "You got too many religions to take care of—it's like they're scared *somebody's going to not let their kid go here if Emmett Vossedek knows less than he should about Hindus one day. Now how many people in this place give a fuck about Hindus?"*

"I don't know," Goody answered. "But we should. We should give a fuck about all of them."

"You're crazy—you think they care about us?"

Goody nodded. "If they're good Hindus, they do." He turned to Pick. "I think maybe that's the point. He's saying that's what we're all supposed to do."

Pick looked at him. "You are fuck plain out of your mind, you know that?"

"Keep reminding me," Goody said. "I might forget."

After chapel they borrowed bikes to ride out to Rossmiller's Creek, an underused park about five or six miles from school, where they liked to hang out and throw rocks. Some beavers had started a dam there, and Pick and Goody were providing tactical help—aiming for just the right places on the banks, to loosen things up for them.

"People only use religion to keep everyone else in line," Pick said. "It's propaganda through and through. Gimme the matches."

The creek was also a great place to get high, when they were flush enough to have something, which was gratefully the case today: Armstrong had visited his cousin at Rutgers again, who was financing his way through business school by selling opiated hash, in quarter-ounce and smaller amounts. Goody and Pick pooled their resources and bought three grams, for this weekend and the next—longer if they really disciplined themselves.

"They want you to behave a certain way," Pick went on, "so they throw Jesus at you. Look at history, for Christ's sake."

Goody shook his head. "It wasn't propaganda when it started though."

"You think he was the Son of God?" Pick asked. "I didn't think you guys were allowed to."

Goody crumbled up some more hash and dropped it into the pipe bowl. "To me, Jesus is . . . he's like the older brother, you know? Like the ultimate older brother." He lit a match, and kept sucking in till a couple pieces caught and he got a good hit. "I mean, God is the father, right? Everybody at least agrees with that."

"Everybody who believes in God."

Goody looked at him, to see if he could actually mean that. He passed the pipe and matches. "Well when you're a kid, you know, your father . . . he's this powerful thing. He's this—"

"—Asshole. My father, anyway." Pick took his hit, coughed out most of it, and huddled over the matches to try again. Goody pulled his coat over both their heads, so it could help block the breeze.

"He's this force," Goody went on. "And he's above you and he's mysterious and everything comes from him. And then Jesus, he's like your older brother—he explains your father to you. He's off to the side, just a little. And from there he interprets things. So that you can understand what the hell is going on sometimes."

Pick looked at him. "That's what the Jews think?"

"I don't know what the Jews think. Nobody ever talks about him."

Pick looked surprised. "Well don't you ask? Guy like you, you'd think you'd be on their asses all the time about this kinda shit."

"Every time I ask somebody, they cough or sneeze or something," Goody told him. "Then they change the subject."

"That's fucked," Pick said, and threw a rock to underscore how fucked it was. He bent down for a fresh supply, from the pile they'd collected ahead of time. "So if God is the father, then who's the grandfather?"

"What do you mean?"

"I mean, does God have a God?"

"No. Of course not. God's God. All there is."

"And there's nobody bigger."

"There can't be anybody bigger."

"But we're made in his image, right?"

"That's what it says."

"So, if we're made in God's image, and we have a God, then God should have a God too. And if he doesn't, what else can it mean except there isn't one? Case closed."

Goody laughed. "I don't know what the name for it is," he said, "but you just did that thing where someone can sound completely right about something, and still be dead wrong."

"It's called Logic. Gimme the matches."

"You have them," Goody pointed out, and Pick discovered that he did. Goody got out the rest of their first gram, and together they knocked off three more bowls before it was time to head back to school, and sign themselves in before dinner.

They looked across the creek, surveying the work they'd done on behalf of the beavers. "What we need are some fireworks," Pick said. "Some M-80's. We could blow that whole stump out, and help those fuckers with their dam."

Goody nodded. "M-80's would do it," he said. "M-80's would definitely take out that stump."

They laughed the whole way back; did daredevil tricks on the borrowed bikes and caught hell for forgetting that dinnertime on Sunday was an hour earlier than it was every other day of the week. But Goody didn't mind; he felt great. It was a perfect afternoon and he was lucky enough to know it at the time. Yet all that night, he thought about what Pick had said, about "Everybody who believes in God." Goody couldn't imagine not believing in God—he could understand people not liking God, or being angry, or feeling like there was no way in. But to not believe at all? Might as well just not believe in the sky, he thought. Might as well not believe in breathing.

And it couldn't have been the hash that kept him up; thanks to Armstrong's cousin there was a nice and steady supply, all year long. And all those other times, Goody slept just fine.

"Well what do you know?" Pick said. "Leave it to you to find this place."

He walked down the aisle and joined Goody in the pew he was in. There was one other person in the chapel; an overweight polka mom, in a quilted jacket and sweat pants with the name "Steamrollers" going sideways down the leg. She bent at the altar, then turned around and passed them on the way out, leaving behind the stale scent of Marlboro Lights, and black licorice.

"A lot of hospitals don't call them 'chapels' anymore," Pick went on. "Did you know that? They have to call them 'meditation rooms,' or 'spiritual centers,' or 'reflective zones,' or some such shit. Sign of the times, I guess. Nowadays people'll throw a class action suit if a traffic light lasts too long."

He looked around, to prove his point; there were several different places to pray in here, depending on who you prayed to and which way you faced. The pews were fixed but there were clots of folding chairs and you could angle them either way. It seemed fair.

"So, I guess you don't have a problem with this," Pick said. "Former Jewish guy, in a Heinz 57 room. Could be a disco ball up there and it wouldn't bother you, right? Could be Elvis before he got fat. You're past that crap."

Goody smiled, softly—as if to say, maybe no one's past that crap.

"And maybe I need more of it," Pick said. "Or just some at all. Maybe I need it to be a box in a stadium, or many roads up the side of a mountain, or angels on a ladder or whatever the hell that other stuff is that people say. I could use something, though. Man could I use something."

He looked over. Goody was watching some candles flicker on a shelf, where you could make a donation in someone's name and light one. The shelf looked like it was moving, shifting from all the shadows tricking back and forth. It was hard to tell which was the illusion anymore.

"Want to hear something funny?" Pick asked him.

"Always," Goody said.

Pick got ready. He looked comfortable at this: collecting his thoughts, running down the mental checklist he relied on, back since Lawyer 101. "Any time we build a case, first thing we do is nail down the timeline. You can learn a lot about things by looking at the order they happened in. So that's what I did with your movie. I went back and put together a timeline. I combed through all the stuff that was available."

He looked at Goody. No reaction. "Anyway—I always thought that the way it happened was, the movie fell apart and then you took off. I never considered it might be the other way around. And then, because I'm a moron sometimes, I finally did. And it was, wasn't it—you went first?"

Goody didn't say anything. Which said everything.

"And right before you did, Laura came to see you—that was the first part. She saw you, you took off, the movie fell apart. And so whatever she told you, that's what made you do it."

Again, Goody said nothing. And again, everything.

"I'm right though, aren't I? You pulled the rug out from your own movie. That's the order it happened in."

"That's the order it happened in," Goody confirmed.

"And the baby," Pick said. "You knew about that all along. That's the thing Laura came to tell you."

Goody nodded. She'd told him, and it all but did him in. In less than a week he was on the run again. And it did nothing. Just like it always does.

Someone opened the door behind them, saw that people were in here already, and left. The candles flickered back into relief. "Maybe Carmine was right," Pick wondered. "My fitness for this shit. Then *and* now. Maybe everyone's right."

Goody looked over. "You really think that?"

Pick nodded slowly. "It's all Laura. They could do without me in a second. But her . . ." He made a little explosion with his hands. "We wouldn't last a day."

Goody had a hard time believing that. "The way your boy looks at you. You're his hero."

"Give him time," Pick said.

The door opened again; this time, the person came in. A businessman, by the look of him. He went straight to the front, pivoted when he got there, then turned around. He looked at Pick and Goody. "Does this shit farm have a priest?" he asked.

Pick looked back at the guy. He'd seen a million like him, and wasn't impressed. He tipped his head towards Goody. "Got one right here," he said. "Zen Buddhist."

"I meant a real one," the guy huffed and left, adding disgust to the list of things that day. They heard something crash out there, and swearing. Sue their fucking heads off, he was promising, and they'd better believe it. The sounds faded away as the tirade moved down the hall. Goody listened, and thought, and waited.

It was time.

"Listen," he said finally. "Pick."

"She's unhappy."

Goody looked over. Pick kept his gaze forward, as if seeing Goody's face right then would kill any chance of getting through this. "Laura. She's unhappy."

Goody's pulse began to race. He thought about Roshi, way early on, at the beginning of Goody's formal training. They were climbing to higher ground, and had come to a section of rapids that had no good place to cross. He had just this long to consider drowning.

"Has she said anything?" he asked Pick.

Pick shook his head, shrugged. "She doesn't have to. You can see it on her, like clothing." He shifted in the pew; call it the hard wood it was made of, but right now he'd be uncomfortable in the sweetest hammock on a perfect summer day. "I'll reach out and she'll pull back. She'll reach out and I'll pull back. You feel like you're shouting through molasses. And then you stop doing even that."

Shouting Through Molasses, Goody thought. Sounded like the title of a book on Zen. Or a *koan,* a teaching riddle that drives a person crazy—for years, sometimes—until the moment comes when they get it, finally get it. And in that moment, brief as it is, they know what it's like to feel sane. *What is the sound of shouting through molasses?*

"She wants us to go see somebody," Pick said, looking pre-defeated about it. "Fuckin' therapy. Everybody's solution has to be God damn fuckin' therapy. Lay it all out, to a total stranger. And then pay them? Rather put my feet in a bucket of scorpions."

Goody laughed, and Pick knew it was at the image, not at him. "Is there anyone?" he asked. "A golf buddy, someone at work. A bartender."

Pick grinned a little, about the bartender. There was a pamphlet on the floor that had fallen off the rack on the pew in front of them. It had the word *Grief???*, with each of the three question marks increasing in size. Pick shoved it out of the way with his foot.

"I talk to you," he said to Goody. "All the time. In the car, especially. I talk to you, and I imagine what you'd say."

Up to his waist in freezing water, Roshi turned and looked back at Goody, who still hadn't moved. The Old Man laughed, shouted "too much attach!" over the roar, and kept going. Even when it was life itself.

Goody turned to Pick. "So," he offered. "Talk to me."

59

Laura

She couldn't find either one of them. She couldn't figure out which one she wanted to find.

She wanted to find Goody.

She wanted to find Pick.

She wanted to find Pick.

She wanted to find Goody.

The more she debated with herself, the more Laura came to know that finding either one of them wasn't what this was about. She was what this was about. Her choices. Her decisions. And how, at certain times in life, everything can turn on which choice you make. Everything.

Will you not get this one simple idea? Will you just repeat, and repeat, and repeat?

Her own life, she felt, had turned more on the bad decisions than the good—how far, really, did she have to look, how much further than the last few hours? She kissed a man who wasn't her husband. She offered herself up to leave with him—she actually thought seriously about how to deal with the kids. So where, in the Pantheon of all her decisions, was the one she'd just made two hours ago? Mommy's going away for a little. Dad will take care of you. And Grandma and Grandpa will come down. Any questions? Don't forget we love you, so much.

If Goody had taught her anything, if only by example, it was the futility of running. Because it doesn't matter where you go—if you're running from something, it stays right with you. Every separate flight brings you right back to where you are. And there's no such thing as a finish line, there's only more running—until finally, one day, in one way or another, the running runs out.

And if Pick had taught her anything, if only by example, it was the futility of standing up to the wind and expecting somehow that it won't blow you over. That fighting harder doesn't always lead to winning, and that the sharpest sword in all of creation is useless, if there's nothing to swing at but air. Laura remembered reading once, that a warrior's greatest weapon is his love; at the time she had a hard time getting that, but now she was beginning to understand—when there's love, real love, there's nothing out there to swing at, there's no need to carry the sword. *No one wins a fight,* she'd told Andy; triumphs are all temporary, and so are defeats. Everything changes, everything becomes its opposite. It's the decisions we make, that make the difference. It's the choices. She knew that now.

She felt her body shaking—an unfamiliar shiver, deep from her core, as if it started in her capillaries and was building out from there. The curtain was pulled now, and she could see it: how she had been fooling herself, even cheating herself, by holding space for Goody all this time. He was her escape; he had been that all along. He was her Get Out of Jail Free card—on long winter nights when she and Pick weren't speaking, on summer drives in the car where the tension was thicker than humidity, Laura would dial into the *What If?* world of imagining life with Goody. How he would understand her intuitively. How his patience would be infinite. How his love would be rock steady and never waver.

She remembered her first apartment, back in Chincoteague; more like a fitted-out screen porch than anything else, all two tiny rooms of it, but her first home all to herself. She remembered how the previous tenants had painted it some awful shade of brownish red, or reddish brown, with possibly some green thrown in—the kind of job that can only be inspired by bad taste and cocaine, in equally grand amounts—and how she'd decided to paint over it, and learned the hard way that you can't do that, you have to strip off the old paint first, otherwise it'll rise up and poke its way through the new color and there goes all your work. Laura had done herself wrong, she realized, and she'd done Pick wrong and the kids as well, by letting Goody in the mix the way she did; by holding Goody out as her own personal safety zone, she had made them all unsafe. And she had to face it—if things had been the other way around, if Pick had been doing what she'd been doing, Laura would know exactly what to call it.

Exactly what it's called.

She was headed back up to the waiting room when she saw Goody. He came out of a men's room, carrying his satchel, dressed the same but looking different somehow. There was something more serious about him; something that meant business. And Laura saw, now, the person he had become—as if the younger Goody was the early prototype, and before her now was the result of years of development and painstaking care. She remembered a piece she'd read about quantum physics, about how a particle can be two places at the same time, but you can't see it travel from one place to the other. The best she could do at the time was accept this to be true, because physicists had come up with it, and because physicists are not known for being wrong about something, once they've worked it all out and announced it. Still though, she couldn't get her mind around it, and understand it the way they did—you can't be here if you're there, and you can't be there if you're here. Also, wherever you are, you have to *get* there from the place you were just before. And yet here was this entirely other universe, deeply infused with our own, where you *could* be two places at once, and you didn't have to get there. Every universe has its own set of rules, she thought. Nothing says you have to understand it. Things just *are*.

But now. With Goody, like this, Laura saw him in two places at once. And then two became five and five became a dozen and then even more. It was like seeing every slide in a slideshow, each at the same time and with equal clarity. You didn't have to take your eyes off one to see the other, you could see them all and with every detail, and every memory that went along with them. And every part of that was completely normal somehow.

"Hi," she said.

"Hi," Goody said back.

She felt shy all of a sudden. A teenager, on a first date, at the mall. "You, um . . ."

"I was in the chapel," he told her. "Pick found me."

"Oh," Laura said.

"He won't be long. I think he just—"

"Stewart, we can't."

Goody stopped, looked at her.

"We can't," Laura said again.

"I know," Goody said finally.

"You do?"

Goody nodded. "He loves you," he told her. "He doesn't know how to say it. He's terrified."

"Me too," Laura admitted. Wondering, one last time, if mutual terror is a place from which to begin things, or end them.

"I've done this before," Goody said. "I know what it's like."

"What?" Laura wondered, "You've done what before?"

"Gone without you," Goody replied. "I've gone without you. I do it every day. So I know what it's like." He looked at Laura. "Pick won't be able to do that. And he shouldn't have to."

Laura took a long deep breath. "Is that enough of a reason?" she asked.

"It is for me," Goody said. And the way he said it brought a whole encyclopedia of other reasons, none of which needed to be said; Laura understood, and agreed, with every last one.

"Me too," she concluded. "it's enough for me too."

Watching him, Laura remembered a line from his book, one of the many passages that would never, ever leave her, describing his heartbreak back then, and the loss. *Like whooshing down a mineshaft*, the line went, *faster and faster, where all it gets is darker, until it's black as ink and the breeze going by becomes ice.* She wondered if that was happening now. If so, she could tell him that she finally knew what it felt like.

"You all right?" Goody asked.

Laura nodded. She could see the affection. And the hurt, and the concern, the weight. And she knew it exactly mirrored her own. They saw straight into each other's heart.

"Okay then. I'll see you upstairs," Goody said. Then he turned for the elevator.

"Stewart—"

Goody turned. Looked at her one more time. "Walking," he pointed out. "Not running." Then he turned again, and went the rest of the way. Carrying his satchel as if he were catching the 5:05 to Massapequa. As if he did that every day.

An older couple came off the elevator, stepping slowly; the husband gripping his I.V. on wheels, like a coat rack. His wife, her hand on his back, listening while he explained the different colored lines on the floor to her, and what each color was assigned to and where it went. He was telling her that earlier in the day he had asked, but nobody knew how the colors were decided on—just that at some point they were. He was curious to know if the same colors meant the same things everywhere, or did each different hospital just choose for itself? But no one had been able to tell him.

"Flora Pankow's a nurse," his wife was saying. "Maybe she'll know."

"Who's Flora Pankow?" her husband wanted to know.

"She's our alternate for bridge. She replaced Helen Parazaider after Helen fell and broke both hips."

"Both hips?"

"Both hips. We can call her in the morning."

The wife noticed Laura watching them; she turned to her as they passed. "He's an engineer," she told her, and somehow, to Laura, that explained everything. Engineers need to *know*. They see patterns, they look for structure, and predictability. To be married to one requires things. And to be one, married to someone who isn't—that requires things too.

These were angels, Laura was convinced, sent to speak to her directly. About what it takes to understand someone, as they are—not as they were or might someday be. What it takes to hold two lives together. What it takes to walk like that, down this antiseptic hallway, parsing out over the meanings of colored lines on the floor. Better and worse, thick and thin, rich and poor, sickness and health and back again, good times and bad, until there's nothing left before you but death do us part—a slow careful walk down the final runway, pushing your fluids on a pole alongside you. The White Mile. He's an engineer. She'll ask Flora in the morning for him. He thanks her. Her hand steadies his back, to keep him from falling.

They got to the end of the hall and turned around. Laura lingered, watching them. Four wide colors, on a floor so shiny you could see their faces looking back. And a quiet and patient promise, to find out what they meant.

60

Pick

" You know what this is like? Agatha Christie."
Everyone looked at Andy. Pick, especially—wondering
how a nine-year-old kid would know who Agatha Christie was.
Or what would make him come up with that just now; at this
point Pick was in enough shock that you could tell him that
both kids were big fans of Baudelaire, and smoking those thin
brown cigarettes, and coming in at four in the morning from a
long night hopping bistros, and he wouldn't wonder at all how
come he didn't know that.

"How is it like Agatha Christie?" Mary asked, on everyone's
behalf.

"Because of the part where all the people get assembled in
one room while someone tries to figure out who the killer is.
That happens in a lot of them."

Pick looked at him. "You read Agatha Christie books?"

"He did a report on her," Laura said. "And that got him
interested, so he dove in."

"Can I read them?" Molly asked.

Andy shook his head. "There're too many words you won't
know. I can read one to you as long as you don't get scared."

"I won't get scared," she said. "The Phantom Tollbooth
didn't scare me, and you read it to me twice."

Pick looked at Molly, feeling overtaken by pride—yet only more isolated, for not knowing that his son was capable of Agatha Christie, and that he read to his little sister at night, and that he knew enough about her to know what her scare threshold was. He was looking out for her. Andy was growing up.

Then Pick felt Laura watching him, and it rammed him back into now, to this moment: a marriage gasping for its life; two kids that he only thought he knew, another one he just found out about who is out there somewhere, and who might not even care to know about him. And add to that, the first adult to ever believe in him was laid out in a coma, while his fully-grown kid was staring at Pick right now in a way that rattled his teeth, and the family matriarch was busy putting her last chance bet down on a lapsed author from Hershey, a runaway monk who was in there right now, with his 'little of this, little of that,' that he'd learned at the feet of great masters. Doing in his way what Pick couldn't do in his—trying to find the combination that would get Henry Griffin to wake up.

So this is your report card, Pick thought. *This is how you've done,* and he felt more helpless and lost than he'd ever felt in his life. *The most precious things in the world and you held them second. And now they're living their lives without you. You let your wife get unhappy, and far away. She could have her bags packed already, and you wouldn't even know. This is how you've done.*

"Have you read Ellery Queen?" Mary asked Andy.

Andy shook his head. "Does she write mysteries?"

Pick watched Chip get a kick out of that, watched him explain to Andy that Ellery Queen was a guy and that Chip had a friend who had all his books and maybe she'd lend one out to Andy while he was here. He watched the interplay between them. He saw Laura watching too. Mary, watching too. He watched glances being traded that he didn't understand.

And then he understood.

"I gotta go to the bathroom," he said. He was already in the hall by the time he was finished saying it.

He was washing his hands when Chip came in. They caught each other's eye in the mirror over the sink.

"Hi," Chip said.

"Hey."

Pick nodded in the mirror as Chip went past. He looked down at the drain and noticed the name stamped in the chrome stopper; he remembered suing that company, for falsely jacking up the stock price and then robbing the pension fund to cover the spread. People were getting laid off in the hundreds, while the CEO who gutted the place took refuge in his custom-built yacht off St. Barth's, complete with second wife and helicopter pad. By the time Pick was finished with him there was no longer a boat, no longer a bank account, the wife and helicopter had both taken off, and the CEO was a guest of the federal government at Eglin, Florida for several years to come.

That one felt great.

He heard Chip flush, and then saw him come back into view on his way to the sinks. Pick watched Chip's reflection in the mirror. The way he did this little squint, a millisecond of a move, before he turned on the water to wash his hands.

Pick knew that squint. He knew that move. He had only seen two people do it: himself, and Carmine.

"You all right?" Chip asked him.

It took Pick a minute to realize that a question had been asked, it had been asked of him, and it was the kind that required an answer. "Math was never my thing," he said finally. He knew that was out of nowhere. He turned off the water but kept staring at the drain. "I learned how to add two and two, though—I did get that far."

"I guess you don't need a lot of math," Chip figured. "You know, as a lawyer. Probably whatever comes up, they have calculators for it."

Pick nodded: yes, they do. "When it's people though, I can still be pretty thick. Some things it takes me a while to catch on. Enough that it shouldn't surprise me."

"I think I know what you mean," Chip said. "I get that way too sometimes."

Pick turned the water back on, actually washed his hands this time and was quick about it. "Genoa salami, though. That was a clue."

Chip thought back, remembered where that came up before. It *was* a clue, no kidding—and clues are part of mysteries and mysteries are what he was lousy at. Although who could have guessed at this one anyway? Not even Ellie probably.

"When did you know?" Pick asked him.

"Not till today."

"Your mom tell you?"

Chip shook his head. "I found the book. Then she told me."

That fucking book.

"You're giving up on him, aren't you?" Chip asked.

"Giving up?"

"Everyone is. Isn't that why you're all here?"

Pick shook his head. "Not giving up," he told Chip. "Just sometimes you have to take a step back and look at something from far enough away. You learn which fights you can win, and which ones you can't."

"So you surrender."

"Maybe not in the way you mean."

"What way do *you* mean?"

Pick thought about it. "I mean sometimes you can force a situation into happening. You really can—you can will things, and muscle them through. Right or wrong, that kind of thing can work."

He looked around to see if there were paper towels; he never liked those blowers. "Other times you can't force things, but you can have some influence, so they're more likely to go the way you want them. And then there are times when the best thing you can do, for everyone, is just stand out of the way and keep your head on as straight as you can, and let things happen the way they need to. You influence them by not being an influence at all." He pulled a few sheets for both of them. "It's a surrender that comes from trust, not defeat."

"That sounds like something my dad would say."

Pick grinned; the kid couldn't possibly know what a compliment that was. Griffin always knew what to say, and when and how to say it. It was the thing Pick admired about him the most, and wanted for himself the most. To make every answer sound like you had a month to think about it.

"But he's not going to make it, though," Chip went on. "Is he?"

Pick didn't know how to answer that. "Listen," he said. "Chip." He realized that this was the first time he'd said the kid's name. *His* kid's name. A kid he was unaware of, as recently as lunchtime. Who'd been kept from him, all his life. "You and I don't know each other. And for my money, the only way this thing could get any more unreal would be if Laura had triplets back then, and two more of you walked through the door. Although I swear if it happens I won't be surprised."

"I'd be," Chip said.

Pick wondered if he'd meant that as a joke; knowing that if he knew anything about him he wouldn't have to ask. "Anyway—I think this is what your dad meant to happen. I think he wanted us all in the same room. Everyone, together— so that whichever way this went, we'd all be here to deal with it, in the here and now, and nobody'd have to go through it alone. Especially you. It's the only thing I can think of that adds up." Pick thought about what Andy had said, about Agatha Christie, and realized the kid might have been more spot on than he knew. Everyone together, and then the big reveal. "Why else would he do this?"

"I don't know," Chip said. "You know him better than I do."

Pick looked at him. He tried not to stare. But he could see the kid's pain, and his anger and defiance—and he could easily, immediately, uncannily recognize it as his own. "Listen. Take it from a guy who's been trying to shut his father out for most of his life—it doesn't work. And you've got a great one. You have the best." He nodded towards the bathroom door, the whole world on the other side of it. "They're the ones who took care of you, when they knew we couldn't—when they knew we'd mess you up beyond belief. And I bet it killed them to have to keep it all a secret."

"So why did they?"

"Because they weren't given a choice. Because sometimes that's how much you want something—especially when it's a kid. And you know what? Look how you turned out."

He dropped the towels in the wastebasket and watched the lid rock back and forth. "So what about now?" Chip asked.

"What do you mean?"

"Is that what you're going to do now? Stay out of my life?"

Pick studied him; in just a few years, this would be Andy. Boy was there ever a train coming. "The one who should decide that," he said, "is you."

He watched Chip take that in, and process it. Battling inside, to come up with some position. "You don't have to know it now," Pick told him. "There's time. And you don't have to come up with an answer alone."

"What, you're going to help me?"

Pick shook his head. "Not just me," he said. "You got a whole family out there."

61

Mary

The sound seemed to come from everywhere and nowhere. An unearthly, haunting tremolo that stopped them all in their tracks.

"What the hell is that?" Andy asked. Pick and Laura shot a look at him, and he blanched; as if a united front from his parents was a brand new, and foreboding, thing to contend with.

"It's Stewart," Mary said, about the sound they were hearing. Bleeding in from the hallway now, and in the door and through the walls, down from the ceiling tiles and vibrating against the windows. It was a low wail, a chant, a baritone moan, and it pervaded everything. It was the sound of heaven and hell, of gods and animals and people's souls.

Laura and Pick stood frozen; Molly and Andy held hands and stared. Chip gripped onto a bookshelf as if the room might start shaking any minute and he'd need to hold tight. And Mary, her face folded into her hands, shed silent tears of hope.

This is what he asked for, Mary thought. *Somehow, Henry knew . . .*

No one knew how long it lasted. It suspended them in time, in thinking, in reason. It captured them and held them in place, like rays from an alien craft.

Somehow he knew.

And then it stopped. The hallways went silent. The whole world seemed hushed, and everyone in the room could only stare, blankly. It had happened without warning, and kept them captive even after it was gone.

It was Goody who broke the spell. He opened the door— looking weary, sucked in, like a patient in these halls himself, who had just decided to unhook all the tubes that held him in bed and go for a walk.

He stood there and looked in at them. Their stillborn expressions; paused, questioning. He gestured loosely out towards the hallway, in the direction of Griffin's room. "We need to consider," he said, "whether the best thing for him is to stay here or move on. And whether the best thing for us is to hold on—or let go."

Mary watched as Goody went over to Chip. "You've been thinking there might be more," he said. "There is. And you'll be able to handle it. You will."

Chip looked at him strangely, and then at Mary, who had no answer for this; there'd been no one else in the room when Chip had said that to her.

"Go in and talk to him," Goody went on. "He needs to know you're going to be okay."

"I will," Chip said. And he left, directly, like he'd been sent on a mission.

Mary watched the door close. Then Goody went over to Andy and Molly. Andy looked impressed, but still on his guard; Molly needed no convincing. In a low voice Goody asked them if he could give them a job to do, and in low voices they said he could, so he told them very quietly that he wanted them to teach their dad about the Beatles, because it was important, and he was never able to do it himself. The kids whispered back that they didn't know anything about the Beatles, so how could they teach their dad? And Goody whispered to them, *ask him to play their music.* Lots of it, and loud. And he promised them that things would change for the better, for all of them, if they did.

"Now don't be alarmed," Goody told them. "But I'm going to give your mother a kiss."

And then he did. He took Laura in between his hands and kissed her on the forehead—gently, curative, sending quiet waves of strength, and energy, and awareness through every part of her—like a fast rushing river, coursing through her memories and taking with it her sadness, her guilts and her regrets—releasing floods of remorse and leaving her cleansed, and refreshed, and complete.

He covered Laura's eyelids and returned her to a summer evening, to the shores of a cobalt lake—the sun still and warm on her neck, horse book in hand, her curious wandering nature forever restored. He whispered something to her; an incantation, ancient and impenetrable, where the words themselves mean less than the vibration they create.

Then Goody lowered his hands and turned to Pick. He took a white scarf out from under his shirt collar, and laid it over Pick's neck like a wreath. Evidently this was something ceremonial, and precious, and all the more sacred to be giving it away. "For your journey," he said.

"I'm going somewhere?" Pick asked.

Goody smiled at him; rubbed his head, playfully, like a father would to a son—like Pick did to his own son. Like fathers do everywhere. "Man of the house," Goody told him. "Do good!" And then he straightened and turned to everyone else. He folded his hands and bowed to them with all the peace in heaven.

And then he left.

No one moved. As if each one felt like they should do something—go after him maybe?—but they couldn't; they were still in the grip. Silent, planted in the same spots they'd been in all along. Enough to have their portraits painted.

Finally, there was a knock on the door. They turned and looked at it like it was a foreign, outrageous possibility. They were braced for anything when it opened.

"Oh—hi..."

It was Ellie. She brought fresh air with her, and the smell of crackled leaves. "They said you'd all be in here," she said. "I asked downstairs."

When no one answered her, she looked a little closer. Seeing them now, seeing the way they were, she stopped, and covered her mouth. "Oh," she said. "Oh, no . . ."

But it wasn't what she thought.

It wasn't what anyone would think.

62

Laura

She found him in Griffin's room. Hands up to his face, tipped forward in the chair next to the bed. His eye was on Griffin's respirator—rising and falling with every breath the man couldn't take on his own. Pick watched it like a metronome.

"I wish I knew how to pray," he told her. Knowing she was behind him, knowing she was listening, that she had come in here to tell him something but would wait. "Should've asked Goody," he said. "Golden opportunity if you want to learn something like that."

He looked down at his hands. *Manicured.* They seemed like a stranger's. "If you decide to leave," he said, "I'd understand why."

"Sandy—"

"I wouldn't make it hard for you. I wouldn't want you to stay just because of that. I know people do."

He looked so small to her, saying that. So far away. "How about I stay then," she offered, "because I want to? Because I do."

Pick looked down, too leery to trust what he'd just heard. "But how can you love me?" he asked.

Laura bit into her lip again. "The real question," she managed to say, "isn't how could I love you, Sandy. But how could I have let you forget?"

"I should be saying that to you."

"Well you can," Laura said. "We both can."

Pick nodded; quietly, as if only now considering the distant possibility of penitent relief.

"I interrupted before," Laura told him. "I'll let you finish." She bent down over Griffin, to say a silent and private goodbye. Standing back up she looked at him, wishing so hard that the last time ever didn't have to be like this. "I hope he knows what you've done for him, Sandy."

"I hope he knows what he's done for me," Pick said.

Laura smiled; crossed back past Pick and went the rest of the way to the door. She turned around one last time. Watching as Pick lowered his head again. He was mumbling something, just barely.

Thank you, was all she heard.

63

Chip

They were outside the hospital entrance, on the same bench that Chip had hurdled the day Mrs. Levering first dropped him off. He remembered the night he watched those doctors out by the canopy, having their smoke; if you told him that happened a hundred years ago, he'd believe it. Now he was here with Ellie—gentle and concerned, doing her best to stay upbeat. Close enough to touch shoulders, Chip felt like they were continents apart.

"So, did you find out what you wanted to know?" she asked.

"I found out more than that."

Ellie nodded. Tentative, checking for signs. "Anything you want to share?"

"Not really."

"Okay," she said. "I get it." And she did, she completely understood. "Then how about this—how about I share something with you?"

"I wouldn't stop you."

She looked at him; he was not handing out free passes. She took a breath to get ready, and then she told him—everything she'd told Mary, and even added a few things. And before he might judge her, she said, "Try being pregnant while you're still in high school. Try thinking with your head on straight when you're scared to death. And try thinking that everyone in the world that you care about could hate and abandon you."

"So, the real reason you broke up with me," Chip said, "instead of all that stuff you told me at the time, was all the stuff you're telling me now."

"Yes."

"And you left me out of all of it."

Ellie nodded. All of it.

"Well. What the hell?" Chip said. "I mean, why not I guess. Join the crowd."

"Sorry?"

He looked at her. "I'm suspended from school, Ellie. I'm off the team. My dad might never wake up again, and I just found out there's this whole other sideshow going on and I have a family in it. And now one more bulletin comes in, and I was almost somebody's father. Except my girlfriend left me out of the loop on that and spent her time hiding from me instead."

"I told you why."

"Because you were scared to tell me before."

Yes, she said, nodding, agreeing, apologizing for everything. What happened, she explained, was that she went a little crazy. Temporarily crazy, under titanic unexpected pressure that made her do everything she did in just the worst possible way. And now, with some time and distance, she could see it a little more intelligently—she could see this whole linked-up chain of mistakes she'd made, horrible teenage unthinking panic moves, and she was trying to separate the wheat from the chaff in terms of what was permanent and what was not.

And was breaking up with him, she wanted to know, one of the mistakes she made that was permanent?

She was asking.

She was saying the words Chip had been waiting for, yearning for—that she'd made a tremendous crashing blunder and wanted to come back. And then she said it all again—expanding, embellishing, apologizing, all of it uniquely and sincerely, all of it a hundred per cent Ellie.

Chip listened—and while he did, every adorable thing that he loved about her came galloping back to him. The way she could start a sentence on a Monday morning before assembly, and finish it by last bell on Friday, and keep you with her the whole time. That she could be going crazy, and *know* she was going crazy, he loved that. He loved that she could be so convinced that a bed would have those ruffle things on it when it didn't, and never would. He loved how she couldn't throw a Frisbee to save her life, and how she wanted to go to Scandinavia one day, and how she hated certain holidays just as much as much as he did, and how she had to be physically held back when people said "guesstimate." He loved how he laughed with her, he loved how they held each other and he loved the way she looked when she saw him in Maine last summer, coming up the path to her house. He loved the way she hugged him and said she'd never let go. He loved the way she meant that, and meant it forever.

But too much had happened, he thought, between that forever and this one. He was different now than he was in Maine; he wasn't even the same person he was a week ago.

A week ago, Nihaminy mattered.

A week ago, his father was living and vibrant.

A week ago, his mother made him a grilled cheese sandwich.

A week ago, she was the only mother he had.

And a week ago, Piccolo and Goodman were just two strange names, belonging to people that you resented very much. And now you know what a critical part they've been playing, behind the scenes, all your life—all along. One of them is your father. One of them, in a total Twilight Zone way, is sort of your uncle. And the girl they

*both loved, is your mom. Your bio-mom, your "bellybutton" mom, the
way they call it sometimes in this world of divorces and separations
and blended families and hyphenated last names and all these things
old people are always losing their shit over, when they're constantly
flapping about how the world is different today, when there weren't
barcodes, when you could call a business number and get a real person
on the phone, when seashore beaches didn't have needles and trash
on them, when a gallon of gas cost whatever the fuck it cost, and
when there were only three channels of television, not three thousand,
and there weren't remote controls then, there wasn't anything, just
sagebrush and dust bowls and food rations, and kids who listened to
their parents and sat up straight and saved their money in passbooks
and played music you could stand, and at a volume where you could
hear yourself think for a change.*

*This was his family, Chip thought. These were his people. Two
mothers, two fathers, three brand-new instant grandparents—and
one was Carmine Piccolo!—and a kid brother and sister who he
also had just now learned about. And hey—let's not leave this one
out—next August he could have been passing out cigars of his own.
He could have been graduating college with a four-year-old to feed.
Or not going to college at all.*

"Chip."

It was Ellie. They were still on the bench. Nothing had
changed. Except, of course, everything.

"What?" he asked.

"Well—I could see that you were thinking," Ellie said. "I
just sort of wondered—what about."

"I don't know. I guess I was thinking about a lot of things."

He could feel Ellie bracing herself. "And what did you come
up with?" she asked.

Chip shrugged. "Well, so far, this," he said. "I think you
should have told me this was all going on—*while* it was going
on. I think you should have told me as soon as you found out
about any baby, so we could figure it out together. I mean, you

ended up telling my parents anyway—why not bring me in before all that, and not after?"

"Because I told you, Chip. I wasn't thinking straight. And I don't mean that as an excuse, I just mean that that's the way it is. It's the way it was. You have to know how fast I would go back and do it all differently."

"But that's the thing, isn't it? What you did was final, Ellie. You can't undo it. You can't undo not telling me about it. You can't undo not giving me a chance to get used to it, and weigh in on it, or even tell you what it feels like right now to hear this stuff, because you've already done it. And you didn't have the right to do it that way."

"Excuse me?"

"I didn't mean the *right*—okay? Don't make this about that when it isn't."

"Then what's it about?"

"It's about you should have talked to me, Ellie. Give us a chance to have some time with it. And get some advice—from people who would have absolutely kicked our asses about this, but they also would have helped—and you left us all out of everything, and did this on your own. What am I supposed to say to that?"

Ellie took a breath. Collected herself. Chip lowered his head and rubbed his neck, looking down at the bench, at the initials people had carved there, with the little hearts and arrows. How many of those lovebirds are still together, he wondered. How many more initials had they come to know since they dug their points into this wood right here. And would it have mattered at the time, if they knew? Nothing is permanent. Not one damn thing.

"Okay, let's say this," Ellie tried. "Let's say we had talked about it, and we did the whole family council thing, and laid it all out. And they kicked our asses and gave us advice and it still came to this: you and I were too young to be parents. And adoption, let's just say for any reason, was discussed but decided against. And they all decided that what I ended up doing was the only option."

"How could it have been the only option, Ellie? Two of the people in this deal are the ones who adopted *me*."

"Let's just say, okay? Let's just say that in these circumstances, hypothetically, everybody agreed on the same thing, and that's the thing that happened. And what I want to know is, could you still love me? And could there still be a possibility?"

"Well give me a minute, okay? You've had time to deal with this—I haven't."

Ellie nodded. "Why don't I give you the future to deal with it," she offered.

Chip looked at her. At the only face he had ever loved so hard. "I'm not sure," he said finally, "that the future is yours to give."

He hadn't meant for that to sound so cold, or to have Ellie start to cry as a result. He really didn't know what he meant; those were just the words that came out of him. But she did cry—quietly, bravely—and Chip knew it was for real and she wasn't trying to pull anything. So he held her, and he looked over her shoulder at the street across from the hospital, and the neighborhood across the street, and he imagined other neighborhoods and other streets further beyond. He hadn't expected to grow up like this, all in one week, shot from a cannon into adulthood, without the usual step-by-steps along the way. He hadn't expected any of this. Who could have?

He held Ellie tight while she cried. And this much he was convinced: the next time Mrs. Wainscot asked him if he felt like he was alive, truly alive, Chip knew what the answer would be. And he wouldn't have to hesitate to say so.

Epilogue

The death of Henry Griffin settled in on the valley like a cold, heavy fog, touching and affecting the people who lived there whether they knew the man or not. Time didn't stop; there was no crackle of thunder, no darkening sky—nothing so dramatic as would embarrass a humble soul. Instead, something more like an awareness came—a moment of clarity, that knocked on people's doors and sat at their tables and made them slow down a bit, enough to stop and think—about an old friend, or a current one, about a lost love, or a found one, or of loves and friendships never known at all.

A kid raking leaves over in Nanticoke would stop and feel it; the two widows who walked past the dorms every day, would feel it on their way to the Orthodox Church. In stores and houses everywhere, in police stations and beauty parlors and banks—in every corner and fold of the valley, people would go over to their thermostats, and tap them—just to see if they had stopped, or were still working. And then, standing there, they would start to think. Later, maybe, they'd pick up a phone and call someone, or write them an actual letter, or think they should, or wish they had. Maybe they'd be nicer to the people they came across for a while. Or even longer than a while.

Maybe.

The funeral was on a Tuesday and the whole school got off. Mary gave the eulogy; she talked about a man whose heart was as deep as the ocean. And whose gift was the gift of listening—and how that was what made Henry a true teacher, a true educator, whose value was evident and lasting. Whose salary at its peak wouldn't equal pocket change to some of the students who had passed through his doors. All because he listened to them, and made them feel heard.

The school chapel wasn't big enough for the memorial, so the Methodist church across the street offered their sanctuary, which soon spilled over into people waiting outside, in the coldest beginning of November in fifty-seven years—and even though they couldn't hear, and couldn't see, they assembled there, so they could honor him. They were as quiet as snow.

Later someone had the idea of ringing the campus bell for Mr. Griffin; then someone else said that anyone who wanted to should be able to line up and take a turn. What no one knew, or could have predicted, was how many people would want to; that the line would be as long as it was, and how much stamina each person would have to stand there and not give up until they'd told the whole world.

Finally, something had to be done about it. The mayor of Kirby showed up, with squad cars, and ended up announcing that each person would be limited to three rings only, and then have to leave, and no one could come back a second time. It was just too much disturbance, he said. Babies couldn't sleep. House pets were jumping at walls. People were calling in thinking it might be the flood again.

And just when the Mayor had the whole thing settled, an enormous Cadillac barreled up and Carmine Piccolo got out and pushed right past him, and past the half dozen cops surrounding him—and went straight to the head of the line where he grabbed that rope and tugged on it like nobody's business, until his hands were blistered and raw.

Mary stayed behind at the church, listening to the bells; then she used the distraction to slip home undetected. She cleaned out the refrigerator of all the food that people had brought, and then all the food that had been in there before that. Then she scrubbed the inside walls and each separate shelf with baking soda—just to be busy, but it felt so good that she did it again, and then a third time. She went into the front room and fell asleep on the sofa, hearing geese outside and wondering what they were still doing up north this late. She started thinking that it might be time for her to go somewhere too. Travel, and see things, even if she'd have to see them alone. She didn't worry about the school because she knew it'd be all right without the Griffins. Mary knew her husband would be missed, and not forgotten—she'd heard that they were going to officially call their house the Griffin House, with a plaque out front and everything. So Henry's name, and his legacy, would be around that place for a long, long time.

They talked about him on the campus, of course. They talked about him in the Blue Knight Diner, too, and also at Piccolo's, where Carmine hung his picture and often paid the check for anyone who recognized it, and who had known Henry Griffin well enough to tell a good story about him. Since there were no bad stories, he picked up a record number of tabs.

And in countless scattered households where there was a successful Pocono Valley graduate—and there were many, many of them, everywhere—candles were lit and prayers were said, and memories shared and lessons passed on, about a man whose strength in the belief of each person's best qualities, whose talent for seeing their talent was unlike any other, and how that touched them, and strengthened them, and emboldened them for life. A man for whom that bell rang, for seven straight hours—cold November hours, mountain hours, with a line of people waiting that threaded through the campus without a single word of complaint. A man who brought people together—whose last dying act was to round up three of them, and call them here, out of love for the person he cherished the most.

His son.

Mrs. Levering got the office ready for Griffin's successor, a provost from Vanderbilt whose husband had family near Scranton. She brought fresh flowers in, and new file folders, and an updated contact sheet with every number and address the woman might need. Still, there were times when it was all she could do not to burst—standing in the open doorway, she'd see the scuff mark in the polished wood of Griffin's desk, where his head had hit and slid down. The mark looked like the stroke from a wide paint brush, and for that reason she decided to leave it that way and not allow herself or anyone else to remove it, until the day it went away on its own. *Because in the end,* she thought, *that's what life is. It's the stroke of a paint brush. It's the mark we leave, and no one has the right to wipe that out.*

The Nihaminy game went off without Chip at quarterback. He watched from the sidelines while Pocono Valley lost a squeaker in the final minutes. Most of his teammates said they understood, and were madder at Scotchmeyer than anyone else, for coming up with such a lame and unprofessional kind of punishment, that hurt a lot more people than Chip; they didn't *all* get caught in the girls' dorm, did they?

And without Chip to throw the ball, Coach Milpitas was forced to go to the running game, where somehow Randy stepped up, and played all four quarters with more heart and intensity than most people, besides Chip, ever knew he had. His parents had come in from Utah to watch, because they knew there'd be scouts there—from Penn State, and Pitt, and West Virginia, and of course, from B.Y.U. Randy got Chip to come along afterwards, for moral support when he dropped the big one that he never wanted to play football again. And anybody who didn't like it could go to hell—or back to Goomer's Gulch, or wherever.

When that was done, Randy asked Chip if he wanted to go over to Cindi Lindberg's and get fucked up with some of the guys from the team, and when Chip said no, he understood. Randy went alone, was the hero of the place, and he and Janet Pardini claimed the top bedroom, the master bedroom, because they were the reigning couple at the school now, and that's the way it worked.

Cindi Lindberg enjoyed her party, as she had enjoyed most of them. She liked these people; she had grown up with a lot of them, and some of the boarding students especially had become friends who she knew would last for a lifetime. There is nothing like the people you meet in high school, she was told, and this was the day she believed it.

She spent most of the evening on the pool patio, where there was an outdoor heater and she could think about things and listen to the party from a distance. She was good-naturedly propositioned a few times, and each time she good-naturedly said no. She was in love with someone, she said, and wouldn't say who—only that he wasn't available right now, but he mattered enough to be patient.

Chip stayed home and looked at college guides. There were a few schools around Boston that sounded good, and two in Colorado, and of course USC and UCLA, for the climate alone—on the dampest, coldest, darkest winter weekends, Chip and his dad would always watch the West Coast games, where it was three hours earlier, incomparably sunny, with bright noisy colors everywhere and people in the stands wearing shirtsleeves, and cheerleaders who looked so pretty they couldn't be real.

And even though he knew he'd never suit up at either place, Chip applied to both. There were always intramurals, and you could play them all year round. January, in a t-shirt. He liked that.

Ellie sought out Mrs. Wainscot, because she needed help with Spanish and she needed help with life; Mrs. Wainscot told her the Kenya story, only this time with a different twist—the emphasis on being your own person and not traveling clear around the world just to see a boy, unless it was a place you'd been wanting to go to anyway.

When love is strong enough, Mrs. Wainscot told her, it is no different than water: it finds its own way. There's very little you can do to stop water and it's just the same with love, she said—and the ones who seem to do best in life are the ones who learn, somehow, how to float on top of both.

Pick and Laura went home and cobbled back into their routines; Laura wrote notes to the kids' teachers for the time they missed, and thought about getting Andy a tutor for his math, which had been lagging, but then decided against it. It was more about motivation with Andy than it was about being behind, and Laura didn't think that a kid his age having a tutor already was such a good idea anyway. And when Molly started coming home from school with drawings that had sunshine in them for the first time since she lost her sister, Laura cried the kind of tears she didn't know she had it in her to cry anymore. Tears of joy, wizened joy, that told her everything might just be all right after all—and instead of that presence she had so long felt inside, the clutching hammering yaw, she now felt something different. She felt loved, and looked after, and forgiven—thoroughly, blessedly forgiven. It was a relief she'd never known. It was liberation.

It didn't get the kids out of the house any faster in the morning, but she did start to relax a little, and build a fire sometimes and just sit there warming while everyone was gone, and she'd go into the city more and more often and meet Pick for lunch, and listen to his strategies and tell him she loved him. When she brought up that she was thinking of getting a dog for the kids, Pick swallowed but didn't argue. The joy would be worth the work, she said, and the family could use the injection; they both knew she was right.

She got out her camera again and started taking pictures, of all of them, and she framed them herself and put the new ones up around the house. She made an appointment with her old agent, who was thrilled to hear she was back and would be ready to show again. He had been waiting, he said. He'd been waiting.

And Pick went back energized to his calling in life: drawing blood from negligent bastards who were screwing innocent people whose only mistake was trusting what they read on the label, or following what the directions said, or believing in the integrity of a brand name, or in the innate goodness of people who aren't innately good, when there's profit to be had.

But he did come home early most nights—and he had long quiet dinners with Laura where he didn't take phone calls, and he gave Iris a raise because there'd be a whole lot more for her to do now, and he let everyone in the office know that they could still call him at home—any of them could, for any reason, but it had better be a really damn good one.

He wrote a long letter to Carmine, on monogrammed stationery with a fountain pen he got when he passed the bar. It could be years, he wrote, before he could untangle all the things Carmine had done, and his motives behind it all, but Pick did recognize that things were more complicated than he could have known at the time, and admittedly he couldn't say what he might have done, or might ever do, in the same situation himself. He just hoped it would never come up.

On a separate page, Pick raised the idea of Carmine coming out to the house—over the holidays maybe, or maybe summer— give the dust a chance to settle by then, and spend a little time with the kids. He'd also invite Chip to come, of course, and Mary too. A family gathering, where they'd have some time to start getting to know each other. Laura offered to move her studio down to the basement, and they could fix up the rooms the psychiatrists had used, and do them over for guests.

Pick looked up from the letter and saw her, at the table cutting a mat for one of her pictures. Laura looked up and saw him too, and smiled, and it filled his every emptiness to feel that. And now Pick could see it—he could blessedly see it—that she was his, that he was hers, that they'd been bound to each other, from the start. And that the things he had wanted to believe in, all his life, really could be true. He had someone he was crazy about, who wanted him to kiss her. Lots of times. And he would. And he did.

As for Goody—they didn't know what to think. Laura and Pick would talk about him, and guess and wonder about him; it was a relief and even a kick to have him out in the open and back up front in their lives. And they knew, finally, what Goody had known all along—that things will be as they're meant to be, even if they aren't what you want them to be—and that the price you pay when you love someone, can really knock you cold sometimes.

They no longer harbored the need to protect him, or to protect themselves from their memories—their memories were good ones now, and they knew undeniably that the three of them had all shared a precious and irreplaceable gift. They were grateful. They spun theories about him.

And if they knew there was a drugstore in Hershey where the Trailways still stopped, by a bench under a sycamore tree on an avenue that was really named Chocolate, and that inside the store they'd still sell you a brick of the Original that you couldn't get anywhere else, then they would like to have pictured Goody doing that, and taking one to his mother, so she could see him, and they could share it, and she'd know that her son was home now—that wherever he had been and wherever he might be going, he was finally, and peacefully, home.

As gently as it came, then, the death of Henry Griffin gathered itself up; and like a cool, northern breeze it began to move—swirling into the creeks and the eddies, down the trickling waterfalls, every misty particle collecting, combining, joining up with bigger streams, on their way to the Susquehanna, the muddy river—sweeping out of the valley and turning south, bound for the Chesapeake and eventually out to sea. Where life began, where life is renewed—and where so many things, if you give them enough time, will return somehow, and begin again.

The End

Song List

Acknowledgments

A lot of years went by between the birth of this story and the book it finally became. There have been many, many angels along the way—it would take another whole book to thank them all. But for now, all my humble and endless thanks, to:

Amy Ferris, Andy Ross and Brooke Warner, who believed in this book enough to make it come true. Lauren Wise and Shannon Green at SparkPress, for putting up with me, and everyone at BookSparks, who put their expertise on the line. Stacey Powells for her help with the permissions, and Gigi Levangie and Richard C. Morais, for your kind and gracious words of support;

Steve Breimer, the absolute exception to every single lawyer joke you've ever heard;

Amy Young and Allison Coleman, who keep so much unpleasantness at bay. God I love you ladies;

Grand Master Cha Sok Park, who loved me like a father and made damn sure I learned my lessons. Anthony Robbins, for all that crackpot talk about Destiny—I'm glad I gave it a shot;

Conrad Hall, who saw the potential in a clueless kid out of college, determined to make movies. Phil Rogers, for spotting me at 23, and Dave Warden, who took me on as a client years before it would ever pay off;

Ed Mitchell, *consigliere*, who let me sleep on his couch until I earned my way back West;

Gary Foster, who turned a no into a yes on a goofy little love story where the two people don't even meet. Richard Fischoff, Claire Harrison Morton and Sandy Golden for helping move it along. Mike Medavoy for the green light. Meg and Tom for being in it, and Nora for bringing it home;

Robert Schwartz, for the two we made together. Brian Grazer, for the two we almost did; Robert Lamm and James Pankow, for the music and the inspiration—working with you even briefly was the coolest damn thing;

David Kirkpatrick, for casting me in the role of Sidekick as we ride into Act Three; Tab and Deb and Rosa and the Story Summit family, you legendary beasts;

My brother Joe, who never stopped looking out for me; my brother Jon, the first one in the audience—for all those car rides where I drove you both nuts; Barbara and Stevi, Gene and Jessie and Gene and Genna. I wrote *Iron Will* for you guys;

Mike Solomon and Elliott Miller, my brothers in soul and spirit. I trust you with everything;

Kenny Loggins, not just for your friendship but you got me to Peru, and that's how I met Michelle. Suzan Pelfrey and Melinda Farrelly for being there while it happened;

Dave Barry and Michelle Kaufman, Don and Carol McQuinn, Kiel Murray and Phil Lorin, and Joel and Lisa Canfield. You figured out marriage better than anyone I know;

Chuck Lull, June Lull, Pat Loftus, Dave Rinehimer, Rosa Lane, Dot Smith, Liz Usarzewicz, Esther Wainstein, Lenny Iorio, Sig Roos, Liza Roos Lucy, Monroe Rockmaker, Iris Berley Davis, Chuck Kellner, Les Robbins, Carol Nelson, Marilyn W and Janie K, for what you brought to these stories;

David Muhlfelder, Jerry Goralnick, Todd Dimston, Mark Faulkner, Mike Cacia, Nick Busco, Brooke Beazely, Francesca Carlow, Barbara Abbagnaro, Mark Faulkner, Alan Ritsko, Don Berman, Carla Murray, Seido Ray Ronci, Laurel Walter, Marianne Younkheere, Tom Hemphill, Pat Meyers, Gary Bosco, Mary Pfaff, Amy and Martial Robichaud, Debra Arch, Chip Rodgers, Donna, Caroline and Jamie Netschert, Elke and Dan Kim; Debra Arch again, Nat Magin, Alex G, Zelma, Shirley and Anne K;

Pat Osman, Myrna Fleishman, Soonae Choi, Pamala Oslie, Justina Vail, Pam Erwin, Caroline Thibeaux, Nicki Bonfilio, Mackenzie Champ, Barbara Carey, Stephen Eidlin Cohen, Judith Halevy, Mike Leoni, Sara Anderson, Alexander Kousnetsov, Stephanie Arnold, Chris Vogler, Rich Krevolin, Michael Hauge, Beverley Parkinson, Wendy Randall, Sara Jaqua, Laura Critchley, Andrew Gemmell, David Wolpe, Eileen Wolpe, Noah and Julia Ben Shea, David Katz, Kate Rodger, Lauri Ringer, Ellen H Schwartz, Caprice Crane, Deborah Reed, Carol Mason, Kristin Hannah, Christina Baker Kline;

My students at H-B Woodlawn, Laguna Blanca, the Bay School and O.S.A. It's not a cliché, I learned more than you did;

The people I grew up with on Green Street and beyond—you are the spaces between the words, and I only hope I've made you proud. Ronnie G and Nancy and lunch buddy Stacey Ellis;

Eric and Dennis Freedman, because you don't often get first cousins who are also your heroes. And for that one cherry tomato in Rome, that made its way to Chapter 37;

Ben and Betsy, who joined this family with Full Knowledge. And Lyra, the Magnet, strong enough to pull a grandfather across a whole country;

Thomas, Shane, Tori and Sarah—you will always be Sims and you will always be mine. In a world forever changing, this will stay the same;

Jenny and Greg—you've lived with this story your whole damn lives, and I never would have finished it but for you. I hope it's been worth it;

Ella and Ecco, you crazy knucklehead dogs—you truly did save me;

And finally, my wife Michelle, artist of the heart. You showed this stubborn Russian how to not be here alone. You're the hand I get to hold, and the pillow I get to share. I love you, Sunshine.

photo © Greg Arch

About the Author

Jeff Arch grew up in Harrisburg, Pennsylvania, where he spent two of his high school years at a boarding school much like the one depicted in *Attachments*. In the '70s, he studied film/tv/theater production at Emerson College in Boston and then moved to Los Angeles, where he worked as a concert lighting designer and toured the country with national rock and reggae acts while teaching himself to write screenplays on the side. Years later, married and with a young family, he was teaching high school English and running a martial arts school when heard the call to write again; in 1989, he sold the school he'd built, rented a small office, and gave himself one year to write three screenplays. The second of those—a quirky romantic comedy where the two lovers don't even meet until the very last page—sold almost immediately, and *Sleepless in Seattle* became a surprise megahit worldwide. For his screenplay, Jeff was nominated for an Oscar, as well as for Writers Guild and BAFTA awards, among others. His other credits include the Disney adventure film *Iron Will*, New Line's romantic comedy *Sealed With a Kiss*, and the independent comedy *Dave Barry's Complete Guide to Guys*. His script for *SavingMilly*, based on Mort Kondracke's searing memoir, earned the 2005 Humanitas Nomination, an honor Jeff treasures. Jeff is a father, stepfather, father-in-law, and grandfather. *Attachments* is Jeff's first novel.

SELECTED TITLES FROM SPARKPRESS

SparkPress is an independent boutique publisher
delivering high-quality, entertaining, and engaging
content that enhances readers' lives, with a special focus
on female-driven work. www.gosparkpress.com

So Close: A Novel, Emma McLaughlin and Nicola Kraus. $17, 978-
1-940716-76-3. A story about a girl from the trailer parks of Florida
and the two powerful men who shape her life—one of whom will
raise her up to places she never imagined, the other who will threaten
to destroy her. Can a girl like her make it to the White House?
When her loyalty is tested will she save the only family member
she's ever known—even if it means keeping a terrible secret from
the American people?

The Half-Life of Remorse: A Novel, Grant Jarrett. $16.95, 978-1-
943006-14-4. Three life-scarred people are brought together to
confront each other thirty years after the brutal crime that shattered
their lives, and as the puzzle of the past gradually falls together, the
truth commands a high price.

Enemy Queen: A Novel, Robert Steven Goldstein, $16.95, 978-1-
68463-026-4. A woman initiates passionate sexual encounters with
two articulate but bumbling and crass middle-aged men, but what
she demands in return soon becomes untenable. A short time later
she goes missing, prompting the county sheriff to open a murder
investigation.

The Cast: A Novel, Amy Blumenfeld. $16.95, 978-1-943006-72-4.
Twenty-five years after a group of ninth graders produces a *Saturday
Night Live*-style videotape to cheer up their cancer-stricken friend,
they reunite to celebrate her good health—but the happy holiday
card facades quickly crumble and give way to an unforgettable three
days filled with moral dilemmas and life-altering choices.

Tracing the Bones: A Novel, Elise A. Miller. $17, 978-1-940716-
48-0. When 41-year-old Eve Myer—a woman trapped in an
unhappy marriage and plagued by chronic back pain—begins
healing sessions with her new neighbor Billy, she's increasingly
drawn to him, despite the mysterious circumstances surrounding
his wife and child's recent deaths.

About SparkPress

S parkPress is an independent, hybrid imprint focused on merging the best of the traditional publishing model with new and innovative strategies. We deliver high-quality, entertaining, and engaging content that enhances readers' lives. We are proud to bring to market a list of *New York Times* best-selling, award-winning, and debut authors who represent a wide array of genres, as well as our established, industry-wide reputation for creative, results-driven success in working with authors. SparkPress, a BookSparks imprint, is a division of SparkPoint Studio LLC.

Learn more at GoSparkPress.com